04930212

OFF THE RECORD

OFF THE RECORD

A Jack Haldean Mystery

Dolores Gordon-Smith

This first world edition published 2010
in Great Britain and in 2011 in the USA by
SEVERN HOUSE PUBLISHERS LTD of
9–15 High Street, Sutton, Surrey, England, SM1 1DF.
Trade paperback edition first published
in Great Britain and the USA 2011 by
SEVERN HOUSE PUBLISHERS LTD.

British Library Cataloguing in Publication Data

Gordon-Smith, Dolores.
  Off the record.
  1. Haldean, Jack (Fictitious character) – Fiction.
  2. Murder – Investigation – Fiction. 3. Detective and
  mystery stories.
  I. Title
  823.9'2-dc22

ISBN-13: 978-0-7278-6974-6 (cased)
ISBN-13: 978-1-84751-304-5 (trade paper)

All Severn House titles are printed on acid-free paper.

Severn House Publishers support The Forest Stewardship Council [FSC],
the leading international forest certification organisation. All our titles that
are printed on Greenpeace-approved FSC-certified paper carry the FSC logo.

Typeset by Palimpsest Book Production Ltd.,
Falkirk, Stirlingshire, Scotland.
Printed and bound in Great Britain by the
MPG Books Group, Bodmin, Cornwall.

To Peter, with love

AUTHOR'S NOTE

In 1877, the thirty-year-old American genius, Thomas Edison, recited the nursery rhyme, *Mary Had A Little Lamb,* into a mouthpiece attached to his new invention, a tinfoil covered cylinder he called a 'phonograph'. He finished the nursery rhyme, rotated the cylinder – and his own voice spoke back to him. Edison had invented recorded sound.

The early tinfoil phonographs had many limitations. The foil ripped easily and was impossible to copy. What *could* be copied – what, in fact, started the recorded music industry – was the gramophone and record, invented in 1887 by Emil Berliner. Berliner's gramophone records were simple to play, cheaper to make and much louder than Edison's cylinders.

Oddly enough, had Berliner's gramophones not been so spectacularly successful, tape recording might have become the norm much earlier. Valdemar Poulsen, a Danish inventor, made the first 'tape' machine (he actually recorded on to fine wire) in the 1890s, but it was the gramophone, with its box, wind-up handle and horn, that became one of the iconic objects of the early twentieth century.

The gramophone was seized on by literally hundreds of manufacturers and it's virtually impossible to say how many different types, from the tiny Mikiphone, the size of a large pocket watch, to luxury models in lavishly-made wooden cabinets, were produced. It seemed impossible that anything could replace the gramophone in the home.

Then, in the early 1920s, came radio. Records, which were recorded by a refined version of the method Edison had worked out forty-odd years earlier, suddenly sounded flat, tired and outdated. To survive at all, gramophone manufacturers had to face the challenge and radically improve the sound. The challenge was met by electrical recording and reproduction, and the race to produce a workable electrical recording system is what lies behind the story of *Off the Record*.

ONE

I t was the summer of 1899 when Charles Otterbourne first came to Stoke Horam. Charles Otterbourne was thirty-six years old, an earnest, if rather humourless man, with a great deal of money and a strong philanthropic urge.

He walked through Horam Woods, crossed the stepping-stones over the river Lynn at the bottom of the valley and up the gentle slope to the unremarkable Hertfordshire hamlet of Stoke Horam. Neither the village, with its twenty-two agricultural labourers' cottages, or the green with its grazing geese pecking beneath the washing hung out to dry, had anything to detain him, so Charles continued up the slope to the thirteenth century and mercifully unrestored church of St Joseph of Arimathea.

The church itself made little appeal to him; Charles had strict Evangelical views and found no pleasure in ancient stones, but the view from the churchyard changed his life.

St Joseph's stood on a knoll, some distance from Stoke Horam, commanding a view of hedged-in rolling fields of grain and pasture and stands of trees. An occasional line of smoke and a distant whoosh of steam marked out the line of the Eastern Counties Railway.

Sitting on that windswept gravestone, sandwiches from his knapsack uneaten in his hand, Charles Otterbourne had a vision. He had visited Thomas Edison's famous Invention Factory in New Jersey, a vast scientific complex of laboratories, factories and buildings. He couldn't do anything on that scale, of course, but he could do *something*. His own village supported by his own factory, could easily be connected to the world by a branch line to that railway. New century, new railways, new roads, new beginnings . . .

By 1924, Charles Otterbourne's transformation of Stoke Horam was so complete, it was difficult to remember life before he arrived.

Otterbourne's New Century Works produced scientific and optical instruments, typewriters, telephones, dictating machines and gramophones but, perhaps dearer to Charles Otterbourne's heart than the factory, was the village.

The farm labourers' cottages – picturesque but insanitary – were hemmed in by Ideal Homes, complete with plumbing, gardens and – a stunning innovation – electricity from the Otterbourne generator. The tiny post office which, in Stoke Horam's previous incarnation, had also acted as a general store, tobacconists and sweet-shop, had expanded into separate establishments in a new parade of shops along the High Street and had been joined by a grocer's, a butcher's, an ironmonger's, a haberdasher's, a draper's and a fishmonger's.

There were allotments and a non-conformist chapel. There were tennis courts, a sports field, a Workman's Institute for lectures and concerts and the Otterbourne library. The library boasted a marble bust of Charles Otterbourne himself, complete with laurel leaves and an off-the-shoulder toga, erected, so the plaque underneath it said, by his grateful employees. If the gift of the bust was not quite as spontaneous as the plaque indicated, it was, nevertheless, sincere.

An innovation Charles Otterbourne had not planned was the War Memorial, listing, among the dead, his two sons, Alfred and Robert. A tombstone in the chapel graveyard covered the grave of his wife, Edith, who had died soon after her sons.

If life in Stoke Horam under Charles Otterbourne's benevolent rule had a fault it was, perhaps, that all this undoubted well-being came at the expense of a certain amount of liberty. Charles Otterbourne saw this as a virtue, not a failing. People needed to be organized. He applied this rule impartially to his own family and his employees alike.

When his daughter, Molly, had shown a worrying interest in an unsuitable man (Justin Verewood, a workshy Bloomsbury poet) he had organized her marriage by forbidding Verewood and heavily approving of Stephen Lewis, a fair-haired, grey-eyed, intelligent man with an engaging smile and a wicked sense of humour. Mr Otterbourne, who hadn't registered the smile and was oblivious to humour, only knew that Captain Lewis, lately of the Queen's Royal West Surrey's, had an outstanding war record and good grasp of business. The marriage was, of course, a success. Molly said as much when he asked her.

One common feature of English village life – the local pub – was missing. Charles Otterbourne had, very early on, identified betting and alcohol as twin evils. Drink and any form of gambling earned instant dismissal. There was no redress. For those workers who did conform to his philanthropic tyranny, there was a well-paid job, a decent home, a doctor on call and provision, in the form of the compulsory pension fund, for their old age.

The pension fund. Hugo Ragnall, Charles Otterbourne's secretary, looked uneasily at the eggs and bacon on his plate. Why on earth he had taken eggs and bacon from the dishes on the sideboard, he didn't know. Habit, he presumed. Fried bread, too, he realized with a twist of revulsion. The smell made his stomach churn and he abruptly pushed his plate away.

'Are you all right, Hugo?' asked Molly. 'You don't seem quite yourself this morning.'

Not quite himself? That wasn't a surprise. *She doesn't know about the pension fund.* 'I'm fine,' he lied, forcing himself to drink his coffee. Molly heard the break in his voice and her puzzled look changed to concern.

She was a kindly soul, thought Ragnall, seeing the look. His heart sank as he thought of Molly. She would be caught up in the whole stinking mess and there was absolutely nothing he could do. 'I didn't sleep very well last night,' he said, knowing he had to respond somehow or other.

And that was true. It had been past one o'clock before he had finished work last night and what he found hadn't made for a restful night.

Steve Lewis, Molly's husband, rustled the newspaper. 'That's too bad,' he remarked over the top of the *Daily Telegraph*. 'Mr Otterbourne wants you to enthuse to this Dunbar chap today. Tell him how wonderful we are and all that sort of thing. I still think Dunbar's someone to treat with caution,' he added.

Oh, good God! Ragnall had forgotten about Dunbar. It could have been the war or increased taxes or cheap foreign imports or simply the fact that philanthropy on a grand scale cost far more than it used to, but the stark fact was that Otterbourne's New Century products weren't the money-spinners they once were. They needed to expand and Charles Otterbourne had approached Andrew Dunbar, a gramophone manufacturer from Falkirk, with useful connections in Scotland and the north of

England. It made good commercial sense for the two compa-
nies to come together and Dunbar, as far as Ragnall could
make out, was interested. The price he had quoted though was
pretty hefty, far more than the size of his firm justified. He
had, to summarize his letter, something up his sleeve, something that would change the whole future of recorded sound.
Steve's advice had been to look elsewhere. Dunbar, he said,
had a reputation as a very tough customer indeed.

Charles Otterbourne was intrigued, however, and asked for
more details. The something up Dunbar's sleeve turned out
to be Professor Alan Carrington.

And that, tantalizingly, was as much information as Andrew
Dunbar was willing to commit to a letter. He was arriving
that morning, complete with Professor Carrington and the
Professor's son, Gerard.

'Professor Carrington?' Steve Lewis had said with interest,
when he had been told of the proposed visit. 'Dunbar may be
on to something after all. Professor Carrington's a relative of
mine. Our families quarrelled years ago, so I've never actually met him, but he's something fairly fruity in the science
line. As far as I can gather, the Professor's a genius, or next
door to it, at any rate. I've run across his son, Gerry, a few
times. He's a scientific type too, but quite human. I don't
know what either of them are doing, tied up with a second-
rate outfit like Dunbar's.'

Lewis folded up his newspaper, scraped his chair back, and
felt in his pocket for his pipe.

'Not in here, Steve,' pleaded Molly. 'It makes the room
smell so.'

Lewis laughed. 'All right.' He inclined his head towards
Ragnall. 'D'you fancy a pipe outside, old man?'

Ragnall stood up, grateful for a chance to escape the breakfast table. The two men walked out on to the terrace and down
the steps into the garden.

'What's wrong?' asked Lewis quietly, taking out his tobacco
pouch. 'You look done in.' He hesitated. 'You haven't come
unstuck on the horses again, have you? You needn't worry,
Ragnall. I'll see you're all right. You know I'll always give
you a hand.'

Ragnall very nearly smiled. 'No, it's nothing like that. It's
damn good of you though, Lewis. I do appreciate your help,

but it's nothing to do with horses or cards or anything like that.' He swallowed. 'It's a lot more serious than that.'

Steve Lewis's eyebrows shot up. '*More* serious? What the devil is it?'

'I can't tell you here,' said Ragnall with a glance back at the house. 'Let's get further away.'

Lewis looked surprised but said nothing until they reached the sundial. Ragnall took a deep breath and, gripping the bowl of the sundial, braced his arms. This was going to be hard.

'Do you like Mr Otterbourne?' he asked eventually.

Lewis looked startled. 'Of course I do.' He glanced towards the house. It was a solid Edwardian building, long, low and comfortable in the sunshine. Ranged along the terrace, which ran the length of the house, were French windows, opening on to the various rooms. The room at the end was Charles Otterbourne's study and, brief against the glass, a dark movement showed them Charles Otterbourne himself. 'Besides that you'd be on to a hiding to nothing if you started finding fault with the man.' There was a cynical twist in his voice. 'The marble bust of him in the library was erected, so the plaque says, by his grateful employees. That tells you something. He's universally beloved.'

'Why?' asked Ragnall quietly.

'Why?' Steve Lewis raised his eyebrows again. 'You know as well as I do.'

'Just tell me.'

'You're being very mysterious about this, Ragnall,' Lewis complained. He shrugged. 'All right, since you insist.' He put a match to his pipe. 'He's a good man.' Ragnall's silence invited further comment. 'OK, I admit it. I find him a bit hard to take sometimes. He knows what's good for us and makes sure we get it, good and strong, but I'll say this for him. He practises what he preaches.'

'Are you sure?'

Lewis looked puzzled. 'Yes.'

It was no wonder Lewis looked puzzled, thought Ragnall. He drew a deep, juddering breath. 'He's a crook.'

'He's a *what?*'

Ragnall swallowed. 'I've been going through the accounts.' He ran his hand through his hair. 'I've been meaning to sort them out for months. That old dodderer who was here before

me left things in a dickens of a mess. I don't think they've
ever been properly tackled.'

'What's the problem?'

'It's the pension fund,' said Ragnall wearily. 'I don't know
how to tell you, but it's a fact. I know the company's gone
through a rough patch, which probably explains it, but Mr
Otterbourne has been taking money from the pension fund.'

There was a moment's shocked silence. Steve Lewis froze,
his eyes wide, then swallowed a mouthful of smoke the wrong
way and broke out in a fusillade of coughing. 'You old devil,'
he said, gasping for breath. 'You had me going for a moment
there. You looked so damn serious I nearly believed you.'

'It's true.'

'Drop it, won't you?' said Lewis, glancing uneasily round
the garden. 'I know you're pulling my leg but it's not really
very funny, you know.'

Hugo Ragnall sighed deeply. 'I'm serious. The pension fund
isn't Mr Otterbourne's money. Everyone who's ever worked
here has contributed to it and the fund is virtually empty.
There's enough in it to pay the weekly outgoings, but that's
it. The capital behind it, the capital built up over years, has
vanished.'

'You must be mistaken.'

'I'm not!' Ragnall lowered his voice urgently. 'I tell you,
Mr Otterbourne's embezzled the funds. His signature's on the
cheques. I believed in him, you know?' he said bitterly. 'And
he's nothing but a hypocrite. A damned, white-haired, pompous
old hypocrite.'

Lewis was pale. He was obviously finding it hard to speak.
'It's unbelievable,' he said eventually. 'Have you said anything
to him? What's his explanation?'

Ragnall looked horribly uncomfortable. 'I don't know. I took
the accounts into the study before breakfast. I said there was a
matter I needed to discuss but I simply couldn't bring myself
to speak. He was sitting there, looking – oh, looking so blinking
saintly – that I just couldn't find the words. He said, "Ah,
Ragnall, the accounts," and that was more or less it.'

Lewis put his hand to his mouth. 'We'll have to talk to him
this evening,' he said after a while. 'Both of us. We can't do
anything before then, not with Dunbar and the Carringtons
coming.'

Ragnall winced. 'No, we can't. If he could pay it back, then perhaps it'll be all right, but there's nearly seventeen thousand pounds missing and I know he hasn't got that sort of money spare. The firm's in a bad way, Lewis. Since the war, it's hardly broken even. It looks prosperous, but it isn't.' He was silent for a few moments. 'I don't know how I'm going to get through today. I can't bear the thought of facing him with this hanging over us.'

Lewis sank his hands in his pockets. 'It's tough, isn't it?' he said after a pause. 'I wish I could disappear for the day. You too, of course. You haven't any ideas, have you?'

'There's always your Uncle Maurice,' said Ragnall slowly.

Lewis snapped his fingers. 'That's it! Uncle Maurice! Of course! He's still ill, ill enough to warrant a visit.' He looked up with a relieved smile. 'Well done. I'll think of something for you.' Lewis glanced towards the study. 'I'll have to tell Mr Otterbourne what we're doing. Go round to the garage and get into the car. I'll drop you off at the station.'

Lewis went up the steps into the study. Charles Otterbourne looked up as he came into the room. 'Ah, there you are, Stephen. I've been studying an article by Professor Carrington.' He tapped the papers on the desk in front of him. 'Did I understand you to say the Professor is a relation of yours?'

'Yes, that's right,' said Lewis. His glance slid across the room to where the accounts lay in a manila file on the table. Did Charles Otterbourne have the slightest idea of what they contained? 'As I said before, I've never actually met him. There was a family disagreement, you understand?' His voice was deliberately casual. 'I've run across his son, Gerry, a few times. According to Gerry, the Professor is nothing short of a genius. Apparently he's a real absent-minded scientist and has the dickens of a temper.'

Mr Otterbourne looked startled. 'That sounds rather alarming. I trust we will get on well enough. Mr Dunbar hasn't given me any details of Professor Carrington's work in his letter, but says I am bound to be interested.' He obviously didn't have an inkling of the bombshell contained in that manila folder. 'I was going to send the car to the station but perhaps you would like to meet them instead.'

Lewis tried to look stricken. 'I'm sorry, sir, but I won't be here. I've had a letter from my Uncle Maurice's housekeeper.

Apparently his chest is very bad again and I thought I'd run down and see him.'

Mr Otterbourne was clearly put out. 'That is very inconvenient, Stephen.'

'Oh, I don't know, sir,' said Lewis easily. 'After all, you don't really need me and poor old Uncle Maurice is pretty ill, you know.'

Charles Otterbourne's lips thinned. 'As you wish.' He turned his head dismissively. 'Ask Ragnall to come here.'

His tone, the autocratic tone of a monarch dispensing with his subjects, suddenly irritated Lewis. 'Ragnall's out for the day, too, I'm afraid.' Mr Otterbourne looked downright affronted. 'He seemed very seedy at breakfast,' Lewis explained rapidly. 'Molly was concerned about him. He told me he'd slept very badly and thought he might be coming down with something. I thought of packing him off to bed, but he said he'd rather not. I didn't think he was in any fit condition to talk to either Mr Dunbar or the Carringtons, so I asked him to go along to Stansfields, the timber people. He's already left.'

Mr Otterbourne drew himself up. 'I should have been consulted first. You have overstepped your authority, Stephen. In future I would ask you to remember that Ragnall is not here to come and go at your say-so.' He frowned. 'Stansfields? We've not dealt with them before.'

'No, but their quote was substantially lower than White and Millwood's.'

Charles Otterbourne steepled his fingers together. 'Quality needs to be paid for. That is one of my guiding principles. We cannot cut corners. You say Ragnall has actually left?'

'Yes, sir,' Lewis said. 'You wouldn't have wanted him around today. He was really under the weather.'

'I would have liked to have judged that for myself. I am not at all pleased.' He frowned at Lewis over the top of his pince-nez. 'If you are going to see your uncle, you'd better be off. Do you intend to return this evening?'

'Oh yes,' said Lewis, involuntarily glancing once more towards the folder. He swallowed. 'I don't think I've got any choice.'

TWO

Professor Alan Carrington was, thought Molly, one of the most alarming men she had ever met. Although his name was English enough, there was a sort of foreign arrogance about him, a scary, down-at-heel but aristocratic foreign arrogance. Like Count Dracula, she said to herself and immediately wished she hadn't. Professor Carrington would make anyone nervous without thinking of vampires. He was tall and spare with high cheekbones, a beaky nose, brilliant blue eyes and nervous, thin hands that were continually in motion. His tweed jacket and grey flannels were shapeless with age, the pockets distended with papers, and bagged at the knee and elbow. Hamilton, the butler, took his shabby hat and coat with a barely perceptible lift of his eyebrows, but it was clear that he thought his master's latest guest was a very odd fish indeed.

The Professor was abstracted and irritated to the point of rudeness by the conventional pleasantries. He was clearly far more interested in a wooden crate, about the size of a tea chest, which Eckersley, the chauffeur, together with Gerard Carrington, carried into the hall. He stood by it defensively, arms folded across his chest, Gerard Carrington and Andrew Dunbar on either side.

It was while Charles Otterbourne was sketching out the day – tour of the factory, tour of the village, lunch – the Professor shook himself impatiently and cut Mr Otterbourne off in midsentence. 'Are you going to buy Dunbar's firm?'

Charles Otterbourne, for once taken completely aback, stammered to a halt. 'I . . . er . . .'

'You can't ask things like that, Dad,' said Gerry Carrington, completely unruffled by his father's abruptness. Dunbar, a short, stout man, pulled at his moustache in a deprecating way. His eyes, Molly noticed, were fixed on her father. In the face of Professor Carrington's overwhelming personality, it was difficult to think of anyone else, but Molly was suddenly aware she didn't like Mr Dunbar. Steve said he had a tough reputation, but she also sensed coldness about him, a wary, calculating quality. If her father did do business with Mr Dunbar, he would have to be very careful he didn't come out the loser from the deal.

'Well,' demanded Professor Carrington. 'Are you?'

Charles Otterbourne coughed in a bring-the-meeting-to-order way. It had never failed to obtain respectful silence but it failed now.

'Because if you are, I suggest you cease to waste any more time and examine my machine forthwith.'

'Your machine?' queried Mr Otterbourne.

'Yes, sir, my machine!' the Professor barked. He put his hand on the wooden crate. 'This machine. Great heavens, sir, you do know what I'm talking about, I presume?' In the face of Charles Otterbourne's blank enquiry, he whirled on Andrew Dunbar. 'I understood this man was interested in my work. He seems completely ignorant of it.'

Andrew Dunbar's accent, that unmistakable Edinburgh twang, grew stronger under stress. 'You cannot talk to Mr Otterbourne in that fashion, Professor. You ken these things are not decided in minutes.'

'Exactly,' agreed Charles Otterbourne gratefully. 'I shall be more than happy, Professor, to examine your machine.' His gaze dropped to the crate. 'You will understand, I trust, that I cannot possibly give a decision on these far-reaching commercial matters without careful examination of all the possible implications.' Alan Carrington sighed mutinously and folded his arms again. 'What does your machine actually do?'

'It records and plays sound, sir!'

'But we—'

'Electronically!' Professor Carrington ran an impatient hand through his hair. 'It utilizes electronics.'

'It's unlike any other machine,' murmured Dunbar.

Alan Carrington ignored the interruption. 'I wish to know with whom I am dealing. If, sir, you are to be responsible for the money necessary to develop my machine, naturally you have a right to understand exactly how it works and what its capabilities are. If you are not, I will bid you good-day.'

'Steady on,' said Gerard Carrington easily. 'You can't go marching off, Dad. We've only just arrived.' He smiled, a warm, friendly smile.

Molly caught her breath. Gerard Carrington had curly

brown hair, mild blue eyes, rumpled clothes and gold-rimmed glasses and Molly suddenly realized he was a very attractive man.

Gerard Carrington must have heard her little intake of breath, for he turned to her as if eliciting her support. He pushed his glasses firmly on to the bridge of his nose with his index finger. 'I know Steve's been called away, Mrs Lewis, but I suppose we're relatives too, in a manner of speaking, aren't we?' He smiled once more. 'After all, Steve's my cousin. As a matter of fact, as we are relations, I suppose you should call me Gerry. Everyone does.'

Molly couldn't help smiling in return. 'Of course I will. And you must call me Molly.'

Gerry looked at his father again. 'You see, Dad? We can't go yet. We're with members of the family, and it would be very bad manners. Besides that, Mr Otterbourne wants to show us the factory and the village and so on, don't you, sir?'

Mr Otterbourne was about to answer but Alan Carrington beat him to it. 'Why on earth should I want to see the factory, let alone the village? I presume, sir, as you are a gramophone manufacturer, you are capable of manufacturing my machine. That is all I need to know.'

'Let me have a word with Mr Otterbourne, Professor,' said Andrew Dunbar in a conciliatory way. He drew Mr Otterbourne aside further up the hall. Professor Carrington scuffed his feet and taking his pipe from his pocket, stuffed it with an untidy wedge of tobacco, lit it, and dropped the match on the floor. Gerard Carrington looked at Molly in a resigned plea for understanding that seemed to make them allies. She liked the feeling. Molly heard phrases such as *difficult, genius* and *truly extraordinary,* in the mutter of words along the hall, but whether that referred to the Professor or his machine she couldn't tell.

'We've decided to change our plans,' said Charles Otterbourne after a few minutes' intense conversation. 'If Professor Carrington is agreeable, it would perhaps be as well if he explained his work to me right away.'

'Just as you like,' grunted the Professor through puffs of smoke.

Molly saw her father control his temper with an effort.

'Molly, my dear,' he said turning to her, 'I intended to escort Mr Dunbar around the factory this morning. That, I'm afraid, is no longer possible. Could you take care of him and Mr Carrington?' He cast an unfriendly glance at the Professor before turning back to Dunbar. 'I'm sorry to have to change the arrangements at such short notice but I can escort you round the factory this afternoon.'

Dunbar regretfully shook his head. 'I'm very sorry, Mr Otterbourne, but that won't be possible. I understand you've got a fine concern here and I would like to see it very much. Perhaps we can make an appointment for another day?' There was a definite gleam in his eye. 'I'm sure we can work together to our mutual benefit. However, I must be away back up to town. There's a meeting of a learned society I'm pledged to attend, you understand. The Professor is giving a paper, aren't you, sir?' Alan Carrington nodded agreement.

With his plans for the day in ruins, Charles Otterbourne gave in with reasonable grace. The two Carringtons carried the wooden crate into the study. Gerard Carrington appeared a few minutes later. 'The guv'nor's well away,' he said with a grin. 'He's giving poor Mr Otterbourne the full works. He won't be finished for at least an hour, probably longer.'

'Would you like to see the village?' asked Molly. 'We can drive down in the car or we can walk if you'd rather.'

Andrew Dunbar shook his head. 'Thank you, Mrs Lewis, but I'll have to decline. I have some papers I intend to discuss with your father and I'd appreciate some time to look at them. I meant to read through them on the train, but I didn't have the opportunity.'

'The guv'nor wouldn't stop talking,' explained Gerry Carrington. 'He was on good form, wasn't he Mr Dunbar?'

'He was very loquacious,' agreed Mr Dunbar. 'And very informative. Is there a room I can use, Mrs Lewis?'

'You can have the library,' she said. 'You'll be free from inter-ruption in there.' She turned to Gerard Carrington. 'Shall we have coffee in the conservatory, Gerry?' She felt mildly self-conscious as she said his name but he obviously liked her using it.

He smiled warmly. 'That'd be nice.' His smile broadened. 'Now the guv'nor's safely taken care of, I can relax for a bit.'

The remark gave her the oddest sense of kinship with him.

He obviously cared about his father and that protectiveness was something Molly was very familiar with.

The Professor didn't fit into the world but neither did Dad. Molly suddenly knew Gerry Carrington would understand how she felt about her father. He was vulnerable. Dad had to have the world run by his rules; he simply couldn't cope in any other way. He had to be surrounded with an armour of deference because without it, he would be as helpless as a crab without its shell. He was, as Steve said, a pompous old tyrant with no sense of humour. She knew that, but there were worse failings, weren't there? He might be an old tyrant, but he was a kindly old tyrant and she loved him. Steve was usually privately and cheerfully disrespectful about her father but every so often, he was serious. 'It's crazy, Molly,' he protested. 'Why on earth do we all have to live by his rules? We're not children.'

'We don't have to,' she said. 'We just have to pretend.' It was kinder that way. So in London she danced, drank cocktails and went to card parties, and Steve couldn't understand that, for Dad's sake, she was willing to lead this odd sort of double life, but it was for Steve's sake, too. She didn't like the double life; she seemed to have been on edge for ages. It was so difficult to simply relax. Gerry, she thought, would understand. The knowledge made her feel slightly shy.

They sat in the conservatory together. Gerard Carrington seemed completely at home, talking about their surroundings, his father and Steve. He really was a remarkably easy person to get along with.

'What does your father's machine actually do?' she asked. 'What makes it so special?' She half-expected to be told it was too difficult for her to understand – Steve usually made a joke if she asked a question – but Carrington looked at her with a sort of hesitant enthusiasm.

'Do you really want to know? To put it very simply, it uses electrical impulses to record and play at length on to a magnetized ribbon.'

'Hasn't that been done before?' asked Molly, a wayward memory coming to her aid. 'Wasn't there a man called Poulsen? I've heard my father talk about him.'

Carrington looked at her with undisguised admiration. 'Spot on. I must say how refreshing it is to meet someone who has an intelligent interest in the subject.'

She felt ridiculously flattered. Steve teased her and Dad declaimed but neither told her she was intelligent.

'The guv'nor's machine is an improvement on Poulsen's. He developed a system of storing electrical signals on magnetized steel wire some time ago now but the sound was terribly distorted when it was replayed. On this machine the sound is very clear.' Carrington leaned forward enthusiastically. 'The guv'nor's come up with the idea of magnetic ribbon wrapped round a cylinder. It's tricky to use at the moment and he'll have to come up with some easier way to manipulate the ribbon but the principle's sound enough.'

'Perhaps it's a silly question,' said Molly doubtfully, 'but I don't see how a sound can be electrical.'

Carrington grinned. 'It's a first-rate question. It really all goes back to Michael Faraday. As you know, Faraday's major discovery was that a magnetic field can induce an electrical current, yes?'

Molly nodded to indicate she was comfortable with Faraday and magnetic fields.

Carrington flushed with pleasure. 'You really do know something about this, don't you? Now as far as sound recording and reproduction are concerned, the trick is to turn sound waves into an electrical impulse. Lee De Forest is doing some pioneering work on this in the States and some exciting breakthroughs are being made in the field of thermionic emissions. If you take an equation where K is Boltzman's constant . . .'

He broke off, noting the glazed expression in Molly's eyes. 'Perhaps I can explain it without maths,' he said tactfully. 'A sound can be converted into an electrical impulse by using a carbon-filled microphone.' He gave a wriggle of enthusiasm. 'You see where this is going? The sound waves vibrate the microphone diaphragm so they're converted into a varying electrical current. If you wrap an iron pole within a coil of wire surrounded by a permanent magnet – we're back to Faraday again – an electrical field is produced and we can use that to make a picture, so to speak, of the sound waves.'

'But you still need a way to turn that picture of the sound waves into actual sound.'

'Exactly!' Carrington pushed his glasses up the bridge of his nose. 'My word, Molly, I'm enjoying this conversation. I've never met a girl like you before. We can hear the sound by using a device which picks up the changes in the magnetic field, converting it to an electrical signal which is amplified so it's powerful enough to make a diaphragm vibrate and reproduce the recorded sound waves audibly. You'll appreciate there's more to it than that, but that's the gist of it,' he said, looking at her happily.

He was so appreciative she felt a rush of pleasure. There was a button missing on his shirt, she noticed. She suddenly wished she could sew it back on for him. She had the oddest desire to look after him. It was the Otterbourne fault, she thought with a rueful stab of recognition.

'Anyway, that's the theory behind the guv'nor's machine,' said Gerry, picking up his coffee. He raised an interrogative eyebrow. 'You were wary of him, I know.' She rushed to deny it, but he shook his head. 'He can be difficult but he's had a lot to put up with. He had to retire early.' He drank his coffee. 'I'm glad he's got this project to work on. He needs something to occupy his mind, to stop him from brooding. He likes to have me around, which is just as well. I can step in if he's getting too outrageous. I understand what he's talking about, you see, but I'm a bit of a plodder compared to him. He really is outstanding but he does find ordinary life very awkward. If things don't go the way he wants them to, he doesn't have any way of coping.' He smiled at her. 'We do, don't we?'

The insight could be nothing more than coincidence, but it seemed so apposite, it took her breath away. She was saved from having to answer by the maid, Dorcas, coming into the room. The cook wanted to consult her about lunch and Molly, putting down her cup and saucer, followed her to the kitchen.

Hamilton, the butler, passed the biscuit tin to Eckersley, the chauffeur. The two men were good friends and always took their morning cup of tea together in Hamilton's pantry, secure from the listening ears of the womenservants. Hamilton liked to be able to express an opinion without any danger of having it gossiped about in the village. 'So what did you think of the Professor?' he asked.

Eckersley dunked his chocolate biscuit, raising his eyebrows expressively. 'I think he's a couple of screws loose, Mr Hamilton, and that's the honest truth. I thought I was picking up a tramp when I saw him at the station.' He bit into his biscuit reflectively. 'He's got a shocking tongue on him, to say he's meant to be a gent. I mean, we've had scientific types before and plenty of them, but I've never seen the like of him, shouting and losing his temper and carrying on. I reckon young Carrington's got his work cut out for him, looking after his Pa. More like his keeper, he was. He seemed a nice enough bloke but his Pa's a right one and no mistake.'

'Old Man Otterbourne was put out,' said Hamilton. 'He was as close to losing his temper this morning as I've ever seen, and that's saying something.' He nodded his head towards the door. 'When I took their coffee in to the study they were at it hammer and tongs. I heard them.' He adopted a high-pitched voice. ' "Don't be an absolute fool, man!" That's what the Professor said, true as I'm sat here, *and* a good bit more. His nibs didn't like it above half, especially as I was in the room.'

'What was he going on about?' asked Eckersley with interest, reaching for another biscuit.

Hamilton shrugged. 'Something to do with that machine of his. Edison or something or other came into it.' He laughed. 'His Highness had a face like thunder. I don't think he's ever been spoken to like that in his life.'

Eckersley grinned. 'It won't do him any harm.' He stopped short. The door opening on to the kitchen garden was ajar and from somewhere very close at hand came a sharp crack. Eckersley thrust his chair back and stood up abruptly, his body poised, listening keenly. 'That was a gunshot.'

'It can't have been,' said Hamilton.

Eckersley waved him quiet. 'It was. I know what I'm talking about. That was a gun.'

'It'll be a poacher in the woods,' said Hamilton uneasily.

Eckersley shook his head. 'No. It was too close. Come on, we'd better have a look and see what's happening.'

Hamilton unwillingly got to his feet, sobered by Eckersley's complete seriousness. The chauffeur was right; he'd served in the army for two years and did know what he was talking about when it came to guns.

'I reckon it came from the back of the house,' said Eckersley. 'Shall we go along the terrace? It's quickest.'

Hamilton was shocked. 'We can't do that! What if the master sees us? We'd better take a look in the hall.'

Eckersley's mouth hardened into a straight line. 'All right.'

On the other side of the green baize door the hall was deathly quiet. Once again, Eckersley stood, poised and listening. 'The study,' he said softly. 'Can you hear it?'

Hamilton did hear it then, a little choking sob followed by rapid breathing. Straightening his waistcoat and squaring his shoulders, he pushed open the door of the study.

Professor Alan Carrington was kneeling on the floor, a gun held loosely in his hand. Beside him the body of Charles Otterbourne lay sprawled out on the hearthrug. He looked round as the door opened but said nothing.

Hamilton looked from the Professor to the horribly still body on the rug. There was a great dark patch by Mr Otterbourne's ear. For what seemed an endless space of time, Hamilton couldn't take in what had happened and then Eckersley spoke.

'You've killed him!'

The Professor got to his feet and stared at them. 'I killed him?' He looked at the gun in his hand. '*I killed him?*'

Hamilton was shaking. 'You bloody murderer. Yes, you killed him.'

The Professor's face twisted in fury. 'What the devil are you talking about? I'll have you know I've done no such thing, my good man.'

It was the *my good man* that did it. As if someone had broken a spell, Hamilton started forward, Eckersley by his side. 'Don't you *my good man* me. You've killed him.'

The gun came up in the Professor's hand and Eckersley made a dive for his arm. The Professor grunted and struggled. Hamilton tried to catch hold of him and, with a deafening blast, the gun went off, the bullet zinging off the marble of the fireplace. There was an utter confusion of shouts, blows and grabbing hands, then the gun went skittering along the floor and the three men fell into the hall in a heaving, struggling, yelling mass.

Hamilton felt a hand between his shoulder blades, pulling him away, and found himself looking into a distorted, shouting face he dimly recognized as that of Gerard Carrington. He fell back, panting, as Carrington wrenched Eckersley away from the Professor. The hall was suddenly full of people all demanding to know what was happening. Gerard Carrington had hold of his father's arm and the womenservants surrounded Hamilton. Molly Lewis was with them. She was speaking too, but Hamilton couldn't make out the words.

Hamilton, his chest heaving, straightened his clothes and pointed a shaky hand at the Professor. 'He killed him,' he said, raising his voice to carry over the torrent of questioning voices. 'He killed the Master.'

There was a fresh chorus of voices. Mr Dunbar, he mechanically noticed, had come out of the library and was staring at the Professor.

'I don't believe a word of it,' said Dunbar robustly, plunging his way past the group and into the study. Gerard Carrington, keeping a firm grip on his father, went after him. Molly followed. She was so utterly bewildered she scarcely grasped the sense of what Hamilton said. The Professor was talking, a non-stop flow of words, but she couldn't make out what he said.

Then she saw her father's body and screamed.

THREE

Molly, after that first scream, stood bewildered and silent, her hand to her mouth. Dad was lying sprawled out on the rug before the hearth, one hand flung wide. Papers were scattered round him on the floor, flapping lazily in the breeze from the open French windows. In the garden beyond, the lawns stretched out in the green glory of a spring day. She knew there was an avalanche of voices round her, a meaningless torrent of noise. A blackbird hopped across the grass and Molly stared at it, trying to see anything but that grotesque thing on the rug, the thing that had been her father. The blackbird pecked a worm from the grass, snapping at it with its beak. Molly gave a little cry as this innocent violence seemed suddenly too much to bear.

She felt her maid, Susan, put her hand on her arm. 'Come with me, m'am. You shouldn't be in here. It's not right.' Susan's voice was kindly but Molly didn't want to go. Mr Dunbar was still kneeling beside her father. It was hard to take in how quickly everything had happened.

Dunbar looked up, his face grave. 'He's dead, all right,' he said, looking to where Professor Carrington stood, Gerry beside him. 'You did this, sir?'

'No, I damn well didn't,' said the Professor testily. 'Gerry, for heaven's sake, can we go?' He ran a shaky hand through his hair. 'There's no point staying here any longer. We'll have to get my machine packed up, I know, but then I really think we should leave.' His gaze slid past the body on the rug. 'It's obvious that Mr Otterbourne can't help us any more and we have no further business here.'

Gerry's grip tightened on his arm. 'Dad, shut up!' He looked at Molly, his face harried. 'I'm sorry. It's just his way of talking.' He turned to Hamilton and Eckersley. 'Is there anywhere I can take my father? Somewhere we can stay until the police arrive?'

'The police?' broke in Professor Carrington. 'Bless my soul, boy, what do you want the police for?'

Dunbar stood up, his hands behind his back, his chin thrust

forward. 'There is a man lying dead, sir, and you have to account for it.'

The Professor flinched back as if he had been struck a physical blow.

'For God's sake,' said Gerry desperately, 'will you leave this to me?' He looked at Hamilton and Eckersley once more. 'Is there anywhere?'

Molly found her voice. 'You'd better go into the library,' she said shakily. 'It's across the hall.' She shook off Susan's hand. 'Don't worry. It's all right. I'll be all right.'

In a ghastly parody of his usual manner, Hamilton showed them across the hall into the library. With Gerry beside him, Professor Carrington sat bolt upright on the leather sofa.

'The police,' said Molly to Hamilton. 'Please phone the police.'

Inspector Gibson paused by the open door of the library where Sergeant Atterby was solidly keeping guard. 'Is he in here?' he asked in an undertone.

'Yes, sir,' said the sergeant quietly. 'Him and his son, Gerard Carrington.'

'Has he said anything?'

Sergeant Atterby puffed out his cheeks in wry agreement. 'He's done nothing *but* talk, sir,' he said in low voice. 'I'm beginning to wonder if he's all there. He hasn't mentioned Mr Otterbourne but he's gone on and on about a lecture he's supposed to be giving tonight.' Sergeant Atterby shrugged. 'I couldn't understand a word of it. He's not shut up.' He cast a glance back into the room. 'I know he's a professor, sir. I reckon we might have a real mad scientist on our hands.'

'You mustn't believe what you read in magazines about scientists, Sergeant,' said Gibson, uneasily aware that the Sergeant was voicing his own thoughts.

'He's not normal, sir,' said Atterby with conviction. 'That young chap, Mr Carrington, he's all right. He's worried, I can tell. He knows what's happened. He's tried to get his father to talk about it, but the Professor just ignores him.'

This, thought Inspector Gibson, was going to be difficult. On the face of it, there didn't seem to be much doubt about what had happened, certainly not in view of the menservants' evidence.

He had been shown the study first where Charles Otterbourne still lay with papers scattered around him. On the table were more papers, scribbled over with mysterious-looking diagrams and a box about the size of a gramophone without its horn. The gun, an automatic, belonged to the house. Mrs Lewis's husband had used it during the war. Hamilton, the butler, couldn't say if it was usually kept in the study but Mr Lewis might have left it there.

The Inspector drew a deep breath. It seemed like an open and shut case but he was wary of arresting the Professor out of hand. For one thing, he was a professor and therefore a man to treat with respect. But what was really making him pause was Hamilton's and Eckersley's assurance that the man was off his head. Inspector Gibson had never had anything to do with loonies before and Hamilton's confident assertion that the Professor would end up in Broadmoor unsettled him. 'Mad as a hatter,' Hamilton had said *and* he had witnessed the Professor quarrelling with his master. It worried him that Sergeant Atterby so obviously agreed with them.

He squared his shoulders and walked into the library, motioning to Sergeant Atterby to follow him.

The Professor was sitting on a leather sofa beside a younger man who was, presumably, Gerard Carrington. Despite his shabby clothes, the Professor had a real presence, thought Gibson. His eyes were very bright. Unnaturally bright, perhaps. He gave an official cough. 'Can I have a word with you, sir?'

'At last!' Professor Carrington got to his feet. 'How long will this take?'

'I'm afraid I can't say, sir,' said Gibson. 'I must ask you to tell me exactly what happened.'

'I've gone through this endlessly,' said Professor Carrington, clenching his fists in frustration.

'Dad,' said Gerard Carrington warningly. 'This is a police officer. Just answer his questions, will you?'

The Professor sighed in exasperation. 'Very well.' He braced his arms against the back of the sofa. 'If you insist, I'll go through it again. I had an appointment with Charles Otterbourne to discuss my new recording apparatus. The sound itself is recorded on to magnetic ribbons by means of . . .'

'What did you actually do, sir?'

'I invented it.'

Inspector Gibson began to wonder if Professor Carrington was pulling his leg. 'What did you actually do with regard to Mr Otterbourne, sir?'

Alan Carrington glared at him. 'Nothing.'

Inspector Gibson coughed once more. 'You must have done something, sir. Let me just run through the facts of the case as I understand them. You had an appointment with Mr Otterbourne, yes?'

Professor Carrington looked at him wearily. 'So I've said. It was to discuss . . .'

Inspector Gibson held up his hand. 'Never mind that for the moment, sir. You'd been with Mr Otterbourne in the study, yes?'

'Yes, of course I was. Great heavens, man, do you usually state the obvious?'

He glanced at his watch. 'Can you hurry up? I want to catch the train back to London and the best service departs in little over half an hour.'

Inspector Gibson heard Sergeant Atterby's quick intake of breath. Surely, *surely* the man must know he was in danger of being arrested for murder? 'I'm afraid you might have to miss the train, sir,' he managed to say. He held up his hand to cut off Alan Carrington's torrent of words. 'I need to get to the bottom of what occurred this morning. The butler served you and Mr Otterbourne with coffee at approximately quarter past eleven.' Alan Carrington looked blank. 'The butler stated he heard you speak very sharply to Mr Otterbourne.'

'The butler should mind his own business,' said Carrington distractedly. 'I might have been a little impatient. It's a fault of mine, I'm afraid. Mr Otterbourne seemed unable to grasp the utilitarian value of thermionic emissions and I was probably more abrupt than the occasion demanded.' He glanced up. 'You might have heard the process referred to as the Edison effect. It can be demonstrated by . . .'

Inspector Gibson hastily intervened. 'Never mind that, sir. You say there was no personal disagreement between you and Mr Otterbourne?'

'No.' The Professor looked puzzled. 'Why on earth should there be?'

Inspector Gibson ignored the question. 'About ten or fifteen minutes later, the butler and the chauffeur heard a shot. They found you in the study, holding a gun.'

Alan Carrington ran his hand through his hair. 'I've explained all that,' he complained. 'And I must say, I thought both the menservants behaved in a disgraceful way.' He dropped his gaze and looked away. 'I don't know what came over them.'

Gerard Carrington stood up. 'Listen to me, Dad.' He spoke slowly and clearly. Professor Carrington unwillingly raised his chin and looked at his son. 'Mr Otterbourne is dead.' Professor Carrington flinched. 'The police think you shot him.'

He ignored his father's murmur of *ridiculous*. 'You were found holding the gun. How did that come about?' The elder man swallowed but said nothing. Gerard Carrington took a deep breath. He spoke very deliberately, spacing out the words. 'Did you shoot Mr Otterbourne?'

Alan Carrington started back as if he'd been struck. 'Of course not! Gerry, you mustn't say such things, even in jest.'

'Then tell us what happened.' Again, Gerard Carrington spoke very deliberately.

Professor Carrington covered his face with his hands. 'I went out of the room. It was a call of nature, you understand. I was only a few minutes at most. When I came back in he was dead.' He dropped his hands. 'I suppose he committed suicide but why he should do any such thing, I do not know. He seemed perfectly in control of himself before I left. I was astonished. He was lying face down on the floor with a gun beside him. As I went to turn him over, the menservants burst into the room and demanded to know what I was doing. Their manner was abrasive in the extreme.'

'You actually had the gun in your hand, I believe,' said the Inspector.

'I picked it up, yes.'

'And you threatened the butler with it.'

'I did no such thing!' said Carrington indignantly. 'I told him to stop talking nonsense – he was babbling that I had shot his master – and I told him to stop.'

'Whilst holding the gun.'

'What the devil was I meant to do with it?'

Inspector Gibson glanced at Sergeant Atterby and took a deep breath. 'Professor Carrington, I'm afraid I have to ask you to accompany me to the station.'

'To catch the train?' asked the Professor hopefully.

Gerard Carrington caught hold of his father's arm. 'Dad, you're being taken to the police station. Stop pretending you don't know what's going on. You're being arrested.'

'Arrested?' repeated Alan Carrington. '*Arrested?*'

'Yes. For the murder of Mr Otterbourne.'

And Alan Carrington started to laugh.

It was nearly nine o'clock that evening when Gerard Carrington returned to Stoke Horam House.

Steve Lewis was standing by the fireplace in the drawing room, his elbow on the mantelpiece, talking earnestly to a sandy-haired man about his own age. He broke off abruptly as Carrington was shown into the room. 'Gerry! I can hardly believe what's happened. I was at Uncle Maurice's. I've only just got back. Why didn't someone try and get hold of me?'

'I knew you were there,' said Carrington. 'Your wife said so when we first arrived. Uncle Maurice is Colonel Willoughby, isn't he? I don't know his address or if he's on the telephone or not.'

'He's not on the phone but Molly should have sent a telegram.'

Carrington shook his head. He was speaking mechanically, forcing himself to think of the words. 'Your wife was knocked sideways. The doctor packed her off to bed with a sleeping draught.'

'Yes, Hamilton told me she'd taken it pretty hard.' Steve Lewis looked critically at Carrington. His face was paper-white and he was swaying on his feet. 'Sit down, Gerry.' He walked over to the sideboard and picked up the whisky. 'Can I get you a drink?'

Carrington sank gratefully into a chair, resting his forehead on his hand. 'Thanks. It's been awful.' He took the whisky and soda from Lewis. 'I hoped you'd be here. I wanted to explain things. There aren't any real excuses but I don't know if my father's responsible for his actions.'

The sandy-haired man looked at him curiously. 'Excuse me, Mr Carrington, but do you believe your father's guilty? I'm Ragnall, by the way, Hugo Ragnall, Mr Otterbourne's secretary.'

Gerard Carrington spread his hands wide in a hopeless

gesture. 'He more or less has to be, doesn't he?' His mouth trembled. 'He's always had a shocking temper but there's more to it than that. The last couple of years have been pretty grim. He got caught in a Zeppelin raid during the war and had to be pulled out of the rubble. That affected him very badly, but when my mother died he went to pieces. He simply couldn't cope. If he doesn't like something he just ignores it.' He looked at Lewis. 'I've told you something of this before. After my mother died it was as if she'd never existed, but every so often he'll say something that proves he knows how things really are. It drives me up the wall. The police don't know what to make of him. He's not said anything at all for the last few hours. He didn't seem to know I was in the room with him. I telephoned Sir David Hargreaves, his doctor, and he's on his way. He might get him to talk but as soon as the police learn his medical history, I'm afraid they'll simply shut him away.'

'His medical history?' asked Ragnall.

'He's always been unstable,' said Carrington flatly. 'It was my mother's death that finally pushed him over the edge. He had a complete nervous breakdown. He had to give up his post at Cambridge and eventually there was nothing for it but for him to be admitted as a patient in a mental asylum. He was released a couple of years ago.'

'A mental hospital?' repeated Ragnall slowly. He shot a look at Lewis. 'Maybe I'm wrong.'

Lewis sucked his cheeks in. 'It's difficult, isn't it?' He hesitated. 'Look, Gerry, I know things look black for your father, but there could be another explanation.' He glanced at Ragnall. 'That's what we've been discussing.' He drew a deep breath. 'You tell him, Ragnall. It's all to do with the firm's pension fund.'

Gerry Carrington listened in growing bewilderment and with many interjections. 'But that doesn't make any sense either,' he said when Ragnall had finished. 'Even if Mr Otterbourne had been dipping into the pension fund, surely that's not such a big deal? It's his firm, after all.'

'It's a very big deal,' said Ragnall. 'Mr Otterbourne might have thought of it as the firm's money but it's theft. The pension fund is made up of both voluntary savings and compulsory contributions from the workers. That money was invested safely, mainly in gilt-edged stock. Those stocks have been sold out and the capital has vanished.'

'Do you see now, Gerry?' asked Steve. 'I tell you, he wouldn't want to face the music. His reputation would be ruined and, for a man like him, that would be impossible to live with.'

'I still don't see it,' said Gerry. 'From what you've told me, Mr Otterbourne didn't know you'd tumbled to it. Besides that, he wouldn't discuss the firm's affairs with my father. For one thing, the guv'nor wouldn't have a clue what he was talking about.'

'That's true enough, Mr Carrington,' said Ragnall, 'but, as I understand it, your father stated he left the room. Mr Otterbourne could have easily have picked up the accounts and realized exactly what I'd found.'

'I knew him well,' said Steve Lewis quietly. 'He wouldn't want to be remembered as a suicide. He could have realized the game was up and, knowing Professor Carrington would more or less be bound to be blamed, shot himself in order to incriminate him.'

Gerard Carrington started to his feet. 'No,' he breathed. 'No, he couldn't. No one could.' His voice quavered. 'Could they?'

Lewis shrugged. 'I tell you, I knew the man. He lived for his reputation. It meant everything to him.'

'But this could let my father off the hook,' muttered Carrington. 'I thought he'd lost his temper and perhaps didn't know what he was doing, but he could have been telling the truth all along. Is there any way of proving it? If we could show that Mr Otterbourne did know he'd been found out, it might make all the difference.'

Ragnall and Lewis swapped glances. 'We could look in the study,' suggested Ragnall. 'I know where I left the accounts. If they've been disturbed, then that would surely tell us that Mr Otterbourne had looked at them.'

'Come on,' said Lewis. 'The body was taken away this afternoon but I don't think anything else has been touched.'

The three men walked into the study. There, on the floor, was the manila folder. Ragnall stooped down and picked them up. 'These are the accounts,' he said breathlessly. He opened the folder, flicking through the papers. 'He must have looked at them.'

'Come on!' said Carrington urgently. 'We have to tell the police.'

They drove to the police station in Lewis's car. As they drew up outside the station, Carrington noticed a black Rolls-Royce parked nearby. 'It looks as if Sir David Hargreaves has arrived,' he said. 'It's just as well. Even if Dad's not guilty, he's still in a pretty bad way.'

Sir David was standing by the desk in the police station, talking to Inspector Gibson. Three other policemen were in the room. They all looked very solemn. Sir David looked up as Carrington, Lewis and Ragnall came in.

'Sir David,' said Gerry Carrington. 'It's good of you to come, sir.' He stopped, chilled by the sudden silence in the room and the grave faces of Sir David and the policemen.

Sir David glanced at Inspector Gibson, then came forward and, looking at Gerard Carrington compassionately, put his hand on his arm. 'I'm sorry to have to break the news, Mr Carrington, but your father is past my help. The Inspector found him in his cell.' He paused. 'I'm afraid your father is dead. He took his own life.'

FOUR

For the first couple of weeks or so after her father had died, Molly found it hard to work out exactly what was happening and why. She had loved her father and he had betrayed her. She was grief-stricken, hurt, but, most of all, angry. A chilled, hard anger that ripped into her emotions like ice ripping away the top layer of unshielded skin.

She'd refused to believe it at first. Dad *couldn't* be a thief. Everything he'd stood for, every rule he handed down, every hoop he'd made her jump through was undermined by that one stark fact. Her father was a crook.

Ever since her mother died she had protected Dad from the world, shielding him from unkind remarks and cynical appraisal. Why? Because she believed he believed in his ideal of an ideal life for ideal workers.

It was so quixotic, so unattainable and so worthwhile that she loved him for it. She had enough worldly knowledge to see how some regarded him as nothing more than a self-serving, unctuous, pompous hypocrite. The knowledge had hurt. And now the cynics were proved right. Her father *was* a self-serving, unctuous, pompous hypocrite. All her past happiness had been poisoned and she'd been trampled by those feet of clay.

To make it worse, at the one time in her life when she wanted to hide like an injured animal, she was forced to parade her scarred emotions for public enjoyment in the press. Not that she could feel any emotion any longer. She was numb. The tidal wave of publicity that had engulfed her drowned everything, so that the inquest, the funeral, the horrible, endless questions about her father, seemed like little islands of events in a featureless sea.

One thing she had been sure about, and that was she didn't want to stay in Stoke Horam. Every room in the house, every cottage and building in the village, reminded her of Dad.

Steve proposed a move to London and found a ground floor flat in Mottram Place, off Sackville Street. The domestic distractions of moving house were a welcome relief. There were practical decisions to be taken, such as furniture and food and where everyone would sleep. Steve solved that tricky problem by cutting the domestic staff down to a cook and two maids and suggesting Hugo Ragnall should live out. She found the new arrangements unexpectedly agreeable and she was glad to escape to the anonymous bustle of London.

She should, she knew, be grateful to Steve. He seemed to have inexhaustible energy as he flung himself into work, defying the speculators who hovered round, waiting for the crash. 'Every penny,' he vowed to a fascinated public, 'will be repaid. Not one of Otterbourne's employees will come off worse.' Which, if it wasn't quite true, was true enough to satisfy the press. He plunged his own money into the firm, cut the unprofitable lines, sold off some of the cottages and land and re-opened negotiations with Dunbar. He tried to comfort her and she should have been grateful, but she seemed incapable of feeling anything; she was completely numb.

It was a fortnight after her father died that Steve came into her dressing room. Molly was in front of the mirror, brushing her hair. They had been invited to dinner with Mrs Soames-Pensford, a neighbour in Mottram Place. Mrs Soames-Pensford was, Molly dully knew, a kind-hearted, gossipy soul with three chattering daughters. Steve wanted to accept the invitation and she went along with as little enthusiasm as a puppet on wires.

He leaned forward and gently took the hairbrush from her hand.

'Shouldn't you be dressing for dinner?' she snapped, irritated by his presence.

He flicked his finger along the bristles, then leaned forward and ran the brush through her hair. 'We've plenty of time.'

'Steve . . .' she began wearily.

'You used to like me doing this,' he said softly. His fingers caressed the back of her neck and she moved involuntarily. The light from her dressing table lamp caught the faint golden stubble on his chin. She had liked him stroking her hair. He hadn't done it for a long time. 'You've got beautiful hair,' he said, looping a dark-brown lock round his finger. 'It's the first thing I noticed about you. It's such a rich chestnut, with deep red lights. That, and your smile.'

He smiled, that wickedly engaging smile, and she knew he

wanted her to smile back. When she didn't, he dropped his
hand. 'Come on, Molly. We used to have fun, remember?'
He picked up her lipstick and idly twisted it in and out
of the tube. 'I used to be able to make you laugh. You used
to like me clowning around.' He leaned forward and, looking
in the mirror, blobbed a smudge of red lipstick on his nose.
'You remember?'

'Steve, don't be a idiot,' she said, amused despite herself.
'You can't turn up for dinner wearing lipstick on your nose.'

'It comes off, doesn't it?' he said worriedly scrubbing at
the mark. 'Oh, Lord, it's gone everywhere. Molly, how the
dickens do I get this stuff off? I don't mind being Koko the
Clown for you but the Soames-Pensfords will think I'm off
my chump.'

'You need some cold cream,' she said laughing. She picked
up the tub. 'Here, bend down and let me wipe it off for you.'

He stood obediently still while she rubbed his nose. 'That's
it, I think.'

He caught her hands and kissed them. 'That's better. I
haven't seen you smile for ages.' She couldn't help but smile
as she felt the warm strength of his hands. 'My word, I'm
tired,' he added inconsequentially and, for the first time, she
noticed the shadows under his eyes. 'I wish I hadn't said we'd
go out tonight, but we can't ignore the neighbours. You need
to make some new friends, Molly. You've spent too long
brooding.' He kissed the top of her head. 'You've seemed very
distant, these past few weeks.'

She said nothing, but relaxed her head against his chest,
enjoying the sensation of his hand on her cheek.

'I've invited Gerry round for dinner tomorrow,' he said after
a while.

She broke away. She couldn't help it. 'Gerry?'

'Yes.' He drew her back to him. 'Molly, what on earth's
the matter? Don't you like Gerry? I've noticed you stiffen up
before when I've mentioned his name.'

'It's silly, really, Steve.' She swallowed and plunged on.
'I can't think of Gerry without thinking of that dreadful day.'
That was partly the truth; true enough that she had clung to
it as an explanation to herself. But – and she hardly wanted
to acknowledge it – the other reason she winced at the thought
of Gerry was guilt. Steve's hand stroked her neck gently.

For some reason that made the guilt worse. She liked Gerry; liked him a great deal and, what's more, was well aware that he liked her. Their only time alone had been that shared coffee in the conservatory but those few minutes blazed in her memory.

'So that's it,' he said thoughtfully. 'I had wondered if . . .'

She looked up in sharp, startled wariness. 'What?'

He kissed her again. 'I was being stupid, I suppose,' he said with a rueful smile. 'Imagining things. I have imagined them, haven't I?' he asked with sudden anxiety. 'It'd . . . Well, it'd hurt like the dickens if things went wrong between us, Molly.' His hands trembled on her skin. He was very strong and very sturdy and very good-looking in a solid, Anglo-Saxon way, but he seemed so suddenly vulnerable that she felt tears prick the back of her eyes.

'Oh, Steve,' said quietly, getting to her feet.

'Molly! Don't cry.' He reached out a finger and wiped a tear from her cheek. 'I couldn't manage without you, you know. You're my wife,' he said with a surge of feeling. 'Mine. I love you. You . . . you do love me, don't you?'

With her head on his chest, hearing his quick breathing and the rapid beat of his heart, his arms encircled her. He kissed her once more, very tenderly, then with growing passion. 'Shall we,' he murmured, 'be late for dinner?'

At six o'clock on a glorious evening in early July, eight weeks after what the newspapers called the *Double Tragedy at Stoke Horam*, Jack Haldean sat in the smoking-room of the Young Services Club watching Hector Ferguson pick out a tune with one finger on the piano.

This was not how Jack had planned to spend the evening. After being stuck in the office of *On The Town* all day, he had dived into the club for something to eat and was heading for the park, with warm and affectionate thoughts of a pint of bitter on the way, when he was buttonholed in the lobby by Ferguson.

'Haldean! The very man!' Ferguson dropped his voice. 'Can you spare me a few minutes?' He lowered his voice further. 'It's confidential, you understand? I've been worrying away for weeks now. I couldn't think what to do or who to ask, and then I saw you.'

Although he didn't know Ferguson well, Jack liked the earnest, red-headed young Scot. Ferguson had a passion and a talent for jazz, both as a composer and a pianist. Jack had hardly ever heard him mention the shipping office where he worked but he could talk enthusiastically for hours about jazz.

At the moment, however, Ferguson wasn't talking at all. He stood by the smoking-room piano, picking out notes in an embarrassed way. 'I'm sorry, Haldean,' he said. 'I don't know what to do for the best. When I saw you in the lobby, you seemed like the obvious person to talk to but I'm not sure how to start.'

'Close your eyes and take a stab at it, old thing,' suggested Jack, covertly glancing at his watch. Honestly, if Ferguson didn't get a move on, the pubs would be closed.

Ferguson turned back to the piano. 'This thing needs tuning,' he muttered irrelevantly.

'Ferguson,' said Jack warningly. 'You didn't lug me in here to agitate yourself about the piano.'

'Sorry.' Ferguson took a deep breath. 'It's about Stoke Horam. You remember what happened there?'

Jack sat up attentively. This sounded promising. 'Considering it was in the newspapers for weeks, I should say so.'

Ferguson brought down his hands in a chord, closed the piano lid in a gesture of finality, and turned round. 'Have you ever heard of a man called Andrew Dunbar?'

'Andrew Dunbar? The name rings a bell but I don't know why. Who is he?'

'He's my stepfather.' Hector Ferguson went to the door, shut it, and walked back to the piano with his chin lowered and his hands deep in his pockets. 'He lives in Scotland but he comes down to London fairly often. He's separated from my mother and he hasn't got a lot of time for either of us.' He looked up with a faint smile. 'I may say the feeling's mutual. He's the owner of Dunbar's, the gramophone manufacturers. He was on the spot when Charles Otterbourne committed suicide.'

'Was he, by jingo?'

'Yes . . .' Ferguson hitched himself on to the stool. 'I know you've got friends in the police. I wondered if you ever got to know what went on behind the scenes.'

'Sometimes,' said Jack cautiously. 'I haven't any special knowledge of what happened at Stoke Horam though.'

Ferguson looked deflated. 'Haven't you?' He drummed his fingers on the wood of the stool. 'I'm not sure how to put this, but since Professor Carrington and Mr Otterbourne died, my stepfather has been a very happy man.' He tapped a cigarette on the back of his hand and lit it nervously. 'He's never been able to conceal his feelings, Haldean, and he was delighted with how things turned out.'

'It sounds a bit ghoulish. Why should he be so happy?'

'I don't know.' Hector Ferguson pulled nervously at his cigarette. 'You see, on the face of it, Mr Otterbourne's and Professor Carrington's deaths, particularly the Professor's, should have made things very difficult for him, but he's been on top of the world. It's very odd, especially when you understand how much he likes money.'

'I don't suppose he's unique in that.'

Ferguson smiled fleetingly. 'No, I don't suppose he is, but he's a canny customer, and no mistake. Professor Carrington built a new type of gramophone for my stepfather. When that machine's ready for production, it'll be a very valuable commodity indeed. Professor Carrington had absolutely no business sense and my stepfather got him to sign a contract giving him the rights to the machine. That contract was little more than daylight robbery. I've heard him gloat about what a shrewd deal he'd pulled off. So far so good, yes?'

'Yes, from your stepfather's point of view,' said Jack with a shrug. 'Not so good for Professor Carrington, I'd say.'

'Exactly. When the Professor died, my stepfather should have been devastated. I don't suppose he cared tuppence about the Professor but he cared about his machine. He was hoping to make a considerable profit from it, so I wasn't surprised when I heard he'd asked Gerard Carrington, the Professor's son, to take over his father's work.' Hector Ferguson clasped his hands together with a frown. 'I made it my business to meet Carrington. I wanted his opinion of what happened at Stoke Horam.'

'Which is?'

'Which is the story in the newspapers was essentially true,' said Ferguson with a shrug. 'Gerard Carrington believes Mr Otterbourne committed suicide. I can see why my stepfather approached Gerard Carrington. He's a scientist at the University of London and, in many ways, a much better bet than his father. He's not as brilliant as the Professor, perhaps, but he's a much more reasonable type. He's the ideal man – perhaps the only man – to bring the new machine to a point where it's ready for production.'

'Couldn't that be why your stepfather's so pleased?' suggested Jack. 'I mean, I don't know much about science and so on, but to get someone to step into the breach like that must have been a huge weight off his mind.'

Ferguson glanced up. 'You'd think so, wouldn't you? However, Gerard Carrington is nobody's fool and he's arguing the toss about the contract. I expected my stepfather to be furious, but he isn't. He's completely and utterly smug. Somehow, in some way, things have worked out for him. He's as pleased as punch. I can't get to the bottom of it, but I'm sure there's something funny going on.'

Jack looked at Ferguson thoughtfully. He was alive with anxiety. 'What's eating you? There's more to this than a suspicion that your stepfather has brought off a smart piece of business.'

Ferguson took a deep breath. 'It's the Stoke Horam suicides, Haldean. Two men died in very peculiar circumstances.' There were white lines etched round his mouth and his eyes were narrow with tension. 'My stepfather's ruthless. And he's very happy.' His meaning was obvious.

'Do you think he's responsible?' asked Jack, quietly.

'I don't know!' exploded Ferguson. He made a chopping motion with his hand as if to physically fend off the suggestion. 'Charles Otterbourne and Professor Carrington committed suicide. The coroner said so.' He stopped, catching his breath. 'I know,' he added wearily. 'Anything else sounds ridiculous.' He met Jack's eyes squarely. 'I said I didn't like him. I admit that, but I know what he's capable of. I don't know what he did or how he engineered it, but I'm sure the full truth hasn't come to light. I don't know what to do. Everything seems so cut and dried but it's *wrong*.'

'Why don't you go to the police?'

'And tell them what?' demanded Ferguson. 'I haven't got any evidence. I'd be laughed at or, worse than that, be accused of having my own axe to grind.'

Jack finished his cigarette in silence. 'What if I have a word with my friend, Bill Rackham? He's a Scotland Yard man. He'll be discreet, I know.'

Ferguson looked relieved. 'I'd be very grateful. I might be

barking up the wrong tree. If my stepfather's innocent, I'll be glad to hear it. It's just that I can't get it out of my mind that he might not be.'

'The Charles Otterbourne case?' said Inspector William Rackham thoughtfully.

Jack had abandoned his plans both for the pub and the park to follow up his promise to Ferguson. They were in Rackham's rooms off Russell Square, the upper floor of an inconvenient but beautifully proportioned Georgian building. The sash windows stood open, the last of the evening sun gilding the well-worn carpet and comfortable chairs.

'Help yourself to whisky, Jack,' Rackham said, gesturing to the decanter on the sideboard, 'or there's beer, if you'd rather.' He moved a heap of newspapers off the sofa and sat down. 'It's certainly a puzzle about Dunbar. I don't know why he should be so happy.'

Jack took the cork out of a bottle of Bass and, pouring out a glass, sat down in the opposite chair. He and Bill Rackham, a big, untidy ginger-haired Northerner, were good friends, and Jack trusted his judgement. 'So you don't think there's anything in it?'

'I don't know what there can be,' said Bill. 'I'd have said Dunbar was very much a loser from the affair. I went into the Otterbourne case fairly closely at the time as I had a hunch – incorrectly as it turned out – that we would be called in. After you telephoned I looked up my notes. The coroner brought in a verdict of suicide on Charles Otterbourne, I know, but in the first instance it looked as if Otterbourne had been murdered by Professor Carrington.'

'The Professor hanged himself while he was under arrest, didn't he?'

Rackham nodded. 'That's right. Gibson, the officer in charge of the case, had to endure a reprimand from the coroner which, I think, was probably deserved. After all, Professor Carrington was clearly unstable and shouldn't have been left alone. His son said as much, and so did his doctor. I did wonder, though, if the Professor's suicide made the coroner's verdict a bit more sympathetic than it might have been.'

'You mean Professor Carrington could have murdered Otterbourne after all?'

'It's a possibility, isn't it? However, the coroner heard the evidence and, although there didn't seem any real reason to doubt his verdict, it all seemed a bit neat.'

'It's got a closed-off quality about it, hasn't it?' agreed Jack. He stretched his legs out on the footstool with relief.

'How's your leg?' asked Rackham, seeing his mouth contract briefly. Jack had had a slight limp for as long as Rackham had known him, a souvenir of the war, but he had recently broken his leg badly and, although the bone had healed, the limp had worsened.

'Not bad,' Jack said dismissively.

'Come off it,' said Rackham, seeing the lines of strain on his friend's dark, rather gypsy-like face. 'It looks like it's giving you the pip.'

Jack smiled broadly. 'All right, Mister Detective-Inspector, sir, you've got me bang to rights. I'm being a brave little soldier. I hope you're suitably impressed. My wretched leg hurts like sin and I've been on my feet for ages. I did a bit of digging in Fleet Street before I came to see you. Stanhope gave me the background to the case.'

'Stanhope of *The Messenger*?'

'That's the lad. Stanhope was disappointed with the Stoke Horam case. He was all geared up to shock us with sensational revelations, when it more or less petered out.'

'I wouldn't say it had petered out, Jack,' countered Rackham. 'The papers were full of it for weeks. With the not-so-saintly Mr Otterbourne on the one hand and a genuine mad scientist on the other, the press had a field day. Ernest Stanhope doesn't know when he's well off.'

'He meant as a crime,' said Jack. 'Like you, he thought the verdict on Charles Otterbourne was very sympathetic to Professor Carrington. His money's on the Professor for murder. However, that's not what's eating my pal, Hector Ferguson. He didn't want to come right out and say it, but he's worried, granted how pleased Dunbar is, that his stepfather might be the real villain of the piece.'

Rackham's eyebrows shot up. 'Dunbar murdered Charles Otterbourne, you mean?'

'That's about the size of it.'

'Can you rely on Ferguson? It sounds as if he may have it in for his stepfather.'

'He admitted he didn't like him,' said Jack with a shrug. 'He said he was a ruthless beggar. I had the impression Ferguson was trying to be objective. He's a very thoughtful Scot. You know the type, Bill. He'll worry away at a thing for ages before he comes to a conclusion, but when he has worked something out, you can be sure he's got a rock-solid line of argument to back him up. He's not someone to make an accusation lightly and, to be fair to him, he hasn't done that.'

'And Andrew Dunbar is happy with the way things have worked out.' Bill took a cigarette from the box. 'That's interesting, but I can't see it adds up. Dunbar was hoping Charles Otterbourne was going to buy his firm. Therefore it's to Dunbar's advantage that Otterbourne was alive to put the deal through. So on that count, Dunbar's out of it, yes?'

'Absolutely,' agreed Jack.

'Now, as I understand it, Professor Carrington was Dunbar's star prize. He'd agreed to make this marvellous machine at a knockdown price for Dunbar. I can't see why Dunbar would kill Otterbourne and he certainly wouldn't do it so as to incriminate the Professor. Professor Carrington wouldn't be any use to Dunbar if he was tried and hanged.'

'Could Gerard Carrington be in league with Dunbar, perhaps? No, that won't work, not if he's trying to negotiate a fairer contract.'

'Exactly, Jack. Dunbar would hardly conspire to murder if it meant he was going to be out of pocket over the deal. I suppose Gerard Carrington could have turned nasty afterwards,' he added thoughtfully.

'Yes, but Dunbar wouldn't be happy about that, would he? He'd be hopping mad.'

'True enough,' agreed Rackham with a frown.

'Say Charles Otterbourne didn't commit suicide,' said Jack. 'Is there anyone else in the running, apart from the Professor?'

'There's the servants, of course. They gave evidence at the inquest, but I can't see they'd have anything to gain. Gerard Carrington, but we've more or less covered him. I can't see why he'd murder Charles Otterbourne. It could be to his advantage that his father died, perhaps, but I don't see how he could have done it, as his father was in a cell at the police station. Professor Carrington was certainly alive when he left. Inspector Gibson testified to that effect.'

'So he's out of it.' Jack ran a hand through his dark hair in a dissatisfied way. 'Anyone else? Chuck the lighter over, Bill. What about the bloke who caused a sensation in court when he blew the gaff about Mr Otterbourne's jiggery-pokery with the pension funds?'

'That's Hugo Ragnall, the secretary, but not only didn't he have anything to gain, he wasn't there. He'd discovered the fraud the night before. The following morning he told Stephen Lewis, Otterbourne's son-in-law, what he'd found and the pair of them had decided to confront Mr Otterbourne after Professor Carrington and Dunbar had gone. Neither man wanted to be around during the day. Stephen Lewis said that the thought of trying to act naturally with the bombshell of the pension funds hanging over them was too much, so they made their excuses and disappeared.'

'Yes, I can see it would be difficult,' agreed Jack. 'Do you know where they got to?'

'Lewis went off to his uncle's, a Colonel Willoughby, and Ragnall came up to London for the day.'

'Stanhope mentioned Stephen Lewis,' said Jack. 'He's pitched in and saved the firm. It looked as if the company might go under but Lewis turned it round. According to Stanhope, Lewis restored a lot of confidence in the business and it looks as if it's going to pull through. What about Mr Otterbourne's daughter?'

'She was knocked sideways by her father's death, by all accounts. He was a dictatorial sort of beggar though, and she might have resented it. Having said that, there was no particular reason why she and her husband should continue living with her father if she didn't want to. It seems a bit extreme to bump him off when all she had to do was move out. Besides that, she was in the kitchen talking to the cook when it happened.' Rackham shook his head. 'It was an odd case altogether, Jack. There's all sorts of threads that could have lead somewhere but it all seemed to be done and dusted. With the two verdicts of suicide it was never put under the spotlight as a murder investigation would have been, but if it was murder, then the chief suspect has to be Professor Carrington.'

'But there's the happy Mr Dunbar.'

'I'm blowed if I know what he's so happy about.' Rackham ran his hand round his chin. 'Leave it with me. I don't know what I can do, but I can look at the files again. You never know, they might suggest something.'

Steve Lewis and Gerry Carrington looked up as Molly came in to the study. 'I wondered if you had finished?' she asked with a smile. She glanced at the clock. 'Would you like to join us for dinner, Gerry?'

For the last five weeks, Gerry Carrington had been a regular visitor at the flat. Steve, after that surprisingly acute moment of insight, never mentioned his fears again. Not that, thought Molly, looking at her big, fair-haired husband affectionately, there was anything to be jealous about. She'd allowed herself to be silly about Gerry, which was stupid of her. It didn't stop Gerry being as pleasant, as rumpled and as undoubtedly brilliant as ever, but it didn't mean anything to her now. He was simply Steve's cousin and friend. That was it, she told herself, stamping on the odd wayward contradiction her mind threw up.

Steve welcomed her acceptance of Gerry with frank relief. Gerry was, according to Steve, the only man on earth who could change Professor Carrington's work from a heap of wood and wires and reams of indecipherable diagrams into a useable machine. And, if only they could negotiate a deal with Dunbar, that machine would make Otterbourne's profitable again. The two men had been working since lunchtime. They were meeting Dunbar tomorrow, and Steve hoped that would result in a concrete deal.

Gerry Carrington stood up. 'I won't stop for dinner, thanks. It's very kind of you, but no. I think I'd like an early night.' He stifled a yawn. 'By jingo, I'm tired.'

'You're not the only one, old man,' said Steve, trying not to yawn in turn. He stood up from the table, stretching his shoulders. 'Still, I think we've got something concrete to show Dunbar. That was a very worthwhile session, Gerry.' He glanced at the papers on the table. 'I'll go through these this evening and put our ideas in some sort of order. I want to check the figures with Ragnall but, with any luck, we've got a workable scheme to present to Dunbar tomorrow.' He walked to the sideboard. 'Have a drink before you go, Gerry,' he said hospitably. 'Sherry for you, Molly?'

'Thanks,' she said, taking the glass from him. 'I'm glad it's gone well. What are you going to say to Mr Dunbar?'

Steve and Gerry exchanged looks and laughed. 'We're going to tell him he can't have it all his own way,' said Gerry. He tapped the folder with his forefinger. 'With these plans I can produce a commercial model but I'm jolly well not going to unless Dunbar puts some more money on the table.' He let out a worried breath. 'I can't tell you how wary I feel about Dunbar. The last few times I've met him he's been unbearable.'

Steve looked at him quickly. 'So you've noticed that, have you?'

Gerry Carrington nodded. 'It's unmistakable. He's horribly smug about something. Maybe he thinks he can get one over on me, but I've told him I'm not going to be bound by that disgraceful contract he signed with my poor father. He's got something up his sleeve, but I don't know what. I don't trust him.'

'I don't trust him either, but what I want to ensure is that once Dunbar *has* got the machine, he doesn't simply up and sell his firm to one of the big boys such as H.M.V. or Victrola. Otterbourne's hasn't had a new product for years. We need your machine, Gerry,'

Molly wrinkled her forehead, puzzled. 'I don't understand. No one seems to like Mr Dunbar so why doesn't Gerry simply make the machine and sell it to us? Or to H.M.V. or whomever,' she added. She looked at Gerry. 'I'd rather you sold it to us, of course, but I suppose you can sell it to anyone you like.'

'Because Dunbar's got the original model,' said Gerry. 'It belongs to him. Unfortunately, there's no two ways about that. There's also a question of patents. Dunbar got my father to take out a patent on certain important components that I've used. And, although I could say that the two machines are different, the lawyers would have a field day arguing about it in court. Besides that,' he added, in a different voice, 'I want people to know it was my father's machine.' His voice was very quiet and Molly's heart gave an unexpected little tug. 'It was his machine, you know. I've tidied it up and made it useable, but he was the brains behind it. He lived for his work and I'd like him to be remembered for that.' He sipped his whisky. 'Incidentally, talking about my father, I had a letter from Colonel Willoughby about him a couple of weeks ago and I still haven't got round to replying. I've been busy, I know, but I can't really think what to say.'

'Colonel Willoughby?' repeated Steve. 'Uncle Maurice, you mean?'

'Yes. I don't know what to make of it. It was a very stiff and proper letter. He said he offered his sympathies. As he loathed my father, I'm not so sure he was offering anything of the sort.'

Steve grinned. 'He's a ferocious old devil but his bark's worse than his bite. He expects life to be conducted on military lines. I'm quite fond of him in an odd sort of way. You've never met him, have you, Gerry?'

'No. The family quarrel goes back years.'

'What was it about?' asked Steve. 'I never knew the details.' He paused, delicately. 'Faults on both sides, perhaps?'

Gerry laughed ruefully. 'Not really. I know the guv'nor could quarrel with virtually anyone but this wasn't down to him. My grandfather was a Lithuanian. He was terribly clever but as poor as church mouse. After my grandmother died he found it a real struggle to look after my father. He worked for Sir Josiah Carrington, who owned a string of coal mines. He saved him a fortune by improving his pumping engines and Sir Josiah, as a reward, more or less adopted my father.' He grinned. 'Unfortunately, from my point of view, Sir Josiah had very strict views about inherited wealth. He left all his money to found Carrington Hall, Cambridge, but he did provide for my father's education and bestowed his surname on him.'

'So your name isn't really Carrington at all?' asked Molly. For some reason, that disturbed her. It seemed dishonest, somehow, to have one name and call yourself another.

A spark of resentment showed in Gerry's eyes. 'It's the name I've always used. The family name has about nineteen syllables in it, so I don't intend to change. Part of the trouble was that my father looked so foreign and the Willoughbys don't marry foreigners. When my mother *did* marry my father, all hell broke loose. My mother's name was scored out of the family Bible and so on and so forth. I can't think why the colonel wrote to me.'

'A sense of duty?' suggested Steve.

'Maybe.' Gerry rolled his whisky round his tongue. 'In a way, I suppose it was good of him to write. I really must reply. Did you say he was ill?'

'He's been ill,' said Molly. 'He came back from India a few months ago. The change of climate got to him and he nearly went under with bronchitis. He wrote to me, too.' She hadn't cared for that resentful look and wanted to restore the fellow-feeling between them. 'I didn't like his letter at all. Stiff and proper were about the kindest things that could be said for it. I've never met him, either, Gerry, and, quite frankly, after that letter, I don't really want to.'

Steve looked at Molly's disapproving face and laughed. 'Don't take it to heart so. He must have been stumped for something to say. A man like Uncle Maurice loathes publicity and he would have hated seeing the news splashed all over the papers.'

Gerry finished his whisky. 'None of us exactly enjoyed it. I don't suppose it'll be forgotten for a long time yet.' He looked at the clock and smothered another yawn. 'I'd really better be going. I'll see you tomorrow, Steve.'

'Steve,' said Molly thoughtfully, after Gerry had gone. 'Did you know Gerry's name wasn't really Carrington?'

'But it is Carrington,' he said, puzzled. 'He told us so. I knew about his Lithuanian granddad, if that's what you mean.' He pulled her to him. 'Don't be such a goose. It isn't important.'

'No,' said Molly. 'No, I don't suppose it is.'

In the bedroom of his bungalow in the village of Stonecrop Ash, Oxfordshire, Colonel Maurice Willoughby, late of the First Battalion, The Bedfordshires, folded up the newspaper – a careful reading of *The Evening Standard* was part of his inflexible nightly routine – and, leaving it on the bedside table, got ready for the night.

He was relieved to see there was nothing about that fool, Otterbourne or that lunatic, Carrington, in the paper. He had known Carrington (not that that was his real name, of course!) would come to a bad end.

Neither of his sisters had shown the slightest sense or respect for family tradition in the men they'd married. All the Willoughbys had been service people as long as anyone could remember. It was ingrained in them. Agatha's marriage to Walter Lewis, a City type, had been just about acceptable, but Edith had married Carrington in the teeth of her father's horrified disapproval.

By jingo, that had been a scene and a half but Edith had inherited the family streak of stubbornness and no mistake. Colonel Willoughby stroked his moustache into place with a wry smile. He couldn't help admire that in a way. It showed spirit, at least. There was nothing admirable about the Otterbourne's of this world. These fellers who set themselves up to change the world were all the same: starry-eyed dreamers, socialists and hypocrites, the lot of them.

A spell in India would have sorted him out pretty damn quickly. *Juldi* as they used to say. *Juldi!* It meant quickly. Damn quickly. There was no one he knew now who would understand the word, he thought wistfully. No one who could understand his longing for those days of purpose and discipline, of an ordered world shot through with the intense heat and dazzling colours of India. No, there were very few friends left and not much family to speak of. Carrington's son – he was still waiting for a reply to his letter – and Stephen, of course. He sighed.

Although Stephen was a likable boy with a decent war record, he lacked the spirit, the grit, of the men he'd known in India. He smiled grimly. This truly was a new world with new ways. He didn't, he thought, as he drifted into sleep, care much for it.

It was the noise that woke him. He stirred uneasily in his bed, drifting on the edge of sleep. The noise, a stealthy, creaking noise, sounded again. With the sense of danger very near, the need for action pulled him towards wakefulness. He mumbled the word *khitmagar*, but his khitmager and all the servants belonged to another Maurice Willoughby, a younger Maurice Willoughby, who had lived half a world away in India.

'*Koi hai?*' Is anyone there? He said it out loud, abruptly shaking off sleep. He sat up in bed, wincing as he jarred his knee. Arthritis and all the discomforts of old age flooded back. There was someone in the next room. For a moment his hand went to the bell, then hesitated. If he rang the bell, what would happen? Not a rush of able-bodied menservants excitedly offering help, but Mrs Tierney, the housekeeper, sleepy and worried, asking what was the matter. No. He was the only man in the house. It was his house and his responsibility and he had never shirked responsibility.

He swung his legs over the side of the bed, listening. There was definitely someone in the next room. Damnit, hadn't he been told? 'There's been a spate of burglaries in the villages roundabout, sir,' Horrocks, the village constable had said only last week, looking over the gate into the garden. 'Make sure your windows and doors are properly fastened. You can't be too careful.'

He reached for his dressing gown and his walking stick. There it was again! He was being robbed, by Gad. Robbed! A cold anger started to grow. He wasn't a rich man and that some thief should feel free to simply take what he had was beyond belief.

He didn't light the oil lamp. There was no point giving the beggars any more warning than he had to. In the dim gleam from the wedge of moonlight that fell across the carpet, he half-saw, half-felt his way to the chest of drawers and took out an electric torch and his heavy service revolver. He slipped the torch into his dressing-gown pocket and opened the door into the hall of the bungalow as quietly as possible. He intended to creep out but with one hand holding the door handle and the other his revolver, his stick slipped out from under his arm, just missed the runner of carpet, and clattered to the wooden floor.

Colonel Willoughby drew his breath in with a gasp, waiting for a shout, a thump, a sound of alarm from the dining room. Nothing happened. Slowly, and with one hand against the wall for support, he reached down and retrieved his stick. He'd got away with it, he thought with grim satisfaction. He'd show them. He'd catch Constable Horrocks' burglars for him. No village thief was going to get the better of *him*. Now for the dining room. He'd didn't have an elaborate plan of action. No, the simpler the better. He'd swing back the door, switch on the torch and shout, 'Hands up!' If that didn't stop their little games he would be very much surprised. His stick was a nuisance, but he'd manage.

He paused for a moment outside the dining-room door to get his breath back, then, grasping the revolver firmly, lent his stick against the wall, pushed open the door and clicked on his torch. In the brief glow of the electric bulb he saw the burglar's eyes, gleaming above the scarf wrapped round his chin. Hiding was he? He'd show the feller, by Gad!

The Colonel lunged forward and pulled away the scarf, desperate to see his enemy. The stranger's face contorted in savagery and, for the first time, the Colonel felt a jolt of fear. He felt the crunch of intense pain, then his world disappeared in a jagged sheet of light.

FIVE

Hugo Ragnall stepped into the hallway of the flat in Mottram Place, took off his hat and coat, handed them to Connie, the maid, who was waiting patiently to hang them up and, concealing a yawn, adjusted his tie in the mirror. 'Where's Mr Lewis, Connie?'

'He's having breakfast, sir.'

'Good-oh.' One of the best features of breakfast in the Lewis household was coffee. Mr Otterbourne, although eschewing alcohol, had insisted on the finest Mocha and Molly Lewis kept up the tradition.

'Morning,' said Steve Lewis from behind the newspaper as Ragnall walked into the morning room.

'Would you like some coffee, Hugo?' asked Molly, reaching for the pot.

'Yes, please,' he said, rubbing his eyes. 'I'll take it into the study, if you'd rather I didn't disturb your breakfast.'

'Sit down for few minutes,' said Lewis, halfway through his scrambled eggs and bacon. 'We've got a fair old amount of work to get through but there's no need to start just yet.' He looked at his secretary critically. 'You seem tired.'

'I'm not surprised. It's the pillow my landlady wished on me. I'm sure it's stuffed with rocks.'

'You look tired yourself, Steve,' said Molly, with wifely concern, seeing the dark patches under her husband's eyes. 'I've said before that you're working too hard. What time did you get to bed last night?'

'I don't honestly know,' Steve confessed. 'It took me ages to get Gerry's ideas and mine into some sort of order. We'll go through the paperwork this morning, Ragnall. Gerry and I are meeting Dunbar at one o'clock and I want to be absolutely certain of my ground. I intended to come straight to bed,' he added to Molly, 'but when I finished, I had a nightcap and what was intended to be ten minutes with the newspaper. I'm ashamed to say I fell asleep on the sofa.' He ate his eggs thoughtfully. 'There's no point denying I'm worried about today. I know Gerry's got right on his side, but if he tries to lay the law down to Dunbar, the entire deal might go up in smoke. The top and bottom of it is that Gerry can't stand the man.'

'You can't blame him,' said Molly. 'I don't like Mr Dunbar very much, either.'

'Which is why,' said Steve, 'I'm so concerned to get our part of the deal tied up so tightly. I haven't finished yet,' he added between mouthfuls of bacon. He nodded towards Ragnall. 'I'll show you the costs I've worked out. Gerry's not concerned with that part of the business, of course, but I promised I'd bring him up to date before we have lunch with Dunbar.'

He broke off as the maid came into the room with a telegram on a silver salver. With a puzzled look he took the envelope and ripped it open. As he read it, his face altered. Molly was shocked by his expression.

'Steve? What is it?' she asked quickly.

He handed the telegram to her. 'It's Uncle Maurice,' he said in bewilderment. 'It's from his housekeeper.'

Molly took the telegram from his outstretched hand. *'Regret inform you Colonel Willoughby victim of attack,'* she read out loud. *'Condition serious. Come at once. Tierney.'*

Ragnall gaped at her in astonishment. 'Colonel Willoughby's been *attacked*?'

'What on earth can have happened?' said Molly. 'He can't have been attacked. No one would harm an old man, surely?'

Steve took back the telegram, his forehead creasing in a frown. 'That's what it says. I wish to God he was on the telephone.' He turned back to Molly. 'I don't know what's happened but I'll have to go and see him.'

'Of course you will,' she said quickly.

'Who would want to hurt an old man like that?' He looked at her in disbelief. 'I can't credit it. This is the absolute devil.' He drummed his fingers on the table. 'Oh, my God, and there's so much else to *do*. It couldn't have happened at a worst time. Ragnall, wait for me in the study, will you? Jot a note to Dunbar and cry off the meeting. I can't possibly see him now. Tell him what's happened. You can say 'unforeseen family circumstances,' if you don't want to go into too much detail. He's staying at the Marchmont Hotel in Southampton Row.

If you hurry you can catch the post. Do it now and I'll have a word with you before I go.' Steve looked utterly distracted. 'I need to give you some instructions for the day.' He stood up, turning to Molly as Ragnall left the room. 'I'll have to get a move on. I can hardly believe it. Uncle Maurice! I know he's difficult at times, but . . .'

'What does that matter, Steve? This is awful.'

'I know!' He looked at her in utter frustration. 'It would happen now! I really needed to see Dunbar.'

'Can't Hugo Ragnall go in your place?'

Steve shook his head. 'He's got appointments of his own. They could be cancelled, but Dunbar's such a tricky devil that he's bound to put one over on him. Besides that, if there're any documents to sign, I have to do it. What's really worrying me is Gerry's temper. Damn!' He looked at her, struck by a sudden thought. 'Can you help?'

'Me?' exclaimed Molly. 'Of course I will, but how can I? I don't know anything about business. Even if I did, Mr Dunbar wouldn't talk to me. Not seriously, I mean.'

Steve shook his head. 'That's not what I meant. You're quite right about Dunbar, but can you see Gerry? After he's talked to Dunbar, I mean? They won't be able to decide anything about Otterbourne's but I want to know what Dunbar's agreed to about Gerry's machine. If Gerry knows he's got to tell you what happened, he might manage to keep the lid on his temper.'

Molly hesitated for a brief moment. The thought of meeting Gerard Carrington alone was oddly unsettling. 'All right.'

Steve breathed a sigh of relief. 'Thanks. That's something, at any rate. You'd better telephone the university and leave a message for him.'

'If I arrange to meet him at five we can have tea together.'

He kissed her forehead briefly. 'Make it a Lyon's or an A.B.C. or something. He probably can't run to anything more extravagant.' He squeezed her shoulders. 'I'll probably have to stay at Uncle Maurice's for one night at least, but I'll let you know. Damn!' He left the room in a rapid stride.

Molly walked into the hall and, with a deep breath, picked up the phone.

At quarter past five that afternoon, Mrs Evelyn Dunbar, a stout, well-dressed, grey-haired lady, leaning heavily on an ornate walking stick, stood impatiently by the large mahogany desk which dominated the marble-clad lobby of the Marchmont Hotel. There was no one on duty. If she had been more familiar with the Marchmont Hotel she would have realized how unusual that was. 'Disgraceful,' she muttered. 'Absolutely *disgraceful*,' and, for the third time, rang the brass bell on the counter, keeping up the peal until a distracted-looking clerk shot out of a door marked *Private* and hurried across the lobby to the desk.

'I have been waiting,' said Mrs Dunbar, in an unmistakable and irritated Scottish burr, 'for a full five minutes. If you and the rest of the staff in this hotel intend to ignore the bell, why have one at all?'

'I'm terribly sorry, madam,' said the clerk. 'There's been a . . .' He hesitated and swallowed, mindful of Mr Sutton, the manager's, snarled instructions. *Answer that bloody bell, will you, and for Pete's sake, don't let on to any of the guests!* 'There's been a slight hiccup in routine, madam,' he said with an attempt at a smile. 'I really do apologize. How may I help you?'

'I telephoned earlier in the afternoon and requested a note be delivered to one of your guests, a Mr Andrew Dunbar.' She raised an imperious eyebrow. 'I trust that note was delivered?'

'Yes, Madam,' said the clerk hurriedly. The question seemed to throw him off-guard. He swallowed once more. 'Mr Dunbar, you say? I . . . I . . . Yes, of course it would have been delivered.'

The grey-haired lady looked at him sharply. 'You seem very uncertain on the matter. Never mind. Mr Dunbar *is* here, isn't he?'

The oddest expression flickered across the clerk's face. 'Mr Dunbar? Yes, he's here all right. But . . .'

'Mr Dunbar is unaccountably late for our appointment. I would be grateful if you could send up to his room requesting him to join me *at once*.'

The clerk looked downright harried. 'I'm sorry, Madam, there may be a problem. What name is it, please?'

'Dunbar. Mrs Andrew Dunbar.'

The clerk gulped. 'I do beg your pardon, Mrs Dunbar, but I think it would be as well if you came and had a word with the manager. There's been an accident . . .'

* * *

Sergeant Butley looked carefully round the second-floor hotel room. It was getting on for half past five and he should have gone off duty nearly half an hour ago. However, duty *was* duty and if a guest at the Marchmont Hotel chose to shoot himself after hours, so to speak, then it was all in the day's work. Apparently the man's wife was downstairs. He'd have to see her before he left.

He sighed unhappily and looked at the rigidly still body slumped across the desk. Andrew Dunbar, a stout, middle-aged, balding manufacturer of wireless and gramophone sets, resident in Falkirk, Scotland. Suicide.

Sergeant Butley's face lengthened. It wasn't easy talking to relatives after a death, even when it was an accident. Suicide made it that much worse.

He looked at the fleshy cheeks and sprawled arms and shook his head. On the desk lay a sheet of hotel writing paper inscribed with two words; *Forgive me*. Beside the paper was a fountain pen, its cap carefully screwed back on. The gun, a neat automatic pistol, was loosely clasped in Dunbar's hand.

'It's funny how often they come to a hotel to do it,' offered Constable Flynn. 'Think they'll save trouble at home perhaps.'

'Maybe,' agreed Butley.

'Or,' continued Flynn, 'they could want one last night of living it up.' He looked round the room appreciatively. 'It's nice here, isn't it?'

'Not if you're dead,' said Butley dryly. Although not an imaginative man, he was conscious of a feeling of depression. The Marchmont was clean and comfortable with a reputation for good service, but as the gateway to the next world it was so . . . so *ordinary*.

The curtain flapped and through the open window came the sounds of a fine summer evening in London. The hotel overlooked Southampton Row with all its bustle and traffic. A car backfired in the street below and Sergeant Butley nodded in recognition. It sounded just like a shot. That, presumably, was why no one had heard the gun. It would be easy to mistake the noise, and you'd never dream it was a shot you'd heard. Talking of the shot . . . Sergeant Butley tilted his head critically to one side. 'Constable Flynn?'

'Yes, Sarge?'

'Just have a look at where this bullet went in. Right at the back of his head.' Constable Flynn knelt down beside the body and peered closely. 'Do you notice anything?'

'It's an awkward way to shoot yourself, sir. Why, the bloke must've twisted his arm right round. I . . . I don't see how he could have done it.'

'Neither do I,' said Butley slowly. 'By cripes, my lad, this isn't suicide.' He swallowed. 'It's murder.'

Inspector William Rackham waited as the Divisional Surgeon completed his investigation. 'Well?'

'It's murder, all right,' said the doctor.

Rackham nodded to Butley. 'Well done, Sergeant. Good work. What can you tell us, Doctor?'

Doctor Morris wiped his thermometer and put it back in its case. 'You can have a report with all the fancy language after the post-mortem but I can't see it'll tell you much more than I know already. There aren't any burn marks round the wound but that, by itself, doesn't constitute a case for suicide.' He nodded towards the gun held limply in Dunbar's hand. 'There frequently aren't any, especially when an automatic pistol has been used. What is significant is the angle the gun was fired at. I won't say that it's impossible for a man to shoot himself in that way, but it's virtually impossible. I don't think it's on the cards. The other thing to notice is this.' He stooped down on one knee beside the body and pointed to Dunbar's outstretched hand. 'You can see for yourselves how stiff the corpse is. He's absolutely rigid, which, I may say, is very common in brain injuries. Rigor's very little guide in these cases. It often sets in immediately. However, if you look at this hand which is holding the gun –' Doctor Morris lifted the index and forefinger of the right hand, '– you can see that this hand, and this hand only, is flexible. And what that means is that someone moved this hand after death.'

Rackham smiled grimly. 'They've tried to be clever, haven't they? What about the time of death, Doctor?'

Morris glanced at his watch. 'It's just gone half past six. It's a warm day, which will affect things but, on the other hand, the window's open, which has cooled the room. I'd say he died between half past three and about half past five. If I had to make a guess it'd be roundabout four to half past or thereabouts, but that's only a guess, mind. It's impossible to be any more accurate.'

'He was discovered at five o'clock,' said Sergeant Butley. 'The chambermaid came in with fresh towels and found him.'

The doctor raised his eyebrows. 'Did she, by Jove? That narrows down the latter end of the timescale. We're fortunate that the body was discovered so soon.'

'He would have been discovered very shortly in any event, sir,' volunteered the sergeant. 'His wife should have had afternoon tea with him.'

'His wife?' said the doctor. He glanced round the room with a puzzled frown. 'Did she have another room? She obviously wasn't staying in this one.'

'She's not staying here at all, sir. Apparently Mr Dunbar and his wife were separated.'

'I had her escorted home,' said Rackham. 'She lives in Kensington. Her son lives with her and she says he should be home from work when she arrives, so she won't be alone. She was pretty upset, poor woman.' He saw the doctor's expression. 'And no, before you get up in arms in her defence, I didn't ask her any questions. I didn't think she was up to answering any.'

The doctor subsided. 'That's very restrained of you. Is she a suspect?'

Rackham frowned. 'Technically, yes. Actually?' He shrugged. 'I doubt it. I'll speak to her tomorrow. What I do need is someone who saw him this afternoon. Sergeant Butley, can you start making enquiries of the hotel staff? I've already seen the chambermaid, of course, but if you find any other witnesses, let me know and I'll interview them as soon as I can.'

A knock sounded on the door and Constable Flynn looked into the room. 'The photographer's here, sir.'

'Tell him to wait a few minutes,' said Rackham. 'I won't be long.'

He waited until Sergeant Butley and Doctor Morris had left the room, then walked to the window and lent against the sill, looking round the room. He wanted some time to himself to put his thoughts in order.

Andrew Dunbar; it was odd to think it was only a couple of days ago he had discussed Andrew Dunbar with Jack. That conversation was a real bit of bad luck for someone. Even if

Butley hadn't spotted the faked suicide, Rackham would have smelt a rat as soon as he heard Dunbar's name. Rackham looked at the body lying stiffly across the desk and pursed his lips. It now seemed more likely than ever that the whole truth about the Stoke Horam suicides hadn't come to light.

He stood beside the body, his head tilted to one side. Dunbar was well dressed, in a conventional morning suit of striped trousers and dark coat. His clothes gave very little idea of what he was like. He frowned. Hotel rooms were essentially anonymous, and that, speaking as a policeman, annoyed him. However, even here Dunbar must have left some imprint of his personality on the room.

He walked round the room, pausing at the heavy oak wardrobe. Inside were two leather suitcases stamped with the initials A.W.D. and, hanging from the rail, a collection of suits and coats. Rackham noted the tailor's name and shrugged. Nothing there, as far as he could see. The drawers revealed, as expected, gloves, ties and collars. On the bedside table were two magazines, *The Windsor Magazine* and – this made Rackham smile – *On The Town* containing a story by Jack Haldean. A pill box quickened his pulse for a moment but proved to contain nothing more exciting than Doctor Trotter's patent liver pills. Skirting round the bed, and noting that Andrew Dunbar favoured an old-fashioned nightshirt rather than pyjamas, he passed by the washstand and came to the desk under the window.

It was nearly impossible to look at anything but the body, but Rackham dragged his attention to the desk. A pamphlet forbiddingly entitled *The Proceedings of the Otorhinolaryngological Society* caught his eye. *Otor* . . . What on earth was that? No wonder Dunbar apparently preferred Jack Haldean for light reading. An open leather folder was at the rear of the desk, containing a few sheets of paper which Rackham turned over, carefully holding them by the edges. They contained lists of figures and some names that he recognized. Lewis, Carrington and Otterbourne's, the gramophone makers. Once again, the Stoke Horam suicides came to mind. He was glad he had looked at the Stoke Horam files only yesterday. Because of that, he knew exactly who these men were.

There was a note on hotel paper beside the blotter. *Mrs Dunbar telephoned. She will meet you in the lobby for tea at quarter to five*. Rackham clicked his tongue. That was one appointment the poor beggar hadn't kept. A letter lay open beside the blotter, the envelope beside it postmarked Sackville Street, 10.23, 15th July. Posted that morning, then. Without touching the paper, Rackham made a copy of the contents.

It was an apology from Stephen Lewis of 47A, Mottram Place for not attending the meeting that afternoon because of *unforeseen family circumstances*. Taken together with the papers in the leather folder, it was clear that a meeting had been arranged for that afternoon between Dunbar, Lewis and Carrington. Although Lewis hadn't been there, Carrington probably had been. At the very least, the man was an important witness and might, just might, be the man they were looking for. Rackham was aware he was running ahead of evidence but he couldn't resist the train of thought.

He looked once more at the rigid body, trying to discern the character from the face but it was difficult to see any character in the flabby, set face. Both the ruthlessness and the happiness that Jack's pal, Hector Ferguson, had talked about had been wiped clear.

Hector Ferguson had wondered if his stepfather had been the real villain at Stoke Horam. He'd thought, not to beat about the bush, there was a real possibility that Andrew Dunbar had murdered Charles Otterbourne and left Professor Carrington to carry the can. In Rackham's opinion, there was no two ways about it. If Professor Carrington hadn't hanged himself, he would've been charged with Otterbourne's murder. And if Hector Ferguson could work that out, so could Gerard Carrington. Gerard Carrington, so Carrington's doctor, Sir David Hargreaves, had testified at the inquest, had been highly protective of his father.

It was a motive. A conditional, unproved, perhaps improvable motive, but he couldn't ignore it. He pulled himself up short. A compelling motive, yes, but one that, in light of the Coroner's verdict, it would be hard to argue in court. He needed evidence.

Some little discrepancy about the suicide note nagged him. The paper was tucked into the corner of the blotter and something wasn't quite right . . . Rackham clicked his tongue. That was it! The ink stains on the blotter were blue, but the note itself was written in black ink, which had been allowed to dry. Rackham gingerly picked up the fountain pen on the desk and unscrewed the cap. The ink in the pen was blue, not black and, as if to confirm it, a bottle of Swan's blue ink stood to one side. There was certainly no other pen on or near the desk. That meant the murderer had used his own pen to write the note. After the medical evidence, he had little doubt that it was murder and not suicide, but this clinched it.

He looked round the room once more and nodded in a satisfied way. Murder.

Gerard Carrington spent the following night in police custody. The afternoon after his arrest he was charged with the murder of Andrew Dunbar; and Bill Rackham went to see Jack Haldean.

Rackham reamed out his pipe, tapped the contents tidily into the ashtray, and reached for the tobacco jar. 'I've got a puzzle for you, Jack,' he announced. 'What on earth does –' he took a deep breath – 'Otorhinolaryngological mean?'

Haldean looked startled. 'Where on earth did you dig up a word like that? Do you need special training to say it? I haven't a clue.'

Rackham looked rather pleased. 'I knew I'd do it one of these days if I tried hard enough. Found a word you didn't know, I mean.'

'Hold on,' said Jack with a smile. 'This is a challenge, isn't it? Is it something to do with Dunbar?' Rackham nodded. 'Blimey. The rudiments of knowledge are coming back to me. It's Greek, or at least, it's derived from Greek. *Oto* means ear, I think, and *rhino* means nose as in rhinoceroses. What's the rest of it? *Laryngological*? Well, *laryn* is throat as in laryngitis – a word like that would give you laryngitis – and *logos* is either creative thought or word, as in the Gospel of St John.'

'*In the beginning was the Word*, d'you mean?' asked Rackham.

'That's the one. So how many bits of words have we got?' Jack counted them off on his fingers. 'Ear, nose, throat and word or thought.' He grinned suddenly. 'It sounds medical but, as it's to do with Dunbar, I'd say it was sound. Recorded sound, at that. Am I right?'

'I don't know about the Greek,' said Rackham, 'but it's recorded sound, all right. Dunbar had a pamphlet in his room,

The Proceedings of the Thingamabob Society. He also had a copy of *On The Town*, by the way, with one of your stories in it.'

'Bless his cotton socks. It's the nicest thing I've heard about him. I do wish people wouldn't bump off my readers. I don't approve of it, you know. You're certain he was bumped off, aren't you?'

'Certain. Apart from anything else, the door was locked and there was no key in the room. The chambermaid who found the body used her pass key to get in.'

Jack made a dissatisfied noise. 'And you've arrested Gerard Carrington.'

'Which is why I'm here. I'm not sure about Carrington. It's a simple explanation and I like things to be simple.' He hesitated. 'I just wonder if it's too simple.' He looked appraisingly at his friend. 'You've got reservations, too, haven't you?'

'Perhaps . . . Tell me, Bill, on a purely human level, do you think Carrington is guilty?'

Rackham tamped the tobacco firmly down in his pipe. 'I don't honestly know,' he said seriously. 'On the one hand, it's a good case. It's circumstantial, but sound.' He hesitated. 'There's *something* though, Jack. I said as much to the Chief but, given the evidence, we had no choice but arrest Carrington. He didn't do himself any favours, I must say. He's an argumentative devil.' He puffed his cheeks out in discontent. 'What can I say? I've got that niggling feeling there's something wrong and I can't put my finger on what it is.' He looked at his friend ruefully. 'I hoped if there was anything wrong with the case against Carrington, you'd be able to spot it.'

'Do you really mean that?'

Rackham nodded. 'Oh yes,' he said seriously. 'I want to see the right man in the dock. The trouble is, Gerard Carrington was alone with Dunbar all afternoon and it's blinkin' difficult to see who else *could* have done it. I know both of us have got Stoke Horam in mind, but that's not why I arrested Carrington. No, I arrested Carrington on the evidence alone. And, I may say, that evidence seems very clear-cut.'

'Simple, in fact,' put in Jack.

'Yes . . .' Rackham put a match to his pipe and sucked in a mouthful of smoke. 'Murders often are. We know that he and Dunbar quarrelled that afternoon. We've got two independent witnesses to that. Dunbar and Carrington had lunch at one o'clock and Dunbar requested coffee to be served in his room. The waiter who brought the coffee, an Italian called Antonio Miretti, distinctly heard the two men quarrelling. That was about twenty past two. They were, in his words, going at it hammer and tongs. He heard raised voices from outside the room and when he went in with the tray, both men were on their feet and looking pretty agitated. The second witness is one of the porters, Walter Parker. At half past three or thereabouts he took a telephone message up to Dunbar. The two men weren't actually quarrelling at that point, but Parker reckoned there was an atmosphere you could cut with a knife.'

'Which, given that Dunbar was murdered shortly afterwards, is what you'd expect him to say,' said Jack. 'I doubt if he or anyone else could resist the temptation to be in on something as sensational as murder.'

'Absolutely,' agreed Rackham with a grin. 'However, in fairness to Parker, he did remark to Rice, the head porter, after he'd delivered the note, that the two jossers in 206 seemed to have taken the hump about something and no mistake.'

'That sounds authentic enough,' agreed Jack. 'What was the message? The one that Parker delivered, I mean?'

'It was from Dunbar's wife, Evelyn Dunbar, saying she'd meet him in the hotel lobby for afternoon tea at quarter to five. I found the note in Dunbar's room. She arrived early and was sitting in the lobby when Carrington, who she's met a couple of times, came through the hotel lobby at what was virtually a run. He saw her, muttered an apology and dashed past her. That was at half past four. She remembers the time as Carrington drew attention to it, saying that he had an appointment and would have to rush as he was afraid of being late. The clock in the hotel lobby's accurate, by the way. I checked it. She's certain about the time. You see where that leaves us, Jack? As the body was found at just gone five, it doesn't leave much time for anyone else but Carrington, especially when you add in five to ten minutes for arranging the suicide and all those shenanigans.'

'It leaves some,' said Jack. 'I agree anyone else would have to be pretty nippy though. What about Mrs Dunbar herself? After all, she was on the spot and I know she's separated from her husband. Couldn't she have done the deed?'

Rackham pulled a face. 'I thought about her, of course, but I just can't see it somehow. She struck me as a dopey sort of woman. I daresay if she tried to make a murder look like suicide, she'd make a complete botch of it.' He grinned. 'She's very keen on Higher Powers and Guidance.'

'Good God,' muttered Jack.

'Exactly. She was very shaken though. She wasn't pretending, unless she's a terrific actress. Besides that, she's not physically up to it. She crocked her ankle a couple of weeks ago. If she had gone up to Dunbar's room, she would have needed the lift and the lift-boy is positive that he didn't take her.'

'She could be putting on the dodgy ankle, though, couldn't she?'

'I saw her doctor. He confirmed she had twisted it badly.'

'That sounds fairly convincing,' agreed Jack. 'How did she react when the news broke?'

'She wasn't heartbroken, but, as she'd been separated from Dunbar for some time, I wouldn't expect her to be. I let her go home and interviewed her the day after the murder. Her son was with her, by the way, your pal, Hector Ferguson. He seems a nice enough chap. He'd taken the morning off work to be with her when I called. He said he hadn't known his step-father was in London, but Dunbar came down fairly often, and always stayed at the Marchmont. That's borne out by the hotel people, by the way. Dunbar was a frequent guest.'

'How did Mrs Dunbar know Dunbar was in London?'

'She didn't know, until the day he arrived. She'd written to Dunbar at the company's offices in Falkirk and received a note from the manager, Mr Bryce, to say Dunbar was in London for a few days. She knew he usually stayed at the Marchmont, so rang the hotel, confirmed he was actually a guest, and, as we know, instructed a note to be delivered to him.' Rackham chewed his pipe stem. 'I dunno. It seems so unlikely that she'd be the murderer. As you'd told me there wasn't an awful lot of love lost between Ferguson and his stepfather, I thought he might be a possible, but he'd been at work the previous afternoon and was certainly at home when his mother arrived, escorted by one of my men.'

'Did you check his alibi?' asked Jack. 'I don't want to sound overly suspicious, especially as he's a friend, but it's as well to be sure.'

'I thought so too. He's a clerk at the Shanghai and Oriental Shipping Company in Leadenhall Street. The office closes at half past five and the clerks have to sign out. I saw Mr Wallace, the manager, who checked the register. Ferguson left the building at twenty-five to six, so he's comfortably in the clear. You see why I kept on coming back to Carrington, Jack? He really does seem to be the only reasonable possibility. I wish to goodness we could get a clear time of death,' he said, relighting his pipe. 'I know it's asking a lot, but the doctor can't narrow the time down. I've grilled everyone in the hotel I can think of, but no one seems to have heard a shot. I bet they did, mind, but it'd be easy to mistake it for a backfire, especially as the windows in the room were open.'

'Has anyone mentioned a backfire?'

Rackham shook his head. 'No, dammit, they haven't. I've asked, you can be sure.'

'Did Carrington really have an appointment or was that an excuse to get away from Mrs Dunbar?'

'Yes, that's true enough. Mrs Lewis met him for tea at the Lyon's Corner House, Leicester Square, to hear how the meeting with Dunbar had gone. Her husband, Stephen Lewis, should have been at the meeting that afternoon but he was called away to his uncle's.'

Jack reached for his whisky. 'Yes . . .' He swirled the liquid round in his glass. 'Don't you think this burglary at Colonel Willoughby's seems a trifle contrived?'

Rackham's eyebrows shot up. 'Contrived? It can't have been, Jack. Colonel Willoughby was attacked with a cosh and badly injured.' He looked quizzically at his friend. 'Come on, what's on your mind?'

'There are two possibilities. Because of the burglary, Stephen Lewis has a very complete alibi for the day.' He grinned. 'You must remember that my imagination is warped by writing detective stories, where a complete alibi is very suspicious indeed.'

'Unless it happens to be true,' Bill countered with a laugh. 'That won't wash, Jack. The Colonel's a game old bird. The man who attacked him had a scarf wrapped round his face but the Colonel pulled it off. He didn't recognize the man and he'd certainly have recognized Lewis.'

Jack pulled at his earlobe. 'That rules my other idea out of court. Carrington is Colonel Whatsisname's nephew too, isn't he? I wondered if Carrington staged the burglary.'

'Why, for heaven's sake?'

'Because it got Stephen Lewis out of the way for the day, leaving Carrington a clear run at Dunbar. However, if the Colonel saw the man, that idea's not on the cards.'

Rackham looked at him sharply. 'Hold on a minute, Jack. You might be on to something. Gerard Carrington has never met his uncle. Mrs Lewis mentioned it. Colonel Willoughby *wouldn't* recognize him. By George, I wonder if you're right?'

'Could you show Colonel Willoughby a photograph of Carrington?'

'I suppose so,' said Bill, suddenly doubtful. 'The trouble is, even if he says it was Carrington, I don't know if I'd believe him. After all, he only had the briefest of glimpses of the man, before he was attacked. He suffered severe concussion. I'm surprised he can remember anything at all. It'd be far too easy for him to say he was certain when he was no such thing. I'll keep the idea in mind, though. It's an interesting possibility. Going back to Dunbar's murder, I'll tell you what did strike me as odd. Carrington made no secret of the fact he and Dunbar had fallen out. You'd expect him to try and conceal the fact, wouldn't you?'

Jack shook his head. 'If the waiter and the porter had seen them, Carrington would know there were witnesses. He'd be an idiot to try and hush it up. Did Mrs Lewis tell you what the argument had been about?'

'It centred on this new gramophone which Carrington's father invented. Apparently it's going to be worth a lot of money. Dunbar insisted that he owned all the rights to it and Carrington was arguing the toss. That's Carrington's version of the quarrel as well, by the way.'

Jack reached for the cigarette box. 'That could be a pretty decent motive. I know we've been distracted by thoughts of revenge for Stoke Horam, but it could be good old solid cash at the bottom of it. If it is worth a bundle, then Gerard Carrington might very well think the most straightforward way out of his legal tangle was to bump off Dunbar.'

'That's what I thought,' agreed Rackham. 'And, oddly enough, so did Gerard Carrington. He denies murdering

Dunbar but admitted that life would be a lot easier without him. Again, I thought that was a rum sort of thing for him to say.'

Jack shrugged. 'It seems a bit rash, I grant you, but as he'd told Mrs Lewis as much, he probably thought it was as well to admit it.' He frowned. 'It's a problem, isn't it?' He leaned back in his chair and blew a smoke ring at the ceiling. 'I wish I knew Carrington. It's so much easier to understand what someone's capable of if you've actually met them. He's got a post at University College, hasn't he?'

'That's right. He's a scientist. His speciality is electronics.'

'And he is, we presume, a bright lad?'

'Very bright, I'd say,' agreed Rackham.

Jack tilted his head to one side. 'How bright?'

'Good grief, Jack, I don't know. I didn't ask to see his school report.'

'OK, let me put it another way,' said Jack with a laugh. 'Granted he's bright, would you say he had the usual amount of common sense?'

Rackham looked bewildered. 'I haven't a clue.'

Jack sighed. 'Would you say he was a pleasant bloke, or did he strike you as arrogant?'

'How on earth should I know? I merely arrested the man. It's not a social occasion. What the dickens has his common sense got to do with whether he's guilty or not?'

'It's got everything to do with it. Help yourself to another drink, by the way. It's perfectly possible, as we both know, to be unbelievably bright but have no common sense. If a man's overbearingly arrogant, then he'll do exactly as he pleases without any thought of how others will see it. The effect would be much the same. If Carrington's got no ordinary common sense – and I'm damned if I know how else to describe it – then the case holds up. But if he has . . . Well, it doesn't add up.'

Rackham walked to the sideboard and picking up the bottle, measured the whisky into his glass. 'How?'

'Oh, for heaven's sake!' said Jack in frustration. 'For a start, I gather the idea is that the crime was not premeditated.'

'Yes, that's right. Even if he did stage the burglary at Colonel Willoughby's, Carrington couldn't *know* Stephen Lewis was going to rush off to Oxfordshire. He might have hoped as

much but he couldn't know. He says he was very surprised
Lewis didn't turn up.'

'Didn't Lewis let Carrington know he couldn't be at the
meeting?'

Rackham shook his head. 'No, and that fits what evidence
we've got. Mrs Lewis telephoned the university. One of his
colleagues, a Doctor Austen, took the message. We found the
note in Carrington's letter rack at the university. It says nothing
about Lewis being called away but simply asks Carrington to
meet Mrs Lewis at the Corner House in Leicester Square at
five o'clock that evening. Dr Austen confirmed that was the
original message. He was very stuffy about it. It isn't, he
informed me, the crusty old beggar, his place to act as an
unpaid secretary for junior members of the Department. You
see what that means?'

'I know what you want me to say. Carrington thought Lewis
was going to be there.'

'Exactly. Now common sense or not, he can't have planned
to commit a murder with a third party looking on. Therefore,
Jack, it was not premeditated.'

'So why did he take a gun?' asked Jack softly.

'Because . . .' Rackham stopped.

'Because there was a gun there. What sort of gun was it,
by the way?'

'A Webley .32,' said Rackham absently. 'It's a handy little
thing. They're very commonplace. It's not a Service calibre
but lots of blokes used them during the war as a second pistol.'
He rested his chin on his hands. 'I see what you're getting at.
As a matter of routine, I've asked for the pistol to be traced,
but I don't know if we're going to manage it. It's well-used
and was probably either brought second-hand or picked up as
a souvenir during the war.' He looked up. 'Carrington denied
it was his, but that's only to be expected. It could have belonged
to Dunbar, I suppose.'

'It could,' agreed Jack. 'Yes, that's perfectly possible.' He
drew on his cigarette. 'Look, if Carrington took the gun with
him on the off chance, or it really did belong to Dunbar, then
that's the end of it. But if he wanted to convince us it was
suicide why did he make such a poor job of it? He shot the
bloke at an impossible angle, wiped the gun and put it in
Dunbar's hand, ignoring the fact that he's as stiff as a board

and he has to crack the fingers open to do so. Then he writes a suicide note using his own pen, apparently not noticing that Dunbar's pen is just by the blotter.'

'Maybe he was worried about fingerprints.'

'With two hands' worth of relevant fingerprints lying beside him? Maybe. He then leaves the room, being careful to lock it behind him and pocket the key, thus telling everyone it's a set-up, and leaves the hotel as fast as he can. You see what I mean about common sense, Bill? On that showing, he hasn't got any.'

'He could have panicked,' said Rackham. He chewed his pipe-stem for a few moments. 'It's a difficult one. When I interviewed him, he stated he hadn't killed Dunbar and seemed to expect me to take his unsupported word for it. He cottoned on about halfway through the interview where my questions were leading, and started to go on and on about proof. He had an absolute bee in his bonnet about it. I think he might just be a brainy dumb-bell, Jack. When I told him that he should have a solicitor, he looked at me blankly and said he didn't know any solicitors. It was quite an uphill job to persuade him he really ought to be represented. When I actually arrested him, he didn't offer any physical resistance, but I've never known anyone *talk* so much.'

He glanced up at his friend. 'Your objections are absolutely sound but all this about what you or I or any reasonable man would do is so much hot air.' He scratched his ear. 'It's a puzzle, isn't it? Look, it's asking a bit, I know, but d'you think you'd be any wiser if you met him? The Assistant Commissioner wouldn't have any objections, I'm sure, not after the Culverton case. He was singing your praises for ages after that.'

Jack didn't reply for a time. 'I don't know,' he said eventually. 'I suppose I could get an impression of what he's like, but there's nothing to say it'll be right. Besides that, how would it affect you? It's one thing chewing it over in private, but I don't want to set myself up against you in public.'

Rackham shook his head. 'You won't be. The Chief knows I've got reservations. He had a good idea I was going to talk things over with you.' He gave a quick smile. 'You'd be doing me a favour, Jack. If I've made a mistake, quite apart from the principle of the thing, I really would prefer to know about it before it came to court.' His smile broadened. 'Now that's common sense, if you like.'

'In that case,' said Jack, 'I'll do it.'

SIX

J ack stood by the oak-stained table. It was a functional table, with strictly functional chairs. He shivered. He hadn't expected Brixton Prison to be jolly but the drabness of the surroundings laid his spirits low. Why were institutions always painted in dark green and yellowing cream? And why did they always smell, vaguely and disagreeably, of old cooked cabbage? At least he could walk out into the sunshine after the interview, unlike Carrington, poor devil. He knew it was his imagination, but he felt dingy and unwashed, as if the atmosphere were clinging to his clothes and skin.

A noise in the corridor made him look up. The warder opened the glass panelled door and ushered into the room a man who was, presumably, Gerard Carrington.

'You'll remember the rules, won't you, Major Haldean?' said the warder. 'I'll stay outside the room. I won't be able to hear what you say, but I would like to remind you that no object may be passed between you and the prisoner.'

Carrington waited until the warder had left the room. 'I don't think I'm allowed to walk around, either,' he said, drawing out a chair. 'It's a frightful nuisance remembering what I can and can't do. Er . . . Won't you sit down?' He smiled fleetingly. 'I would ask you to make yourself at home, but it's not an invitation I imagine you'd want to take up.'

Jack sat down, his sympathies firmly engaged. It hadn't been much of a joke, but any remark that verged on the light-hearted was nothing less than heroic under the circumstances. He liked the look of Carrington. He was a tall, thin-faced man with curly brown hair, mild blue eyes and gold-rimmed glasses. He had a faintly distracted expression, as if perpetually surprised by his surroundings and at first glance seemed a bit weedy, an impression helped by his clothes. He wore a brown sleeveless pullover, which looked as if it had seen better days, and a button was missing from his shirt. However, his shoulders were broad and his mouth firm. Stubborn, thought Jack, summing him up in a word. Let him get his teeth into something and

he'd be stubborn. He had a rumpled look, as if he had slept
in his clothes. He was willing to bet that Gerard Carrington
would always look rumpled, no matter if he were in Brixton
Prison or the Savoy Hotel.

'I suppose you're wondering why I'm here,' he began.

'Well, I was, rather,' said Carrington. 'Major Haldean, is
it?' He took in Jack's light grey suit and blue tie and gave a
puzzled smile. 'When they told me I had a visitor, I assumed
you must be from the solicitors, but you don't look as if you
are.' His forehead creased in a frown. 'Are you a reporter?'

Jack shook his head. 'No. It's a little difficult to explain,
but Inspector Rackham is a friend of mine.'

'Inspector Rackham?' Carrington drew back in wary defi-
ance. 'He arrested me. I don't know if I should say anything
more. Certainly not until I know exactly why you're here.'

Jack took a deep breath. Carrington must be sick of answering
questions and was understandably suspicious of a stranger. 'In
the past I've been involved in working out what actually
happened in a couple of cases where things were pretty obscure.'

'You're Jack Haldean, aren't you? I've read about you in
the papers.' Carrington's voice had a cynical twist. 'You say
you're a friend of Inspector Rackham's. He thinks I'm guilty.
Why does he need you to confirm it?'

'Inspector Rackham doesn't need me to do anything of the
sort.' Jack's voice was measured. 'I know he arrested you. In
the face of the evidence, he couldn't do anything else.' He
looked away, apparently examining his fingernails. 'Inspector
Rackham is a very fair-minded man. He had sufficient reservations about you to wonder if all the facts had come to light.
Because of what I've done in the past, both he and the Assistant
Commissioner of Scotland Yard, Sir Douglas Lynton, trust me
enough to let me see you and ask a few questions.'

Carrington caught his breath. 'They think I might be innocent? Do you?' There was a sudden strength of hope in his
voice, which shook Jack. For some reason it was far more
convincing than any declaration of innocence and yet a guilty
man could hope for freedom too.

He looked up. 'It means I've got an open mind.'

The eager light faded from Carrington's eyes. 'That was
too much to expect, I suppose,' he said softly. 'Still . . .' He
sat up, alert and expectant.

He reminded Jack of a child who, longing for a treat, has been met with the words, *wait and see*. Poor devil. 'Let's get the obvious question out of the way first of all,' he said, trying to make his voice matter-of-fact. 'Did you kill Andrew Dunbar?'

'Well, of course I didn't, but it seems so hard to make anyone believe me.' Carrington looked at him with bewildered irritation. 'I always thought a man was innocent until he'd been proven guilty. What the police seem to think of as proof doesn't tie in with any notion of scientific evidence at all. I've said again and again that Dunbar was alive when I left the hotel. I can't see why they can't simply take my word for it. I mean, why should I be lying?'

'Because you've been accused of murder,' said Jack dryly.

'But I didn't do it!'

'Mr Carrington, why did you leave the hotel in such a hurry?'

Gerard Carrington looked at him with a mutinous expression. 'I've explained that. I was going to have tea with Mrs Lewis. Apart from anything else, I wanted to find out why Steve hadn't showed up. Whatever's wrong with that?'

Jack sighed. 'Well, I'm afraid, you know, it looks as if you were running away from the scene of the crime.'

'That's ridiculous!'

'No, it's not.' Jack's voice was calm. 'It's a perfectly understandable assumption. What time did you arrive at the Lyon's?'

'It was just after five. I was in a rush because I was late. I'd stayed far too long with Dunbar and hadn't realized the time.'

'Can you tell me about your disagreement with Dunbar?'

Carrington firmly pushed his spectacles back on the bridge of his nose with his index finger. 'It was a bit more than a disagreement. I've never pretended otherwise. It was about my father and his machine.' Carrington looked at him questioningly. 'I don't know if you've heard of it?'

'It's a new sort of gramophone, isn't it?'

'It's a jolly sight more than that.' Carrington interlinked his fingers thoughtfully. 'Technically speaking, it's a huge step forward. My father was brilliant.' His voice altered. 'The trouble is, once he'd understood something, he couldn't see why anyone else couldn't understand it as well. Things were so obvious to him he really couldn't grasp that it wasn't self-evident.' Carrington's voice faltered. 'He . . . He could be an awkward beggar.'

'He'd had a nervous breakdown, hadn't he?'

Carrington sighed. 'You can call it a nervous breakdown if you like. I suppose it's as good a description as any other.' He looked at Jack appraisingly. 'You know, I really think you might understand. I said he was outstanding. As a matter of fact, I think he was a genius.' Carrington caught the flicker of scepticism in Jack's eyes. 'I don't mean it as a compliment,' he said wearily.

'Don't you?' asked Jack, startled.

'No. His work meant more to him than anything else in the world. He was so removed from ordinary concerns that he was horribly isolated. A genius – a real genius – is, you know. Even I couldn't follow him when he really got underway. He was driven by a vision that was virtually incomprehensible to the rest of the world.' He gave a tired smile. 'He used to talk non-stop to my poor mother. She couldn't grasp what he said, but she was there, at least. When she died, he went to pieces.'

Jack was silent for a moment. Like most people, he cheerfully bandied the word *genius* around as a shorthand term for *very clever*. With sudden insight he realized it meant much more than that. Professor Carrington had been at the top of his profession. Without any conceit he would know he had equals but no superior. There was no one to knock the edges off, no one to keep him humble. Jack shuddered. Alan Carrington would always be alone.

'D'you know, I think I've just understood something,' Jack said slowly. 'It's the meaning of the word. Genius can mean supernatural power. We talk about a good or evil genius inhabiting a place or a person, setting them apart. I've never really seen why before, but I think I do now.'

'You do understand,' said Carrington softly. He buried his face in his hands. 'D'you know, that's such a relief?' His voice wavered. 'Mrs Lewis understood as well. That's why . . .' He broke off abruptly, then took off his glasses and polished them on his handkerchief. 'She understood,' he said, more to himself than to Jack. His hand slowed as he continued to polish his glasses.

Jack looked at him sharply. Carrington's face was shielded

by his hand. He was sure the man had turned away to hide his emotions. He had a good idea that with a little careful probing he could draw those emotions out into the open. It would be as easy, pointless and cruel as pinning a struggling butterfly to a card. Poor devil.

Carrington put his glasses back on and, sitting upright, straightened his pullover, and drew a deep breath. 'Anyway, perhaps you can see why my father was such easy game for a shark like Dunbar.'

'Was he really such a shark?' asked Jack.

'Absolutely he was. My father thought he was wonderful. He wasn't remotely practical himself and always had an exaggerated respect for practical men. He had as much worldly knowledge as a babe in arms and was about as helpless. He ran across Dunbar at a meeting of a learned society. I'll say this for Dunbar, he really knew his stuff.'

'This society – it wouldn't be the Otorhinolaryngological Society, would it?' asked Jack with a grin. 'I have to gear up before I say that.'

'That's the one,' said Carrington in surprise. 'It's a dickens of a title, isn't it? Dunbar was a member, which must have taken the guv'nor off guard. He'd expect any fellow-member to be a scientist, with a purely theoretical interest in the subject. Dunbar suggested that my father should put some of the ideas they'd discussed into concrete form by making a working electronic machine. The guv'nor was delighted. He saw it as a purely academic exercise. It never occurred to him – and I could never get him to realize – that once it was developed it would be a very valuable commercial property. Dunbar realized it,' he added wryly. 'Dunbar was out for every penny he could get.'

'Is it really so valuable?'

'I'd say so.' His eyes brightened. 'The system my father came up with has the potential to make acoustical recording obsolete. I'm not exaggerating. He transformed both the quality of the sound and the length of the recording. You can see what a giant step forward that is. The absolute limit of a disk played at seventy-eight revolutions a minute is four and a half minutes. Three is much more common. Theoretically, the guv'nor's system can record and play for hours at a time.'

'Hours?' asked Jack, sceptically. 'That seems a pretty big claim. Besides that, who would want hours of recorded sound?'

'Have you ever seen a film, Major Haldean?'

'Well, yes . . .' Jack's eyes widened. 'I see what you're getting at.'

Carrington craned forward excitedly. 'Can you imagine it? Instead of having to read what the actors said, you could actually hear them say it. It's not just speech, either. Any sound at all can be recorded and played. Just think what that would do to a film of a battle, say, or even something as ordinary as a street scene. It would make the whole thing come alive in a way that just isn't possible at the moment.'

'It would be like being there,' said Jack slowly. 'I'm beginning to understand why this is so valuable.'

'I've replicated my father's experiments,' said Carrington, his eyes alight. 'His system needs work, of course, but he'd done it.' He took off his glasses and polished them absently once more. 'He experimented, as others before him, with recording on wire but he believed a much better sound could be obtained by using a metal ribbon. The sound he was able to reproduce was truly extraordinary and Dunbar realized that. The way things were shaping up, Dunbar was going to have a genuinely revolutionary system and my father would be left with nothing. I was delighted when Dunbar approached Otterbourne's. Mr Otterbourne had a reputation as an ethical man and I hoped there would be fair play.' He slumped back in his chair. 'Well, you know what happened next.'

Jack swallowed. The coroner had said Professor Carrington was innocent; he had a sudden, vivid impression of a brilliant, vulnerable man caught like a fly in a spider's web, threshing helplessly as his struggles brought the waiting horror ever closer. 'What did you think of the coroner's findings? Were you satisfied?'

'Satisfied?' Gerard Carrington looked blank.

'Do you think,' said Jack, choosing his words carefully, 'they arrived at the correct verdict?'

Carrington paled. 'You know what happened to my father. He was unjustly accused, Major Haldean. I know that now, but, at the time, even I wondered if his temper had got the better of him.' The muscles in his throat contracted. 'I've blamed myself for that, but it was only later the truth about the pensions and so on came out. That explained why Mr Otterbourne took his own life. It made sense afterwards but at the time I was bewildered. The guv'nor didn't help. He tried to deal with it as he dealt with any situation he couldn't cope with. He ignored it. I shouldn't have left him.' He put a hand to his mouth. 'I told him I'd be back and when I did return, it was all over.'

'It must have been difficult,' said Jack awkwardly.

'Of course it was difficult! What the devil does that matter? He *needed* me. He always did. You were in the war, weren't you? I wish I'd been able to fight. Because of my father, my mother begged me not to go. My cousin, Steve – my God, how I envied him! He got the D.S.O. No one's ever questioned his courage or his patriotism. My grandfather was a foreigner and, even now, even someone like Mrs Lewis thinks I'm not quite English. It matters, you know?' His mouth trembled. 'I wanted to *prove* I could do it. I was desperate to join up.' He touched his glasses. 'My eyesight was a problem, but I could have rigged the test.'

'It's as well you didn't,' said Jack sharply. 'I mean it. One knock, one nudge, your spectacles have gone and, without good eyesight, you're a danger to yourself and to your men.'

'So I was told,' said Carrington miserably. 'I allowed myself to be persuaded. I knew how much Dad needed me, so I let myself be classified as unfit for service. I finished my degree and knuckled down to academic work on soundwaves.' His face twisted. 'It's not very heroic, is it?'

'You were probably a damn sight more use at home than in France. There's more than one sort of heroism.'

'It's good of you to say that,' said Carrington. He gave a long sigh. 'In the end, what did it matter? He needed me and I wasn't there.'

Every instinct Jack possessed urged him to offer some comfort but he couldn't think of any words that wouldn't seem unbearably clumsy. He forced himself to ask the next question. It was cruel, he knew, but he had to see Carrington's reaction. 'You don't have any doubts that Mr Otterbourne did shoot himself?'

Gerard Carrington rose from his chair, his eyes gleaming. The warder outside tapped on the window and he subsided, his body rigid. 'Are you trying to say that my father *did* kill him?'

'Not exactly,' said Jack. 'But there were other people in the house.'

'But . . .' Carrington broke off. 'Someone else shot him, you mean?' Jack could see the idea take hold, then Carrington shook his head regretfully. 'I can't see it.' He started to speak once more, then broke off.

'What is it?' prompted Jack. Carrington remained silent. 'If you've got any doubts at all about the verdict on Mr Otterbourne, I'd be very obliged if you'd tell me.'

'I didn't have any doubts at the time,' said Carrington slowly, 'but since then, I've wondered.' He ran a hand through his hair and took a deep breath. 'I shouldn't tell you this. It won't make life any easier for me, I know, but I've wondered if Dunbar could have been responsible.' He looked at Jack with narrowed eyes. 'You don't seem surprised. I thought you'd be astonished.'

'It's not the first time I've come across the notion.'

Carrington leaned forward. 'Isn't it? On the face of it, it seems a ridiculous idea, but I kept coming back to it.' He grinned cynically. 'You can see why I didn't want to say anything. I'm in quite enough trouble as it is without saying I thought Dunbar could have murdered Mr Otterbourne and shoved the blame off on to my father. That's handing the police a motive on a plate. And –' he shrugged '– it's only an idea.'

'Why did it even cross your mind?' asked Jack. 'You must have had a reason.'

Carrington clicked his tongue. 'I've asked myself the same question. At the time, he was horrified, or I thought he was, at any rate. I didn't pay him much attention.' He clasped his hands together so the knuckles showed white. 'But since then, yes, I've wondered. The first time I saw him after my father died was at the inquest and, although he acted perfectly properly and said all the right things, I knew he didn't really mean any of it. His attitude was all wrong.'

Jack felt a prickle of excitement. 'His attitude?'

'He was *pleased*,' broke out Carrington. 'At first I thought I must be wrong. I argued the toss with myself dozens of times but I couldn't get rid of my impression. For some reason, Dunbar was pleased that Mr Otterbourne had died.' He glanced up. 'I don't know about my father. Perhaps that was too painful for me even to contemplate, but I'm sure about his reaction to Mr Otterbourne's death. As time went on I became more and more uneasy about working with him.'

'You did work with him though.'

'What choice did I have?' asked Carrington with a shrug. 'I didn't make a meal of how I felt but I didn't try and conceal the fact I had reservations about him either. Quite apart from what might be nothing but fancy, I had legitimate grounds to feel pretty iffy about him. Dunbar knew that, but he had no choice but to turn to me. I must be about the only person in the world who had a sporting chance of understanding my father's notes.'

He polished his glasses once more. 'Dunbar had taken possession of Dad's machine. That was perfectly legal and I had no grounds for complaint. However, he needed me to make it work. I've got some ideas of my own, too. The machine is essentially the guv'nor's, but my version will be a great deal easier to operate. I've started work on the new machine. I'm not there yet, but it's only a matter of time. Now, I'm not my father. Dunbar might have exploited him, but I was damned if he was exploiting me. There are parts of the new machine which are mine. I want to be able to use the process in other machines and, furthermore, I wanted a licensing agreement so I would get a payment for every model sold. That was what the argument was about.'

'Did you come to an agreement?'

Carrington shook his head. 'No. I don't know if we ever would have done. I'll be honest, it's easier now he's dead. All I want to do is develop that machine, not argue endlessly about who owns what.'

He broke off suddenly and looked round the bare room. He swallowed convulsively and put a hand to his mouth. 'Just for a moment I'd forgotten where I was. I can't believe this has happened,' he said passionately. 'I was thunderstruck when the Inspector told me Dunbar was dead. I assumed he'd had a heart attack or something. I couldn't see the point of his questions. When I was arrested I couldn't credit it was a serious accusation. Then, when I realized they *were* serious, I asked them to produce proofs. I still haven't been shown anything that I would consider as a proof and they won't admit they're wrong. They are wrong, though. After all, if a man comes to an erroneous conclusion, then either his chain of reasoning must be false or his premises can be contradicted. It's a matter of logic or a matter of fact. But they won't give me their premises and when I say their chain of reasoning is at fault I can see they either don't understand – although God knows what's so hard to grasp – or simply think I'm lying.' He swallowed. 'All the ways I've ever used to present an argument seem to be redundant.' His voice trailed off. 'I don't know what to do.' He suddenly looked very frightened and oddly, vulnerably, young.

Jack leaned forward, willing confidence into the man. 'Look, Mr Carrington, you're in a rotten position. Tell me, do you have any friends?'

The fear faded from Carrington's face. His forehead creased in a frown. 'Of course I do. Why do you ask?'

'Say one of your friends makes a statement that you can't objectively prove or disprove – that they had measles as a child, for instance, or that they had a chop for dinner – do you believe or disbelieve them?'

'I believe them. Why shouldn't I?'

'And if one of those same friends said they'd seen a ghost, what would you think then?'

'A ghost?' Carrington repeated, puzzled. 'I'd probably think they were joking.' A smile twitched the corner of his mouth. 'Either that, or they'd been making a night of it.'

Jack smiled too, but he wanted an answer. 'And if they were serious? And sober?'

'Utterly serious? I can't say I believe in ghosts but I'd think they'd probably seen *something*. What it was is another matter.'

'So your belief or disbelief hinges not so much on what you're being told, but on who says it?'

'I suppose so. Yes, of course it does. There are some people I'd trust to tell me the truth, even though it may sound peculiar.' He hesitated. 'That's only common sense, isn't it? To trust the people you know are trustworthy. You might not always be right, of course.'

Jack breathed a sigh of satisfaction. Common sense; indefinable but unmistakable. He nodded in agreement. 'That's ordinary life, isn't it? We can't possibly check the truth of what everyone says. We wouldn't have time, for one thing and, for another, we wouldn't have many friends left by the time we'd finished. Now the police don't know you, Mr Carrington. Your account of what you did sounds odd to them and not only haven't they got enough information about you to take your statement on trust, they wouldn't be allowed to let such personal considerations enter into it. I know very little about science, but I imagine that when presenting a scientific argument, you point to the results of various experiments and justify your theory because of those results. Unlike your hypothetical friend and his ghost, the personality of the man conducting the experiments doesn't affect the outcome.'

'No, it doesn't, unless you think he falsified his results. But if the experiment can be repeated and the same result reached, then that's objective truth.' Carrington relaxed, happy to be on familiar ground. 'You can debate his conclusions, of course.'

'And that's the position the police are in.' Jack shifted in his chair, linking his fingers together. 'They have the objective fact of Andrew Dunbar's murder to account for. Their conclusion is that you murdered him. We want to debate that conclusion, but we can't do it by asking them to show their proofs. They haven't got any, in the sense you mean. What they have got is a chain of inference, shaky as it may be, and that's all they need. In court your actions will be examined as if you had shot Dunbar. You might say that's a false premise, but it's what they'll be acting on. All they have to show is that it's beyond reasonable doubt that you killed Dunbar. It's not scientific. It can't be, any more than a friend who says he saw a ghost can be judged scientifically. It'll simply be the jury's opinion based on your actions. We have to see it from their point of view. If you can provide an innocent and reasonable account of your actions, then we've got a chance.'

Carrington gave a fleeting smile. 'Is this meant to be cheering me up?'

'It's meant to stop you asking for scientific proof of their accusation. Science, in your sense – real science – where the truth of a proposition can be tested by a series of experiments, won't help us. Dunbar's murder was a unique event and, as such, has unique characteristics. You can't reproduce the exact event to see if the same consequences occur.'

Carrington gazed at him. 'I see. Yes, of course, I see.' He rubbed his hand through his hair anxiously. 'No one's put it quite like that before but it's obvious, really. I've been using the wrong methodology,' he added, more to himself than to Jack. He suddenly looked very unsure of himself. 'But if science won't help . . .' He drummed his fingers on the table. 'I've been rather stupid, haven't I? I . . . I don't know what to do. When Inspector Rackham came to interview me, I obviously put his back up. I got on better with my solicitors but I could tell they didn't understand my point about the nature of the proofs against me. They didn't explain it as you've just done.' He gave Jack a worried glance. 'It's partly arrogance, I suppose. No, let me be honest. It was arrogance. I was so stunned when I was accused and I found the idea so idiotic, I demanded they should prove it, really prove it, I mean. I realized they didn't know what I was talking about. It seemed so ridiculous they couldn't understand what I meant.'

'It could be shock, too,' said Jack. 'You were grasping for a way of looking at things which seemed familiar.'

Carrington nodded eagerly. 'That's right. I wanted their proofs.'

'But Inspector Rackham thought he'd answered your question, because he does know what proof means in the courts' sense of the word. It means, if I can put it like this, the balance of probabilities.'

'I see,' said Carrington again. He put a hand to his mouth. 'Oh, crikey. It looks . . . It looks as if I'm for it, doesn't it?'

'Not necessarily.' Once more Jack tried to will self-confidence across the table. Carrington looked close to panic.

'Let me take you back to that afternoon with Dunbar. You said you argued with him. Did the argument continue all afternoon?'

'No. I'll give Dunbar his due, he knew how to handle people.' Carrington gave a sudden boyish smile. 'The fact is, I got interested. As I said, he knew his stuff and asked some fairly penetrating questions. I've been working on amplification. That's how to increase the electrical impulse sufficiently to reproduce the soundwaves so they can generate a detectable vibration in a diaphragm.' He grinned. 'I drew pages of diagrams for him.'

'What pen did you use?'

'Pen?' Carrington looked startled. 'I didn't use a pen. I always have a pocketful of pencils. When I'm merely sketching out ideas I always use a pencil.'

'Did you have a pen with you?'

'I think I must have done. I usually carry one in my jacket pocket.'

'What kind of pen do you use?'

'It's a Waterman with a gold nib. Why? Is it important?'

Jack smiled easily. 'Probably not. What colour ink do you prefer?'

'Black, as a general rule.'

Jack's spirits dipped. The suicide note had been written in black.

'Look, what is all this about my pen?' asked Carrington impatiently. 'The police wanted to know about it, too.'

Jack held up his hand. 'Don't worry. I daresay it won't lead anywhere but it was just an idea that occurred to me. These pages of diagrams that you drew – did you take them with you?'

'I'll say. I might have left Dunbar in a better frame of mind than I started with, but I was blowed if I was leaving my work scattered round the room for him to help himself.'

'Yes, I can see you'd be cautious. Did you have a bag or a case with you?'

Carrington frowned, trying to remember. 'No . . . No, I didn't. I just stuffed everything in my coat pockets. It's a bad habit of mine.'

'And doesn't do much for the line of your clothes. When did you realize the time?'

'It was coming up to half four. I suddenly remembered I'd promised to meet Mrs Lewis and realized I was going to be late. I bundled all my things together, but, of course, you can't just leave like that. Dunbar kept me for a few minutes, thanking me for my time and so on. Then I shot off as fast as I could go. I was only a few minutes late in the end. I'm a pretty quick walker and it's not very far.' Carrington looked at him. 'There's not much more I can say.' He paused hesitantly. 'Major Haldean, is there anything you can do?'

'I don't know,' said Jack honestly. 'I'll tell you this much though, Mr Carrington, I'm willing to try.'

Carrington readjusted his glasses. 'That's good of you.' His voice was oddly shy. 'It's very good of you. I've . . . I've enjoyed talking to you. The people here try to be decent enough, but there's not really anyone I can talk to properly. They all seem to know things I haven't a clue about and I feel like a spare part. They're kind enough but . . .'

'They're talking about trivialities and you want to talk about real things?'

'That's it,' said Carrington in eager agreement.

'And yet, you know, ordinary people have a lot to talk about. All you have to do is listen.'

'Listen,' repeated Carrington. 'I can do that, I suppose. Anyone can do that.'

'You'd be surprised how many people don't want to,' said Jack dryly. He got up to go. 'Thanks for seeing me.'

Carrington's mouth twisted. 'I wish I could say "I'll show you out".' He smiled once more. 'And Major Haldean – thanks for everything. I don't want to go overboard, but I do appreciate what you're doing.'

'Keep your chin up. I'll do my best.' Carrington looked so heartened that Jack's conscience bit him. After all, he thought, as the doors of Brixton Prison clanged behind him, cheery remarks were all very well. But where on earth did he start?

SEVEN

He decided to start at the Marchmont Hotel. By means of a long-winded reminiscence of a friend who had supposedly recommended the Marchmont to him, Jack managed to secure room 202, three doors down from what had been Dunbar's room. From Bill's description, the room seemed identical to Dunbar's and, like his, looked out on to Southampton Row.

He was, quite frankly, hoping for inspiration. Like Bill, he thought something about Carrington's story didn't add up. There was a loose thread somewhere that had bothered Bill and bothered him. Carrington bothered him. He unpacked his few belongings thoughtfully. He liked the man, for heaven's sake. He had an engaging, dishevelled charm that was so disarming it could easily – far too easily – be deceptive. He'd run across engaging murderers before.

Half an hour later, he glanced at his watch. Ten past four. My word, it was quiet. Carrington had been seen in the lobby by Mrs Dunbar at half four, so if he had shot Dunbar, it must have been roundabout this time in the afternoon. The Marchmont dozed in the summer afternoon sun, the hum of London traffic in the street below softened into drowsy melody. He opened the dressing-table drawer and took out a Webley .32, weighing it thoughtfully in his hand for a moment. He had brought the Webley second-hand in a fishing tackle and gun shop. Bill was right. Webleys were easy enough to obtain.

A familiar imp of mischief made him grin. This was going to be *loud*. He opened the window, pointed the gun at a piece of blue sky and pulled the trigger.

Although he had been expecting a fairly impressive noise, the sound of the pistol was shattering at close quarters. He hastily threw the gun back in the drawer and slammed it shut, trying hard not to laugh. By jingo, *that* should make someone jump. He opened the door on to the corridor and left it ajar. If someone did come to investigate, they would probably start with an opened door. There weren't, he noticed, any fumes from the pistol to give him away. The Webley, an automatic, used smokeless powder. Picking up a magazine, he sat at the desk and lit a cigarette looking, he hoped, the picture of innocence.

A few minutes later he heard the sound of footsteps followed by a timid knock. 'Sir? Are you all right in there, sir?'

He crossed the room and opened the door fully. Outside stood the chambermaid, a plump woman in her fifties, at a guess, with iron-grey hair. His heart lifted. He'd read the various statements from the witnesses at the hotel and the chambermaid who found Dunbar's body, a Mrs Doris Gledburn, had given her age as fifty-three. With any luck, this was her.

The worried expression on her face cleared as she saw him. 'I'm sorry to disturb you, sir, but I thought I heard a noise.'

'So did I,' said Jack, cheerfully. 'Terrific bang, wasn't it? Goodness knows what it was.' He gestured to the window with his cigarette. 'A car or something, I expect, backfiring in the street. It made an awful racket. It sounded like a gun going off.'

A startled look leapt into her eyes. 'Well, that's it, sir. And . . . And . . .'

'I say!' said Jack, apparently struck by a sudden thought. 'This is the place where that chap, Whatsisname, got shot, isn't it?' He looked at her with sympathy. 'Good Lord, you must've thought it was happening again.' He lowered his voice conspiratorially. 'It was this hotel, wasn't it?'

She looked round and edged a bit closer to the door. 'Well, I don't know as we're not really meant to talk about it. Mr Sutton – he's the manager – doesn't want it spoken about. He's very keen on the Marchmont's reputation and says it'll give us a bad name, but really, I can't see it. It's hardly our fault, is it?'

'I don't suppose it happened because of rotten service,' agreed Jack. To his surprise she smiled.

'He wouldn't have found that here, sir. We're very particular.'

He smiled back. 'I'm sure you are. It's a nasty shock for everyone, though, finding a body.'

She nodded vigorously. 'I know all about that, sir.' She looked at him with a sort of reluctant pride. 'I was the one who found him.'

Jack felt a glow of satisfaction. So this really was Mrs

Gledburn. Not only that, but she was obviously quite happy to talk about what must have been one of the most startling experiences of her life, and he was perfectly willing to let her. 'Good Lord,' he said with flattering interest. 'You actually found him?' He looked behind him in sudden, if assumed, concern. 'It wasn't this room, was it?'

'Oh no, sir, don't you worry.'

Jack breathed a very convincing sigh of relief. 'I'm glad about that. It must have been terrible.'

'Oh, it was.' Mrs Gledburn, glanced up and down the corridor, saw a reassuring absence of senior staff, and shifted her position into an agreeably gossipy stance. 'I've had night-mares about it.' She clasped her expansive bosom and rolled her eyes. 'Nightmares. Just two doors along from here, it was.' Jack put his head round the door and peered solemnly down the corridor. 'I went into the room and there he was, lying all stiff and cold.' She leaned forward impressively. 'Murdered!'

Jack's jaw dropped. *'Murdered?'* he repeated.

'Yes, sir, murdered.' She lowered her voice still further. 'What's more, I think I saw the man who did it.'

The thrill of discovery ran through him. This was new. Mrs Gledburn had made no mention of seeing anyone in her statement. 'You actually saw him?'

Mrs Gledburn leaned forward confidentially, flattered by his interest. 'Yes, sir. Lurking on the corridor he was, leaning against the wall. I didn't know as much then, but he was over-come with guilt, and no wonder! He had his head in his hands, sort of upset like. I caught sight of him before I found the poor gentleman dead, and that put it out of my mind, as you might say. I did wonder if I should tell someone, but I talked it over with the other ladies here and they said it was better to let sleeping dogs lie.'

'Couldn't he have been a guest?'

'We thought about that, but if he was a guest he'd have gone into his room, not stood hanging about on the corridor. It did strike me as he may have lost his way but he didn't want to be seen, not by the way he was acting. As soon as he saw me coming he went down the stairs and I thought, "Hello, what do you want, I wonder?" because we've got to be careful, you know, about robberies and suchlike. Then I went in to give Mr Dunbar his towels and it gave me such a turn, I forgot all about it. They said at first he'd made away with himself, so I didn't think anything of the man for a while. Then, when it came out he'd really been *murdered*, I tell you, I could hardly breathe, when I remembered how close I'd been to the man who did it.'

She shuddered. 'It was a blessing I didn't speak to him. Why, I might have been murdered myself. I read in the paper he was one of these mad scientists, the sort who want to be blowing us up with their nasty bombs and poisoning us with gas and such like, as if we didn't have enough of that in the war. It's not right, is it? I tell you, I could have been struck down as sure as I'm stood here.' Her chest heaved and her eyes closed momentarily at the thought of her narrow escape. 'There's enough trouble in this world without looking for it.'

'Absolutely right,' said Jack, radiating sympathy. 'Would you know him if you saw him again?'

Her face fell. 'I've asked myself that many a time. I looked at the photo in the paper of what's-he-called, the man they arrested, but those pictures are very deceiving, aren't they? It's not like seeing someone properly, like. I *might* do, but I'm not sure. After all, I only had a glimpse of him, and he had his hat and coat on. I don't know if I could swear to him again. Even if I could, I don't want to get mixed up with the police.'

'Didn't you have to talk to the police anyway?'

'Well, I *did*,' admitted Mrs Gledburn grudgingly, 'but that was all about finding the body and so on.'

Jack looked at her thoughtfully. To have found a murdered man almost begged to be matched with a sight of the murderer. It was too good a chance to miss and yet, if she were making it up, he would have expected her to embroider the story with more detail. 'Did he have staring eyes?' he probed gently. Surely she couldn't resist that lure. 'I've always heard that murderers have staring eyes.'

For a moment she hesitated, then shook her head regretfully. 'I couldn't tell you, sir. It'd be different, perhaps, if I saw him again, but I can't bring to mind if he was fair or dark or anything. I think he was a youngish man, but I can't really be sure of that, even. It was him though, and no mistake.' Mrs Gledburn shuddered agreeably once more. 'It makes me go cold all over, thinking about it.'

'And I suppose you heard the shot, too?' said Jack in an awe-struck way. 'I read that it sounded like a thunderclap. Everyone thought there was a storm brewing and one of the maids was so startled she broke a teapot and, when she looked at the leaves, said there was a death on the way.'

Mrs Gledburn smiled indulgently. 'The rubbish that they do write, I don't know. I think they make it up half the time.'

This was so undoubtedly true that Jack mentally congratulated her on her scepticism.

'We didn't hear anything, sir, not me or the rest of the maids, and we would have done, I'm sure.' She sniffed. 'We'd have certainly heard about it if one of us had broken a teapot, murder or no murder. We'd been having a bit of a chat in the Maids' Room at the end of the corridor before I went round with the towels. I was a bit behind as Gladys Street's daughter's just had a new baby and she was telling us all about it.' Her voice softened. 'Eight pounds three ounces, he was and a lovely little boy with a full head of hair.' Her forehead creased. 'It's funny that we didn't hear anything, though. I can't understand it. After all, I've just come from the Maids' Room now and we all heard that car backfiring as plain as plain.'

'Was there any other noise? Perhaps men digging up the street or something?'

Mrs Gledburn shook her head. 'No, there was nothing. If there were men at work outside, we'd have known. This is a very quiet hotel, sir. You can hear a pin drop, particularly in the afternoons.'

'I wonder when he was shot, then? If you didn't hear it, I mean.'

Mrs Gledburn looked perplexed. 'D'you know, that's a puzzle, that is. We must have just missed it, but I don't know how. There's always someone around at this time of day. I don't care what was said in the papers about tea-leaves and such-like, we didn't hear a thing.' There were the sounds of footsteps on the stairs and she regretfully stepped back. 'Well, I must be off. I hope you've got everything you want, sir. I'll be along with your shaving water later.'

The next morning Jack woke up slowly, nudged out of sleep by the hushed but unfamiliar noises in the corridor outside. After the excitement of the chambermaid's revelations about The Man, the evening had passed without further ado. Whoever The Man was, he couldn't be Gerard Carrington, as Gerard Carrington had been in the lobby before the chambermaid started her rounds. That was something but it wasn't enough.

What about the damn gun? Jack put his hands behind his head, lay back on the pillow and stared unseeingly at the bedroom ceiling. Mrs Gledburn had been very sure that no one had heard the shot. It wasn't, thought Jack, remembering the sleepy somnolence of the Marchmont yesterday afternoon, as if there was any background noise to drown out the sound.

Mrs Gledburn had referred to it as a puzzle, and, thinking back to his experiment of yesterday, he wholeheartedly agreed. A silencer fitted to the gun was the obvious answer, but that raised as many questions as it answered.

Dunbar might very well have had a gun, but he'd hardly have a gun and a silencer. A silenced gun was a real assassin's weapon. Gerard Carrington could have used a silenced gun perfectly easily, but if he had thought it through enough to buy a silencer, then he surely would have made a better fist of the job. The supposed suicide had been clumsy enough for Sergeant Butley to see through it right away. Carrington was such an obvious suspect Bill had tracked him down only hours after the crime. And yet . . . It all hung on what a reasonable man would do and a man who was gripped by panic wasn't reasonable. It wasn't *enough,* thought Jack in disgust.

A brilliant shaft of sunlight lanced a spear across the bed, catching thousands of gilded, dancing dust-motes. They were unexpectedly beautiful and he watched, his senses stilled. The curtain flapped and the dust-motes abruptly vanished. A brief dance and then into darkness, he thought, chilled.

He knew there was something he had missed. Think! But no thoughts came. It couldn't be suicide. The angle of the bullet, the missing key, the wrong colour of ink on the note. Nothing there.

He snuggled back further into the crisp pillows. The noises in the corridor grew closer; comfortable, start-of-the-morning, cup-of-tea-soon noises with the chink of crockery and discreet knocks on doors. He could hear the shrill young voice of the post-boy following the chambermaids. Tea, plain biscuits, letters. *Post, sir!* There wouldn't be any letters for him, of

course. Bullet, key, ink . . . He sat bolt upright. Ink, pen . . .
Post! That was it, *surely* that was it. He needed to telephone
Bill and then he had to post a letter. The chambermaid knocked
and with a broad smile he called, 'Come in.'

He had an idea.

It was quarter past four that afternoon when Bill Rackham
knocked on the door of Jack's hotel bedroom. 'I got the information you wanted,' said Bill, pulling out a chair and sitting
down, after Jack had relieved him of his coat and hat. 'I've
spoken to that precious chambermaid of yours, too,' he added.
'I'd have liked to have been here when you fired off that gun,
I must say.'

'I feel a bit guilty about that,' said Jack, offering him a
cigarette. 'It gave her the dickens of a fright, poor woman.'

'Poor woman be blowed,' said Bill heartlessly. 'It serves
her right. Why on earth she couldn't tell us she'd seen a man
in the corridor, I don't know. How did you get her to come
clean? I thought you reserved your devastating charm for real
lookers, not stout grey-haired ladies in their fifties.'

'I appealed to her motherly instincts,' said Jack with grin.
'Devastating charm, indeed! It makes me sound like Gigolo
Joe. I got more out of her than you did, though.'

'Don't be so smug,' said Bill. 'At least she's amended her
statement, which is something. What I hadn't really taken on
board is how odd it is that no one seemed to hear the shot.'
He lit his cigarette and looked at Jack with a puzzled frown.
'Could the gun have been silenced?'

'Now that's an interesting question,' said Jack. He opened
the desk drawer and brought out a small, stout, blue-covered
book. 'This is the *Text Book of Small Arms*. I knew I had a
copy somewhere. I went home and dug it out this morning.
This is what it says about the Webley.' He opened the book,
ran a finger down the index, then flicked through the pages.
'Here we are. Webley .32 automatic. First produced in 1906
– it's astonishing they've been around for that long – weight,
twenty ounces, length, six and a quarter inches, magazine
capacity of eight rounds and – listen to this – a muzzle velocity
of nine hundred feet per second. What d'you think of that?'

'Nothing much,' said Rackham. 'You'd still have to be pretty
nippy to dodge it, if that's what you're getting at.'

'Idiot,' said Jack impatiently. 'Don't you see, Bill? With a low muzzle velocity like that, a Webley, unlike most guns, can be effectively silenced. You can't silence a revolver and you can't silence the crack of a high velocity bullet – although, come to think of it, if you stand close enough to your target you don't have to – but you can silence this. There'd be some noise but it'd sound like a flat *whiz* rather than a shot.'

Bill smoked his cigarette in silence for a few moments. 'All right. It could have been silenced, I grant you, but that's not to say it was. Silencing a gun isn't something that would occur to most people, is it? I've used a Webley myself. It was the standard pistol issued to the Metropolitan Police, but it never crossed my mind it could be silenced. That's pretty technical knowledge.' He frowned unhappily. 'Silencing the gun doesn't seem to square with the clumsy way in which the suicide was arranged. I can't work it out. We would have bought the idea of suicide, you know. All it needed was a little more care in the details and Dunbar would have been chalked up as dead by his own hand.' He looked up. 'You spoke to Carrington. Could he be the sort of person who would look up all the technical guff about the gun and then make a complete hash of the actual carrying-out of the plan? That seems to me the sort of mistake a clever person might make.'

'Yes, it does,' said Jack uneasily. 'However, you said yourself you weren't a hundred per cent convinced it was Carrington and, now the chambermaid has decided to tell us what she saw, we do have another man on the spot.'

'So we do. The youngish man who she just might – or might not – recognize if she saw him again? That narrows it down to about fifty thousand or so. I'll have fun finding him. Anyway, you asked me about the letter Dunbar received, the one from Stephen Lewis.'

Jack looked up alertly. 'Yes?'

'The postmark shows it was sent from Sackville Street at ten twenty-three. There were plenty of fingerprints on the envelope, including a set from Dunbar himself, but the actual letter only had two sets of prints. There's one set from someone unknown. Those, I imagine, belong to Stephen Lewis, or Lewis's secretary, at any rate. There's another set of prints that belong to Dunbar. All of which,' he added, looking inquisitively at Jack, 'is exactly what we would expect to find.'

'Carrington's prints aren't on it, are they?'

Rackham shook his head. 'No. He could have handled it if he wore gloves, I suppose.'

'I think that's a bit of a blind alley. The prints tell us Dunbar read the letter though, don't they?'

'As far as we can tell, yes. You asked me to check if they seemed naturally placed. They certainly seemed so. I don't think there's any doubt about it. What's your idea?'

Jack hunched forward in his chair. 'It's fairly simple,' he said. 'How did you know that Stephen Lewis should have been at the meeting?'

'Because he told us so,' said Rackham. 'Carrington said so too. And, of course, we found the letter from Lewis beside Dunbar's body.'

'Exactly,' said Jack. He stopped as a knock sounded at the door, followed by a youthful shout of 'Post!'

He opened the door. Two doors along the corridor, a boy in hotel livery stood with an open satchel over his shoulder and a handful of letters in his hand.

'Letter for you, sir,' said the boy helpfully, pointing to the envelope he had left in the rack outside the room.

'Just make a note of the time, would you?' Jack murmured to Bill, then, raising his voice, called to the boy. 'Come here, son.'

'What is it, sir?' asked the boy, trotting towards them. He was a stocky, crop-headed, intelligent looking lad of about fourteen and was clearly very happy to have a legitimate reason to stop and chat.

'What's your name?'

'Henry Ellis, sir,' said the boy. He sized Jack up and found him worthy. 'My pals call me Harry.'

Jack grinned. 'And have you worked here long, Harry?'

'I've been here nine weeks, sir,' said Harry.

'Do you always bring the letters round at this time in the afternoon?'

'More or less, sir. I takes them round in the morning, too. Eight o'clock and half past four, those are my times.'

'And do you always knock and shout "Post!"'

'Well, yes, sir,' said Harry defensively, sensing a possible reprimand in the offing. 'I'm sorry if I disturbed you, sir, but it's what I've been told to do, see? Mr Rice, the head porter, he told me particular. He said I had to knock because if a party was waiting for a letter, if I didn't knock they wouldn't know it was here, would they? It's only what I've been told to do, sir.'

'It's all right,' said Jack with a smile. 'You're not in trouble.' Harry, although still wary, relaxed. 'Were you here the afternoon Mr Dunbar was murdered?'

The boy's face lit up. 'The geezer in 206? Cor, I should say I was!' He grinned happily. 'That was exciting, that was. Old Ma Gledburn – she's one of the chambermaids – she was in a right old state, weeping and carrying on. She found him, and my word, she didn't half squawk. You could have heard her a mile off, the way she went on.' He frowned in remembered outrage. 'I wanted to have a look but they wouldn't let me. It wasn't fair, that. I only wanted to *look*.'

'Ghoulish little beggar,' interjected Rackham without heat.

Harry looked at him with an expression of injured innocence. 'It wouldn't do any harm, would it? Not just having a *look*. Old Mrs Gledburn, she kept on saying as how he'd shot himself but he didn't, did he? It's better'n that, ain't it? He was murdered. I've never seen a geezer who's been *murdered* afore.'

'Did you see him before he was murdered?'

Harry's eyes filled with longing, then he regretfully shook his head. 'No. I can't say I did. If I'd a-known what was going to happen, I'd have copped a look at him special, but he was just an ordinary gent.' He sniffed. 'I wished I'd a-known.'

'But you did bring a letter for him that afternoon, didn't you?'

'Oh yeah. I did that all right.'

Rackham shot a quick glance at Jack. 'Did you, by Jove?' he said quietly. 'Did you knock on his door, Harry?'

'Oh yes. I called, "Post!" like what I've been told to do and he called back.' Harry adopted a squeaky, supposedly posh, voice. '"Right-oh," He didn't come to the door,' he added broodingly. 'I'd a-seen him if he come to the door. I'd liked to 'ave seen him, as he was going to be murdered.'

'What time was it?' asked Rackham. 'When you delivered his letter, I mean?'

Harry ran a hand through his hedgehog hair. 'It would a-been about this time, sir. It always is, unless suminck goes wrong, and there weren't nothing wrong that afternoon.'

'Twenty to five,' muttered Rackham. He drew himself up to official height. 'Now look here, son, I'm a police officer. Why didn't you tell us any of this before?'

'No one asked me! That flatty who was here—'

'Sergeant Butley,' put in Jack.

'Yes, him. He asked who'd seen the bloke who was murdered and I didn't see him, did I? That's what I've been telling you.'

'All right,' said Jack. He felt in his pocket for some loose change and held out a shilling. 'Here you are.'

Harry pocketed the shilling with a lop-sided grin. 'Thanks, guv. You ain't a flatty, are you?' Jack shook his head. 'I didn't think so. More class.'

'Cheeky little beggar,' said Rackham, once they were back in Jack's room. 'Just because I can't go tipping shillings to witnesses he thinks he can cheek the police. Either I or Butley should have spoken to him before now, though.' He glanced at the envelope in Jack's hand. 'Who's your letter from?'

'Me. It's just a blank sheet of paper. I posted it to myself this morning.' He held out the envelope. 'I wanted to replicate the letter Stephen Lewis sent to Dunbar and, as you can see from the postmark, this was posted this morning at Sackville Street and postmarked ten twenty-three, just as Lewis's letter was. I wanted to check what time it would arrive here.'

'Twenty to five,' said Rackham absently.

'Can we assume that Lewis's letter arrived at more or less the same time? Twenty to five?'

'I suppose so. I don't see why it shouldn't.'

'And Mrs Dunbar saw Carrington in the lobby at what time?'

'Mrs Dunbar? That was . . .' Rackham broke off and swallowed. 'My God, Jack, she saw him at half four. She's certain she saw him at half four.' He sat down, his face pale. 'That's ten minutes before Lewis's letter arrived. Dunbar read that letter. Carrington has to be innocent. Dunbar was alive when he left him.'

EIGHT

A look at the head porter's day book confirmed it; on the fifteenth of July, the day Dunbar was killed, the post office had delivered the afternoon post to the hotel at twenty past four. Rice, the head porter, confirmed that if the ordinary routine of the hotel had been carried out – and he was certain it had been – then Young Ellis would have started on his rounds about half past four, reaching the second floor and Room 206 around twenty to five. The murder, said Rice, pulling at his walrus moustache meditatively, fixed the day in his memory. If there had been anything out of the way, he would have remembered it, sure as eggs were eggs.

Sir Douglas Lynton, Assistant Commissioner of Scotland Yard, also pulled at his moustache, but in his case it was irritation rather than thoughtful reflection that was the chief emotion. 'Damn it, I thought it was an open and shut case!' He glared at Rackham and Haldean. 'You're absolutely convinced of the facts? Carrington couldn't have shot Dunbar after the letter was delivered, I suppose?'

'Absolutely, sir,' said Rackham with a glance at Jack. This was a possibility they had explored earlier. 'Mrs Lewis confirms that Carrington met her at the Lyon's in Leicester Square just after five. Even if he'd taken a taxi, he couldn't do it in the time allowed and there would be the risk that the taxi driver would remember him. There's no doubt that Dunbar really did read Stephen Lewis's letter, sir. I had the fingerprint department go over it with a fine toothcomb once I'd realized how important it was. They're certain Dunbar was alive when he handled it.'

Sir Douglas looked at them grumpily. 'I can't really argue with our own fingerprint people.'

Rackham nodded. 'It seems conclusive to me, sir. Besides that, I can't help thinking that if Carrington had any idea of how important the letter was, he'd have found some way of drawing it to our attention. He's never mentioned it. I thought there was something I'd overlooked but it was Major Haldean who actually pinned down exactly what it was.'

'I suppose you're to be congratulated, Major,' said Sir Douglas unenthusiastically. He looked at the file on his desk and sighed. 'There's nothing for it. We can't go ahead now. But, damnit, if Carrington didn't murder Dunbar, who did? If the man was alive at twenty to five and dead twenty minutes later, it comes down to a matter of split-second timing.'

'Or luck, sir,' put in Rackham.

'Or luck,' agreed Sir Douglas dryly. 'Quite considerable luck.' He leaned back in his chair. 'Well, there's nothing for it. Carrington will have to be released. I still think there's a chance he's our man, but we can't afford to go ahead now.' He raised a quizzical eyebrow at Jack. 'If Major Haldean has another inspiration and works out how Carrington could have done it after all, I don't want to have scuppered our chances because he's already been tried and acquitted. The law won't let us bring a man to court twice for the same offence, even if we're certain he's guilty. As the case stands, we haven't a hope. Not now.' He looked at the file gloomily. 'You'd better go back to the beginning, Rackham.' He tapped his finger on the file. 'There's Dunbar's wife. She might know something.'

He read the notes for a few moments. 'Dunbar's her second husband of course,' he said thoughtfully. 'We know they were separated, so she might be a possible.'

'I don't think she could manage to climb the stairs to his room, sir, and she didn't take the lift.'

'Maybe,' said Sir Douglas, unconvinced. He read on for a few moments then looked up with a different expression. 'Good Lord, I've just realized who she is! Evelyn Dunbar is Evie Grace. That was her stage name, of course.'

Jack looked at Bill. No, the name didn't mean anything to him, either.

Sir Douglas was surprised by their lack of reaction. 'You've heard of Evie Grace, surely? The fair singer of Scotland, The Bluebell of the North? No? Perhaps you're too young, but she was famous in her day. She was the star of a string of shows – light operettas, I suppose you'd call them – at the Majesty. She was a wonderful actress with a wonderful voice, too. The audience used to hang on her every word.' He smiled indulgently at Rackham and Haldean's blank expressions.

'They used to play one of her songs as the troop ships left for the South African war. Every errand boy in London whistled it. *A Barefoot Prince*. That's it. *A Barefoot Prince* from *The Golden Touch*.'

'I've heard of that,' said Jack intelligently. 'It was a huge hit.'

'*The Golden Touch*?' said Rackham. 'We had the music in the piano stool at home.'

'Everyone did,' said Sir Douglas absently. 'My word, she was a lovely girl, with huge blue eyes. I suppose nowadays a show like *The Golden Touch* would be thought terribly sentimental but it suited her down to the ground. She was a sweet little thing. Fragile, you know? Not at all like these modern, hard-bitten girls, all lipstick and cigarettes and skirts up to their knees. My word, if we saw an ankle it was a real thrill.' He recalled himself with a sigh from his Edwardian youth. 'She must have had a hard time of it when she was young. I'm not surprised she changed her name. It isn't generally known, but her mother was Violet Cautley.'

'Violet Cautley?' repeated Rackham, puzzled, but Jack was ahead of him. 'You mean the Cautley poisoning case, sir?'

'That's the one. It was about 1875 or thereabouts. Donald Cautley was an opium-eater, a philanderer, and known to be a violent man. Violet Cautley was a wispy, pretty bit of a thing who made a good impression on the jury. She was acquitted but that probably had as much to do with the sympathy she aroused rather than any regard to the facts of the matter. Cautley was poisoned with antimony. It was argued that Cautley had taken it himself and the jury, despite some fairly strong evidence to the contrary, decided that was the truth of the matter.'

'Are you suggesting these things run in families, sir?' asked Jack.

Sir Douglas laughed. 'No. Not in public, at any rate. Officially Violet Cautley was innocent.' He closed the file. 'I'll leave it with you, Rackham. Let me know how you get on.'

'Can I come with you?' asked Jack as they clattered down the stairs from Sir Douglas's office. 'I wouldn't mind meeting Mrs Dunbar.'

'I suppose so,' said Rackham. 'It's not by the book by a long chalk, but you wouldn't be involved in the first place

unless I'd asked you to take a hand. I wouldn't mind getting
your impression of her.' He looked uneasy. 'You know I said
I didn't believe Evelyn Dunbar could have murdered her
husband? I mentioned her dodgy ankle, I know, but the real
reason was that I just couldn't see her doing it.'

'You said, as I recall, that she'd have to be a brilliant actress.'

'Yes,' agreed Rackham slowly. 'And now Sir Douglas has
just told me that she was.'

Mrs Dunbar's house in Essex Gardens, Kensington, was part
of a pleasant, quietly prosperous, mid-Victorian terrace, with
neat sash windows, whitened steps, and an oak front door
with a brass lion's-head knocker gleaming in the evening sun.
A tall, elderly parlour maid admitted Jack and Bill into the
hall and, after a short wait, ushered them into a comfortably
furnished drawing room where Mrs Dunbar was waiting for
them.

She was not alone. With her was Hector Ferguson, who looked
understandably surprised to see them, and a middle-aged, plump,
cheerful-looking man with a round, good-natured face who spoke
with a precise Edinburgh accent. He was introduced as Mr Robert
Bryce, the manager of Dunbar's Gramophone Company. He had
come down from Falkirk to accompany Mrs Dunbar and Hector
Ferguson to a meeting with Stephen Lewis.

'I hope we're not interrupting your plans, Mrs Dunbar,' said
Rackham, taking in Mr Bryce's and Hector Ferguson's evening
dress.

'No, indeed, Inspector,' said Mrs Dunbar. 'We've already
dined. You'll excuse me not getting up,' she added, patting
the walking stick beside her. Jack raised his eyebrows involuntarily. It was difficult to see the fragile Evie Grace of Sir
Douglas's memories in this grey-haired, stout woman, dressed
soberly and correctly in widow's black, but as she spoke, he
amended his first impression. Her voice had a husky richness
which imparted Drama to the simplest sentence. Her eyes
were a striking, guileless china-blue that implied helpless
dependence on the Big Strong Man she was looking at. Jack
didn't quite believe in that dependence. Clever? Perhaps not;
but shrewd certainly.

'We met Captain Lewis this morning and I found even that
excursion exhausting.' She gave a little laugh. 'Still, even though

my wretched ankle stops me from getting about as I would like, I shouldn't complain, should I? Everyone has been so very kind and when I think if it wasn't for my accident *I* might have been the one to discover poor Andrew, I can only say that I feel guided.' She clasped her hands together with a stricken expression. 'It seems dreadful to even think of it now, but I was annoyed with Andrew for being late. If I had been able to manage the stairs, I would have gone to his room and then . . .' She shuddered. 'So often in my life I have felt *guided*. It is a great thing,' she added, 'to feel protected by a Higher Power.'

There was a weary sigh from Hector Ferguson.

'It is only,' continued Mrs Dunbar, ignoring her son, 'when I have ignored the promptings of my inner nature and succumbed to the so-called wisdom of the world things have gone wrong.'

'What on earth are you doing here, Haldean?' demanded Hector Ferguson brusquely.

Mrs Dunbar winced at his tone. 'Hector,' she said faintly. 'Don't be so abrupt. You know it upsets me. But,' she added, looking at Jack, 'I understand that Hector spoke to you about my late husband.' Her eyes circled. 'I was terribly upset when I learned of the suspicions that Hector had allowed to fester. The idea that poor Andrew was concerned in any underhand activity was completely monstrous, as events have so sadly proved.'

Ferguson shifted uneasily in his chair. 'We've been over all this before, Mother. You were as puzzled as I was, you know you were.'

'That is beside the point, Hector,' she said in a much more business-like voice. 'It doesn't matter. However inexplicable your stepfather's moods may have been, I cannot think they were a proper subject to be discussed outside the family. To suggest, as you did, that he profited by the sad events at Stoke Horam is completely unacceptable.'

'It was only what you thought yourself,' said Ferguson defensively. 'Yes, I know I was wrong, but you were worried, you know you were.' He glanced at Mr Bryce. 'We all were, weren't we?'

Mr Bryce cleared his throat. 'It was a concern I shared with your mother, Hector. I did not expect to be quoted on the matter.'

Rackham seized on the salient point. 'So Mr Dunbar's change of mood was noticeable, was it? And you noticed the change after his visit to Stoke Horam?'

Mr Bryce bit his lip. 'Yes,' he agreed reluctantly.

'And you thought it odd, sir? Granted the circumstances, I mean.'

'I thought it very odd, Inspector,' said Mr Bryce cautiously, with a glance at Evelyn Dunbar. She nodded almost imperceptibly for him to continue. 'You know Mr Dunbar had come to an arrangement with Professor Carrington? Mr Dunbar, quite justifiably, congratulated himself on the deal he had worked out. There was no two ways about it, he stood to make a great deal of money from Professor Carrington's machine. And, to be fair to him, he had a sincere interest in sound and wireless and was always interested in any new advances for their own sake.'

'Especially if he thought he could make a profit from them,' interjected Ferguson.

Mr Bryce shook his head. 'You mustn't be too cynical. He really did understand the subject. That's why he was so enthusiastic about Professor Carrington's work.'

'And why you, I and everyone else who knew him thought it was so peculiar when he acted like a dog with two tails after the Professor bought it.'

'Not immediately,' countered Mr Bryce. 'That wasn't his first reaction.'

'All right, if you say so. But it wasn't long before he picked himself up.' Hector Ferguson looked defensively at his mother. 'I know you don't like me talking about it, but it was very odd. He loved money and was always looking to make a profit.'

'That is the nature of business,' put in Mr Bryce.

'I don't dispute that. What I did wonder was why, once the Professor had died, he should suddenly be so cheerful about things. It wasn't natural.'

'He must have been relieved when he realized that the machine was going to be developed after all,' suggested Jack.

'By Gerard Carrington, you mean?' asked Mr Bryce. 'No, that wasn't it.'

Ferguson nodded agreement. 'He cheered up before Gerard Carrington came on the scene.' He lit a cigarette. 'I still say it's odd.'

'I don't want to talk about it,' sniffed his mother, looking close to tears. 'I don't want anyone to talk about it. You know things were difficult, Hector.' She clasped her hands round her knees and swallowed deeply, looking at Jack and Rackham. 'You must understand. Hector is a dear boy but he felt my wrongs very deeply.' The dear boy, Jack noticed, rolled his eyes at this point. 'He will always seek to make things better for me, by taking my side in any agreement, in any dispute,' – Ferguson sighed once more – 'and, of course, to blame Andrew for the slightest disruption comes easily to him.' She shook her head wearily. 'I should have never married again. In my heart of hearts I knew we were not suited, but I allowed myself to be swayed. I was very foolish. I blame myself entirely.'

Ferguson raised his eyebrows expressively and drew on his cigarette. 'That wasn't exactly what I was getting at, Mother.' He glanced at Jack. 'To get back to what I was saying, why are you here? I wouldn't have thought there were any questions left to answer. After all, you've nabbed Gerard Carrington, haven't you?'

'Poor Mr Carrington,' said Mrs Dunbar distantly. 'I liked him. I cannot believe he planned such a wicked crime. Andrew must have upset him. If Andrew had a fault, it was that he could be a little abrasive at times. Poor Mr Carrington must have simply answered to the impulse of the moment. I'm sure it was all a misunderstanding. I do hope he's treated kindly. I cannot bear to think of him languishing in prison.'

'He isn't,' said Rackham.

'What?'

'It's like this, ma'am,' said Rackham, clearing his throat. 'There have been a few further developments.' Mrs Dunbar exchanged worried glances with Mr Bryce and sat forward expectantly. 'Some new facts have come to our attention.' He couldn't help but pause for effect. 'We now believe Gerard Carrington to be innocent.'

There was an abrupt, rigid silence.

Mrs Dunbar, who had been listening to Rackham with a gentle smile, froze. Her smile, fixed in place, became a rictus grin. Mr Bryce started and muttered an exclamation under his breath, staring at Rackham. Hector Ferguson, his eyes wide and his freckles suddenly vivid against his pale skin, swallowed a mouthful of smoke and choked on his cigarette.

'No,' whispered Mrs Dunbar, and then, in a stronger voice, 'no! You have to be wrong, Inspector.' She glared at Ferguson, who was still coughing. 'For heaven's sake, Hector, will you please stop making that dreadful noise. Go and get a drink of water.' There was a definite command in her voice.

Ferguson recovered himself. 'I'm all right.' His eyes were fixed on Rackham.

'Hector, *go away!*'

Rackham held up a placatory hand. 'Perhaps it's better if Mr Ferguson stays, ma'am. After all, this concerns him.'

Mrs Dunbar turned to him with frightened apprehension. She took a deep breath before she spoke. 'What do you mean?'

'I mean that it concerns Mr Ferguson because it was his stepfather who was killed.'

Mrs Dunbar shut her eyes for a second. 'Yes,' she said, recovering herself. 'Yes, of course.'

'What are these new facts, Inspector?' asked Mr Bryce. 'I thought there was no doubt about Gerard Carrington's guilt. After all, Mrs Dunbar herself saw Carrington leave the hotel and his manner impressed you very unfavourably, did it not, Mrs Dunbar?'

She nodded vigorously. 'That's so. As soon as I heard what had happened I felt instinctively he was guilty. He has to be guilty. There wasn't enough time for anyone else to have done it.'

'There was, as a matter of fact,' said Rackham. 'We have evidence that proves your husband was alive when Mr Carrington left the hotel.'

'You can't have!' she wailed. 'He was *dead*. I know he was dead.'

Rackham looked at her appraisingly. 'How can you be so sure?'

Her mouth quivered ominously. 'I just know it. I . . . I sensed it.' She burst into tears. 'Gerard Carrington must be the man,' she said between sobs, dabbing at her eyes with a handkerchief. 'I felt sorry for him, of course I did. Andrew could be very difficult.' She swallowed noisily. 'Or . . . Don't you think Andrew must have killed himself? After all, he wrote a note to say he killed himself. Can't we all just say that's what happened? It'd be so much better if we could simply accept Andrew killed himself.'

'Unfortunately, we know that's not the truth,' said Rackham.

'Excuse me, Mrs Dunbar, why does it upset you so much?' asked Jack.

Mrs Dunbar couldn't bring herself to answer.

'Don't you see, Haldean?' said Hector Ferguson, his face still pale. 'If Gerard Carrington is innocent, someone else must be guilty.'

Mrs Dunbar burst out into renewed sobs. 'Hector, don't! Don't say another word!' She looked up from her handkerchief. Her eyes were suddenly calculating. She took a deep breath, squashed the handkerchief in her hand, and sat up straight. There was a regal quality in her bearing which demanded respect. It was, thought Jack, startled by the change, as if another personality had overlaid the fussy, tearful, slightly silly woman of seconds before. When she spoke, her voice matched her bearing.

'I know, Inspector, that I must be a suspect.'

For a moment no one spoke. Mrs Dunbar threw back her head, facing Rackham with dignity. Her expression showed an acceptance of the blows of fate. It was a gallant challenge to the man before her. Blimey, thought Jack, her voice could still a theatre. *A theatre . . .*

Rackham shifted unhappily in his chair. 'I wouldn't put it as bluntly as that, ma'am.'

Her hand flicked to one side. It was one of those gestures which, small in themselves, are magnified to huge emotional proportions. It would live in an audience's memory forever. Her very weakness was so compelling that it forbade the use of strength. Only a complete monster could crush such a delicate creature.

Bloody hell, thought Jack, this is the dickens of a performance. He immediately felt ashamed of doubting her aching sincerity.

'It's no use,' she said, with the ghost of a heart-rendingly brave smile. 'I'm a woman of the world and I realize how damning the facts must seem.' She took another deep breath.

'Andrew and I separated, as you know. What you perhaps do not know is how much I gained by his death.'

'Mother,' said Ferguson in a slightly dazed voice. 'What are you saying?'

She looked at him squarely. 'I know exactly what I am doing, Hector. I would rather put all my cards on the table sooner than have my affairs discussed behind my back later. The police will make it their business to find out anyway.' She turned to Mr Bryce. 'I have never concerned myself overly much with money but you, I know, have a far better grasp of the details than I could ever hope to achieve. You will oblige me by spelling out the position to Inspector Rackham.'

Mr Bryce gave an agonized cough. 'What, now?'

'Yes, now.'

He shrugged unhappily. 'If you say so. In a nutshell, Inspector, Mrs Dunbar inherits everything.'

'So my income has gone from the allowance Andrew made me to what, Mr Bryce?'

Mr Bryce swallowed. 'It is a little difficult to say exactly. The firm has not been doing at all well in recent years. Do you really want me to discuss the details now?'

'Yes. Tell everything. Everything, I say! An accused woman must hold nothing back!'

Mr Bryce sighed unhappily. 'Just as you like.' He looked at Rackham over the top of his glasses. 'Mrs Dunbar had a considerable amount of money of her own when she married which – and I cannot help but feel you were badly advised, Mrs Dunbar – because it was not protected by any form of trust, became the property of Mr Dunbar.'

'It is not in my nature to hold back. My lawyers urged caution but I despise anything that smacks of meanness. I trusted Andrew. I gave him everything.'

Mr Bryce gave a little cough. 'As you say, Mrs Dunbar. When you separated Mr Dunbar agreed to make you an allowance of . . .' He hesitated once more. 'Do you really want me to cite actual figures, Mrs Dunbar?'

'Do it!' she commanded, her face a tragic mask. 'If you do not, I will. It was little enough in all conscience. He flung me a pittance, a trifling bagatelle, the crumbs from his table.'

Looking round the snug drawing room, Jack couldn't help wonder at the size of some of the crumbs.

'You have been in receipt of nine hundred pounds a year,' said Mr Bryce with a touch of reproof in his voice. He clearly didn't think nine hundred a year was too crummy either.

'Nine hundred,' she echoed. 'A mere competence when I had never been accustomed to consider money.' She allowed a few moments' silence for contemplation of her plight, then her voice took on a firmer note. 'But now, Mr Bryce, what is it now?'

'I have already warned you that the firm is not doing as well as could be hoped. However, Mr Dunbar did have an income from various stock holdings and a sizable amount in the bank. You should be comfortably off, Mrs Dunbar.'

'Exactly.' She clasped her hands together and looked earnestly at Rackham. 'You see, Inspector? Andrew – poor Andrew – could never have realized what his petty economies meant to me. I existed on a shoestring, scrimping and saving, eternally penny-pinching and making do. Now I shall be a rich woman.' She opened her hands wide. 'The world is mine once more.'

'I wouldn't put it like that exactly,' said Mr Bryce. 'You can not afford to be too extravagant, you understand.'

She looked at him coldly. 'It isn't a matter of mere money. There is a richness of spirit that cannot be entered in a clerk's ledger. I have regained my freedom. It is not something that can be assessed in mere monetary terms, but to me it is a pearl of great price. I am my own woman once more; free from the shackles I so blindly placed upon my own wrists. I know what you are thinking, Inspector!'

This was so unlikely to be true Jack had to look away for a moment.

'Even now, although you fight to conceal it, I can see the suspicion, the growing doubts, the stark accusation in your eyes.'

'No you can't,' said Rackham, stung.

She ignored him. '*J'accuse!* That is what is in your heart. I know I had a lot to gain. I realize what interpretation could be put on it if I tried to hide the fact. My poor mother suffered at both the hands of the press and the bar of public opinion. I have learned that it is better to reveal everything!' She cocked an eyebrow at Rackham. 'You know who my mother was? She was,' she said, not waiting for an answer, 'Violet Cautley.' She caught Rackham's expression. 'I see you know the name. Even now, her name is a byword. She was hounded, Inspector, positively *hounded* and her life made unbearable but she was innocent, as I am innocent of this monstrous accusation.'

'I haven't actually accused you of anything yet,' said Rackham in desperate self-defence.

'It is in your mind!' She raised an arm as if to shield herself. 'Can you understand my emotions? Would I – would any woman – want to endure what my mother endured, to be the subject of ill-nature gossip and speculation?' With a wave of her hand she put this option to one side. 'Find out what you will, Inspector, but you will find I am innocent. I know that as a gentleman, you would take my word but as a policeman, you are forced to be nothing more than a calculating machine, collecting crumbs of *facts*.' She made the word *facts* sound slightly indecent. 'It will tell you nothing but what you know in your heart to be true.'

Rackham reddened and ran a finger round the inside of his collar. 'Unfortunately, Mrs Dunbar, that's about the size of it. Collecting facts, I mean. Tell me, when did you last see your husband?'

She sat back with a wistful, reminiscent smile. 'The last time? How sad that sounds. It is, perhaps, a mercy of Providence that sometimes the future is not ours to apprehend. Sometimes, I – foolish as women are, swayed by a desire to pierce this veil which clouds us – sometimes I have yearned to see beyond, to see further than the few steps which the Merciful All-Knowing illuminates for us.'

Hector Ferguson gave a short sigh. 'The last time you saw my stepfather was the afternoon he returned from Stoke Horam. That's what? Nine or ten weeks ago now. It was the day Charles Otterbourne and Professor Carrington died.'

'So it was,' she agreed distantly. 'Poor Andrew was perturbed.' She unleashed another wistful smile. 'Although we could not live together, Andrew occasionally liked me to accompany him to public events. There was a dinner that evening he wanted me to attend. You might not know this, Inspector, but I was on the stage before my first marriage. The public were very kind to me. Andrew was well aware that, in my own small way, I am still held in regard.'

'He would wheel you out if he thought it would influence a deal,' said Ferguson.

Mrs Dunbar's lips tightened momentarily. 'There are still people for whom I evoke fond memories of their youth. And if I could help Andrew, why shouldn't I? He was still my husband, after all. And – and it was nice to meet people and know that I am not entirely forgotten.'

'Excuse me, Mrs Dunbar,' said Jack. 'But if you hadn't seen your husband for a couple of months or so before his death, how were you so sure of his change of mood?'

She said nothing for a moment.

'I told you, didn't I?' said Ferguson. 'Don't you remember? We talked about how odd it was.' He looked at Jack. 'It was after that I started to wonder who I could ask about it and eventually I thought of you.'

'That's right, Hector,' she said with a tinge of relief. 'Yes, you told me about it.'

Hector Ferguson stubbed out his cigarette. 'I saw him about two weeks after Charles Otterbourne and the Professor copped it.'

'And that was the last time you saw him, wasn't it, Hector?'

Ferguson looked at her thoughtfully. 'Yes,' he said after a slight pause. 'Yes, it must have been. You're quite right, you know, Mother. It is funny to think you've seen someone for the last time. He'd come down to meet Captain Lewis. I thought he'd be beside himself about Professor Carrington's death but he wasn't.'

'He had been,' said Mrs Dunbar with a touch of reproof.

'That may be so, but he got over it pretty quickly, didn't he? He was going to meet Captain Lewis and talk things over with him. Perhaps he had the idea about asking Gerard Carrington to work on his father's machine then, but if he did, he didn't mention it.' He looked at Mr Bryce. 'Do you know when it was decided Gerard Carrington should take over the work?'

'It was later that same week,' said Mr Bryce, after a moment's thought. 'As you say, Mr Dunbar had come to London to see Mr Lewis and it was then the arrangement was made.' His round face crinkled unhappily. 'It was an awkward situation.

We – the firm, that is – have a clear right to Professor Carrington's machine. Mr Dunbar hoped that Gerard Carrington would complete his father's work under the same terms that Professor Carrington agreed but Gerard Carrington refused to be bound by that contract.' He stopped and looked at Mrs Dunbar with an apologetic air. 'I know you have reservations about Captain Lewis, Mrs Dunbar, but in my opinion if it hadn't been for his intervention, I believe Mr Carrington would have been a great deal more awkward about matters.'

Mrs Dunbar bridled. 'Captain Lewis! Don't talk about Captain Lewis to me! Andrew should never have got involved with Otterbourne's. I distrusted Stephen Lewis from the moment I saw him.'

Hector Ferguson wrinkled his nose. 'Did you, mother? I thought you got on perfectly well.'

She drew herself upright. 'Naturally, Hector, I did not parade my feelings, but I have them, all the same. I do not expect you to understand my reasons. I have never concerned myself with matters of business.'

'Which is why you asked Mr Bryce and me to accompany you to the meeting.'

'But I do understand *people*,' she continued, as if Ferguson hadn't spoken. 'Stephen Lewis has a shifty expression. Not only that, but he has grey eyes.'

'What on earth have his eyes got to do with it?' said Ferguson in bewilderment.

'I have never trusted anyone with grey eyes. You may laugh, but the eyes are the window of the soul. Grey eyes are the token of a treacherous nature.'

'You can't honestly intend to run a business based on what colour someone's eyes are, Mother. It's crazy.'

'It is nothing of the sort, Hector. This whole idea of an association with Otterbourne's has been nothing but trouble from the word go. It was a disaster from the start. For all his reputation, in my opinion Mr Otterbourne had a most un-desirable love of publicity with his so-called good works and his model factory and his model village and making sure everyone lived model lives. It was nothing but unwarranted interference and busy-bodying. Andrew might have had his faults but at least he was content to let his workers simply be, without constantly telling them what they should do and

how they should live and what they should think. Charles
Otterbourne was nothing more or less than a dictator and eventually he showed himself to be the fraud he always was. I am
not an unfeeling woman. No one who has lived my life could
be. Heartbreak has been my lot. I have known tragedy. I have
supped sorrow with a spoon. I would not mock or jeer at the
depths of misery which force self-annihilation, yet I tell you,
I believe Charles Otterbourne received nothing but his just
desserts. The mills of God grind slowly, Hector, but they grind
exceedingly small.'

There was a stunned pause from the men in the room. Jack
bowed his head as if moved beyond words. What he was actually doing was trying desperately not to look at Bill. He knew
that if he did, he couldn't help but laugh.

Mr Bryce made a *hrumm* noise. 'And yet, Mrs Dunbar,
the offer from Otterbourne's is a good one. I understood you
were perfectly satisfied. Captain Lewis is, I know, keen to
proceed with the deal and I would be failing in my duties if
I did not urge you most strongly to consider it.'

Evelyn Dunbar lifted her head and looked at him squarely.
'I will not entertain the notion.' She shuddered. 'Stephen Lewis
is not to be trusted. I know that glamorous, handsome type, with
their smooth speech, fine clothes, slick manners and easy
charm. I've seen any amount of Captain Lewises in my time.
Stage-door Johnnies, the lot of them!'

'Lewis isn't like that,' protested Hector Ferguson. 'You
make him sound like a tailor's dummy. He's a good-looking
beggar, I suppose, and he knows how to enjoy himself, but
you can't hold that against him.'

'I know, Hector,' said Mrs Dunbar repressively. 'I am never
wrong about these things. Andrew trusted him and he paid
the penalty.'

Hector Ferguson brought down his hand with a thump
on the leather arm of his chair. 'For heaven's sake,
Mother! Are you saying that Stephen Lewis murdered my
stepfather?'

She winced. 'Murder is a harsh word, Hector. But yes, I
think it's possible. More than that, even.'

'That's the third theory you've been certain of in as
many minutes!' said Ferguson in exasperation. 'First Gerry
Carrington killed him, then he killed himself and now you've

accused Stephen Lewis. What earthly reason have you got for suspecting him?'

'You may mock intuition, Hector, but there is such a thing in this world as *guidance*.'

'It's guiding you up the garden path this time,' he said shortly. 'Come on, Mother, you can't be serious. Stephen Lewis can't have bumped off my stepfather. He was nowhere near the place. I read as much in the paper.'

She closed her eyes in the manner of a Pre-Raphaelite mediaeval saint. 'I make no claims to cleverness. There was a time I regretted that. Learning was something that, no matter how earnestly I desired it, was not mine to command. And yet, there was a purpose in that, as there is in all things. I have come to see that what the world calls learning is flawed. True wisdom knows the human heart. My intuition is never wrong.'

Ferguson snorted dismissively. 'Apart from the times it's not right. Wisdom or no wisdom, I can't see how Lewis could be in two places at once.'

This time Jack couldn't help looking at Bill. Bill's eyes crinkled and his mouth was suspiciously tight. It was a good few moments before he could say anything but when he did, his voice, much to Jack's admiration, was level. 'Mr Ferguson is quite correct, Mrs Dunbar.'

'It's unfair to Mr Lewis that you should harbour such suspicions,' put in Mr Bryce. 'The offer from Otterbourne's is very good. I'm not dismissing intuition, you understand, but it would be very awkward for us to deal with Mr Lewis if you take against him. It's bad for business.'

'Business!' murmured Mrs Dunbar, subsiding back against the sofa.

Mr Bryce pursed his lips. 'I'm afraid you will have to consider what is best for business, Mrs Dunbar. The firm is yours and you have to take the decisions. I will, of course, advise you to the best of my ability but the decisions are yours.'

'Mine as well,' put in Ferguson. He hesitated, looking at his mother's bowed head. 'I was looking forward to it. I've got plans, things I want to do. You *liked* my ideas. You said you wanted me to run the firm.'

Mrs Dunbar put her hand to her forehead. 'That is no longer possible, Hector. I will probably sell the firm.'

Both Mr Bryce and Hector looked startled but it was Ferguson who spoke. 'You can't do that.'

'Can't I? Correct me if I'm wrong, Mr Bryce, but as I understand it, the firm is not doing as well as it once was.'

'Unfortunately, that is so. We are, I may say, not alone. These are very hard times for any gramophone manufacturer. The quality of sound on the wireless is excellent and records have slipped out of fashion.'

'Records sound tinny and outdated,' said Hector Ferguson. 'That's why my stepfather was so enthusiastic about Professor Carrington's machine. We might not have seen eye to eye about lots of things but he was right about that. If this machine is all it's cracked up to be, we'll go great guns.' He leaned forward, his eyes bright. 'Can you imagine it? As I under-stand it, we'll be able to reproduce a sound that's so close to the real thing you'll hardly be able to tell the difference. I know musicians who can fill a dance floor. If we can capture any of the excitement of that sound, we'll make a mint. It's not just musicians, either, it's singers too. At the moment, no one bothers much about singers. All the attention is given to band leaders but – I was thinking of you, Mother – you were famous *because* you were a singer. There's no reason why a singer shouldn't be a star.'

'Now that,' said Mr Bryce in a pleased sort of way, 'is the kind of radical idea that we need.'

'You can't give it up now, Mother, you really can't. What's the problem? You were all for it earlier on.'

'You seem to think, Hector, that I am running the firm solely for the benefit of you and your friends.'

'That's not—'

'You have, I know, ambitions to be a musician.'

'I *am* a musician,' said Hector, flushing. 'What on earth's got into you, Mother? You've always encouraged me before.'

'If you are serious, Hector, you should study. Paris, perhaps, or even New York. I've heard you talk about New York often enough.'

'I don't want to go to New York,' said Ferguson mutinously. 'Not now. You said I could run the firm.'

'Don't be silly, dear,' said his mother with a lightning smile. She picked up the pair of gold-wire framed spectacles she wore on a chain round her neck, carefully put them on, and stared at her son without speaking. Then she laughed. 'Look at you. You're far too young to tie yourself to an office desk. It's all for the best. You don't want to be bothered with business at your age. You'll be far, far happier in New York.' There was an edge to her voice. 'Trust me.'

NINE

'**M**rs Dunbar,' said Bill Rackham, once they were out of the house and safely out of earshot, 'takes the biscuit. She must be the most appalling woman I've ever come across. I couldn't believe it when she insisted on telling us about money and her freedom and so on. *A pearl of great price*. I've never heard anything like it. It was down-right embarrassing, to say nothing of all that toe-curling stuff about supping sorrow with a spoon, or whatever it was.'

They crossed the street, walking towards the tube station. Essex Gardens was one side of a square. In the middle of the square was a tree-lined, railed-off garden which, as the notice detailing Regulations For Use beside the iron gates informed them, was restricted to Residents Only. The shady paths and open lawn were, in a picture of prosperous middle-class content, occupied by a scattering of householders and, correctly Secured On A Leash, a bevy of well-behaved dogs, all enjoying the evening sun.

'I mean,' said Rackham in disgust. 'Look at this place! It's hardly a picture of grinding poverty, is it? To hear her talk, you'd think she'd been forced to take in washing.'

'It was a wonderful performance,' said Jack with a grin. 'I wonder if the Bluebell of Scotland has become a thistle. Or, to put it another way, if she was spiking your guns?'

Rackham looked at him. 'You mean all that nonsense was intentional? It can't have been. You'd have thought the silly woman *wanted* to be arrested.'

'Maybe she did.'

'Following in her mother's footsteps, you mean?' Rackham sighed impatiently. 'She's such a blinkin' drama queen she's probably rubbing her hands together at the thought of appearing in court. I know people do confess to crimes they haven't done. They want the attention, I suppose. She's half-baked enough to be one of them.'

'She didn't actually confess, though, did she?'

'No, she stopped short of actual lunacy.'

'And yet she was demonstrably on the spot and she certainly had a motive. Like you, I think nine hundred quid a year is nothing to be sneezed at, but if she'd really had money to burn before she married Dunbar, she probably did resent it. And I know she put it oddly, but she *has* regained her freedom now Dunbar's dead. What she's done is present you with the points that tell against her wrapped up in way that means you can't really take her seriously. After all, say you did arrest her. What would happen?'

'If she treated a court to a fraction of the nonsense we've just heard, I imagine most of the jury would die laughing. You can never tell, though. Some of them might think she was a tragic victim. It wouldn't wash though, Jack. Once her doctor gave evidence that her ankle really was crocked, she'd be acquitted.' He looked at his friend inquisitively. 'What's on your mind?'

Jack clicked his tongue. 'She's an actress, Bill. She looks like an unremarkable middle-aged lady. Before she rang the bell on the desk at the Marchmont Hotel no one from the hotel had taken any notice of her.'

'So what?'

'So our unremarkable middle-aged actress could easily come into the hotel, complete with a change of clothes and a different hat. She could get up to Dunbar's room, do the deed and be back downstairs without anyone really noticing she'd been there in the first place.'

'But her ankle was crocked.'

'Her ankle might have been crocked but that doesn't paralyze her from the waist down, does it? She is still capable of movement. How were you so sure that she hadn't taken the lift up to the second floor?'

'I asked the lift boy. When I was called to the Marchmont I saw Sergeant Butley. He was waiting in the manager's office with Mr Sutton, the manager, Mrs Gledburn, the chambermaid who'd found the body, and Mrs Dunbar. Mrs Dunbar was so upset I sent her home. We've got to be careful of interviewing witnesses when they're in a state. I don't like doing it and any statement they do make would probably be deemed inadmissible as it was obtained under duress. However, before she left, I collared the lift boy and asked him if he'd taken Mrs Dunbar up in the lift. I wanted to ask him while it was still fresh in his mind. He was positive he hadn't.'

'But he didn't know Mrs Dunbar, did he? I bet he didn't recognize her as such, but remembered what she was wearing. If he was asked to identify a lady in green tweed with a cloche hat, say, it wouldn't occur to him to him she could possibly be a woman in red, for instance, with a fox-fur collar and a wide-brimmed panama with a veil and a feather.'

Rackham bit his lip. 'That's true enough. You're right, dammit. I'll tell you something else, too. She must have said about a dozen times how awful it was to think of her husband lying dead upstairs while she was sitting alone in the lobby, waiting for him. I didn't think anything of it at the time, but she did insist upon it. She told the manager he must have seen her, sitting quietly in the lobby, not knowing what dreadful news awaited her – I think those were more or less her exact words – and he agreed, of course.'

'He would, under those circumstances. He wouldn't want to argue with a newly bereaved woman. I can't imagine the manager was feeling any too bright, either.'

'No, he wasn't. I can see he wouldn't want to contradict her. At the time I thought he probably hadn't noticed her at all, but it's odd, you know, how convincing that sort of inno-cent-sounding statement can be. I have to say I didn't take Mrs Dunbar seriously as a suspect. Her account of herself seemed so credible that I didn't really doubt it.'

They walked for a couple of minutes in silence. 'If Mrs Dunbar did murder her husband, she must have planned it,' said Rackham. 'It can't have been impulsive, not if she changed her clothes and so on. How would she know he was alone?'

'She might not be certain, but she could have hoped for the best. She certainly saw Carrington leave the hotel, so she'd have known he was out of the way. She'd asked to have tea with Dunbar, hadn't she? If he intended to keep that appointment, he'd probably rid himself of any other guests beforehand. And if, by chance, he wasn't alone?' Jack shrugged. 'She hadn't committed herself in any way. All she'd actually done is turn up for afternoon tea. That's not a criminal offence.'

'I don't like this,' said Rackham after a little while. 'It's beginning to sound all too plausible for my liking. What's her motive? I know she told us about money and freedom and so on, but none of that is new. She's been separated from Dunbar for about five years. Why should she decide to take action now?'

'She wasn't too happy about Dunbar's association with Otterbourne's. That's new.' Jack frowned. 'It doesn't seem enough though.'

'I couldn't understand why she was so worked up about that. After all, Mr Bryce said they stood to make a lot of money out of it.'

Jack suddenly stopped dead. 'Bill! That's it! *Mr Bryce.*'

'Mr Bryce?'

'Don't you think he knew a lot about her? He's the manager of the firm. Why on earth should he know how much Mrs Dunbar had to live on? That's nothing to do with the running of the company, that's strictly private.'

'I don't know if that woman knows the meaning of strictly private,' muttered Rackham. 'I see what you mean, though. D'you think they might be more than friends?'

'I think it's possible. After all, he knows a lot about how she's situated and they clearly got on well enough.' Jack cocked an eyebrow at his friend. 'It's all speculation, I know, but it could be a motive.'

Rackham was unconvinced. 'Isn't she a bit old for that sort of thing? She must be fifty-odd if she's a day.'

'And that's too old, is it? Think about it, Bill. Here's a woman who's been discarded by her husband. She's used to admiration. She must have resented it. It's only natural that she should. I know she talked about 'Poor Andrew' but I didn't get any impression she was fond of him and I know Hector Ferguson couldn't stand the man. From what we've heard, Dunbar wouldn't have wanted a divorce. He'd have to make her some sort of settlement and, by the sound of things, that would have seriously dented the apple cart, if not overturned it altogether. Then, along comes Bryce, who thinks she's the caterpillar's boots, and, all of a sudden, life without Dunbar seems very attractive indeed. All that high falutin' stuff about freedom needn't have been made up, you know. It's always easier to exaggerate an emotion that's really there, rather than invent one from scratch.'

'It's possible,' said Rackham. 'By jingo, Jack, it really is possible, isn't it?' He swallowed. 'They could have planned it out between the two of them. When I first interviewed

Mrs Dunbar, she said she'd written to Dunbar in Falkirk and Bryce replied, saying Dunbar was in London.' He puffed his cheeks out unhappily. 'Is she capable of it, though? Maybe I've been totally taken in, but I find it hard to believe she could actually hold a pistol to Dunbar's head and pull the trigger.'

'Bryce?' suggested Jack softly.

'Bryce was in Falkirk.' Rackham's lips thinned. 'Or so I've assumed. At least Mrs Dunbar told me that Bryce had written to her from Falkirk. That's something I can find out. There was a man in the corridor. I wonder if the chambermaid would recognize him?'

Jack's landlady, Mrs Pettycure, poked her head round the door of her sitting room as he came in to the hall. 'Is that you, Major? A Mr Carrington's been on the telephone. He's rung twice, wanting to speak to you. He's at a Captain and Mrs Lewis's. He wants you to slip over and see him. Very insistent, he was.' She felt in the pocket of her apron. 'I've got a note of the address here.'

'It's all right,' said Jack, picking up his hat. 'I know where it is. If he rings again, tell him I'm on my way.'

Stephen Lewis answered the door. 'Major Haldean? It's good of you to come.'

He certainly was a good-looking beggar, thought Jack, remembering Mrs Dunbar's censorious comments, but he wasn't any sort of empty-headed stage-door Johnny. Captain Lewis struck him as a decisive, intelligent man who was not only worried but wary as well.

'Hector Ferguson brought us the news. I believe you called to see him earlier this evening. He'd just finished telling us what was what when Gerry himself turned up.' Was it Jack's imagination or was there a slight reservation when Lewis said his cousin's name? 'We're all pleased, of course. Very pleased. It's just that . . .' He broke off and ran a hand through his hair in a bemused way. 'I don't mind telling you, though, it's knocked us all for six. But please, come into the sitting room.'

The fashionable sitting room was warmly lit by shaded lights glinting off polished mahogany, glass, silver and the rich leather bindings of books. There were four comfortable brocaded armchairs, a sofa, a grand piano and a large, ornate gramophone with records in a mahogany case beside it. To a man freshly released from Brixton prison, it must have seemed like a vision.

Molly Lewis and Gerard Carrington stood up as he came into the room. It wasn't, Jack thought, as they came forward to greet him, just the furniture that had drawn Gerard Carrington here.

Molly Lewis was a quiet, self-contained woman in her early twenties, attractive in a square-necked turquoise silk dress with her chestnut hair cut fashionably short. Her jaw was too determined for beauty but she looked an extremely capable sort of person. Judging by the quick, encouraging glance she gave Carrington, she certainly felt protective towards him. She had, Jack thought, a maternal nature, the sort of woman who needed to look after someone. An Otterbourne trait? That probably wasn't a bad guess, remembering the way her father had organized everyone's lives for them.

'It's very good of you to come and see us, Major,' said Molly Lewis. Her fingers clasped together nervously. 'Gerry's free and that's wonderful of course, but we don't *understand*.'

Carrington's shoulder twitched as if he was about to put a soothing hand on her arm. He hesitated, thought better of it, then stuck his hands in his pockets. His face was gaunter than Jack remembered but he still had the same air of rumpled bewilderment. 'Were you responsible for my release?'

Jack nodded.

Carrington put a hand to his mouth. 'Thank you,' he said at last. 'I'm more grateful than you could ever realize but . . . but I don't know why I'm free.' He pushed the bridge of his glasses back up his nose. 'No one explained anything. They just said I could go.'

Hector Ferguson, who had gravitated towards the piano as naturally as a compass needle points north, looked up with a sheepishly embarrassed expression. 'Thank goodness you're here, Haldean. Everyone's bombarding me with questions and I don't know any answers. I was so bowled over when you turned up at home I never thought to ask you the whys and wherefores. I felt such an idiot when I realized I hadn't actually asked you any details.'

Molly Lewis swallowed convulsively. 'We're worried, Major. Is it over? Is Gerry safe?'

Stephen Lewis turned from where he was standing by the sideboard with the soda siphon poised over a glass of whisky. 'Soda in yours, Haldean? Right you are. To put it bluntly, we're all having kittens that Gerry could be arrested once more.'

'I think you can rest easy about that,' said Jack, taking the glass Lewis offered him.

Gerard Carrington shut his eyes momentarily, his shoulders slumping in relief.

'So what happened?' asked Stephen Lewis, busy once more at the sideboard with the siphon and the whisky decanter. 'We'll understand if it's all hush-hush, but we're dying to know the truth. Help yourself to something to smoke, by the way. There's some decent cigars in the box or cigarettes if you'd prefer.' He handed round the drinks then sat down in the chair across from Jack, looking at him inquisitively. 'I don't know if you can tell us about it?'

'I can't see why not,' said Jack, reaching for a cigar. As succinctly as he could, he told the story of the letter. Although outwardly at ease, one part of him stood back, observing everyone's reactions.

Hector Ferguson was frankly jumpy, his eyes abstracted and his lips occasionally moving as if he were conducting a soundless inner dialogue. Molly Lewis and Gerard Carrington listened intently. Carrington, he thought, was so wound-up he was just this side of a breakdown. He had seen men look like that in the war, strung out by exhaustion, fear and frayed nerves. Molly Lewis, sitting beside him on the sofa, obviously knew how great a strain Carrington was under. She inclined towards him and her hand moved every so often as if she wanted to reach out and comfort him.

Jack shot a glance at Stephen Lewis. He was certainly listening to Jack – his questions had been very much to the point – but his attention was focused on his wife. His hands were clasped together so tightly his knuckles were white. He's a possessive man, thought Jack, with sudden insight. He's possessive and as defensive and alert as a wary guard dog. Molly Lewis had better watch her step.

When he had finished, Gerard Carrington looked at him blankly. 'So that's it? My God.' His eyes screwed shut and he buried his face in his hands. 'It's so trivial. That letter would have been so easy to overlook. I wouldn't have stood a chance. Thank God you wrote to Dunbar, Steve.'

'Yes,' said Lewis slowly. 'If it had gone by a different post or if I hadn't written at all, things might have been a bit tricky, old man.'

'Things are still tricky,' put in Hector Ferguson. 'Not so much for you, Carrington, but for anyone else with a motive.' He looked at Jack. 'You heard my mother this afternoon, chucking accusations around.' He smiled nervously. 'It was all hot air, of course. After you'd gone, both Mr Bryce and I told her she was talking nonsense, but she couldn't resist the drama of seeing herself as the chief suspect.'

'Your mother?' asked Stephen Lewis, his forehead furrowing. He turned to Jack. 'Is she a suspect, Haldean?'

'I'm afraid so,' said Jack.

This bald affirmation knocked the wind out of Ferguson's sails. He stared at Haldean, aghast. 'She can't be! Not seriously. She's just not capable of it. The trouble with my mother is that she can't help but give a performance.'

A performance. Yes, it had been the dickens of a performance. He'd thought as much at the time and, what's more, he could remember exactly when the natural woman gave way to the performer. *Don't you see?* Hector Ferguson had said. *If Gerard Carrington is innocent, someone else must be guilty.*

Hector Ferguson was as pale now as he was then. He was worried about his mother or – Jack mentally sat back – was it the other way round? Was his mother worrying about *him*? Hector Ferguson hated his stepfather. Oh, dear God. That made so much sense. With a sickening feeling, Jack suddenly realized how much it explained.

If Evelyn Dunbar knew her son was guilty, she would pull out all the stops to throw them off the scent. It was at least as likely as her staging a double bluff to conceal her own guilt. It all stacked up.

Evelyn Dunbar had been sorry for Gerard Carrington. As long as Hector was safe, she could afford to be openly sympathetic but with Carrington cleared, Hector was in danger again. That's when she'd changed her tune. First of all she'd volunteered herself as a suspect and then tried to throw suspicion on Stephen Lewis. Hector Ferguson had been looking forward to running the firm, but his mother had unexpectedly wanted him out of the way, safely across the Atlantic in New York. His alibi; Ferguson had an alibi. Come tomorrow, he must get Bill to take that alibi apart. He wanted to *prove* Hector Ferguson was innocent. And if he couldn't . . .

'What on earth did she say, Ferguson?' asked Lewis. 'I know you said she relished the role of chief suspect, but that's nonsense. You say she was chucking accusations about. Whom did she accuse?'

Ferguson twisted with embarrassment. 'She didn't mean it!'

'*Who?*'

Ferguson took a deep breath. 'You.'

Lewis's jaw dropped and for a moment he, Molly and Carrington sat frozen in shock. Then he laughed incredulously. '*What?*'

'It's crazy, Lewis,' said Ferguson miserably. 'Ask Haldean.'

Lewis whirled to face Jack. 'She said it to you? With Inspector What's-his-name in the same room?'

'I don't think Inspector Rackham thought she was serious,' said Jack quickly.

'She said it for *fun?*'

'Not fun, exactly,' said Jack. 'She was worried.'

'Worried? What's that got to do with it? She must be off her head. I didn't want Dunbar dead.'

'Please, Lewis,' pleaded Ferguson. 'Don't take any notice of her. She gets silly fancies.'

'It's a bit more than a silly fancy, it's insane! Can't she see that? I can't possibly have bumped off your ruddy stepfather.'

Gerry Carrington cleared his throat. 'You were at Colonel Willoughby's, weren't you, Steve?'

'Absolutely I was. Tell her, Ferguson. We need to nip this nonsense in the bud.'

'The trouble is, I don't know if she'd believe it,' said Ferguson miserably.

Lewis put his glass down with an irate click. 'Good God, I haven't made it up!'

'Of course you haven't, Steve,' said Molly. 'You left for your uncle's as soon as you got the message. It's a ridiculous accusation and Mr Ferguson knows it.'

'Exactly,' said Ferguson, grateful for her support. He looked at Lewis apologetically. 'My mother knows you and my stepfather didn't always see eye to eye, that's all.' He attempted to smile. 'I wouldn't take it personally.'

'It's hard to see how I can't take it personally. It's important, Ferguson. She's not merely some middle-aged woman, she's the owner of Dunbar's. You've got to make her see sense.'

'I tried,' said Ferguson.

Lewis blew his cheeks out in exasperation. 'This is absolutely ridiculous. Apart from anything else, it's going to play the devil with business.' He slumped back in his chair and drained his whisky. 'What about the merger?' he demanded. 'That's still on the cards, isn't it?'

Ferguson swallowed. 'Er . . .'

'For crying out loud! This has got past a joke. What am I meant to do? I can hardly ask Uncle Maurice to tell her I was with him. The poor old beggar was in rotten health to start with and this burglary business has just about put the tin lid on it. I don't know if he's going to recover. He's certainly in no fit state to trot up to London just to convince your mother she's talking out of the back of her neck.'

'Could Mr Ferguson go and see him?' asked Molly.

'I'd rather not,' said Ferguson quickly. 'After all, what on earth would I say? I can't tell a complete stranger my mother's got a bee in her bonnet that his nephew's bumped off my stepfather. He'd throw me out neck and crop, and I don't blame him.'

'Perhaps,' said Jack, 'she might believe Carrington.' He looked at Carrington. 'He's your uncle too, isn't he?'

Carrington looked startled. 'Yes, he is, but I've never met him.'

Jack knew that perfectly well. That was why he suggested it. Colonel Willoughby hadn't recognized his assailant. If Gerard Carrington could be brought face to face with the Colonel, Jack wanted to be there to see it. Sir Douglas Lynton, the Assistant Commissioner, had been heartily sceptical of Carrington's innocence. The burglary might be nothing more than coincidence but the opportunity to bring Carrington and his uncle together was too great to be missed.

'Why should Mrs Dunbar believe me?' continued Carrington.

'She would,' said Ferguson confidently. 'She likes you.'

'I could go, I suppose,' said Carrington thoughtfully. 'I never did reply to his letter and I should have done, you know. I'm not at all sure of my welcome, though. Will you come, Steve?'

Lewis laughed sardonically. 'Not on your life.' He glanced at Ferguson. 'If I turned up your mother could argue I influenced the poor old beggar into saying what I wanted him to say. I'll leave this one to you, Gerry.'

'I'll come with you if you like,' said Jack. 'I can't swear to it, but I'm sure my Aunt Alice, Lady Rivers, has mentioned a Colonel Willoughby. And, granted it's not just a social call, it might be useful to have an impartial observer along. We can run down tomorrow, if that's OK. Would your mother believe me, Ferguson?'

'Heaven knows what my mother can believe,' said Ferguson. 'She might. She's like the Red Queen and can believe six impossible things before breakfast. Not that,' he added hastily, encountering a look from Lewis, 'she wouldn't have any reason not to believe Haldean. Or Carrington, come to that.'

'Do you mind, Steve?' asked Carrington. 'After all, I know I should see him, especially as he's ill, but I don't like the idea of checking up on you.' His face lengthened. 'The more I think about it, the less happy I am. With all due respect to your mother, Ferguson, it's a silly idea.'

'I know,' agreed Ferguson quickly. 'I couldn't agree more.'

'You go, Gerry,' said Steve Lewis, flicking the ash from his cigar. 'You too, Haldean.' He laughed cynically. 'With Mrs Dunbar trying her level best to convince the cops I'm a murderer, I need someone to tell her and anyone else to whom she sees fit to mention it that it's a loopy idea. The sooner, the better.'

TEN

The next day Jack had an early start. He called to see Bill Rackham, who greeted him with distinctly modified rapture.

After hearing his latest idea, Bill Rackham buried his head in his hands. 'Let me get this straight, Jack. After persuading me that Evelyn Dunbar isn't off her rocker but capable of conspiring to murder with Sonny Boy Bryce, you're now telling me that Hector Ferguson is your most favoured candidate?'

'I wouldn't go as far as that, but he is a possibility, isn't he?' Jack glanced at his watch. 'Anyway, I'll leave it with you. I can't stop. I promised I'd call for Gerard Carrington. We're going to see his Uncle Maurice. Ferguson rather tactlessly told Stephen Lewis that his mother accused him of bumping off the dear departed. Lewis wants someone to make it clear to her that he was too busy smoothing pillows and generally being an angel in the sick-room to be doing anything of the sort.'

'He doesn't honestly think we'd take her seriously, does he?'

'No, I don't think he does, but if Mrs Dunbar goes round muttering accusations, it'll make the proposed merger a bit awkward.'

'Yes, I can see it could lead to a bit of a frost. Why are you involved? Sheer kindness of heart?'

'Not really. I thought it might be interesting to be there when Carrington met his uncle. You remember I had the idea that the burglary was contrived?'

Rackham sat up. 'By jingo, I see what you mean.' He clicked his tongue. 'I can't see it, though, Jack. If Carrington thinks his uncle might recognize him, he'd hardly invite you along to witness it, would he?'

'You wouldn't think so, but he might be prepared to brazen it out. I thought it was worth doing, anyway.' He picked up his hat. 'I must be off.'

He drove to Carrington's rooms on Tavistock Square and,

drawing the Spyker up outside a block of flats dwarfed by the bulk of University College, pipped the horn cheerfully.

After a couple of minutes the door opened, Carrington came out, stopped, indicated with a complicated wave of his hand and shrug of his shoulders that he would be back shortly, and disappeared back into the house. Jack grinned, took off his motoring gloves and, sitting back, lit a cigarette.

The front door opened again. Carrington came out, paused, felt his head, went back for his hat, came out once more and joined Jack at the car.

'It's awfully good of you to take me,' he said, climbing in over the side. 'I've never actually learned how to drive.'

'Haven't you?' asked Jack, pulling away from the kerb. 'I bet you know more about engines than I do, though.'

'The theory, perhaps,' agreed Carrington, diplomatically. 'I wish my uncle was interested in science,' he added in a worried way. 'It's hard to think what we can possibly have in common. I hope he's not going to be difficult,' he added, his worry visibly increasing. 'I sent him a telegram to say we were coming but he's never met me and he might resent my turning up with a complete stranger. Perhaps I should have gone by myself. That didn't occur to me.'

'As a matter of fact, I've got an introduction,' said Jack, to whom it had occurred. 'You know I said I thought my Aunt Alice had mentioned a Colonel Willoughby? One of her old friends is a Reverend Colthurst, who knew your uncle out in India.'

Now this was true, but, until last night, Jack had been unaware of the Reverend Colthurst's existence. He'd telephoned Aunt Alice and asked her if she knew anyone who might have been in India at the same time as Colonel Willoughby. As the whole point of his journey was to see the Colonel together with Carrington, he didn't want to spend his time in Stonecrop Ash kicking his heels in the parlour while Carrington had a tête-à-tête with his uncle. Aunt Alice phoned back less than half an hour later with the name and necessary biographical details of a Samuel Colthurst, now retired and living in the next parish but two, who had been an army chaplain. 'I've been instructed to convey Mr Colthurst's good wishes and sympathies.'

Carrington's face cleared. 'That's just as well. At least it'll give us something to talk about.'

'Was your uncle in India for a long time?'

'Most of his life. From what Steve tells me, this country doesn't suit him. He only came back a year or so ago and went down with severe bronchitis almost immediately. He almost bought it then. He recovered, but it left him terribly weak and more or less confined to the house. It's a rotten shame, because I gather he'd been a very active, out-of-doors type. There was this horrible attack, too.' He sucked his cheeks in. 'I'm glad I've made the effort to see him. It sounds as if the poor old beggar might not have long left.'

Colonel Willoughby's house looked as though it was on parade. It stood up to attention, a smart brick box of a bungalow on the outskirts of the village, with a shining black-painted door and window frames, set squarely at the end of a gravel path flanked by rows of regimented flowers.

No doubt it was far pleasanter and more convenient to live in than the straggling, wriggly-roofed houses of Stonecrop Ash proper but there was no doubt which was nicer to look at. Sentimentalist, Jack told himself as he and Gerry Carrington opened the gate and walked down the path. It's just a pity it didn't seem possible to combine the picturesque with modern drainage.

Taking a deep breath, Carrington raised the highly brassoed doorknocker. 'Mrs Tierney?' he asked, raising his hat to the white-aproned, comfortable-looking woman who answered the door. 'I'm Gerry Carrington and this is Major Haldean. I sent you a telegram.'

Her face fell. 'Mr Carrington?' She ran her tongue round her lips. 'I . . . I don't know how to tell you this, I'm sure, but I showed your telegram to the Colonel and he said he wasn't going to see you, not no how.' She had a soft, Irish voice which was a delight to listen to. Honest distress showed on her face at Carrington's crestfallen expression. 'He didn't approve of your little bit of trouble, sir.' That was, thought Jack, a tactful way of referring to an arrest for murder. 'I'm terribly sorry.'

A bell jangled in the hall behind her. Mrs Tierney looked utterly distracted. 'That's the Colonel wanting to know who's here, I expect.'

'Look,' said Jack kindly. 'Why don't you let us step into
the hall for a moment while you go and see what it is the
Colonel wants? You could say I've got a message for him
from Mr Samuel Colthurst. I believe he knew him in India.
If he really won't see us, we'll trundle off nice and quietly.'

The bell jangled again. 'Well . . . if you would just step
inside,' said Mrs Tierney with a glance over her shoulder. 'I
can't see that's going to hurt.'

'This is a turn-up for the books,' said Carrington quietly
after her departing figure. 'I am sorry, Haldean. I didn't think
the old man would take it like this.'

'It's a bit rough on you, I must say.' Voices, muffled by the
distance and a shut door, came to them. 'Someone sounds
upset. Hello, here's Mrs Tierney again.'

She walked towards them, smoothing down her apron. 'I
told the Colonel you were here,' she said quietly, 'and he says
if you've got a message from Mr Colthurst he'd better hear
it and you're to go in, please? But he's not happy, sir. You
know he's ill?'

'That's partly why I'm here,' said Carrington.

'Well, you will remember that, won't you, sir? You'll have
to make allowances for him. He's had a very bad time.'

'We'll remember,' promised Carrington and, with a grimace
at Haldean, followed in Mrs Tierney's footsteps to the end of
the hall and into the bedroom.

Colonel Willoughby was sitting up in a stiff-backed winged
armchair. He had a white military moustache and fierce blue
eyes. Jack was irresistibly reminded of being summoned to
the Headmaster's Study. 'Which one's Carrington, eh? That'll
be all, Mrs Tierney.'

Carrington waited until the door closed behind her. 'I am,
Uncle.'

The old man winced. 'Never thought I'd hear you say that.
Come closer, boy!' Carrington stepped up to the chair. The
Colonel drew his breath in. 'Yes . . . You've got a look about
you I recognize.'

Jack froze. He couldn't help it. Carrington, however, seemed
unperturbed.

'I've always been told I take after my mother.'

'So you do,' said the Colonel thoughtfully. 'Yes, that's it.'

Was it really just a family resemblance the Colonel had

seen or was there more? Carrington could have been prepared for this, but his manner seemed entirely natural.

'Edith was a stubborn girl,' continued Colonel Willoughby. 'Still, she made her bed and she had to lie on it. What d'you want with me, eh? Money?'

Carrington flushed. 'Certainly not.'

'Really? Because you're not getting any. Everything I have goes with me, young man, so if you were looking for rich pickings, you'd better look elsewhere. I've told Stephen as much. I'm not having anyone think I'm trying to buy attention. There'll be nothing for a pack of relatives to squabble over, take my word for it.'

Carrington drew himself up to his full height and for a moment looked as fierce as his uncle. His fists clenched, then he swallowed, pausing before he spoke. 'I think we'd better leave. I appreciated your letter on the death of my father, sir, and would like to apologize for not replying. I'm sorry that you misinterpreted my motives for coming and I'm sorry to have bothered you. We'll leave you in peace. Come on, Haldean.'

The old man looked at him and nodded. 'You looked exactly like Edith then. She had a temper, too. I shouldn't have said that. My apologies. Sit down. Please. Got yourself mixed up with the police, didn't you? I don't like the idea of a member of my family being involved in that sort of thing. Stephen wrote to me about it. I'm glad to see you're out of prison at any rate.' He turned his gaze to Jack. 'Major Haldean?' Unconsciously Jack stood to full attention. The Colonel's voice, although weak, held exactly the same intonation as he'd heard on the barrack square. 'I believe you're acquainted with an old friend of mine.'

'Yes, sir. Mr Colthurst. He's a neighbour of my aunt, Lady Rivers. He sends you his good wishes and trusts you will enjoy a speedy recovery.'

Colonel Willoughby acknowledged the familiar name with a nod. 'I think there's little chance of that,' he grunted. 'He always did hope for the best. Comes of being a parson, I suppose. I haven't got much time for parsons as a general rule, but Colthurst wasn't a bad chap. How're those daughters of his?'

'Married with children, sir.'

'He'll like that. Being a grandfather will suit him. Is he in good health?'

'Yes, sir.'

'Tell him I appreciate his concern. Obliged, sir.' He looked at Carrington once more. 'So you're young Gerard, are you? If it's not money you're after, what do you want?'

'I wanted,' replied Carrington, picking his words carefully, 'to see you.'

The Colonel gave a short laugh. 'Before I died, eh? It sounds as if you nearly beat me to it. You've got a lot of your mother about you. You've got her mouth and a certain look. It's very familiar. Are you sure that's all you had in mind?' He waved a hand. 'No, don't answer that. I can see it is. Odd thing. I didn't want to see you but I'm glad to have met you. D'you get on with your cousin?'

'Yes, I do.'

'Glad to hear it. You've turned out better than I'd hoped for. Pity about your father.' His eyelids flickered, then shot open again. 'I haven't got much to leave but it's going to Stephen.'

'I'm glad to hear it, sir.'

'Good.'

'Pity I never knew you.' His voice was fading and his eyes closed momentarily once more. Carrington glanced at Jack with a 'let's go' look but he was halted by the Colonel jerking himself awake. 'Why did you say you'd come?'

'I wanted to see you, sir. After all, apart from Stephen, you're my only living relative.'

'He's a good boy, Stephen,' muttered the Colonel. 'He doesn't take after his mother. Just as well. Agatha didn't have a patch of Edith's spirit. Not much to look at but a kind heart. Comes to see me.' He put a hand to his forehead. 'What happened to me? Something did. I can't remember.'

'You were hit by a burglar, sir,'

'That's right. Damned scoundrel. Stephen came.' His eyes closed again and his head sunk down on his chest.

Mrs Tierney was at the far end of the hall, waiting for them. 'He's asleep now,' said Carrington. 'Can I have a word with you, Mrs Tierney?'

'We can go into my sitting room,' she offered, leading the way.

'I didn't realize my uncle was so weak,' said Carrington, after they had sat down in the comfortable room.

'He's ailing, sir, there's no two ways about it. Mind you, his chest was never very strong. He had this awful bronchitis and the doctor nearly gave up on him then, but what can you expect? It must be a big shock coming from India to here and he was taken poorly right at the start. I've been more nurse than housekeeper, and that's a fact.'

'Don't you have a nurse?' asked Haldean. 'I'd have thought he needed one.'

'We did have one, sir, but the Colonel didn't like the fuss. I do all that's needed, sir. I've looked after him for nearly a year now, ever since he got back from India. There's some who won't go to an Indian gentleman, what with wanting curry and bogurrah and kedgeree and such-like and being used to different ways, but I've always got on with him.'

'I'm sure he's fortunate to have you,' said Haldean sincerely. 'This dreadful attack he suffered must have caused a lot of extra work.'

'As if I should mind about that! Whoever attacked him was a fiend, sir, a fiend, to strike down a poor old man like that. I heard a terrible groaning in the middle of the night and went into the dining room and there was the poor Colonel, stretched out and weltering in his blood. The doctor expected to lose him, but the Colonel's a fighter through and through.'

'You sent for the Colonel's nephew, didn't you?' asked Jack, remembering that Mrs Dunbar had to be reassured. Stephen Lewis wouldn't thank them if they'd taken the trouble to visit and then neglected to mention him.

'I did, sir, as soon as I could. Constable Horrocks sent the telegram for me, as I didn't like to leave the Colonel. Mr Lewis arrived at lunchtime and it was a relief to have a man in the house, knowing there were these burglars about, I can tell you. I've always appreciated Mr Lewis's visits. He's such a nice, quiet, well-spoken gentleman and always grateful for any trouble you take. He's the only relative the Colonel has – saving you, sir,' she added, nodding to Carrington.

There didn't seem much doubt about that, but he might as well make sure that Mrs Dunbar had no room for argument. 'He left the same afternoon, though, didn't he?'

'Indeed he did not, sir. He stayed overnight, as you'd expect, and would have stayed longer, if it wasn't for neglecting his business in London. He left after tea the next day. I remember that, because it was the last of the raspberry jam I'd made and I had to open the blackcurrant. He's very partial to black-currant, is Mr Lewis. After what had happened to the Colonel, it made me feel as if things were getting back to normal to do something as ordinary as make a bed, air the room and cook the dinner. I'm very fond of Mr Lewis. He's a pleasure to cook for, and so appreciative, too. "I'll have what's easiest," he says, "Or I'll go to the pub if you'd rather." "Indeed you won't," I said, and made him a nice cutlet with blackberry tart and custard to follow. He said it was the best fruit tart he'd ever had and I could see he'd really enjoyed it. I'd bottled the fruit myself and the poor Colonel can't take it because of his false plate, so there were two bottles unopened.'

Even Mrs Dunbar couldn't argue with this welter of detail, Jack decided. Mrs Dunbar could be reassured. Not that, he thought uneasily, Mrs Dunbar had ever really doubted it. Her accusation of Stephen Lewis had surely never been anything more than a smoke screen to cover either herself, Mr Bryce or Hector Ferguson. He hoped Hector Ferguson's alibi held up. He liked Hector Ferguson.

But Bill Rackham had severe doubts about Ferguson. Bryce, he reckoned, was in the clear, even if Jack had probably been right about the manager's relationship with Evelyn Dunbar. Dunbar's manager had, according to Inspector Frazier of the Falkirk police, been innocently managing the day Dunbar was killed. However, Inspector Frazier had added a note that there was a persistent rumour in the small and censorious world of Falkirk society that Mr Bryce's concern for Mrs Dunbar was thought to be a little more than seemly.

'An affair?' asked Jack, when he called into Scotland Yard on his return from Stonecrop Ash.

Not really; it didn't seem to have got that far. Bryce, in Rackham's opinion could be counted out and Colonel's Willoughby's semi-recognition of Gerard Carrington was so semi, nothing could be based on that either. But Hector Ferguson on the other hand . . .

Rackham had hopes of a Mr Wilfred Wallace, the senior clerk of the Shanghai and Oriental Shipping Company. Although he had affirmed Hector Ferguson's alibi, there was a hesitation in his manner that was promising. He proposed to leave Mr Wallace to think things through overnight before paying him another visit tomorrow.

The next day a crisis broke out at *On The Town*, resulting in a frenzied telephone message to Haldean's rooms.

'For Pete's sake, Jack,' said Archie Keyne in a harried way as Jack walked into the magazine office at eleven o'clock that morning. 'I said it was *urgent!*'

'Calm down, old bean. It's less than half an hour since you phoned.'

'I know, I know, but this month's issue's up the spout unless we can do something quickly. Have you got a ten thousand worder?'

Jack tapped his briefcase. 'All present and correct. What's up? I gather from what you said to my landlady there's something adrift.'

'We can't run the lead story for at least another couple of issues, and we need another one. You haven't got poisoned beef or pork or anything in your story, have you? It's useless if you have.'

Jack raised his eyebrows. 'Er, no. That's a fresh approach to literary criticism, Archie. I haven't really stressed the meat *motif*. My victim gets knocked off by an electrified window-frame. It's rather well worked out, actually. You see . . .'

'Yes, yes, yes, yes, yes,' said Keyne impatiently. 'As long as there isn't any meat in it, I don't mind. He's not a politician, is he?'

'It isn't a he, it's a she. Why this down on the roast beef of Old England? You haven't become a vegetarian, have you?'

'I'm likely to become a cannibal if I don't get a bit of co-operation. The new issue of the *Piccadilly* is out this morning and they're running virtually the same story as us. A cabinet minister gets bumped off from eating a poisoned chicken casserole.'

'That's a neat trick,' said Jack admiringly. 'Poisoning a casserole, I mean. Everything's mixed up, you see.'

Keyne contented himself with a look. 'Ours is about poisoned shepherd's pie and a Home Secretary but the principle's the same. Damn these ruddy writers. It's hard enough to tell the magazines apart as it is and if we start running the same stories at the same time, we haven't a chance.'

'D'you know,' said Jack, mildly, 'when I first started this

writing game I had no idea that the lack of shepherd's pie would prove essential to success.'

Keyne propped his chin on his thumb. 'An electrified window frame, eh? Have you got the girl looking through it?'

'I don't think so.'

'Put that scene in. We can use one of the illustrations to the shepherd's pie story.'

'I could make it her reflections or thoughts or something – you know, looking back into the past.'

'Yes, that'd do it. Take a look at the other pictures we've got and see what you can work round them.'

'Can't I have at least one picture of my hero?'

'Is he young and clean-shaven?'

'No. Middle-aged and bearded. The beard's important.'

'Damn! Never mind. We must have an illustration of a bearded bloke somewhere in stock. Use that. One chap in a beard looks much like any other and they all look like Methuselah. The pictures can mean anything. It's the words around them that are important. Get Radcliffe to work on it and give him instructions for the cover. We'll have to run your story as the lead. Can you let me have it, complete with pictures, by five o'clock?'

'I'll try. Although what my readers would say if they knew I was writing stories to fit the pictures rather than the other way round, I don't know.'

'They'll love it. This isn't art, it's business.' Archie Keyne made an impatient noise as the telephone on his desk rang. 'Yes?' he barked down the phone. He glanced at Jack. 'Yes, he's here.' He covered the mouthpiece with his hand. 'It's a Hector Ferguson. Don't even think of leaving the building.'

'Relax,' said Jack, taking the phone. 'Ferguson?'

'Thank God!' said Ferguson. 'I rang you at home but your landlady said you were at work. I need to talk to you.'

Talk? Ferguson's voice was cracked with worry. Bill said he was going to approach the Shanghai and Oriental again. It sounded as if Ferguson had realized something was in the air. If Ferguson wanted to talk then he wanted to listen but he couldn't – simply couldn't – let Archie down.

'Can we,' said Ferguson, 'meet for lunch?'

'Sorry,' said Jack, performing a complicated manoeuvre as he shrugged off his coat whilst continuing to hold the telephone.

He heard Archie's sigh of relief. 'I'm going to be here until at least five, probably later.'

'Can you come to the house, then?' begged Ferguson. 'I'll be alone. I . . . I could do with talking things over. I think I might have made a fool of myself.'

ELEVEN

Ferguson, thought Jack, was in a state. The ashtray beside him was overflowing and, even though the window was open, the room stank of cigarette smoke. He'd downed a whisky and soda that was obviously not his first of the afternoon in record time and was working his way through another. Jack couldn't help wondering what Mrs Dunbar, who was attending a matinée with Mr Bryce, would say when she got home. He hoped, because it had been a very long day, he wouldn't be around to hear it.

Jack glanced at his watch, that particular hope fading fast. The man simply wouldn't get to the point. 'Ferguson,' he demanded, interrupting a rambling narrative about jazz, New York and mothers, 'why did you want to see me? You said you'd made a fool of yourself. How?'

Ferguson cut off mid sentence, baulked visibly. 'It's the police,' he said at last. 'I know they've been digging away about me. Tommy Paxton, who works at the Shanghai and Oriental, says they've been round again. If they ask him, I know he'll tell them what I did. He's . . . he's a good sort, Tommy, but he can't tell lies. Not to the police.' He broke off. 'I don't know what to *do*, Jack.'

His mouth trembled in ineffectual anger. '*Bloody* Dunbar! I've always hated him.' He looked at Jack in bewilderment. 'What was I supposed to do? I was only a kid when my mother married him but I knew he was a swine. He loved finding fault with me. *Spare the rod and spoil the child.* That's what he would say. Then he'd take me into his study and beat seven bells out of me. I . . . I used to imagine killing him.'

Jack chilled. 'Did you?'

'Oh, yes. I used to comfort myself with it. Horrible, isn't it? True, though.'

'What on earth did your mother say?'

'Most kids get a tanning occasionally, don't they? I imagine I deserved some of them but he really loved walloping hell out of me. When my mother realized that, she left him.' He nearly laughed. 'Most people couldn't understand it, you know? You know how grown-ups talk over your head when you're a kid? If you keep quiet you hear all sorts of things you're not meant to. He was thought to be a good husband. He didn't have affairs or get drunk.' Ferguson broke off and took another gulp of whisky. 'No one seemed to notice how cold hearted he was, how money-grubbing. He was an elder of the church and so respected but if he worshipped anything, it was money. I hate churches, especially those Scottish ones.' He finished his whisky. 'My mother wanted a divorce.'

'Did she?'

Ferguson raised his head at the question. 'You didn't know that. I shouldn't have told you, should I? We've been trying to keep it quiet.' He looked at the empty glass in his hand. 'Perhaps I've had a couple too many, but what does it matter? You'd have found out sooner or later.'

'I knew she couldn't be happily married. She was separated, after all.'

'Yes, but a divorce is different, isn't it?' said Ferguson, walking to the sideboard and pouring himself another drink. 'He didn't want one. Dunbar, I mean. He'd have to make her a settlement and he didn't want that. It's true, you know, what she told you the other day. It really is all her money. It isn't fair.' He leaned against the sideboard. 'And then there's that poor beggar, Bryce. He thinks the world of her. You'd guessed, hadn't you?' Jack nodded. 'I knew you had. My stepfather guessed as well. I ask you, what would any normal man do? If they knew, I mean.'

'I imagine they'd be angry,' said Jack cautiously.

Ferguson laughed harshly. 'I would. You would. Not him. Not holier-than-thou Dunbar. He kept Bryce close to him for the sheer pleasure of seeing him squirm. It's damned hard to get a job at his age and poor old Bryce had to put up with it or starve. My stepfather loved getting one over on someone. I like old Bryce. He's a decent sort. And it was all so painfully innocent, you know? There wasn't anything dodgy going on, I'll swear to it.'

'Ferguson,' said Jack awkwardly. 'Should you really be telling me all this?'

'Why not? You knew already. Most of it, anyway. Besides, you're a pal.' He took another drink. 'S'right, isn't it? I know what's bothering you,' he added with bleary insight. 'You're trying to work out who killed that swine. You think I've said too much.'

'It might be difficult for your mother, you know. To say nothing of Mr Bryce.'

Ferguson raised his head. 'It's all right. There's no way on God's earth she would have laid a finger on him. She's too soft. So's Bryce. Nice bloke. I like him.'

'Even so . . .'

'For God's sake, Haldean, they didn't do it! I know they didn't do it. Look, I can prove it!'

He put a hand in his pocket, took out a key with a fob, and threw it on to the table.

Jack gazed at the key. He could see a number on the fob. 206. The number of Andrew Dunbar's room. He stared at Ferguson. His face was pale, his eyes unnaturally bright. 'How did you get hold of that?'

'I was there! Don't you understand? I was there.' He buried his head in his hands. 'I can't stand it. I know the police are getting closer and closer, but I didn't do it.' He looked at Jack helplessly. 'I wanted to tell you. I know I'm going to be found out. The police are after me, aren't they?'

Jack didn't see anything for it but to agree. 'They're checking your alibi.'

Ferguson made a sound between a laugh and a sob. 'Alibi? Oh my God, I haven't got an alibi. I lied. It wasn't meant to be an alibi, just an arrangement between me and Tommy Paxton.'

'This chap you used to work with?'

'Yes. We junior clerks were supposed to be there until five o'clock but you know how it is. Everyone wants to slope off early at some time. The senior, Old Wallace, was dead easy to fool. We've all done it. If you wanted to go early, you got someone to initial the register for you. Wallace never noticed and, if he asked where Mr so-and-so was, someone would say they'd been called to Dispatch or Advance Orders or some-where. It didn't happen very often. We were never found out.'

'You asked Tommy Paxton to initial the register for you?' Ferguson nodded. 'Why?'

Ferguson put his hand to his forehead. 'Bryce wrote to my mother saying my stepfather was in London. We knew he'd be at the Marchmont. He always stayed there. I tell you, Haldean, I was worried. I knew my mother had just about reached the end of her tether with Dunbar and this divorce business.' His face twisted. 'She was going to cause a scene. She can't help it, you know. She loves a good performance and every so often she lets rip. I didn't want her to have a blazing row with him. It wouldn't do any good and would make things even more beastly for Bryce. She wouldn't listen, though. Bryce said in his letter that my stepfather was meeting Lewis and Carrington and she guessed the meeting would go on all afternoon. She planned to ring the hotel, make an appointment for afternoon tea while he was stuck with Lewis, and nab him before he could vanish. She was stupidly pleased with herself. I tried to argue, but she wouldn't listen. She always thought she was going to win. She never did. Dunbar always came out best. I thought if I was there, I could calm things down, stop her getting out of hand, so I asked Tommy Paxton to sign me out.'

'What time did you get to the hotel?'

'Time?' Ferguson thought for a moment. 'It must have been twenty to five or so. My mother didn't know I was coming. She didn't exactly jump through hoops when I arrived. However, I was there and there wasn't anything she could do about it. She'd sent a message saying she'd meet Dunbar at quarter to five, but quarter to five came and went and he didn't show up. We hung about for a while, waiting, and my mother's temper got worse and worse. She knew what room he was in and was on the verge of going upstairs. If she'd had clapped eyes on him at that moment, there'd have been fireworks, so I said I'd go. She was a bit iffy about it, but her ankle was giving her jip and she agreed.' He broke off and lit another cigarette with shaking fingers.

'What happened?' prompted Jack.

'I found him! My God, yes, I found him. His door was ajar and I pushed it open.' He sucked deeply on his cigarette. 'There he was. I can't tell you how long I was there. Not long. I couldn't believe he was dead until I touched him. It was as if a bomb went off in my head. He was *dead*. I couldn't bring myself to touch him again but I knew he was dead. I backed out of the room and just stood there. I realized I had the key in my hand. It had been on the desk but I can't really remember picking it up. I locked the room. I don't know why. I think I wanted to hide it all. I was in a hell of state. I could hardly breath.'

'Did you think he'd shot himself?'

'I didn't think anything. All I knew was that he was dead. And then . . .' He looked at Jack with wide eyes. 'I hated seeing him, but somewhere, underneath it all, I was pleased. Nasty, isn't it?'

'Understandable, perhaps.'

'Yes? It made me feel wrong. I felt as if *I'd* killed him. It was horrible. A chambermaid came along the corridor. I couldn't speak. I couldn't have spoken to save my life but I knew she'd seen me and I knew I had to get away. I got back to the lobby and there was my mother, still waiting for him to show up. It was a nightmare. She took control, told me to go home, to act as if nothing had happened, and she'd cover my tracks. I did what she said – it was good to have someone tell me what to do – and it wasn't until I was nearly home that it struck me that she thought I'd killed him. And you know what? I couldn't get rid of the idea that maybe I *had*. I wondered if I could have acted in a blind rage, then forgotten what I'd done. I was pleased he was dead.'

Ferguson's voice trembled. 'He'd gone. Everyone could be happy again. I found the key in my pocket and imagined killing him. It felt good. I could have done, so very easily.'

He crushed out his cigarette and lit another one. 'My mother won't talk about it properly. When Gerry Carrington was arrested, she never thought he'd done it. She thought it was me. She likes Carrington. She felt sorry for him. He might have done it, you know? I wouldn't blame him if he had. When you and that policeman said Carrington was free, she panicked. Ever since, she's tried to make me go to New York. She's convinced it's only a matter of time before I'm arrested and . . . and she's right, isn't she?'

Jack looked at Hector Ferguson. His mouth was trembling, he was twitching with nerves, and there were dark shadows under his eyes. 'Why don't we talk to Bill Rackham?' he asked, his voice deliberately calm.

'The *police*?'

'Bill's a policeman, Ferguson, but he's also a good bloke.'

'I've told you! You can sort it out, can't you?'

'Not by myself. You'll have to come clean sometime.'

He was interrupted by the ringing of the doorbell. Ferguson raised his head slowly. His skin seemed oddly mottled, then Jack worked out it was his freckles standing out against his unnaturally white face. He levered himself up from his chair and, walking very slowly, went to the window to see who was at the door. He shrank back, then stood, rigidly poised, the knuckles on his fists showing white.

There were footsteps in the hall as the parlourmaid went to answer the door. Bill Rackham. Jack recognized his voice.

'It's him,' Ferguson muttered. Like someone who had forgotten how to walk, he stumbled into the hall.

Bill, who was standing on the doorstep, raised his hat as Ferguson appeared. 'Ah, Mr Ferguson. If I could just have a word . . .'

With an explosion of movement, Ferguson hurtled forward. He thrust a hand on to Rackham's chest, pushed him away, and shot down the steps. Taken completely by surprise, Bill staggered, missing his footing and fell to one side.

'Ferguson!' yelled Jack. 'Come back!' He shot after the running man seeing, as if in a blur, the startled faces of Bill and the parlourmaid. He took the steps in a single jump, his leg howling a protest.

Ferguson, running hard, nearly cannoned into a couple who were rounding the corner into Essex Gardens. It was Mrs Dunbar and Mr Bryce, arm in arm and heads together. Jack saw Mrs Dunbar's mouth circle as Ferguson skidded to a halt before dodging round them. Behind him, Jack heard the thud of Rackham's feet on the pavement. He ran forward desperately as the shrill note of Rackham's police whistle bit through the air.

At the sound of the whistle, Ferguson stopped and glanced back in horror. Jack had nearly caught him when Bryce's stick entangled in his legs, sending him sprawling. He scrambled furiously to his feet and lunged after Ferguson.

A police constable appeared at the end of the road in answer to the whistle. Ferguson swerved and ducked under the policeman's arm as Jack reached out and grabbed his shoulder. Panic-stricken, Ferguson jabbed first his elbow then his fist into Jack's face. In a blaze of pain, Jack fell back, as Bill, overtaking him, stuck his foot out, bringing Ferguson crashing to the ground. The constable's hand descended, none too gently, on Ferguson's collar, hauling him to his feet.

'What's going on here?' he demanded. 'Who blew that whistle?'

'I did,' said Rackham crisply. 'Inspector Rackham of Scotland Yard. Well done, Constable.' He turned to Jack who was holding a handkerchief to his face. 'Are you all right? Good grief, you're bleeding.'

'He caught me a juicy one,' said Jack in a muffled voice. 'Strewth, it hurts.' Ferguson, safe in the constable's clutches, looked ashamed. 'I'm sorry, Haldean,' he said sullenly. 'I didn't mean to lash out, but when you grabbed hold of me I couldn't help myself. What were you chasing me *for?*'

'Because you were running away, you idiot.'

Mrs Dunbar and Mr Bryce arrived. 'Why are you hounding my son?' wailed Mrs Dunbar, hysterically. 'This is *persecution*. Absolute persecution.' She clutched at Mr Bryce's arm again. 'You tried to save him, Robert. Do something!'

Mr Bryce, swelling visibly, faced Rackham. 'What is the meaning of this, sir!'

The constable majestically interposed, his hand still on Ferguson's collar. 'Do you wish to charge this man, sir?' he said, addressing Rackham.

'I wish to ask this man a few questions,' said Rackham. 'Questions appertaining to the making of a false statement.' He glared at Mrs Dunbar who was muttering *persecution* in an undertone. 'However, there very well could be another charge pending. I was subject to an unprovoked attack and as for you,' he said, rounding on Bryce, 'I saw you deliberately trip up Major Haldean while he was aiding the police in the execution of their duties. That, sir, is assault.'

There was a yelp from Mrs Dunbar. 'No! Not you as well, Robert. I can't bear it!' She clutched at Mr Bryce. 'You saved him, Robert! You saved my son.'

'I think not, Madam,' said Rackham coolly. 'Mr Ferguson, I was going to ask you a few questions in your own house. I must now ask you to accompany me to Scotland Yard.'

Jack cut through Mrs Dunbar's agonized wail of protest. 'You need to go back to the house, Bill.' He nodded towards Ferguson. 'He's got the key of Dunbar's hotel room. It's on the table in the drawing room.'

'No' shrieked Mrs Dunbar. 'No! It isn't true! You can't have it! I won't let you!'

'For heaven's sake, Mother, *shut up!*' said Hector Ferguson wearily. Putting his hand to his mouth, he swayed momentarily. 'Let's get it over with, shall we? Oh, God, I feel sick. It's been hell and I've been a fool. Mother, please, be quiet! I've been expecting this for ages.'

The constable dropped his hand and took out his notebook. 'When apprehended, the suspect remarked, "I've been expecting this for ages,"' he noted with grim satisfaction.

'Oh, blimey,' said Ferguson. He buried his head in his hands. 'Go and get the key. It can't make things any worse.' He turned to Mrs Dunbar wearily. 'I'm sorry, mother. I'm for it.'

'It's looking a bit grim for your pal, Ferguson,' said Bill Rackham, smothering a yawn. He rubbed his eyes and, picking up his whisky, drank it appreciatively. 'I've earned that. It's been a long evening. For both of us, I'd say,' he added. He had promised he would call in for a nightcap and bring Jack up to date and, although the clock was nudging half eleven, had been true to his word. 'He's safely tucked up for the night. It was a relief when he stopped talking. He rambled on and on about how much he hated Dunbar. At one point he seemed to be saying he *did* kill him but he finally decided he hadn't. I'll have to go through the case with the Chief tomorrow but I think he'll be charged, all right.'

Jack reached for the tobacco jar and filled the bowl of his pipe. 'I can't say I'm surprised. He was more or less bound to be arrested after making a break for it.'

'Absolutely. How's your nose, by the way?'

Jack grinned ruefully. 'Sore. I can't blame him for lashing out, though. He was pretty worked up. Besides that, he was a fair way to being bottled.' He hesitated. 'What's your opinion?'

'It's not really a matter of my opinion, is it? I can't smell out crooks like some sort of Witchfinder-General. My life might be a bit easier if I could. We got hold of Mrs Gledburn, the chambermaid from the Marchmont, by the way. She picked him out as the man she'd seen in the corridor. His alibi is a pack of lies from beginning to end. I'm sorry, Jack. I know he's a pal, even if he did take a swing at you, but the case against him stacks up, you know. It's a question of evidence.'

'Yes, I was thinking about the evidence. We know he was on the spot. That's not in any doubt, but what about the gun? Has he ever owned a gun?'

'According to him, no. Apart from during the war, of course.'

'That's a definite enough statement. If you can disprove that, you're in business.'

Rackham cocked an inquisitive eyebrow. 'And not otherwise?'

Jack sighed in exasperation. 'You've got a case. You've got a damn good case. Given the amount of bouncers he's told, I can't see it going wrong. It's just that I don't know if it's true. I don't know if Ferguson is capable of planning a murder. I know he can go off at half cock, right enough,' he added, touching his nose gingerly, 'but the amount of deliberate planning this involves is something else. And, granted he *did* plan it, why should he lose his nerve so spectacularly?'

'Because he was frightened.'

'I suppose so. Oddly enough, I can see Mrs Dunbar planning it but not Ferguson.'

'I'll agree that Mrs Dunbar has a damn sight more to her than I gave her credit for. But if she's guilty, she'd hardly let her son take the rap, would she? She thinks he's guilty, I know. He told me as much. It's a very good case. Jack. Don't you think you might have got too tied up with how much planning was involved? You placed an awful lot of weight on the fact that no one heard the shot, but that could be sheer chance, you know?'

'It seems pretty unlikely to me.'

'Unlikely? Or impossible? Look, Ferguson hated his step-father.'

'With good cause.'

'That doesn't make it less likely, does it? From what he said, I think he had very good cause, but that's the point. He told you he'd imagined killing him, didn't he?'

'As a kid, Bill. Be fair.'

'And kids don't grow up? He dwelt on it at some length when he was talking to me. I know he'd had one over the eight, but once he got launched on Dunbar, it was difficult to stop him. He could have bought a gun at any time. He doesn't have to see off Dunbar at any particular time or in any particular place. All he has to do is want to kill him. You know that.'

Jack shifted uneasily in his chair. He did know that.

'Then he hits the bullseye. Dunbar's in London and his mother's gearing up for a row. So kindly Hector Ferguson says he's worried, says he wants to referee the match, and, if Dunbar had kept his appointment, that might have happened. But it didn't. Instead he has the perfect opportunity to make his dream come true. I'm not saying he's cold-blooded. I don't think he is. He had enough sense left to try and make it look like suicide, but he made a pretty poor job of it.'

'That all sounds horribly likely,' said Jack unhappily. 'The psychology makes sense, too. He gets what he thinks he wants, but falls to bits when he's faced with reality. He told me after he knew Dunbar was dead, everyone could be happy again and they're not, are they? The only thing I would say, is that he was prepared to let Gerry Carrington take the rap and that doesn't square with what I know of him.'

'He was frightened, Jack. You don't know what he'd do.'

'No,' said Jack, in reluctant honesty. 'I don't. Poor old Ferguson. It doesn't look good, does it?'

Inspector Rackham looked at the sandy-haired man standing by the desk. He was smartly dressed, his light summer coat unbuttoned to show a well-cut grey suit. He was, Rackham reckoned, in his late twenties or early thirties. A professional man, thought Rackham, perhaps a young doctor or an accountant. He seemed nervy and ill at ease, but that wasn't particularly surprising. Most men felt a little uncertain of their ground on entering Scotland Yard. 'Mr Ragnall?' he asked, extending his hand, with a reassuring smile. 'I'm Inspector Rackham. I gather you want to see me in connection with the Dunbar case.'

Hugo Ragnall relaxed. 'That's so, Inspector. Is there anywhere we can go to discuss the matter?'

Rackham ushered him into a small room with a table and chairs. Ragnall. The name rang a bell.

'I am,' said Ragnall, 'secretary of the Otterbourne New Century Company.'

That was it! Rackham drew up a chair to the table, looking at Hugo Ragnall with sharpened interest. 'You're the man who gave evidence Mr Otterbourne had misappropriated the pension funds, aren't you?'

Ragnall looked distressed. 'That is so, Inspector. I might

say that I took no pleasure from having to testify to that account, as I always had the greatest respect for Mr Otterbourne. However,' he added with a shrug, 'facts are facts, no matter how unpalatable they are.'

'Exactly, sir,' agreed Rackham.

'Before I go any further, is it true that Mr Ferguson has been charged with the murder of his stepfather? The account in the newspaper wasn't clear.'

'He's been arrested,' said Rackham guardedly. 'He hasn't actually been charged yet.'

Ragnall seemed pleased. 'Then perhaps I am in time, Inspector, to prevent a miscarriage of justice.'

Rackham frowned. 'Could you explain what you mean, sir?'

'Indeed.' Ragnall cleared his throat. 'As I said, I am secretary of Otterbourne's. Incidentally, I may say that I am here with the full knowledge and support of Mr Stephen Lewis and his wife. Mrs Lewis is the proprietor of Otterbourne's, although she takes no active part in the business.' He cleared his throat once more. 'There is no need, is there, to go through the reasons why Mr Lewis was unable to attend the meeting that should have occurred the day Mr Dunbar was – er – killed, is there?'

'No, sir. I know he was unexpectedly called away to his uncle's.'

Ragnall leaned forward. Rackham could sense his anxiety. 'Mr Lewis was concerned about Mr Carrington. You know they are cousins?' Rackham nodded. 'Mr Carrington has an . . .' he paused. 'He has an uncertain temper and Mr Dunbar could be a difficult man.'

'We know all about that, sir.'

Hugo Ragnall smiled suddenly. 'Mr Lewis was, so to speak, on eggshells that Mr Carrington would completely lose his temper.' He grew serious. 'I may say that when it appeared Mr Carrington *had* lost his temper, uncontrollably, as you might say . . .'

'You mean when it seemed Mr Carrington had murdered Mr Dunbar?'

Hugo Ragnall swallowed at this plain speaking. 'Yes. It was a ghastly thing to have happened, but Mr Carrington had very good cause to resent Mr Dunbar. It all seemed cut and dried, Inspector. There didn't really seem any reason to doubt it.' Ragnall took a cigarette from the box on the table and struck a match. 'I didn't like it,' he added. 'Neither did Mr Lewis. You mustn't think he wanted his cousin to be found guilty, whatever the true facts of the case may be.'

That, thought Rackham, was an interesting way of putting it. 'The true facts, Mr Ragnall? Gerard Carrington's innocence has been confirmed, you know.' At least as far as the public are concerned, he added in the privacy of his own thoughts.

'Yes,' agreed Ragnall rapidly. 'Yes, I know it has, Inspector. You mustn't misunderstand me.'

'But you're not convinced?' asked Rackham quietly.

Hugo Ragnall swallowed. 'I . . . I suppose I have to be, don't I?' Rackham didn't answer. 'It's just it seemed so *probable*,' burst out Ragnall, spurred into speech by Rackham's silence. 'We all knew how badly Professor Carrington had been treated by Dunbar. It's only human nature that Gerard Carrington should resent it. I think what really bothered me is that Major Haldean's proof seemed to turn on such a trivial thing. I know Major Haldean is a very clever man, Inspector. I've read his stories and they're very clever, indeed.' He suddenly smiled, oddly shy. 'I think I've read nearly everything he's written. An old friend of mine – he's out in Kenya now – knew him in the war and always had the greatest respect for him. But I do think that very clever people can be misled sometimes.'

'Perhaps,' said Rackham, trying to keep his voice non-committal. He didn't quite manage it. The trouble was, Hugo Ragnall was doing such an excellent job of putting his own thoughts into words.

Ragnall sensed his unspoken agreement. 'It's all very well reading this sort of thing, isn't it? When you actually know the people involved, though, it can be a little difficult to swallow. Ever since Mr Carrington was released, I've been conscious that anyone who knew Dunbar has been under a strain. I don't see how any of us can be implicated, but it's a strain, all the same. You see, if Mr Carrington isn't guilty, who is?'

And that, thought Rackham, was the question. 'We've arrested Hector Ferguson,' he said, his voice as neutral as possible.

Hugo Ragnall nodded eagerly. 'Which is why I've called to see you today. Let me explain. Because Mr Carrington's temper is so uncertain, Mr Lewis asked his wife to meet him to see how the meeting went. However, that would only give him Mr Carrington's point of view, so Mr Lewis asked me to look in on Mr Dunbar around five o'clock or so, to see what his reaction to the afternoon's events had been.'

Rackham sat up. 'You called on Dunbar? Did you see him?'

Ragnall shook his head. 'No. I arrived at the Marchmont sometime before five. I've been trying to think exactly what time it was. It must have been about twenty to five or so. It was certainly after Mr Carrington left. I thought I might see him. When Mr Carrington was arrested, Mr Lewis asked me if I'd seen him, as it would have established what time he left the hotel.'

'You never said anything at the time, sir.'

Ragnall shrugged. 'There wasn't anything much to say, was there? I didn't feel what I'd seen could help or hinder your investigation in any way. Besides that, it's not the easiest thing in the world to admit to being on the spot when a murder's been committed.'

'If you've done nothing wrong you've nothing to fear, sir.'

Ragnall laughed cynically. 'That doesn't quite square up with the facts, does it, Inspector? You might not approve, but I thought it best to say nothing. However, when I heard Mr Ferguson had been arrested, I had no choice but to come forward. You see, I saw Mrs Dunbar.'

'Mrs Dunbar?' Rackham's voice was sharp. 'Did you speak to her?'

'No.' Hugo Ragnall's eyebrows lifted. 'You have met Mrs Dunbar, Inspector?' Despite himself, Rackham grinned. 'In that case, I don't really have to explain myself. Mrs Dunbar, Inspector, can talk the hind leg off a donkey. I sat down in the lounge of the Marchmont. I wanted a few minutes to get my papers in order and to work out exactly what I was going to say to Mr Dunbar. I must admit, my heart sank when I saw Mrs Dunbar and, although it sounds ungallant, took care to stay out of sight. Not only did I want to avoid her if possible, she could only be there to meet Mr Dunbar, and I really did want to speak to him. I couldn't cross the lobby to the stairs without her seeing me, so I decided to wait where I was. I assumed it could only be a matter of minutes before Mr Dunbar joined her and I thought the best plan would be to wait for him to arrive, then pretend I'd only just entered the hotel, and ask for a few minutes' private conversation.'

'Fair enough. What happened?'

'I saw Hector Ferguson arrive. He arrived shortly after I got there.'

'You saw Hector Ferguson?' repeated Rackham blankly. 'Why on earth haven't you said anything before?'

'For the reasons I've already given, Inspector,' said Ragnall unhappily. 'I discussed it with Mr Lewis and we decided it was as well to keep quiet, especially as Hector Ferguson didn't admit to being at the hotel. His story was that he'd gone straight home from work that afternoon and I didn't want to be the one to contradict him. I knew that would cause problems for him.'

'You're probably right there, sir,' Rackham agreed heavily. 'Can you tell me exactly what occurred? This is important, you understand.'

'He talked to his mother for a little while. I got the impression that she wasn't too happy to see him, as they seemed to be arguing. Not violently, you understand, but they had certainly disagreed about something.'

'Could you hear what they said?'

Ragnall shook his head. 'I couldn't hear much, just the odd word. Mr Ferguson seemed to be very impatient. He looked at his watch a couple of times and I heard him say, 'I'll go.' He left Mrs Dunbar and went up the stairs. From what had gone before, I assumed that Mr Dunbar was late and Hector Ferguson had gone to root him out. I looked at the clock as Ferguson went up the stairs. It was five to five when he went upstairs and I was surprised to see him return almost immediately. I heard the clock strike five as he came into the lobby once more. I was startled by his appearance. He was clearly upset.' Hugo Ragnall hesitated. 'He looked as white as a sheet, as if he'd seen a ghost.'

'You're sure about the time, sir?' asked Rackham.

'Certain. I was looking out for Dunbar, you see. I wanted to be ready to nab him when he came down with Ferguson. There was clearly something wrong. I couldn't see Mrs Dunbar's face but I could see his and he looked ghastly. They spoke for a little while – not long – and then they both walked to the hotel entrance. I wondered for a moment what I should do, and decided the best thing was to go to Dunbar's room myself. I knew which room Mr Dunbar was in, of course, so when Mrs Dunbar and Ferguson were out of sight, I went up the stairs.'

'Did you go into Dunbar's room?'

Ragnall shook his head. 'No, I didn't. I reached the top of the stairs and I heard the most awful shindig. There was a woman shouting, clearly in distress. That brought me up sharp. There was a door open a little way up the corridor and the noise was coming from there.' He broke off with a thin smile. 'It was, of course, Dunbar's room. I guessed as much at the time and wondered what the devil had happened. As I watched, a chambermaid shot out of the room, yelling her head off. She didn't see me, but doors started opening all along the corridor. In two ticks the place was going to be seething. I thought of going along to Dunbar's room to see what all the fuss was about, but all I actually did was turn tail and walk back down the stairs.'

'Why was that, sir?'

Hugo Ragnall ran his tongue over dry lips. 'I didn't want to get mixed up in things. I didn't know what was wrong but it was obviously something serious. No one had seen me come into the hotel and I thought it was as well if I simply faded away. After all, what could I do? By the time I got downstairs, Mrs Dunbar was back in her seat in the lobby, but I managed to slip past her.' He put his hand to his mouth and suddenly looked acutely uncomfortable. 'You see, Inspector, I knew Mr Carrington had been with Mr Dunbar all afternoon.'

Rackham didn't say anything for a few moments. 'Did you think Dunbar had been murdered?' he asked eventually.

'No,' said Ragnall, startled. 'No, of course I didn't. But I knew something had happened and I knew Mr Carrington had been there. That's all. I didn't feel I could help in any way. Mrs Dunbar was on the spot and she was the person chiefly concerned, after all.' He shrugged helplessly. 'What could I do? When Mr Carrington was arrested, I said nothing. After all, I hadn't seen him and you must believe me when I say I was sincerely glad when he was released. However, when Mr Ferguson was arrested, that was a different matter.'

Rackham dug a scrap of paper out of the blotter with his

pen. 'And you're absolutely certain that Hector Ferguson entered the hotel after you?' Hugo Ragnall nodded. 'And he was only upstairs for a matter of five minutes?' 'Less, if anything. I'm certain about that.'

Rackham took the scrap of pink paper from the nib of his pen and rolled it thoughtfully between his fingers. Hugo Ragnall, he realized, was still on edge. 'Is there anything else you want to tell me, sir?' he asked.

Hugo Ragnall's gaze shifted to one side and Rackham knew he had touched a nerve. He waited in silence but this time the silence lengthened. 'Mr Ragnall?' he prompted. 'It could be something utterly trivial, perhaps. Something you didn't attach any weight to at the time.'

'There isn't anything else,' said Ragnall firmly. His eyes met Rackham's, but Rackham could see his throat muscles tighten. 'Nothing at all.'

TWELVE

A couple of hours later, Inspector William Rackham and Jack Haldean were in the lobby of the Marchmont Hotel. Under the rather weary eye of the manager, Mr Sutton, who was observing them from the reception desk, they were engaged in an experiment. 'That was just shy of thirteen minutes,' said Jack as Rackham came back down the stairs and into the lobby. 'Shall I try? Sergeant Hawley's still up there. We can see if our times match up.'

'All right,' said Rackham, taking the watch from Jack. 'Wait for my signal . . . Off you go.'

Jack walked rapidly across the lobby and climbed the stairs. Arriving at room 206, he knocked at the door. 'It's Jack Haldean, Sergeant,' he called. 'We're going through it again. Pretend I'm Hector Ferguson, will you?'

There was the creak of a chair followed by footsteps and Detective-Sergeant Hawley, who, for purposes of reconstruction, was playing the part of Dunbar, opened the door.

'Hector?' he said, in deep disapproval, clearly relishing the role. 'What do you want?'

'A few moments with you,' said Jack. 'My mother's waiting in the lobby downstairs. You're meant to be having tea with her, remember? You're late. But look, before we go downstairs, I need to speak to you. Can I come in?'

'I suppose so,' said Sergeant Hawley, standing back.

Jack shut the door behind them. He felt in his pocket and took out his tobacco pouch. 'Would you mind looking at this, sir,' he said, adding as Sergeant Hawley took the pouch with a puzzled frown, 'that's to get you to sit down and take your attention off me for a couple of ticks. I said that last bit, not Ferguson, of course.'

'Inspector Rackham just told me to sit down.'

'Yes, but there must have been some sort of reason why Dunbar sat down. I'm back in character now. I'm Hector Ferguson. Will you look at my mysterious tobacco pouch, sir? If you'd rather, it could be a contract, a will, a map of Treasure

Island or a Tibetan monk's list of the ninety-nine names of God.'

'Very good, Hector,' said Sergeant Hawley with a broad grin and in the tones of a stage butler. He walked to the desk and, tobacco pouch in hand, sat down and examined it with as much rapt attention as a housewife scrutinizing a black beetle in the scullery.

'Now I walk up behind you,' said Jack, 'take out a pistol,' – he aimed an outstretched finger at Sergeant Hawley – 'and pull the trigger. Bang.'

Sergeant Hawley obligingly gave a heart-felt groan and collapsed on the desk. 'I'm dead now, sir,' he said helpfully.

Jack stood stock-still for a moment. 'No one heard the gunshot,' he muttered. 'By jingo, that was lucky. Stay still, Sergeant. I can't concentrate if you move. Now I need to make it look like suicide. I don't know why the silly ass didn't use the pen on the desk but he didn't.' He pulled the blotter towards him and took a piece of paper from the stack. 'What shall I say?'

'The note said 'Forgive me,' muttered the corpse.

'I think I'll write 'Forgive me,' said Jack, ignoring this voice from Beyond. 'If I had planned this out, I'd have brought a note with me but the note was written on hotel paper *and* left an impression in the blotter. There we are. One suicide note. Now all I have to do is wipe the gun. I'd better be careful with this bit. I don't want any fingerprints on it. Put it into his hand and then I've done. All right, Sergeant, up you get. You might as well come downstairs with me.'

The two men walked out of the room. 'Hold on a mo,' said Jack as the sergeant made for the stairs. 'I've got to lean against the wall and repine. That's when Mrs Gledburn, the chambermaid, saw me.' He staggered against the wall and buried his head in his hands. 'Oh deary me, what have I done? Oh deary me, what have I done?' He looked up. 'OK, that's enough grief. Back we go to England, Home and Mother.'

Rackham looked up as they came back into the lobby. 'Twelve minutes,' he said in disgust. 'Are you sure you couldn't do it any faster?'

'Blimey, Bill, we moved like greased lightning. You can't just barge in, shoot someone and pop off. There have to be some social *pourparlers* and we kept those to a minimum, didn't we, Sergeant?'

'We did, sir,' agreed Sergeant Hawley with a smile.

'I think, if anything, we undercut the time,' said Jack. 'If Ferguson was some hard-bitten gangster then maybe, just maybe, he could do it in the time we took, but he isn't, is he? The chambermaid saw him looking stricken and Hugo Ragnall said he was as white as a sheet when he came back into the lobby.'

Rackham clicked his tongue in frustration. 'All right. As we're here we might as well reconstruct Ferguson's own version of events.'

'Shall I be Ferguson again?' asked Jack.

'You might as well. Knock off the time it takes to unlock the door. It can only be a matter of seconds or so.' He looked at his watch again. 'Nearly at the minute . . . Off you go, Jack.'

It was six minutes before Jack returned.

'This is all taking too long,' said Rackham. 'What on earth were you doing?'

Jack reached out his hand for the watch. 'Why don't you try?' he suggested. 'I'll be surprised if you can cut the time down by much.'

Rackham arrived back in the lobby six minutes and forty-five seconds later. 'I see what you mean, Jack,' he said, pocketing the watch. 'I don't see how it can be done in much less.'

'Hugo Ragnall was certain Ferguson was only absent for five minutes, wasn't he?'

'Absolutely certain,' said Rackham disconsolately. 'He's signed a statement to that effect.' He looked at the sergeant. 'All right, Hawley, you can go.'

'Five minutes is pushing it,' said Jack, once Hawley had taken his leave. He pulled up a chair and, leaning forward to avoid the fronds of a potted palm, sat down at one of the low tables that dotted the lobby of the Marchmont. 'I don't know how long you spent wringing your hands and bewailing your fate, but I cut it down to the bare bone. I gathered from Ferguson that he spent some time having the heebie-jeebies. However,' he added with a shrug, 'it was a very subjective impression.'

'Which Hugo Ragnall's impression wasn't,' said Rackham, sitting down. 'Having said that, he wasn't standing there with a stopwatch. On the face of it, there isn't much difference between five and six and a bit minutes or so.' Rackham looked at Jack quizzically. 'Could you talk to him? As you're not official he might be a bit more forthcoming than he was with me.'

'Why, Bill? As you say, there's not much difference between five and six minutes.'

'It's not that so much, but I felt sure there was something he was holding back. It's probably something and nothing, but until I know I can't judge.'

'If you like,' said Jack with a shrug. 'I can't see why he should confide in me, though. I've never cast eyes on the bloke.'

'He knows you, though.' Rackham grinned. 'He's a fan of yours.'

'What?' Jack looked startled.

'He said he'd read nearly everything you'd written.'

'Poor devil. You can get treatment for that sort of thing.'

'And one of his pals was a pal of yours in the war.'

'Really? Who?'

'I don't know, but he's in Kenya now, apparently. As I say, I wouldn't mind if you asked him. There's one thing for sure, though, Hugo Ragnall's statement lets Ferguson out completely. He can't possibly have got up to Dunbar's room, shot him and arranged it all to look like a suicide – even that cack-handed attempt to make it look like a suicide – in five or six minutes.' Rackham took a couple of cigarettes from his case, tossed one to Jack, and lit it gloomily. 'I wish people wouldn't hold things back. If Ragnall had told us what he'd seen in the first place, we wouldn't have ever had Ferguson in the frame, or wasted time thinking about Mrs Dunbar.'

'It'd have saved Ferguson a bad few days, too, poor devil.'

'Absolutely. He should have owned up, as should that precious mother of his.'

'I don't know I really blame him for that. Why didn't Ragnall come forward sooner, though?'

'Because we'd nabbed Gerard Carrington. He didn't think it would make any difference. He didn't want to contradict what Ferguson had said and he was unhappy about being mixed up with the police. He's not the only one who didn't tell us everything. There's the post-boy and your Mrs Gledburn, too.' Rackham gave a discontented sigh. 'The way this is going

I can believe there's a witness out there who saw someone leave Dunbar's room carrying a smoking gun and didn't know it's relevant and doesn't think it'd be nice to mention it. This is less like a murder and more like a conjuring trick. Have you got any ideas? I'm fresh out and the Chief's none too happy about it.'

'There was something,' said Jack, tapping the ash reflectively from his cigarette. 'You said it was like a conjuring trick. Now we've narrowed the time down even further, I couldn't agree more. We've concentrated on a very few people, but couldn't there be a Mr X? Someone that Dunbar did down in business, perhaps? Rather than happening on the odd few minutes when he could get in Dunbar's room by chance, he could be lying in wait for the coast to be clear.'

Rackham looked up, suddenly alert. 'And that means . . .?'

'And that means he, or if it was a Miss X, she, was here. Here, in the hotel, as a guest, in an adjacent room, where he or she could keep a careful watch on Dunbar's comings and goings.'

'You could be right.' Rackham got to his feet and nodded towards the reception desk. 'Let's ask the manager, shall we?'

Mr Sutton greeted them with threadbare politeness. 'Have you finished, Inspector?'

'Not quite, sir.'

'I had hoped this matter would have been cleared up before now. I have the reputation of the hotel to think about.'

'I appreciate that, sir,' replied Rackham, smoothly. 'However, these things take time, you know, and there's a chance you may be able to help us further.'

'We need to see the guest list for the fifteenth of July,' said Jack. 'We're particularly interested in anyone you don't know. That won't exclude them, of course,' he added in an undertone to Rackham, 'but if they're a frequent visitor to the hotel, it makes them a bit more doubtful.'

'Very good, gentlemen,' said Mr Sutton. 'If you would care to come into my office, I will have the Residents' Register brought to you.'

Once installed in the office with Mr Sutton in attendance, Rackham ran through the list of names for the fifteenth of July. 'As far as I can see, there's five rooms which are prime candidates,' he said. 'The two on either side of Dunbar's room and the three facing.'

Jack looked at the floor plan. 'Dunbar was in Room 206, so that's 205, 207 and 217, 218 and 219.'

Rackham turned up the register. '205 was occupied by a Mr and Mrs Carlton Eccles.'

'They're fairly regular visitors,' said Mr Sutton. 'He's a pottery manufacturer from the Midlands. They're a quiet, most respectable couple.'

Rackham nodded, looking at the address. 'Room 207 was empty. Across the corridor in 217 was a Miss Emily Stephenson from Northampton.'

'I am unable to recall Miss Stephenson but one of my staff might be able to help you.'

'In number 219 there's Mr and Mrs Rowland Harris of York.'

'They've stayed with us before,' the manager said. 'A very pleasant and quietly spoken couple.'

'And in number 218 there's a chap who's presumably an Irishman, Mr Patrick Mullaney of Dublin.'

'A most quiet, reserved gentleman.'

Quiet seemed to be the highest praise Mr Sutton could bestow upon a guest, Jack decided. He tapped his finger on the entry for Mr Mullaney. 'I see he booked into the hotel on the thirteenth, but changed his room.'

Mr Sutton readjusted his pince-nez and peered at the entry. 'That's quite correct. Now why . . .? Ah yes, the reason is noted here. Mr Mullaney's original room was on the third floor and he requested a move to 218 so as to be nearer the stairs. I remember now. I dealt with him myself. We make every effort to accommodate our guests' wishes, especially in the case of an elderly man such as Mr Mullaney.'

Rackham looked disappointed. 'Elderly, you say?'

'I don't suppose he had a beard, by any chance?' asked Jack.

'A beard?' Mr Sutton was surprised by the question. 'Yes, he did, as a matter of fact.'

'A long beard?' asked Jack. 'And side-whiskers, too, perhaps? I imagine he wore tinted glasses as well.'

Mr Sutton was puzzled. 'Yes, he did, now you come to mention it, although how you know, I cannot imagine. He explained he had weak eyes and had to shield them from the light. He said he was writing a book on – now what was it? – the Celtic church, as I recall, and was pursuing his researches in the British Museum.

I remember thinking how venerable he looked. Really, quite the model of an elderly scholar.'

'And did Mr Mullaney dine in the restaurant or in his room?'

Mr Sutton frowned in remembrance. 'He dined in his room, as I recall. Yes, that's right. As I say, he was a quiet, reserved gentleman,' he added in reproof.

'Absolutely,' muttered Jack softly. 'That's him.'

'Well, Bill, what d'you think of that?' asked Jack triumphantly as they walked up Southampton Row. 'Have we just had a description of the real murderer or have we not?'

'An elderly, bearded, Irish scholar?'

'The age is simulated, the beard is assumed and the accent's phoney. Add the weak eyes and a retiring habit and you've got a man who defies description. Come on. All Mr Sutton really saw was a mass of hair and a pair of dark glasses. No one nowadays goes round with a beard like an exploding mattress. As my editor said the other day, one bloke in a beard looks like any other bloke in a beard. He has to be dodgy.'

'And how are you going to prove these breathtaking assertions?' asked Rackham mildly. 'Looking for a Patrick Mullaney in Dublin will be like trying to look for a needle in a haystack. You can put it down to experience or divine inspiration or whatever you like but I can't see us finding him to ask him outright. He booked not by letter but in person, hadn't stayed at the hotel before, left no forwarding address, and God only knows where he is now.'

'You could try the British Museum to see if they've got any record of him. But what if he proves not to have existed at all?'

'That'll be damn difficult to prove, Jack.'

'What is it?' asked Jack, looking at his friend curiously. 'I tell you there's a Mr X, produce a man who fits the bill and instead of clapping me on the shoulder, you look as if you're sucking lemons.'

Rackham wriggled unhappily. 'It was something Hugo Ragnall said. It wasn't part of his official statement, of course, but he said it all the same. He believes we got it right in the first place and Gerard Carrington is our man. He's sympathetic to Carrington as he freely admits Dunbar was the frozen limit, but he still thinks Carrington did it. What's more, so does Lewis. He's sympathetic too, apparently, but he believes it all the same. And I must say, I think they've got a point.'

'But I *proved* Carrington couldn't have done it.'

'You made it impossible to proceed with the case against him, Jack. It's not quite the same thing. So an Irishman stayed at the Marchmont. So what? He could be perfectly genuine, you know, even if he did look like Old Father Time. I think what's really bothering me is that Hugo Ragnall was talking about something he knew, which was Carrington's character. Look at the way it's completely taken for granted that Carrington's temper was so uncertain that there was almost an expectation he'd lose his rag with Dunbar. That's why Ragnall was at the Marchmont in the first place and why Stephen Lewis suggested his wife should meet Carrington for tea. If Ragnall's right and Carrington is our man, then we can run round after Mr X forever, without getting anywhere. And you must admit that although we've had some promising leads, the other suspects have turned out to be duds. I've got a feeling that this is going to turn out to be the sort of case where we've got a very good idea who the guilty man is but we'll never be able to prove it.'

'The guilty man being Carrington?'

Rackham didn't answer.

'I think,' said Jack, 'that I'd better take you up on your suggestion and go and see Hugo Ragnall.'

Jack found Hugo Ragnall ensconced by files and papers in the study at Mottram Place, a pleasant airy room overlooking the street. It had been kitted out as an office and Hugo Ragnall was obviously a busy man. As the maid showed him in, Ragnall stood up with a puzzled, although friendly, expression.

'Major Haldean? I heard the doorbell but I thought it was the telegram boy.'

'We arrived at the same time,' said Jack with a smile. 'You'll excuse me dropping in like this, but I understand you saw Inspector Rackham this morning.'

'Yes?' said Ragnall, suddenly alert. 'How's Ferguson?'

'It looks as if he's going to be all right.'

Ragnall breathed a sigh of relief. 'I'm glad to hear it. I felt guilty that I hadn't come forward sooner but it never occurred to me he'd be suspected. It's no joke, telling the police you were on the spot when a murder was committed.' He turned a pencil over and over between nervous fingers. 'Is that why you came? To tell me about Ferguson?'

'As a matter of fact, no. It was just idle curiosity, really. Inspector Rackham mentioned that you knew an old friend of mine, a bloke who's out in Kenya. I couldn't think who it could be.'

Hugo Ragnall's face cleared. 'Oh, I see.' He gave a rather forced laugh. 'For a moment I thought you were going to quiz me about what I'd said to the inspector.'

As that was precisely Jack's intention, he schooled his face into blank innocence. 'Quiz you? About a statement you made to the police? I don't think so. It's not really any of my business, is it? No, I just wondered who this old pal was.'

Hugo Ragnall's mind was obviously running on another track and the question seemed to catch him off guard. 'Your old pal? His name's Carslake.'

This was a bit of an effort, but Jack kept going. 'What, Johnnie Carslake? I've lost touch with him completely but we were great pals at one time. I didn't know he'd ended up in Kenya.'

Ragnall made an obvious attempt to concentrate. 'He's been out there a couple of years. He's the manager of a coffee plantation.'

'I'd love to catch up on his news,' said Jack. Hugo Ragnall was trying hard, but he was as twitchy as a kitten. Why, for heaven's sake? 'I don't know what time you finish for the day but I did wonder if you'd care to have a drink and bring me up to date. There's a very decent pub not far from here, The Floating Light. I don't know if you know it? They do excellent grub, too, if you fancy a bite to eat.'

'I . . . I'd like to, yes,' said Ragnall. 'Yes, I'd enjoy that. Why don't I meet you there in twenty minutes or so?' He tapped the letters on the desk. 'That'll give me time to clear away here.'

'That sounds like a good idea,' said Jack, and would have said more when the door opened and Stephen Lewis, holding a telegram, walked into the room.

'Ragnall, I've had some news . . .' He broke off as he saw Jack. 'Hello, Haldean. I didn't know you were here.' He looked curiously at Ragnall. 'I didn't realize you knew each other.'

'We've only just met,' said Jack easily. 'I hope you don't

mind me barging in, but Inspector Rackham mentioned Mr Ragnall knew an old friend of mine, so I thought I'd look him up.'

'I see. Is there any news of Ferguson, by the way? I was horrified when I heard he'd been arrested. The police made a real bloomer there. Ragnall told me that he'd seen Ferguson at the hotel at the time but it never occurred to either of us that he could be suspected. Least said, soonest mended and all that, especially when Ferguson denied being there. I know why he did it, but he'd painted himself into a real corner, hadn't he? When we got the news I said Ragnall better tell the Inspector what he'd seen. I hope it's going to be all right.'

'I think so, yes. But I'm sorry, I'm interrupting your work,' said Jack, glancing at the telegram in Lewis's hand. 'I was just leaving.'

'It's not work, I'm afraid,' said Lewis, seriously. 'It's bad news.' He held out the telegram to Ragnall. 'I've been expecting it for a while, but that doesn't make it any better. Uncle Maurice died this morning.'

Jack was surprised at the effect of the news on Ragnall. He took the telegram and, as he read it, his shoulders sagged and his face fell in what seemed genuine distress. He read the telegram in silence and handed it back with a sigh. 'My word, Lewis, I'm sorry,' he said. 'He was such a splendid character, a real fighter. I know he was difficult sometimes, but he was a grand old boy.'

Lewis stiffened and Jack realized, with the shock of the unexpected, that he hadn't liked Ragnall saying that. Once before he had likened Steve Lewis to a wary guard dog. Ragnall had stepped over the invisible, possessive line of kinship and Lewis's voice contained a warning growl.

'It's not really your place to comment, is it?'

Ragnall jerked his head back and met Lewis's eyes. 'No,' he said, dropping his gaze. 'No, I don't suppose it is. I'm sorry.'

His authority restored, Lewis relaxed. 'Poor old beggar,' he said. 'I'll miss him.' He sighed deeply. 'I suppose I'll have to think about the funeral.'

Ragnall swallowed. 'The funeral?'

'Yes. I should have considered it before, but I've been putting it off. I was hoping he'd pull through, I suppose. I could do with a hand to get everything sorted out.'

'Yes, of course,' said Ragnall. 'Yes, it'll have to be arranged.'
He broke off for a moment. 'Will Mrs Lewis attend the
funeral?'

'We'll discuss it between ourselves,' said Lewis, adding, in
a fairly obvious hint that Jack should depart, 'It can't be of
much interest to you, Haldean.'

'No, of course not,' said Jack. 'I don't want to intrude. I
met your uncle, though, Lewis. Please allow me to offer my
sympathies.'

'Thanks,' said Lewis absently. 'Yes, you went down with
Gerry, didn't you? It's just as well he did go. I warned him
Uncle Maurice didn't have long left. I'm only sorry to have
been proved right so soon.'

Ragnall cleared his throat. 'I think in the circumstances,
we'd better postpone our drink, Major. We were going to the
pub,' he explained to Lewis. 'We'd better leave it for the time
being.'

'Yes,' said Lewis, looking once more at the telegram. 'Yes,
that might be as well.' He was silent for a few moments then
looked up briskly. 'It seems a shame, though. What did you
say? That you had friends in common? Why don't you come
here, Haldean?' He smiled. 'With any luck, Ferguson will be
able to join us and I know both Ragnall and my wife would
like to talk to you about your stories. They're both regular
readers.' His smile widened. 'And, ever since you got him off
the hook, Gerry's been singing your praises, so I think I'll
invite him, too. You can be assured of a very warm welcome.
Shall we say the day after tomorrow? Half seven for eight for
cocktails and dinner. Will that suit you?'

'That's very generous,' said Jack. 'I'll accept with pleasure.'

Lewis ushered him into the hall. 'I must say I was surprised
to see you, Haldean,' he said as he showed him to the door.
'You're welcome, of course, but did you really look up Ragnall
on the strength of having a mutual friend?'

'More or less,' said Jack easily. 'Talking of old friends, I'm
glad that Hector Ferguson seems to be cleared. Ragnall might
not have thought his evidence was particularly important, but
it's got Ferguson out of a hole.'

'It never crossed my mind that a chap like Ferguson could
be in any danger.'

'Why not?' asked Jack. 'After all, he'd said he'd been at

work all afternoon. You knew that wasn't true. Didn't you have any suspicions?'

Lewis shook his head. 'Not really. Mind you, I knew what Ragnall had seen, so I knew he was in the clear.'

'But both you and Mr Ragnall knew the police had considered Mrs Dunbar. It wasn't really fair to her.'

'Considering Mrs Dunbar had no compunction about accusing me, I can't say I lost any sleep over it,' said Lewis grimly. 'I didn't think she could be serious but it stung, all the same. Look, Haldean, what was I supposed to do? I didn't see Mrs Dunbar or Ferguson; Ragnall did. Both of us thought if Ferguson wanted to tell the police he'd never been near the Marchmont, it was best to let sleeping dogs lie. Ferguson might have bent the truth a little, but the point was that whoever had bumped off Dunbar, it wasn't him. I was in a position to know that was true, so I advised Ragnall to keep schtum and I did the same. Besides that, you must remember that the police had arrested Gerry. It seemed to be an open and shut case.'

Jack paused by the door. 'And you didn't disagree with them?' he asked softly.

Lewis looked at him with a hunted expression. 'What do you want me to say?' he demanded. 'The man's my cousin, after all. It seemed so cut and dried. I didn't want it to be true, but we can't have the world arrange itself to our liking simply because we don't care for the way things turn out.' He dropped his voice. 'You see, I *know* Gerry. He's a brilliant scientist but, just like his father, he wants everything to be black and white. He hates it when things don't go his way.'

'So you found it a credible accusation?'

Lewis met his eyes squarely. 'I don't think I'd better answer that. Gerry's free. It's all turned out for the best.'

THIRTEEN

'One of the things that's getting to me, Bill,' said Jack, giving a final tweak to his white tie in front of the mirror, 'is the calm way everyone – including you – seems to take on board that Gerry Carrington is a murderer but doesn't seem to want to do anything but pat him on the head and say "There, there, never mind, don't do it again. Off you go and play."'

'That's a bit of a low blow, Jack,' complained Bill. He had called in to see Jack before he left for the dinner party at the Lewis's and, glass of gin and lime in hand, was going through the case. It seemed, he said, to have completely stalled. Ferguson had been released and Rackham had drawn a predictable blank at the British Museum when he had enquired after Mr Patrick Mullaney. 'If Gerard Carrington's guilty, I'd like to see him in the dock. I've got no intention of patting him on the head, as you put it. I wasn't sure about Carrington. It's an odd thing, but I've become more convinced as time's gone on, even though you did produce the evidence about the letter.'

Jack picked up his gin. 'I've given myself a headache brooding about that damn letter,' he said seriously. 'If it was a trick, I'm blowed if I know how the trick was done.'

'So you're beginning to wonder as well?' asked Rackham shrewdly.

Jack plumped down heavily in an armchair and sat for a while without speaking. 'Yes,' he said eventually. 'It's not surprising, is it? Carrington's a likable sort, but he's a clever man and, I think, a determined one. He seemed oblivious of the letter but perhaps he has enough brass neck to keep it up his sleeve. If he'd produced that letter in court, he'd be laughing. Maybe all I've done is save him the trouble of being tried. Naturally he had to appear to welcome my help. Maybe he did welcome it when he worked out there couldn't be a case brought against him.'

'D'you think that's the truth of it? I still believe Carrington's far and away the most obvious suspect.'

'He's blindingly obvious, which, of course, bothers me.'
It suddenly struck Rackham that there were dark shadows
under Jack's eyes. 'Go easy on yourself,' he said gruffly. 'I
asked you to look into the case as a favour. You can hardly
blame yourself for uncovering the evidence that was there.'
Jack drained his gin. 'I could almost wish I hadn't, Bill. If
he's not guilty, I don't know if the poor beggar will ever be
free of suspicion, but if he *is* guilty, I haven't made any difference at all.' No, he hadn't; and Carrington, that dishevelled
yet oddly precise man, with a mind full of equations, was
essentially a lie. 'Carrington's free and that would have
happened with or without my help. But if he is guilty, not
only has he really got away with murder, everyone – Stephen
Lewis, Hugo Ragnall, Molly Lewis, Mrs Dunbar and Ferguson
too – is telling him it doesn't actually matter. And that's a
very dangerous state of mind.'
'I see what you mean,' said Bill, his forehead creasing in
a frown. 'And now Colonel Willoughby's dead, that's murder,
too. We have to get to the bottom of this, Jack.'

Stephen Lewis, thought Jack, as Lewis showed him into the
flat, was worried. The sound of music and chatter from the
drawing room was clearly audible in the hall but Lewis seemed
far too distracted to be in the mood for a party.
'Is everything all right?' asked Jack, handing him his coat
and hat.
'Yes,' said Lewis, hanging up Jack's things in the hall wardrobe.
'That is . . .' He sighed in a harried sort of way. 'It's Gerry,' he
dropped his voice. 'I haven't said anything to the other guests,
of course, but you know so much that it's silly to pretend that
everything in the garden's lovely. To be honest, I'm expecting a
few fireworks. When you rang the bell I thought it might be him.
Never mind. Hopefully it won't amount to anything.'
The door of the study opened and Hugo Ragnall looked
out. 'Oh, it's you, Major Haldean,' he said, his shoulders
sagging in relief. 'I thought it might be Mr Carrington.'
'It can't be anything but a misunderstanding,' said Lewis,
assuming a painfully synthetic heartiness. 'You mustn't worry.
I'm sure it'll all be sorted out. The fact is, Haldean, that
Gerry's written a very peculiar letter to Ragnall here, and
we're not sure what to make of it.'

Ragnall's lips thinned. 'You may think it's merely peculiar, Lewis, but I call it downright offensive.'

'Gerry's got the wrong end of the stick, somehow,' said Lewis pacifically. 'I said as much before. Anyway, Ragnall thought he'd better have a word with him in private before dinner and see what it was all about. It'll be something and nothing, I'll be bound. Gerry's overstepped the mark a bit, but he's done what he always does. He's heard half a story, invented the rest, and gone off at half cock.'

The doorbell rang and Lewis and Ragnall exchanged looks. 'That's probably him now,' said Lewis. 'Relax, Ragnall. You mark my words. He'll be all apologies after a few minutes, you wait and see. Haldean, just wait a minute to say hello, will you? He can't be too over the top if he sees you're here.'

'Right-oh,' said Jack agreeably, as Lewis went to answer the front door, adding in an undertone to Hugo Ragnall, 'I hope you get it sorted out.'

'I want an explanation,' said Ragnall grimly as he went back into the study. 'It'd better be a good one, too.'

Gerard Carrington came into the flat like a tornado. He took no notice of Jack but greeted Lewis curtly then, without taking off his hat or coat, stood with his fists clenched, radiating anger. 'Where the devil's that blasted secretary of yours?'

'Calm down, Gerry,' said Lewis, indicating Jack. 'We've got guests in the flat.' Carrington nodded to Jack in a restrained way, then whirled as the study door opened and Hugo Ragnall came into the hall. 'So there you are!' snarled Carrington.

'Yes, Mr Carrington,' bit back Ragnall. 'Here I am. I've been waiting to see you.'

'I bet you have,' said Carrington.

'Gerry,' said Lewis, harshly. 'Get a grip on yourself. I don't know what's wrong, but you and Ragnall had better get it sorted out between yourselves and quickly, too. I'll be in the drawing room.'

Lewis heaved a distracted sigh, giving Jack an expressive glance as they walked towards the drawing room. 'I hope to God those two get it sorted out. The last thing I want is a row, particularly with guests around.' At the door he straightened his waistcoat and squared his shoulders with a tired smile. 'Let's pretend there's nothing wrong, shall we?'

In the drawing room, Hector Ferguson was standing by the gramophone, listening with earnest interest to *That's My Hotsy Totsy Bon Bon*. He glanced up as they entered and gave Jack a rather sheepish look.

Molly Lewis who, cocktail in hand, was sitting with an older woman and three girls, got up with a worried air. 'Was that Gerry at the door, Steve?' she asked Lewis quietly.

'Yes.' Lewis gave her a warning frown. 'Least said, soonest mended, eh?' He raised his voice. 'Let me introduce you, Haldean. These are neighbours of ours, Mrs Soames-Pensford and her daughters, Barbara, Ethel and Phyllis.'

'Major Haldean, I just loved *The Secret of the Second Shroud*,' said Babs Soames-Pensford. 'It was too enthralling for words.' She was a remarkably pretty girl and, if Jack's mind hadn't been on the quarrel in the next room, he would have been more than happy to give her his undivided attention. 'When Molly said you were coming to dinner we were *thrilled*. We've all read it and my mother's reading it, too. We can't wait for her to finish it so we can talk about the ending.'

Jack recalled himself to his social duties. 'I won't give anything away,' he said with a smile, taking the cocktail Stephen Lewis offered him. 'That's very kind of you.'

The music came to an end. The flat was solidly built and he could hear nothing from the next room. Maybe the quarrel would come to his aid. He wanted that talk with Ragnall and, if things went badly, Ragnall would probably be looking to enlist sympathy. Not tonight, not with Lewis there and – if things were patched up – Carrington as well, but tomorrow, perhaps. Bill said that he was sure Ragnall was holding something back. Not only that, but Ragnall thought Carrington was guilty. Real or imagined, Ragnall might have some actual knowledge. If it had got to Carrington's ears, it would account for his furious letter.

'Put another record, on, Ferguson,' said Lewis. 'I've had a half a dozen new pressings from the factory today. They're in the box by the side of the machine.'

'New records, Captain Lewis?' said Babs Soames-Pensford. She sighed wistfully. 'What an exciting life you have. I expect you know all the band-leaders, don't you?'

'Some of them,' said Lewis. 'Why don't you help Ferguson choose a record?' he added gallantly, to her obvious pleasure.

'There's not a bad selection here,' said Ferguson, opening the box and looking through the records with Babs Soames-Pensford. 'All single-sided, I see.'

'Yes, they're new,' said Lewis in an abstracted way. He was clearly thinking about what was happening in the next room, too. 'Just play one, Ferguson, will you?'

'Now this is the stuff to give the troops!' Ferguson drew a record from its paper sleeve. 'Jack Hylton. *Mama's Doing It Now!*'

'I do like Jack Hylton,' said Babs Soames-Pensford happily. 'He's too shattering for words.'

Ferguson jerked *That's My Hotsy Totsy Bon Bon* from the turntable and put it on the piano. Jack winced. For someone who was so positive about the joys of recorded music, Ferguson was horribly heavy-handed with the disks.

'Jack Hylton,' said Ferguson knowledgeably over the music, 'knows how to get a true jazz sound. It's all a question of technique. What it needs is the singer to stand close to the microphone and sing into it, rather than bellowing away like someone at a Sunday concert, trying to get his voice to carry to the back of a hall—'

He stopped short as a loud crack rang out. The Soames-Pensfords gave a squeal of surprise. Jack Hylton played on, loud in the listening silence.

Molly Lewis made a little noise in the back of her throat. She looked at Lewis, her eyes wide and her face suddenly pale. 'What's happened?'

'Nothing, I expect,' said Lewis, in a blustering let's-pretend-everything's-fine way that was more alarming than any amount of honest concern. 'It must have been a backfire from a car. I'll just take a look and see how old Gerry's getting on.' Jack made to follow him to the door but Lewis stopped him. 'Keep an eye on things in here, old man,' he muttered.

'These *dreadful* cars,' said Mrs Soames-Pensford to Molly Lewis. 'It sounded exactly like a gunshot, didn't it? Why, you look quite upset, my dear. It's too bad. Something really should be done. Only the other day, I was crossing Piccadilly and a car made such a *frightful* bang I honestly thought my last moments had come. I was so shaken the policeman on point duty had to catch hold of my arm to steady me.'

Jack strained to hear the voices in the hall. Gerard

Carrington, indignant, Stephen Lewis a brief, indistinguishable low rumble.

'Actually hold my arm!' continued Mrs Soames-Pensford. 'I was so grateful, because I'm sure I would have fallen without his aid. I said, "My good man . . ."' She carried on speaking but Jack wasn't listening. The drawing room was at the back of the flat and looked out on to gardens. He supposed it could have been a backfire, but . . .

Lewis put his head round the door. 'Haldean, can you come here? Ferguson, you too.'

There was a shout from the next room. Lewis spun round and ran, followed by Jack, Hector Ferguson and Molly Lewis.

In the study, Gerard Carrington knelt by the sprawled body of Hugo Ragnall.

It was like a bad dream. It was only a second or perhaps part of a second but Jack saw the scene as if there had been a flash of lightning. Gerard Carrington's ghost-white face, Hugo Ragnall's outstretched hand, loosely holding a gun, the absolute knowledge that Hugo Ragnall was dead. And in the hall, unable to see into the study, Mrs Soames-Pensford, kept up a steady flow of complaint about cars.

'Gerry,' said Lewis, his voice hoarse.

Carrington stood up and backed away. 'No,' he said. 'No. I'm not doing this. I'm not. Not prison. Not again.'

With an explosion of movement, Carrington hurled himself forward and snatched the gun from Ragnall's hand. He was shaking, Jack noted mechanically. Carrington's fear was so strong he could almost smell it. Holding the gun in a trembling hand, Carrington pointed it at them. 'Let me out.'

'Gerry, you can't do this,' said Lewis in a bewildered way. Sudden fury transformed Carrington's face. 'Can't I?'

Jack moved forward and the gun pointed waveringly at his stomach.

'I'll do it!' Carrington's voice was sharp with terror. 'Steve, stay where you are!' The muzzle of the gun suddenly seemed huge. Stephen Lewis moved again and Jack saw Carrington's knuckles whiten.

'Stop!' he yelled.

Lewis froze and Carrington's knuckles relaxed.

'Let me out,' Carrington repeated. With his back to the

bookshelves that lined the wall, he inched his way towards the door, the gun fixed on the men opposite.

'Stand away from the door,' Jack shouted to the women crowding the entrance. 'He's got a gun. Stand right away.' He knew just how dangerous a gun in the hands of a badly frightened man was. 'Let him *through*,' he snarled, his voice savage.

There was surprisingly little noise from the girls as they fell back. A whimper, a cry abruptly cut off, and a series of choking gasps.

Carrington, his eyes fixed on them and the gun at the ready, backed his way down the hall.

'Gerry,' pleaded Molly Lewis. 'Come back.'

His face twisted. 'I can't,' he said, his voice nearly a sob.

Steve Lewis saw his chance and sprang. Carrington jerked the gun up and fired in a thunderous, ear-shattering roar. Lewis was hurled backwards and the bullet ploughed through the ceiling.

A few things happened simultaneously. Molly screamed and flung herself to the floor beside her husband as, with a series of ominous creaks and with ghastly inevitability, the plaster on the ceiling crazed into fragments and fell in a soft whumph of blinding, choking lumps.

It was like an explosion in a flour mill. It was impossible to see and nearly impossible to breath. Through streaming eyes, Jack could see a white haze appear as the front door opened, then it slammed shut once more, plunging the hall back into shifting, dusty darkness.

Everyone seemed to be coughing, then shouting, then coughing again. Beside him, Babs Soames-Pensford kept repeating, 'He's dead, he's dead,' in a bewildered monotone. He heard Ferguson yelling but his voice was lost in the uproar.

Jack, stuck at the back of the group, tried groping his way towards Lewis through the panicking group in the hall, guided by Molly's screams. From behind the green baize door at the end of the hall, the three womenservants pushed their way into the jostling crowd.

He scrambled past Mrs Soames-Pensford and found Steve Lewis more by touch than sight. He was sitting up, supported by Molly, shaking his head blearily. He clutched his arm and his hand came away red. 'Blood!' yelped Mrs Soames-Pensford and crumpled to the floor.

'It's my arm,' Lewis managed to say. 'The devil got my arm.' He closed his eyes and fell against Molly.

Covered in plaster-dust and with his ears ringing from the shot, Jack made his way as best he could to where he thought the front door should be. Eventually his hands closed on the handle and he wrenched it open. He staggered down the steps, holding on to the railings and taking great gulps of fresh air.

A kitchen maid from the opposite flats, who had just stepped out to enjoy a cigarette on the steps down to the area, gazed at him in as much horror as if he were the demon king in a pantomime. She threw back her head and screamed at the top of her voice. A postman and a woman walking a dog stopped in their tracks, open mouthed, as Ferguson and the Soames-Pensford girls, covered in white dust, spilled down the steps behind him. More passers-by, drawn by the shouts and the promise of something utterly remarkable on this quiet, tree-lined street stopped to look and then the housemaid, Connie, her eyes bulging with excitement, elbowed her way to the front, threw back her head and yelled, 'Murder!'

It was incredible how quickly the crowd gathered. The shout of 'Murder!' was taken up, carried down the street and suddenly a ring of densely packed people gathered round the steps, preserving, with an odd sense of propriety, a clear half-circle round the front door. Errand-boys, a postman, respectably dressed clerks, all the servants from the other flats, newspaper sellers, fashionable women, men in flat caps, men in greasy overalls, women in aprons with their hair in nets, dozens of children and innumerable barking dogs. Two taxis squealed to a halt and what seemed to be scores of top-hatted, exquisitely dressed young men leapt out, and took up, in penetrating, high-pitched voices, the cry of, 'Murder! I say, murder!' The taxi drivers got out, took one look and, as one man, yelled, 'Murder!' in a stentorian Cockney bellow.

It was with heartfelt relief that Jack heard the shrill blast of a policeman's whistle. Two constables converged and made their stately way through the crowd which fell back in a wave to let them through. 'It's murder!' yelled a knot of small boys, whooping as if they were at a football match. 'Murder! 'E done it,' added a bristle-headed youth, pointing to Jack. 'That toff in filfy clothes! 'E done it! Murder!'

A policeman's hand descended on Jack's collar. 'What's all

this?' he said. 'Wot's 'e mean, murder?' He looked up at the open door of the flat, still hazy with dust. Stephen Lewis emerged on to the steps. His evening dress was dishevelled and dirty, the ripped fabric of his sleeve was hanging loose and he had blood smeared on his cheek from where he had rubbed his face with his hands.

The crowd gasped and the bristle-headed boy jumped up and down in a paroxysm of delight. 'Cor! That's the bloke 'e murdered!'

'Don't be daft, you silly young shaver,' grunted the policeman, catching the boy a clip on the head with the edge of his cape. 'Get out of it!' He raised his voice to an official bellow. 'Everyone, clear away!'

'I think,' said Jack, wearily, to the policeman still clutching his collar, 'you'd better come inside.'

It was nearly two hours later and Rackham and Jack were in the study together. Rackham was intent on a meticulous analysis of the murder, including a word-for-word account of Carrington's entry into the house, the conversation in the drawing room and the scene in the hall. Rackham even played the records they had listened to. He would never, thought Jack, shrinking from the urbane jollity of the song, be able to listen to Jack Hylton again. The breezy tune and the witty lyrics now seemed jeeringly, unbearably sinister.

Stephen Lewis was with Sergeant Hawley in the drawing room. The crowd had reluctantly dispersed, Molly Lewis had retired to bed, Hector Ferguson had gone home and the Soames-Pensfords had returned to their flat. The doctor and the photographer had been, statements had been taken, and Hugo Ragnall's body had been removed to the mortuary.

'Carrington was furious when he walked into the flat, you say?' said Rackham, prowling round the filing-cases in the study.

'Absolutely blistering, Bill. Hugo Ragnall, poor devil, was pretty worked up, too, about this letter Carrington had written to him.'

'I can't find the letter. Carrington probably took it with him. I don't suppose you've any idea what was in it, have you?'

'Stephen Lewis knows. He was trying to calm Ragnall down

before Carrington arrived and, from what he said, he knew what Carrington had written.'

'Does he, by jingo? He didn't tell me that.'

'I can guess what's in it though,' said Jack. 'I bet you can, too.'

Rackham let out his breath in a long sigh, then, lighting a cigarette, sat down on the study chair. 'It's not very hard to guess, is it? I *knew* Ragnall was holding something back, the idiot. How about this for an idea? We know Ragnall arrived at the Marchmont Hotel the day Dunbar was murdered. He said he didn't see Carrington. What if that was a lie?'

'That's exactly what I was thinking,' said Jack.

'Because if he *did* see Carrington he'd be in a position either to back up his story or to deny it. And, although Carrington was officially in the clear, Hugo Ragnall might have tried a bit of blackmail. Knowing that Carrington was due to attend this party this evening, I bet Ragnall wrote to him, asking for a private word. Carrington, who's not a man to push around, certainly took violent exception to something Ragnall had said, done or hinted. I bet Carrington dashed off a note, denying everything, and came round in person to settle the matter. We know he's got a foul temper and, with both men spoiling for a fight, things got out of hand and Carrington pulled a gun.' He cocked an eyebrow at his friend. 'How's that for a reconstruction?'

'I've always liked Carrington, but it sounds fairly likely to me,' said Jack heavily. 'I know what I heard and saw, and if Ragnall really did know Carrington was lying about the time he left the Marchmont, that'd carry a lot more weight than my inference about the letter and the post-boy and so on.'

'The evidence of the post-boy bothers me, though,' said Bill. 'He wasn't lying, I'd swear to it. Why the devil should he? Unless Carrington had bribed him, of course,' he added thoughtfully. 'But he was taking a dickens of a risk if he did, placing himself at the mercy of a lad like that. I can't see it, Jack.'

'No,' said Jack. His face was pale. 'You know I said I'd been trying to think how the trick might have been worked? I think I know how it could be done.'

'What?'

'It depends on Mrs Dunbar's eyesight.'

Bill looked puzzled. 'How, exactly?'

'It's a question of time. Your expert at the Yard was convinced that Dunbar had opened and read the letter, the letter that was delivered, according to Mrs Dunbar's evidence, after Carrington had left the hotel. Right?'

'Right.'

'Now say Carrington was there when the letter was delivered. Dunbar reads the letter and, maybe while he's reading it, Carrington bumps him off. Carrington knows that the post-boy, a completely independent witness, will be able to fix what time he delivered the letter. All he has to do then is convince someone – anyone – that it's earlier than in fact it is. He goes down into the lobby of the hotel and looks for someone to talk to about the time. There's a couple of ways he could have done it. He could have brushed against someone, apologized, saying he's frightfully sorry but he can't stop because he's got an appointment, makes a point of looking at his watch, exclaims, "It's half four" and he's going to be late. Or, if he saw someone with a newspaper, he could have stopped and asked for the racing results, mentioning that he had a bet on the four o'clock, say. Then he could pretend to see the time, laugh, and say it wouldn't be in the newspaper yet because it's only half past four. You see what I mean? It's a way of impressing on someone's mind that it's half past four.'

'And none of these people are capable of looking at the hotel clock for themselves?'

'We're talking about minutes, Bill. People don't usually give the time to the precise minute. Besides that, it all depends on eyesight, doesn't it? If an elderly gentleman were to have been reading a newspaper with spectacles, he wouldn't be able to see the hotel clock with his reading glasses. It'd only be a blur and, in those circumstances, he's unlikely to check the time with his watch. An elderly man wouldn't have a wristwatch. He'd have a fob watch and to produce it, in those circumstances, would be tantamount to checking up on what this apologetic young man had said. Not only would that be impolite, but as far as the elderly gentleman's concerned, it's a very unimportant incident. Now what *actually* happened is that Carrington sees Mrs Dunbar, whom he knows. He dashes past her, saying he's got an appointment at five and it's half four already.'

'Mrs Dunbar wears glasses,' said Bill slowly. 'She couldn't have seen the hotel clock. When we were at her house and she staged that performance of accusing herself I remember she put her spectacles on and stared at Hector Ferguson. She was warning him to shut up, obviously, but she needed spectacles to see him.' He smacked his fist into his palm. 'It's so simple,' he said. 'So incredibly simple. Bloody hell, Jack, I'm going to get to the bottom of this.' He jerked his head towards the next room. 'Stephen Lewis knows a damn sight more than he's ever told us. I'm going to get the truth out of him if it's the last thing I do. Come on. I've got some questions for that gentleman.'

Stephen Lewis, his arm now neatly bandaged, was drinking a weak whisky and water in the drawing room. His face was drawn and pale. 'Are you nearly finished, Inspector? You'll understand if I say I want nothing more than to get to bed.'

'I imagine you do, sir,' said Rackham with a rather forced smile. 'We won't be much longer, but there are another couple of questions I'd like to ask.'

Lewis sipped his whisky in a depressed sort of way. 'If you must. What do you want to know?'

'It's this, sir. From the very start, you've believed that Gerard Carrington murdered Dunbar. Don't bother to deny it, sir,' he added, seeing Lewis's startled expression. 'I think it's time you told the truth.'

Lewis bit his lip. 'Perhaps,' he said reluctantly.

'Thank you. Mr Ragnall was in the Marchmont the afternoon Dunbar was murdered. His evidence – which he was very slow to give – put Mr Ferguson in the clear. However, it did occur to me to wonder what else he saw.'

'Please, Inspector! Gerry Carrington's my cousin. What do you expect me to say?'

'I expect you, sir, to bear in mind that Carrington threatened your wife and your guests with a gun, shot you, and murdered your secretary. He's a dangerous man and I believe both you and Hugo Ragnall knew just how dangerous he was.' Lewis said nothing. 'Shall I tell you what I think happened, sir?' said Rackham. Lewis put the back of his hand to his mouth but still said nothing. 'Very well. I will. Hugo Ragnall saw Mrs Dunbar and Hector Ferguson at the Marchmont, right enough, but he *also* saw Gerard Carrington.' Lewis met his eyes, then looked away, wriggling unhappily on his chair. 'You knew that, didn't you? You knew that Carrington hadn't left the hotel when he said he had. You knew he'd had the opportunity to kill Dunbar and you knew that because Hugo Ragnall had told you so.'

'For God's sake, yes!' Lewis let out a long, shuddering sigh. 'Gerry always had a filthy temper. I knew that. I was afraid he'd gone off the deep end. He loathed Dunbar and with good reason. I couldn't see that anybody else but Gerry could possibly have shot Dunbar, but I was damned if I was going to be the one to accuse him. Ragnall told me that he knew Gerry's account of the time he'd left the Marchmont was false. I told him to keep quiet. After all, Gerry was in enough trouble without Ragnall knocking another nail in the coffin.' He nodded at Jack. 'When you got him off the hook, I didn't think your explanation added up, but I thought it was all for the best. Ragnall would never have come forward if Ferguson hadn't been in danger. It was one thing not making anything worse for Gerry. It was quite another letting Ferguson carry the can for something he hadn't done. But I still don't see why Gerry went berserk with Ragnall.'

'Did you see the letter Carrington wrote to Ragnall?' asked Jack.

Lewis nodded. 'It was like the ravings of a madman. I couldn't think what the problem was. After all, Ragnall hadn't accused him of murder. He'd kept that under his hat. Gerry should have been grateful to him, not nearly insane with rage.'

Rackham cleared his throat. 'And what if Hugo Ragnall had attempted a little blackmail?'

'He couldn't!' began Lewis indignantly, then broke off. 'Oh, my God,' he said very softly. 'Oh, my God.' He turned his face away. 'Gerry couldn't have intended to murder him,' he said at last. 'He's not like that. Not Gerry. His temper must have got the better of him.'

'He had a gun, sir.'

'I know he had a gun,' said Lewis testily. 'He shot me with the damned thing. He must have meant to wave it round and perhaps scare Ragnall into silence. I don't know what was in his mind. I've stood by him and maybe I've been stupid. But Gerry is a brilliant man. It seemed all wrong that he should suffer for a temporary lapse of temper.'

'Have you considered Colonel Willoughby, Lewis?' asked Jack.

'Uncle Maurice?' said Lewis, bewildered. 'What's Uncle Maurice got to do with it?'

'He was attacked,' said Rackham. 'We think he might have been attacked to draw you off for the day.'

Lewis looked at them blankly, then flushed angrily. 'No. No, you're not telling me that Gerry did that. I just don't believe it. It was a burglar.'

'It was a very convenient burglar, wouldn't you say?'

Lewis stood up and walked to the sideboard where, his movements made clumsy by his bandaged arm, poured himself another drink. He turned around, obviously sunk in thought, then came to a decision. 'Look, Inspector, I might have been stupid but I'm damned if I'm going to carry on being stupid. If Gerry really did attack Uncle Maurice, then he deserves everything he gets. I'll tell you something else, too. I knew what Ragnall had seen. If Ragnall told Gerry as much, then I'm in danger.' He took a long drink.

Perhaps it was his injured arm or perhaps it was his nerves, but Stephen Lewis had gone very white. 'I don't think I'm a coward, but that scares me.'

Jack believed him.

FOURTEEN

The Reverend Matthew Meldreth, Vicar of St Ambrose, Stonecrop Ash, Oxfordshire, looked at Joseph Woollard with a puzzled frown. Mr Meldreth had been vicar of St Ambrose for the last seventeen years and Joe Woollard had been the sexton for twenty-two, but neither of them could remember a situation quite like this.

The Reverend Meldreth picked up his pipe from his desk and absently stuffed it with tobacco from the old and dented pewter jar, a sure sign he was perplexed. Part of the trouble was that he knew so little about Colonel Willoughby. The Colonel had received him with a certain reluctance when Mr Meldreth had called to welcome his new parishioner last September. The Colonel had plied him with a *chota peg*, a Scotch of ferocious strength, complained about the cold, compared England adversely with India and said that no offence taken, he was sure, but he didn't have much use for parsons in the general way.

And that, thought Mr Meldreth, lighting his pipe, more or less amounted to the sum of his knowledge of the late Colonel. About Mrs Tierney, the Colonel's housekeeper, he knew even less. A Roman Catholic, Mrs Tierney took no part in parish life. Even if she had been one of his flock, the Colonel's severe bronchitis, which had plagued him since his return to England, would have kept her tied to the house. However, although he had never been through the doors of St Ambrose, the Colonel was still a parishioner and when he died – a truly shocking business, that! – Mrs Tierney had asked for the Colonel to be buried with the due rites and ceremonies of the church. Mr Meldreth had called upon Joseph Woollard, Sexton, who, in addition to digging out the graves, was also the undertaker.

'I saw Mrs Tierney the day after the Colonel passed away, Reverend,' said Woollard. 'She told me that the Colonel's nephew wanted him to be buried properly, as you'd expect. I fixed him up with a nice bit of elm, with brass handles, as right as a trivet. I called this morning to tell her it was all done and to arrange for the coffin to be taken back to his bungalow, so he could be buried from his own house, which she said was what she wanted. And then, as I'm telling you, she wasn't there. She was gone.'

Mr Meldreth sucked deeply at his pipe. 'When you say gone, Joe, are you sure you mean gone?'

'Yes, Reverend,' affirmed Joe Woollard vigorously. 'Gone to London, so Martha Giles says – she's next door but one and friendly with Mrs Tierney – and no one seems to know when she'll be a-coming back. That was two days ago now, and the funeral's the day after tomorrow, as you well know, and I don't know what to do with the body.'

'But dash it, man, she must have left some instructions. She can't have just disappeared.'

'But she has. I don't know, but London could have gone to her head, like, and she might have clean forgot her duties. Things happen in London.'

Mr Meldreth recalled Mrs Tierney and shook his head. The idea that the pleasant, homely, middle-aged woman should have been seduced by bright lights and wicked ways was too fantastic for words and said more about Joe Woollard's choice of Sunday paper than his sense. In a way, though, he was right. Things happen in London. 'She could have met with an accident, I suppose.'

Joe Woollard acknowledged this less sensational explanation with a downturned face. 'She might have done at that. But what do I do with the Colonel? He can't be buried from his bungalow, not if no one's there to see him off.'

'He'll have to be buried from your workshop, Joe. You'll do it all properly, I know. I'd better get in touch with this nephew of the Colonel's. I presume he's coming to the funeral.'

But that was more than Joseph Woollard knew; nor did he know the Colonel's nephew's address or even his name. And Reverend Meldreth, completely at a loss and after two hours delay, reluctantly telephoned the police.

The first Jack Haldean knew of Mrs Tierney's disappearance was when his landlady, Mrs Pettycure, told him that Mr Rackham was on the telephone and would appreciate a word.

'Jack,' said Bill, his voice tinny on the phone, 'this is just a thought, but when you drove Gerard Carrington to meet his uncle, Colonel Willoughby, did you come across the Colonel's housekeeper, a Mrs Tierney?'

'That's right, Bill. I had quite a long conversation with her. She seemed a very pleasant woman.'

There was a pause. 'Would you recognize her? If she was dead, I mean?'

'Good God, what's happened?'

'That,' said Rackham grimly, 'is what I want to find out.'

The mortuary attendant pulled back the grey cotton sheet from the face of the body on the narrow wooden table. Jack swallowed. 'That's her, all right.' Rackham nodded to the attendant who replaced the sheet.

Jack was silent until they regained the street. He was thankful to be out of the building. In a way, the waiting room, with its scrubbed deal table and institutional chairs, where he had spent minutes that seemed like hours while Rackham completed the paperwork, had been worse than the white-washed mortuary itself. There was a vase of sweet peas on the table. At least no one had tried to pretend the mortuary with its lonely occupant and air laced with formaldehyde was anything but clean, cold and depressing.

'There's a pub across the road,' said Rackham. 'Come on. I think we both need a pick-me-up.'

In the Dog and Duck, Jack swallowed quarter of his pint of Bass in a single gulp. 'My God, I needed that,' he said with feeling. 'The atmosphere of that place seems to stick to your clothes, doesn't it? I'm sure I stink of disinfectant.'

'I hate seeing a woman come off worse.' Bill was pale with emotion. 'It's *wrong,* Jack. You told me she was a decent, kindly soul, and she looked it. How anyone could wish harm to a woman like that beggars belief.'

'What on earth happened to her?' asked Jack.

'She fell under a number eleven bus outside Paddington Station two days ago.'

'The same day Hugo Ragnall was shot.'

'Yes, at half past ten that morning. You didn't see the report in the newspapers?' Jack shook his head. 'It's no great wonder. The papers have been so full of Gerard Carrington that the fact an unknown woman was knocked down and killed hardly scraped in. Compared to Carrington, I don't suppose it's very important,' he said bitterly. 'The conductor and the driver, both of whom were very shaken, said there was absolutely no chance of avoiding her. She staggered into the road and sprawled in front of the bus.' He took a long drink. 'Exactly, they say, as if she'd been pushed.'

Jack let his breath out in a sigh. 'Did they see anyone with her?'

'There was a crowd round the station entrance, but they didn't see anyone in particular. We've asked for the public's help, but so far, no one's come forward. We might have more luck now we've got a definite person rather than an unidentified victim, but I doubt it.'

'Didn't she have any identification on her?'

'Not a thing. I imagine she had a bag of some sort but my guess is that whoever pushed her – and I'm going to take it she *was* pushed until it's proved otherwise – took her bag and scarpered. But what's getting to me is why would anyone want to kill her? By anyone, I mean Gerard Carrington, of course. It seems so pointless.'

Jack ran his finger round the top of his pint glass. 'It could be security. You know I said Colonel Willoughby half-recognized him? Carrington explained that at the time by saying he took after his mother. The Colonel agreed that must be it. But what if Carrington, thinking it over, sees there's a danger? What if, prompted by his visit, the Colonel realized that Carrington was the burglar? Who would he talk to?'

'Mrs Tierney,' said Rackham slowly. 'Damn it, Jack, that makes sense. But look, if Colonel Willoughby knew, or thought he knew, that Carrington had attacked him, why didn't he tell the police?'

'Family loyalty?' suggested Jack. 'He was very ill, too, and might not have been strong enough to talk to the local police. We don't know the Colonel *did* rumble him. That doesn't matter. All it needs is for Carrington to work out Mrs Tierney is potentially dangerous to him.'

'Dangerous,' repeated Bill. 'Carrington's dangerous. Dangerous and clever. According to a Mrs Martha Giles, who's a cook in one of the neighbouring houses and friendly with Mrs Tierney, Mrs Tierney was deeply moved when she received a letter, apparently from the Colonel's solicitors. The letter said the Colonel had left her a substantial legacy. Mrs Giles saw the letter but can't remember the name of the solicitors. The address, she thinks, was somewhere in Holborn.'

'That's a fat lot of good,' put in Jack. 'There's hardly anything but solicitors in Holborn.'

'Exactly. The letter said she would be met by a representative of the firm in the tearoom at Paddington Station. I think he met her, all right.

'Who are the Colonel's solicitors, as a matter of interest?'

'I don't know, but I'll find out. The chances of this letter having come from them are non-existent, I'd say, but I'll ask Stephen Lewis.'

'When's his uncle's funeral?'

'Tomorrow.'

'I hope he's safe,' said Jack, suddenly worried. 'He was downright rattled the other day.'

'I don't blame him. It's his own fault, though. He should have insisted Ragnall told us what he'd seen at the time, rather than covering it up. However, I think I might arrange for one of my men to be present at the funeral. Didn't you tell me that Carrington had a hankering after Lewis's wife?'

'I thought so, certainly.'

'That's another motive,' said Rackham heavily. 'Yes, I'll definitely make sure an officer's there.'

Predictably enough, Colonel Willoughby's solicitors, Grant, Thornton and Grant of Lincoln's Inn, knew nothing of any letter sent to Mrs Tierney and she certainly didn't have a large legacy; the Colonel had left her fifty pounds and four pieces of Benares brass. Stephen Lewis, too, did not profit to any large extent from his uncle's death as most of the Colonel's income was from a pension which had died with him. Less predictably, there was no incident of any sort at the funeral, a state of affairs about which Rackham had mixed feelings. It wasn't that he wanted any harm to come to Stephen Lewis, but he had hoped that the funeral might draw Carrington out into the open. Lewis, visibly shaken by both Hugo Ragnall's and Mrs Tierney's deaths, moved back to Stoke Horam.

It was, said Rackham, incredible how completely Gerard Carrington had disappeared. They were able to find out something of what he'd had done after he'd escaped after Ragnall's murder. Carrington gone back to his own rooms in Tavistock Square, changed his clothes, packed a small suitcase and vanished into thin air. And that, despite Carrington's face staring out of every newspaper, was that.

It was Wednesday, two days after the funeral, that an entry in the agony column of *The Daily Messenger* caught Jack's attention. *Gerry. S.H. on Thursday. Evening. Half nine, summer house. Danger. M.*

'I've seen it,' said Bill Rackham when Jack appeared in his office with the newspaper. 'I telephoned Mrs Lewis and spoke to her as soon as I saw it.'

'And?'

'And she knows nothing about it.' Bill picked up a pencil from the desk and twirled it thoughtfully between his fingers. 'Or so she says. I've been on to the newspaper office. They haven't got a note of who handed in the entry, which is what I expected. People who correspond through the agony column as often as not don't want any record kept.' He raised his eyebrows at his friend. 'You reckoned Gerard Carrington was stuck on Mrs Lewis. What's the chances of his feelings being reciprocated?'

Jack pulled out a chair and sat down heavily. 'I don't know,' he said after a few moments' thought. 'You might be right. She liked him, that was obvious, but everyone seemed to like him. I liked him, for Pete's sake.'

Rackham nodded. 'Yes, but it's her feelings I need to know about.' He tapped the paper. 'If this comes from Mrs Lewis, that means she's in league with Carrington. That opens up a whole range of possibilities.'

'Yes . . . Could Stephen Lewis have placed it? He was frightened, Bill. He might be trying to winkle Carrington out of hiding.'

'Then I wish he'd tell us!' Rackham stood up and stretched his shoulders. 'How much does it take to convince someone that a murderer is a dangerous man? Surely Lewis has learned his lesson by now?' He braced his arms on the desk. 'Tell me I'm right. That entry has to have been placed by either Molly Lewis, or Stephen Lewis using his wife's name. It can't be some plan of Carrington's can it?'

'I doubt it. If Carrington did want to silence Lewis, he'd hardly warn him beforehand. Even if it's an attempt to misdirect him, to lull him into a false sense of security, Carrington would be far better off saying nothing at all. '

'That's what I thought. Well, I don't know who's playing games but there's one thing for sure. I'm going down to Stoke Horam tomorrow and if Gerard Carrington comes to call, I'll be waiting. D'you fancy coming along?'

'Why not? I don't like that entry in the agony column, Bill. I don't like the way things are shaping up at all.'

'There's not much to like, is there?' He looked at the clock. 'I've got a meeting in couple of minutes. It's a conference on the case, as a matter of fact. Why don't you come round for a nightcap this evening? I can bring you up to date and we can plan out exactly what we're going to do tomorrow.'

But the plans which Rackham made, had, he said in disgust later that evening, gone up in smoke. 'Stephen Lewis is an idiot,' he said, topping up Jack's glass. 'We – that's the Chief and I – took it for granted that he'd welcome police protection. I telephoned him to say as much and he hummed and hawed and eventually refused. Apparently he's convinced we'll be spotted and it'll put Carrington off.'

'Doesn't he want to put Carrington off?' asked Jack, taking one of Rackham's excellent Turkish cigarettes from the box on the table.

'No, he wants to bring things to a head. He's scared, I think, but going it alone is stupid in these circumstances and I told him as much. Anyway, whether he likes it or not, I'm damn well going down to Stoke Horam tomorrow and I'm taking some officers with me. If we have to stay outside the grounds, fair enough. It's Lewis's house and we have to do what he says, but my hope is we'll nab Carrington on the way in.'

'Do you think he'll show up?'

'There's a chance,' said Rackham with a shrug. 'After all . . .' He broke off as the telephone on the sideboard rung. 'Excuse me,' he said briefly, picking up the earpiece. 'It's the Yard,' he mouthed across the room, then Jack saw his face change. 'He's done *what*? Right, I see. I think I'd better get down there right away. The local men are there, you say? Good. No, with any luck I'll be able to come by car.' He clamped his hand over the phone. 'Jack, can you drive me down to Stoke Horam? Now?'

'Yes, of course,' said Jack, standing up.

'Thanks.' Rackham turned back to the telephone. 'I'll be there as soon as possible and I'll be in touch as soon as I know anything definite. Tomorrow at the latest.' He hung up the phone and turned to Jack. 'That entry in the agony column could have been a blind after all. Gerard Carrington's just tried to murder Stephen Lewis.'

It took them over two hours to get to Stoke Horam, the pace through the maze of the dark Hertfordshire country lanes frustratingly slow. The facts, as Rackham knew them, were simple. At ten o'clock, or as close to it as made no difference, Gerard Carrington had shot at Stephen Lewis in the garden of Stoke Horam house. Molly Lewis, who had telephoned Scotland Yard immediately afterwards, had actually seen Carrington. It was only a fleeting glimpse, but she was certain it was him. Although unharmed, both Stephen Lewis and his wife were badly shaken and the Hertfordshire police had been called in.

'I doubt we'll be able to do anything tonight, Jack,' said Rackham, 'but at least we're on the spot to start a search tomorrow. The local men couldn't find any sign of Carrington, but that's only to be expected at this time of night. I only hope they haven't destroyed all the evidence by blundering round the garden. Lewis is safe enough for the time being, as long as he stays indoors.'

A constable was on duty at the gates of Horam House. Jack stopped the car and Rackham beckoned the man over. 'I'm Inspector Rackham of Scotland Yard. Have there been any further developments?'

'No, sir, it's all been quiet. Superintendent Clough's here, with four of us men. There are servants in the house, too. I can't see him coming back tonight.'

'No, neither can I.'

The policeman saluted and they drove on.

'I'm not sure about having the place so visibly guarded,' said Rackham thoughtfully. 'Tonight, yes, that makes sense, but we can't keep the house in a state of siege. If we can't lay hold of Carrington tomorrow, I think I'll ask the Superintendent to draw his men off. I want them around, but I don't want them to be seen. I'd like to have Carrington try his luck again.'

'Will Lewis go for that?' asked Jack as he braked the Spyker on the gravel in front of the house. 'After all, you're more or less asking him to act as the tethered kid to Carrington's tiger.'

'It's not up to him to decide how I arrange the policing,' said Rackham. 'After all, he's safe enough in the house and the object of the exercise is to put Carrington out of circulation, not scare him off to try another day. Hello, here's Mrs Lewis.'

The door of the house cautiously opened and Molly Lewis beckoned them in. 'I've been watching out for you.' There was honest relief in her welcome. 'I'm really glad you're here. Steve was so horribly twitchy after it happened that I gave him a sleeping-draught and packed him off to bed.'

'It's probably the best place for him,' said Rackham. 'You actually saw Carrington?'

'Oh yes.' She took a little anxious breath. 'I saw him quite clearly. I couldn't be mistaken. I wanted a walk in the rose garden, as it was such a lovely evening, and Steve was having a cigar on the terrace. Then I thought I heard what must be a badger or a fox or something moving in the rhododendrons. I'd just decided that it really must be a fox, when the bushes parted and Gerry looked out with a gun in his hand. I saw both him and the gun in the moonlight. I screamed and the gun went off. Steve dived for the ground – I thought he'd been hit – then Gerry ran off. I could hear him crashing through the bushes. I got to Steve as quickly as I could. Perhaps we should have tried to chase Gerry, but Steve was far too upset and I . . .' She broke off.

'Don't worry, Mrs Lewis,' said Rackham comfortingly. 'Speaking for myself, I'm glad you didn't decide to go after an armed man in the dark. You did exactly the right thing. Is Superintendent Clough around?'

'Yes, he's in the library,' she said leading the way. 'I'm glad you're here,' she repeated. 'I feel much safer now you're here.'

Superintendent Clough, a stocky man with a military moustache and an abrasive manner, couldn't add much to what Molly Lewis had told them. He and his men had searched the garden thoroughly without result. He was dubious of the wisdom of apparently leaving the way free for Carrington tomorrow but, as the Chief Constable had instructed him to offer every assistance to the Yard, he didn't have much choice but to agree. Nothing, however, could make him like it, and he couldn't refrain from giving the much younger Rackham some lessons, as he phrased it, in practical policing. He intended to spend the next day combing the area for Carrington. That, in his opinion, was how the man would be caught, not lying back supine and waiting for him to strike again. Local knowledge, he said, emphasizing his remarks with a strike of his fist on the table, was the key. The implication, which Rackham could hardly miss, was that although Scotland Yard had failed to find Carrington, he would.

It was two o'clock before Jack went to bed that night. Even though he was tired, a niggle of worry drew him to the bedroom window. Something – he didn't know what – wasn't right. The moonlight, chopped into fragments by the trees, bathed the house in shifting, shadowy, silver spears. And somewhere in those shadows was Carrington. Brilliant, rumpled, likable Carrington with a temper that flared like magnesium fired by a Bunsen burner. He frowned at the darkened garden once more and yawned. Something wasn't right.

Despite his late night, Jack was up early the next morning. The breakfast table was still being laid as he went into the morning room. Mrs Lewis, he was told by the housemaid, who was setting out the dishes on the sideboard, had also risen early and was in the garden somewhere.

It was a glorious summer's day. Jack walked down the steps from the terrace on to the dew-bright grass and felt in his pocket for his pipe. Molly Lewis, a wicker basket of roses in her hand, rounded the path at the bottom of the garden. He was just about to call her, when he heard the sound of a window being raised. He looked back at the house and saw Bill Rackham leaning out of an upstairs window, blinking in the sun.

'Jack? I thought it was you. Stay there, I'll come and join you.' By the time Bill came down, Jack, pipe drawing nicely, was deep in conversation with Molly Lewis.

'This is a lovely place,' said Rackham, once he'd answered her polite enquires as to how he had slept. He meant it. Stoke

Horam House was the epitome of Edwardian domestic comfort, a rich man's house, built of pale yellow sandstone, the glass of the windows silvered in the morning light.

Molly looked at the house and shuddered involuntarily. 'I used to love it. Dad did, too.' She pointed to the room at the end. 'That's where we found him.' She was quiet for a few moments. 'The flat's uninhabitable until the workmen have repaired the ceiling. We didn't have much choice, but I didn't want to come back here. Now I am back, I miss Dad more than ever.' She walked the sundial and stood, her hand resting lightly on the grey stone. 'I remember Hugo Ragnall and Steve standing here, the morning Gerry and Professor Carrington came.' She gave a little shudder. 'You couldn't guess, could you, what was going to happen? Poor Dad. Poor Hugo. I miss him. So does Steve.'

'Did your husband like Hugo Ragnall?' asked Jack curiously. He couldn't forget how Lewis had snapped at Ragnall for his unwanted sympathy about his uncle. The relationship, he thought, was a little more complicated than Mrs Lewis would have them believe.

'Of course he liked him,' she said warmly. Her mouth twisted in a rueful smile. 'When Dad was alive, Steve saw Hugo as a bit of a kindred spirit. If it wasn't for Steve, Hugo would have been sacked before he'd had time to unpack. I don't think Hugo had taken on board what Dad was really like. You had to be careful with my father, you know. I suppose he was a bit of an old tyrant, but he always meant well. He had this absolute thing about drink and gambling but Steve and I enjoyed an odd cocktail and the occasional trip to the races. Steve loves the races. Why shouldn't he? There was absolutely no harm in it, but Dad would have had a fit if he'd known. I knew Hugo Ragnall liked racing, too, and I'd warned him to keep quiet about it. Then, one day – it was last August and Hugo had only been here a week or so – this dreadful man turned up at the house. Fortunately Dad never got to hear about it. Hugo owed him some money for racing. It wasn't very much and Steve paid him off. Poor Hugo would've been in the soup, otherwise.' She stopped abruptly and, lighting a cigarette, pulled on it deeply. 'Dad had such strict rules. They seem so pointless now.' She smoked her cigarette for a little while in thoughtful silence. 'Poor Dad.' She shook herself briskly. 'I suppose you want to see where it all happened last night.'

She walked across the grass to where a stand of rhododendrons fringed the lawn with their polished green leaves and pointed to a path that ran along the bushes. 'This leads to the rose garden. I heard a noise and stopped to listen.' She went on a few paces. 'I was about here.'

The soft earth under the bushes was littered with freshly broken twigs and scuffed with footprints.

'Carrington didn't do all this,' said Rackham. 'This must have been Clough's men last night.'

They glanced up as Molly's name was called from the house. 'That's Steve,' said Molly. 'Do excuse me. I won't be long.'

'Lewis would provide a pretty easy target, standing on the terrace,' said Bill. 'Especially outlined by the light from the windows.'

'Yes,' agreed Jack, 'but it's about a hundred yards, I'd say. That's a long shot for a pistol. That's probably why he missed. I wonder how far back these bushes go?' He plunged in beneath the branches.

'Watch you don't step on any footprints,' called Rackham. 'It looks as if a herd of elephants has gone over it already without you making it worse.'

'Trust me,' called Jack from within the shrubbery, raising his voice to carry through the bushes. There was a loud rustling followed by a sharp cry. 'Ouch! I didn't see that twig. The damn thing got me in the ear. I'm glad these things don't have thorns. Hello! I've found the shell case.'

'I'll join you,' said Bill hastily.

'All right. I've marked the spot where I picked it up. Don't come through the bushes. I'm nearly out of them. Come round on the path and join me on the other side.'

Rackham rounded the corner of the rhododendrons to find Jack sitting on a rustic bench, checking something in a little book. 'What's that?'

'My diary,' said Jack, replacing it in his breast pocket. 'Bill, does anything strike you about the garden?'

Rackham looked at the rose garden, basking in the sun. It was a fine display with massed banks of red, yellow and white roses, set off by neatly-trimmed hedges marking out a grassy path which wound its way through the roses, circling round the stand of glossy rhododendrons back to the main lawn. A light breeze wafted the scent of the flowers towards them. Blue butterflies alighted on the petals like tiny chips of sapphire and a bumblebee hummed on its industrious round. 'Nothing much. What should strike me?'

Jack rubbed his chin with his thumb, leaving a smear of earth. 'I wondered why Gerard Carrington should sneak through the rhododendrons when there's a perfectly good path he could have taken.'

'He wanted to stay out of sight?' offered Rackham.

'But he could do that perfectly well by simply staying in the shadows beside the bushes. There'd be no need for him to sweat through the undergrowth. There's a couple of other things as well, such as . . .' He broke off as they heard Molly Lewis call to them. 'Let me talk to her on my own for a few minutes,' he said quietly. 'I've got an idea.'

'All right.' Rackham raised his voice. 'We're here, Mrs Lewis.'

She came round the bushes into the rose garden. All the worry of the previous night had returned. 'Steve's in a horrible mood,' she said. 'I'd like to apologize in advance. He's like a bear with a sore head this morning.' She looked at the two men. 'Have you found anything?'

'We've found a shell case,' said Jack.

From the house the breakfast gong sounded. Rackham looked up in unfeigned interest. He was hungry. 'I'll get back to the house,' he said.

'And I want to talk to Mrs Lewis about rhododendrons,' said Jack, taking her arm and walking across the lawn. 'You've got a fine display, haven't you? Now they're in flower, I mean. I like the pink and purple against that rich green, but they can be a bit oppressive at other times of the year, don't you think? Not that that would bother you here, because they're far enough away from the house for you not to feel hemmed in, but they can seem a bit encroaching. They grow wild in Spain, you know, and a whole hillside covered in them is a magnificent sight. Your roses are wonderful, too. Are you troubled with greenfly? Beastly nuisance, so I'm told, but it's quite good fun squirting them. I especially like those yellow ones you've got. You know, the ones which ramble over everything.'

She looked at him as if she thought that yellow roses weren't the only things in the garden which rambled. 'Major Haldean, what are you talking about?'

He bent his head towards her. 'I'm trying to put enough distance between us and Inspector Rackham so I can talk to you without being overheard.' He took her other arm and gently turned her to face him. 'You see, Mrs Lewis, I want to know why you made up that cock-and-bull story about Gerard Carrington.'

FIFTEEN

He felt the shudder of defeat running through her body. 'How did you guess?'

Jack shrugged. 'You said Carrington came out of the bushes beside you, but it's not so easy to creep through those bushes without making a row. I know, I've just done it. You said you heard something that could have been a fox, but I must've sounded more like an elephant, and that was in daylight. Why should Carrington come through the bushes? The path would have done just as well. And then there's the moon. We were late to bed last night, and when I looked out of my window, there was a brilliant moon, shining full on the house. We're facing east, so the moon could only have risen a short time before. I nearly twigged it last night and, when I looked in my pocket diary and it gave the time of moonrise as ten to midnight, I knew what it was. You said you'd seen Carrington at ten o'clock *in the moonlight*. And that was impossible. But why did you do it?'

She buried her face in her hands for a few moments. When she looked at him, her eyes were bright with unshed tears. 'I was scared. You can't guess how scared I've been. Ever since Dad died – before then even – I always seem to be on edge. I don't know why. I feel as if I'm haunted.'

'A ghost, you mean?'

She shook her head impatiently. 'No. You think I'm silly, don't you? But I can't rid myself of this dreadful feeling of foreboding. I've felt like this for the last couple of years. When Inspector Rackham telephoned me about that entry in the agony column, I was petrified. It said there was danger. Inspector Rackham thought I'd put it in, but I didn't.'

'Who did, then?

'Gerry?' she suggested helplessly. 'He always read *The Messenger*. We used to tease him about it. I think he was warning me to stay out of the way. There's *danger*, Major Haldean. I couldn't get Steve to take it seriously, but there's danger. I wanted him to get the police here tonight, but he

wouldn't. I wanted you to come, but he wouldn't hear of it. Despite everything that's happened, he couldn't really believe Gerry means any harm and that's stupid!' Her lip trembled. 'I liked Gerry. I liked him so much and . . . and . . .'
'He's in love with you, isn't he?' asked Jack softly.
She stared at him speechlessly for a second, and then tears did come, in great sobs that shook her body. Jack held her to him, cradling her head to his shoulder until she was quiet once more. She wiped her eyes and blew her nose on the handkerchief he gave her. 'Steve guessed,' she said miserably. 'Steve guessed how Gerry felt and he still wouldn't take the danger seriously. He refused point blank to ask for help. It sounds cruel, because I knew he'd have an awful fright, but I needed a reason to get the police here. That's why I did it. I screamed and fired the gun, and said I'd seen Gerry. I hid the gun in the bushes. No one found it and I picked it up this morning. It was in the basket of roses I was taking to the house when you saw me. I hoped the police would come but I didn't realize how much fuss there'd be. I never dreamed I'd be found out.'
'Does your husband know? What you did, I mean?'
She looked at him in horror. 'No, of course not. You won't tell him?'
Jack shook his head. 'Don't worry. I'll have to tell Inspector Rackham, though.' He took her hand. 'There's no need to be scared. He's an understanding man and very discreet.' And likely to be hopping mad, he added to himself. 'I actually think it was very resourceful of you. It worked, didn't it?'
'Perhaps it's worked too well,' she said bitterly. 'It's hit Steve in a rush. He's usually so strong and so capable. It's as if all his confidence has gone. He's in a beastly temper, too.' She dabbed her eyes with the handkerchief. 'I must look a sight,' she said, with a watery smile. 'I don't want breakfast, but I'll have to be there. All I really want is a cup of tea, a wash and some face powder.'
'Let's go back to the house,' said Jack, offering her his arm. 'I'm sure you can slip upstairs unnoticed. And don't worry,' he added, giving her arm a squeeze. 'If Carrington does come today, we'll be waiting for him.'

*   *   *

The only person in the morning room, much to Molly's relief, was Rackham, buried behind a newspaper and apparently uninterested in anything but the headlines and his eggs and bacon. With a muttered excuse she slipped out of the room and Jack, keeping his voice low, brought Bill up to date.

'She did *what?*' he said in disgust.

'She was scared, Bill.'

'I know, I know. You said.' Despite himself, he grinned. 'It's quite funny really, especially when I think it was that pompous ass, Superintendent Clough and his merry men, who were playing hide-and-seek in the garden.'

He broke off as Molly and Stephen Lewis came into the room. Molly was strung-up and nervy and it soon became obvious she hadn't exaggerated her husband's foul mood. She poured herself a cup of tea with shaky hands, clattering the cup on the saucer.

'Do you have to make so much noise?' snapped Lewis, standing beside the sideboard, plate in hand.

'I'm sorry, Steve,' she apologized. 'I'm feeling all to pieces this morning.' She turned to Jack. 'Would you like to see over the factory later on?'

Lewis stared at her. 'What are you talking about?'

'Dad always showed visitors round the factory,' said Molly with an overly bright smile. 'He expected people to take an intelligent interest in what we did.'

'For heaven's sake, Molly, Rackham and Haldean aren't here for the weekend! They're not ordinary guests.' Jack and Bill glanced at each other and tactfully concentrated on their bacon. 'They're here because I was nearly murdered last night.' He held the butter knife like a weapon. 'Murdered, do you hear?'

'We'll see you come to no harm, Mr Lewis,' said Rackham with exaggerated ease. He looked at Molly with a smile. 'I'd very much like to see the factory, but some other time, perhaps?'

'Let's keep up the pretence,' muttered Lewis, sitting down with a plate of scrambled eggs and sausages.

'I'll look forward to it,' said Molly, ignoring her husband.

'I always think of Otterbourne's as making wireless sets and gramophones,' said Jack, stepping in before Lewis could speak again, 'but you do more than that, don't you?'

'We did,' said Molly. 'Steve wants to concentrate on wireless and music, though, don't you, Steve?'

Lewis made a visible effort. 'It's where the money is.' He picked at the food on his plate. 'These sausages aren't up to much, are they? You'll have to speak to the cook, Molly. I don't know why she can't provide a decent breakfast.'

The sausages were, in fact, excellent, and judging from Molly's face, she was about to say as much. 'I've always wondered how a record was actually made,' said Jack, trying to prevent what looked like shaping up into a real row.

With a glance at her husband, who had subsided into a very charged silence, Molly took up the conversational baton. 'We start with the musicians, of course. The studio's in London, and that's where the master recording is made. It's recorded on to a plaster disk, and that's brought here, to the factory, where it's electroplated.'

'Fascinating,' grunted Lewis morosely. 'You should do a talk on the wireless.'

'Once it's electroplated,' continued Molly with an edge to her voice, 'we press it into wax, take a copper electro and nickel-plate it. That's what we use to press the actual record. If it's a brand new recording, we issue it as a single-sided record. We only do double-sided recordings of pieces that have already been issued. We've got lots to choose from. We've got a whole library of master recordings, going back years.'

'It all sounds more complicated than I realized,' said Rackham, picking up his toast.

'It's always been done like that,' said Molly. 'Steve's an expert but he thinks the whole business needs shaking up, don't you, Steve?'

He drew a deep breath and tried hard. 'You know I do.'

'The sound is tinny,' continued Molly, trying hard. 'It didn't matter before wireless, but the quality of sound on the wireless is so good, it makes conventional recordings sound outdated, which is where Gerry's machine comes in . . .' she stopped, biting off her words.

Lewis put down his knife with a thump and buried his head in his hands. 'Gerry! It all comes back to Gerry, doesn't it!'

'Please, Steve,' pleaded Molly.

Lewis abruptly stopped. 'Sorry,' he muttered.

Molly, her cheeks flushed, picked up her tea, clattering the cup once more. She was so edgy that even Jack felt his nerves fray and, although he didn't like the man's temper, he wasn't particularly surprised when Lewis turned on her. 'For God's sake, Molly, can't you do anything right?'

Molly's head jerked back. There was an arctic silence as husband and wife faced each other. Molly put the cup down and stared at her husband, a furious gleam in her eyes.

Jack and Bill squirmed in embarrassed silence. 'Steve,' said Molly in a voice as sharp as the cut of a whip. 'Kindly control your temper.'

His shoulders went back, and he then made an obvious effort. 'I'm sorry.' He dropped his gaze and ran a hand through his hair. 'I really am sorry. I hardly slept last night.' He pushed his plate away and reached for the toast rack. 'Those sausages are foul.' He buttered his toast absently and stretched out a hand for the marmalade and jam glasses in their silver holder. 'It's worse than the war, waiting to go over the top. At least in the war, everyone was in the same boat and you knew where the enemy was.' He spooned some jam on to his toast and looked at it blankly. 'What the devil's this?'

'Jam, Steve,' said Molly thinly. 'Raspberry jam.'

Lewis looked at her blankly. 'Jam? *Jam?* That's the final straw.' He pushed his plate away with loathing. 'I can't stand jam. You know that. I never eat fruit with pips in. Never. It makes me ill. You know that. I hate all these bits of berries. Why on earth did you tell the servants to put jam on the table?'

Molly took a deep breath and glanced at her guests as if seeking moral support. 'I had it put there in case anyone else wanted it.' Her voice took on an artificially bright Mother-knows-best tone. 'We have to think of others, Steve.'

Although Jack disliked Lewis's moodiness, he couldn't help feeling a touch of sympathy for the man. If his nerves were in shreds and he'd had a lousy night, the last thing he'd want was to be addressed – especially in front of guests – as a sulky and recalcitrant three-year-old at a Sunday school treat. 'I know you don't like it,' continued Molly in her 'Now, children,' voice, 'but other people might. Just get yourself some more toast, Steve, and don't make such a fuss.'

'*Fuss?*' It was all he said but his look spoke volumes.

'Could I have some more coffee, please?' asked Rackham,

passing her his cup. He'd seen Lewis's expression, too, thought Jack.

Molly poured him another coffee, obviously glad of the distraction. 'Steve?' she asked. 'Would you like some more?' 'Yes, all right.' He took the cup and frowned. 'This coffee's nearly cold. I can't stand cold coffee.' He pushed back his chair impatiently. 'I'm going to the study.' And I don't blame you, thought Jack. 'Molly, ask for some coffee to be sent in, will you? Hot coffee *if* you don't mind,' he added, obviously trying to grab back some authority.

He left the room, much to everyone's relief. Molly stood up. 'I'm so sorry,' she said. 'I feel dreadful, especially as it's my fault. I'd better go and see to his coffee right away. I really am sorry. I can't apologize enough.'

'Don't mind us,' said Jack, getting up and opening the door for her. 'You acted for the best.' He closed the door behind her.

'Whew!' said Bill, throwing down his napkin. 'Have you ever seen anyone in a worse mood?'

'I thought they just about drew on points,' said Jack. 'I must admit I had a sneaking sympathy for Lewis.'

Bill looked at him in astonishment. 'You must be joking! I've heard plenty about Carrington's temper but it obviously runs in the family. It's just as well he doesn't know last night's affair was a phoney. I felt blinkin' sorry for Mrs Lewis.'

'I know that,' said Jack. 'I was afraid you were going to stick your oar in at one point. It's just as well you didn't. I knew you were itching to leap to her defence.'

'What if I was?' muttered Bill. 'I can't stand hearing a woman being spoken to like that.'

'You're a chivalrous beggar.'

'Rubbish,' said Bill, colouring in embarrassment.

'It's not rubbish, it's true,' said Jack, reaching for the marmalade. 'I mean, take this business. I'd say the one death that really got to you was Mrs Tierney's.'

'What d'you expect?' said Rackham, slightly abashed. 'That's not chivalry, or anything fancy like that, it's a normal human emotion. I'd defy anyone to look at that poor woman, lying all alone in that ghastly mortuary, without being moved. Colonel Willoughby's death was probably unintentional and Andrew Dunbar and Hugo Ragnall were, perhaps, the result of hot blood, but Mrs Tierney? What excuse can there be?

And to sit here and listen to poor Mrs Lewis being spoken to like that after all she's been though, really did take the biscuit. I can't say I wholeheartedly approve of what she did last night, but she was acting for the best, even if she hasn't got any thanks for it. And, I have to say, it was very cleverly done. It never occurred to me that a lady like Mrs Lewis could be telling bouncers. She fooled me, all right.'

Jack didn't answer.

'I didn't take to Superintendent Clough, I must say,' Bill continued, 'but I'd be honestly glad to hear that he had managed to track down Carrington, even if I'd never hear the last of it.' He broke off and looked at his friend. 'Are you listening? You seem miles away.'

Jack, piece of toast halfway to his mouth, knew Bill was speaking but he didn't register the words. Like a searchlight in the fog, he had an idea, an idea so fantastic it seemed to knock the legs from under him. A big idea, perhaps the wrong idea, but an idea. And if he was right, it explained so much. But if he was right, then . . . 'She would have known. *She would have known!*' He didn't know he had spoken out loud.

'What the devil's wrong?' asked Bill.

Jack put down the piece of toast with painful precision. He sat completely still for an appreciable time, then shook himself like a man climbing on to a rock from the water. He turned to his friend. 'Bill, have you got Hector Ferguson's fingerprints?'

'*Ferguson's* fingerprints?' repeated Rackham, puzzled. He stared at Jack. 'What the dickens do you want Ferguson's prints for?'

'Have you got them?'

'They're on file at the Yard.'

'Can I get to see them?' said Jack, standing up. 'If I run up to London, I mean?'

'Yes, of course you can, but you can't leave now. What about Carrington?'

'I'll be back long before half past nine. Tell Mrs Lewis I had an urgent appointment in town but don't mention Ferguson. Come out to the car with me and I'll tell you what I've got in mind.'

It was late afternoon before Jack arrived back in Stoke Horam. He was shown into the library where there was evidently a conference in progress. Molly and Stephen Lewis were sitting at the table with Superintendent Clough and Bill Rackham. Lewis looked up as the butler announced him and, getting to his feet, came forward with his hand outstretched and a rather hangdog expression.

'Look, Haldean, I want to apologize. About this morning, I mean. I was in a foul mood but I know that's no excuse.'

'That's all right,' said Jack, returning the handshake. 'Don't mention it.'

It's good of you to take it so well,' said Lewis with an embarrassed smile. 'Molly pointed out to me exactly how unacceptable I was and, quite honestly, I felt like a heel when I realized how I'd behaved. I tried to find you to say as much, but was told you'd gone up to London.'

'Yes, it was an appointment I couldn't get out of,' said Jack, smoothly. 'It was a beastly nuisance but it couldn't be helped.'

'If Carrington keeps his appointment, we've got him,' said Superintendent Clough, twisting the ends of his moustache. 'Half nine in the summer house. By jingo, I hope he turns up. I've just been running through the disposition I've made of the men.'

'It's a simple enough plan, Jack,' said Rackham. 'The idea is that Mrs Lewis sits in the summer house from about half eight onwards and stays there, apparently alone. There will, of course, be policemen and the menservants lying in wait. If he comes, we'll get him.'

Jack nodded. 'We'll get him, all right. I don't want to sound overly dramatic, but I think it's a matter of life and death. We have to lay hands on Carrington. That's urgent.'

Rackham turned back to Superintendent Clough who was *harrumphing* quietly to himself. 'Superintendent?'

'I wanted,' said the Superintendent with an unfriendly glare at Rackham, 'to have two men in the summer house itself and I still think that's the best plan, eh, what?'

'And I think it would give the game away before we started,' said Rackham firmly. 'Carrington isn't a fool.'

The Superintendent snorted. 'If you say so. What I cannot approve of is the notion that Mrs Lewis should calmly sit in the summer house, waiting for this feller to make an appearance. I really cannot countenance the thought of you putting yourself in harm's way, dear lady.'

'I won't be in any danger,' said Molly quietly. 'Gerry wouldn't harm me.'

The Superintendent sighed. 'Mr Lewis, I appeal to you, sir!'

'The trouble is,' said Lewis slowly, 'is that I'm inclined to agree with Molly. I don't know if Gerry would harm her or not, but if he can't see her, he won't come near the place. But one thing I don't agree with is your idea that I should stay in the house while all this is happening in the garden.'

'Now, Steve . . .' began Molly.

'No.' He stuck his hands in his pockets and smiled ruefully at her. 'I didn't make such a good showing of myself last night, I know. What I should have done is collared him there and then, but I didn't. I'm damned if I'm going to sit calmly in the house while everyone, including my wife, fights my battles on my behalf.' Molly Lewis looked guilt-stricken. Fortunately, Lewis misinterpreted her expression. 'Don't be worried, Molly. You'll be in no danger, as long as I'm there. Don't you agree, Superintendent?'

'I can certainly see your point of view, Mr Lewis. If I were in your position, I'd feel much the same myself. Inspector?'

'It's your house, Mr Lewis,' said Rackham. 'I can't tell you what to do.'

'Good,' said Lewis briskly. He patted his arm and winced. 'That's the second pot shot he's taken at me. I've got a score to settle with cousin Gerry.'

Molly bit her lip and Jack knew she was trembling on the verge of telling the truth.

'We can't take any chances after last night,' he said quickly. Molly still looked uncomfortable. 'It's not just for your sake, Lewis, but everyone will be better off once we get Carrington behind bars. Last night was unfortunate, but it's perhaps worked out for the best. After all, if it wasn't for that, *we wouldn't be here*.'

Molly heard the emphasis and gave him a glance of sheer gratitude. 'Perhaps he won't come,' she said. 'I'm going to my room.'

She was back downstairs in a matter of minutes. 'This was on my dressing-table,' she said shakily, holding out an envelope. Frowning, Rackham stepped forward and took it from her hand. It contained a sheet of paper torn from a small notebook with a single line of writing. As Rackham read it, he swore involuntarily.

I'll be there. Gerry.

The effect of that single sentence was to throw the house into uproar. The servants, said Lewis, had to be in league with Gerard Carrington. Half an hour later, Winnie and Ellen, the kitchen-maids, were in tears, Hamilton, the butler, and Eckersley, the chauffeur, were stiff with fury, the rest of the female staff were veering between outrage and hysteria and Mrs Bassingham, the cook, never, as she said, having been spoken to like that in all her born days, had given notice.

Lewis, white with anger, threatened to sack every one of them, until Superintendent Clough and Bill Rackham, who were, for once, of the same mind, pointed out that tonight of all nights, Lewis needed the help of the servants. It took some heavy tact from Molly and the promise of a substantial rise in wages before things simmered down but, unsurprisingly, the dinner was sparse and badly served and it was a relief when it was over.

One suspicion that Jack had nurtured he was able to lay to rest. Molly Lewis had not written the note. After a few minutes with her alone, he was convinced it really had come from Carrington but that, in the face of the servants' denials, which he also believed, meant only one thing. Gerard Carrington had, somehow, got into the house. Rackham, together with Clough and his men, hunted through the house and grounds without success.

As Jack took up his position in the garden at half eight that evening, he looked back at the house. It wouldn't be difficult to enter. The garage stood clear of the house, separated by a narrow passageway from the laundry, carpenter's shop and gardeners' room which were attached to the main building and formed a single-storey block with a gently sloping roof.

The passageway was a tradesman's entrance, closed by a solid wooden door locked with a key, but it wouldn't take much for an agile man to heave himself up on the door and climb up on the roof. Then, by means of the ornamental balcony that ran beneath the bedrooms, he could easily gain entrance through an open window. There was an open sash window at the end of the upstairs corridor that would do nicely

but really, once a man was on the roof, he had plenty of
choice. As for the ground floor – well, there were three sets
of French windows at the back of the house and both they
and the doors had been open, in this hot weather, all day. All
it needed was nerve.

He had prepared himself for a long wait but the time seemed
endless. Half past nine came and went, dusk ripened into darkness, and only the firefly glow of Molly Lewis's cigarette a
hundred yards away showed any sign of life in the summer
house.

And then he heard it. Molly's voice rang clear through the
summer night. 'You're here!'

Instantly, lights flared out. Jack hurled himself towards them
as police lanterns bobbed and swung across the grass as
Clough's men ran forward. He had a brief sight of Carrington's
face, caught in the glare, then Lewis ran across the grass from
the other side, wildly firing shot after shot from his automatic.
Rackham shouted, Clough yelled, but by the time they got to
the summer house, Carrington had gone.

'He's there!' screamed Molly, pointing to the house. 'Steve's
after him!'

Jack, with Bill close behind, thudded across the lawn to
the open French windows and into the house. There was
plenty of noise in the garden but here, in the morning room,
was silence. They went through to the hall and stood,
listening. From outside came the shouts of the police, but
surely there were sounds from up above? There was the
creak of a floorboard, a series of thumps and then a yell of
savage triumph.

They ran up the stairs to see Lewis and Carrington grap-
pling furiously on the landing. Lewis still had his gun but
Carrington had tight hold of his arm, forcing it upwards. At
the end of the landing was the open sash window. Carrington
wrenched a hand free, slammed it against Lewis's throat and
made a sudden dash for the window. Lewis fell back, choking,
his hand to his throat, cannoning into Bill. Jack pushed past
him in time to see Carrington drop down to the sloping roofs
of the outbuildings. He followed Carrington out of the
window, his feet slipping on the slate of the roof. Behind
him he could hear Rackham call. 'Watch it, Jack, he's got
a gun!'

Carrington, poised on the roof, turned to face him, gun in hand. 'Come and get me.'

'Don't be an idiot,' said Jack levelly. He started forward, balancing on the sloping roof. Carrington screwed up his eyes and fired. Jack threw himself to one side as the bullet zinged off the slates.

Carrington, caught off-balance by the recoil of the gun, flailed at the air wildly and fell, clattering down the roof. Jack missed his footing and sprawled full length on the slates, scrabbling frantically with his hands. He half fell, half rolled down the roof, as three more shots, this time from the window, cracked out. He grabbed wildly for the gutter, his body lurching over the edge. He knew Bill was shouting but couldn't make out the words. The wood of the gutter was slippery with moss and mud. He felt it crumble under his fingers, then it gave way and he fell.

The drop must have been about twelve feet but the gutter had saved him from a headlong plunge. He staggered against the wall of the garage, the breath knocked out of his body. He was in the tradesman's entrance, a well of darkness. Because of the angle of the roof, he couldn't see the open window above but he could hear the furious argument between Rackham and Lewis. From the garden on the other side of the house came the shouts of Clough's men, but here, in the passage, there was only the sound of breathing.

Winded, Jack tried to speak, but could only manage a croak. He heard a shout and the crunch of a blow from above, then a huge noise as someone slid down the roof. A shape hung from the gutter for a moment, then the weakened gutter gave way altogether in a cracking of wood and a rain of splinters and mud. There was an agonized cry, followed by the whimper of a groan.

Jack, his chest like fire as his breath returned, struck a match. Carrington was standing against the garage wall, gun in hand. Lewis was lying at the end of the passage, crumpled against the wooden door. Jack, from behind Carrington, saw the terrified gleam in Lewis's eyes as Carrington raised his gun.

Jack started forward, grabbing Carrington's arm as he fired. The bullet ricocheted from the walls in a terrifying whine of sound. Carrington twisted in his grasp and broke free. Jack propelled forward, fell in front of Lewis, covering him with his body. Getting to his knees and gasping for breath, he struck another match.

'Haldean!' It was Carrington. 'Get out of my way. I don't want to hurt you.'

Jack got to his feet and shook his head dumbly.

Carrington's gun was levelled at his chest. 'If you don't move, I'm going to shoot you.'

Jack's eyes met his in the last of the match's light. Carrington's head went back as if he'd been struck. Jack tried hard and managed to speak. He wished he could see Carrington's face, but he was only a black shape against the gloom of the passage. 'I'm walking towards you. Give me the gun.'

'I'll kill you!' The words were hardly audible.

'Then kill me.'

There was a sound like a sob. Jack reached forward and took the gun from Carrington's unresisting hand. A noise behind him made him whirl and, kicking out, he sent Lewis's automatic flying.

'You shouldn't have done that,' said Lewis wearily. 'It'd be better if I shot him. He's going to *hang*.'

Jack delivered the unresisting Carrington into the care of Superintendent Clough. He talked to Carrington, a soothing flow of words, but the man was sunk in complete apathy. He didn't think Carrington had heard anything of what he'd said.

'Good work, Major Haldean!' boomed Superintendent Clough enthusiastically, rubbing his hands together. 'My word, I'll be glad to have this chap under lock and key and no mistake!'

'Make sure he's treated properly,' warned Jack. 'Inspector Rackham and I will be along to see him later. Can you get hold of a doctor? Mr Lewis fell off the roof. I think he's crocked his ankle. He's in the passage by the garage. See someone attends to him, will you? I wouldn't be surprised if Inspector Rackham needed some attention as well. I'm not sure, but I think he's a bit worse for wear. He's on the upstairs landing.'

He went into the house where he found Bill coming groggily down the stairs, clutching the banister with one hand and holding his jaw with the other. 'That bloody idiot, Lewis, laid me out,' he said. 'He fetched me the dickens of a wallop and I hit my head against the wall. I was trying to stop him loosing off with that damn gun of his.' He blinked at Jack. 'Did we get Carrington?'

'Safe and sound. Come and sit down, Bill. You look all in. Superintendent Clough can see to anything that needs doing.'

Bill sank into a chair in the hall with a groan. 'So it's over,' he said distantly.

'For the time being, yes,' answered Jack.

'For the time being?' asked Rackham with a groan, propping his forehead on his hand. 'What happens next?'

'I need to have a talk with Hector Ferguson,' said Jack. 'But that can wait till tomorrow.'

SIXTEEN

'In my opinion, Lewis,' said Hector Ferguson earnestly, 'it would be a crying shame not to carry on with Carrington's work.'

It was three days after Gerard Carrington's arrest. Stephen Lewis and Hector Ferguson were sitting in the bar of Goodyers, Lewis's club in St James. Hector Ferguson, his whisky completely ignored, was enthusiastically leafing through diagrams. 'I was in Scotland yesterday,' he said. 'My chief engineer's absolutely aching to complete this improved version of the machine. These diagrams are copies, you understand? He's got the originals and, based on what Carrington's already done, he's confident he can have a working machine ready within the fortnight.' He hunched forward in excitement. 'Just think of it, Lewis. In two weeks' time – *two weeks!* – we can change the future of recorded sound. However, I don't want to proceed without your agreement. Carrington's your cousin, after all, and I suppose, not to put too fine a point on it, you are his next of kin.'

'Meaning?'

'Meaning that unless Carrington's made other arrangements, you'll inherit his property.'

Lewis drew back as if stung. 'For heaven's sake, Ferguson, that's pretty cold-blooded. He's not dead.'

Ferguson sucked his cheeks in. 'Can you not treat the situation with a degree of what I might call . . .' He coughed and suddenly looked very uncomfortable. He was obviously choosing his words carefully. 'With intelligent anticipation, Lewis? There's no point avoiding facts. Carrington's been arrested.' He drew his finger across his throat. 'Is there really a chance of any other outcome?'

Lewis looked at him with an appalled expression. 'But even so, man, I can't just wade in and help myself to his property. God knows, Carrington's put me through the mill. If it wasn't for Haldean he would have shot me the other night.'

'So I understand,' agreed Ferguson.

'But even so, it seems wrong. I don't dispute what you're saying, but wouldn't it be more . . . more seemly, I suppose, to wait?'

'And if we do wait,' said Ferguson, hunching forward, 'there's every chance we'll be pipped at the post.' He tapped the table firmly. 'Electrical recording is the next move forward. We're not the only people who are developing this sort of system. The Americans are nearly there and so are the Germans and the Danes. And you know as well as I do that there aren't many prizes for coming second. The winner will scoop the pool and there's a lot of money to be made.'

Lewis took a deep breath and lit a cigarette. 'OK,' he said eventually. 'Let's say, for argument's sake, I agree. I want to be involved.' He raised his eyebrows sardonically. 'As Carrington's next of kin, I should be.'

'And will. Don't worry about that.'

'All right. Who will own the new machine?' asked Lewis cautiously. 'The legal tangle about ownership is a nightmare.'

Ferguson waved the legal tangle to one side, nearly knocking the ashtray off the table. 'That doesn't matter! Well,' he added, seeing Lewis's face, 'of course it does, but it's a secondary consideration. Oddly enough, Haldean asked me the same thing. He wanted to know who owned the rights and how close the machine was to production.'

Lewis drew back. 'What did you tell him?'

'I said who owned what was a very moot point, but in any case it would be some time before the machine could be sold commercially.'

'That's true enough,' said Lewis. 'It'll take some time to set up a production line. This question of ownership really does need to be thrashed out, though. Let me get this straight. You've still got Professor Carrington's original machine, yes?'

'No,' said Ferguson unexpectedly. 'As I said, I was in Falkirk yesterday. I had the Professor's original machine, complete with all the ribbons and various bits and pieces boxed up and sent to you at Stoke Horam. It should arrive today.'

Lewis choked on his whisky. 'Why?'

'Why not? As a matter of fact, you have Haldean to thank for it. It was his idea.'

Lewis's eyebrows shot up. '*Haldean's* idea? What, that you should send me Professor Carrington's machine?'

'And all the bits and pieces, yes.'

Lewis blinked in bewilderment. 'But why? Don't mis-understand me, Ferguson, I'm grateful. I really am grateful, but what the dickens has Haldean got to do with it?'

'Nothing, as such. As I say, he came to see me, principally, as far as I could make out, to see if Dunbar's owed Carrington any money. He thought it could go towards Carrington's defence. At least,' he added in a dissatisfied voice, 'that's what he said.'

'What else could he want?'

'I don't really know,' said Ferguson with a shrug. 'He asked me a dickens of a lot of questions about my stepfather, that's for sure.' He laughed nervously. 'I didn't really care for his manner. I know Carrington's your cousin, Lewis, but I won't be sorry when it's all over.' He caught Lewis's expression and looked away. 'Anyway, I told Haldean that Dunbar's didn't owe Carrington anything but he knew about the machine, of course. I mentioned the Professor and his connection with Dunbar's. I showed him the Professor's original machine and said I didn't really know what to do with it. He wasn't really interested, I could tell, but I asked him for his advice and he suggested sending it to you. I don't know if he meant it – he was quite offhand – but I thought, why not? I'll be frank, Lewis. I wanted to convince you that I was a trustworthy person to work with and I thought, however offhand Haldean had been, it wasn't a bad idea.'

'Well, I'm very pleased to have it, of course. You do realize that I could go ahead and develop it myself?'

'That's the chance I took,' said Ferguson earnestly. 'The Professor's machine is a wonderful achievement, there's no two ways about it, but it's a pig of a thing to operate. Take the ribbons, for instance. They're so awkward to use they'd drive any customer up the wall. In the new version the ribbons are encased in a holder and are easy to handle. The old ones won't work on the new machine, but that's not a problem. We'll simply make new ones. What d'you say, Lewis? Let me complete Carrington's work.'

'I must say I'm tempted,' admitted Lewis.

Ferguson brightened visibly. 'You won't regret it.' He spread his hands out encouragingly. 'We can talk about the finer points of ownership afterwards. The great thing is to have a working machine up and running. If you're still interested in a merger, it's something I'd like to do.'

Lewis ran his finger thoughtfully round the top of his glass. 'It makes sense to proceed, I must say. Quite apart from the huge technical advance, Otterbourne's has taken such a battering that we do need a new product. What about your mother, though? What's her opinion? After all, she owns the company.'

'My mother's happy to let me have my head,' said Ferguson. 'She doesn't want to be bothered with business. You can take it I'm speaking for her. There won't be any trouble.'

Lewis picked up his whisky and drank it reflectively. 'Let's do it,' he said eventually.

'Excellent,' said Ferguson happily, boxing his papers together. 'I'll go ahead and you should hear from me very shortly. I've just taken the lease on a new recording studio. It's in Bridle Lane, Soho. Why don't we meet up there? Under the circumstances, with Carrington and all, it's perhaps inappropriate to give a party, but we should mark the event in some way. I know my mother's interested and she really should be there. Why don't you bring Mrs Lewis? I'll provide cocktails and so on.'

'I'll look forward to it,' said Lewis with a very satisfied smile. 'And I'll look forward to hearing from you soon.'

Molly sipped her cocktail and looked round Hector Ferguson's new studio. It seemed odd, in a way, that the whole evening should be focused on the two modest wooden boxes sitting on the table. Those wooden boxes were, she knew, *It*. The new machine, the Big Advance, the Great Step Forward, as Steve had enthusiastically described it. Ever since he had agreed to Dunbar's producing the new machine a couple of weeks ago, Steve had been like a different person. He had, he said, something genuinely to look forward to. Otterbourne's would merge with Dunbar's and they would have an unbeatable product.

The worry that had clouded him, the worry that had plagued him ever since he received that telegram about his uncle, had vanished. Quite simply, Steve was fun to be with once more.

His arm encircled her waist. 'Shall we dance?' he said, his

mouth close to her ear. The gramophone – a Dunbar's gramophone naturally – was playing a foot-tapping American song, *Do It Again!* 'Or shall I take on Mrs Dunbar?'

'Dance with Mrs Dunbar if you must dance,' she said with a giggle.

'Beast,' he said softly. 'She creaks when she moves. I think she needs oiling.'

'I think she wears corsets. Mrs Dunbar,' she called, turning, 'my husband was wondering if you would care to dance.'

'Molly!' said Steve in apprehension, then moulded his features into a smile as Mrs Dunbar bore down on them.

'That's very kind of you, I'm sure,' said Mrs Dunbar, 'but later, perhaps?' Steve's sigh of relief was so heartfelt it tickled Molly's ear. She gave him a warning nudge with her elbow. He grinned and slipped away to refresh his glass.

'What do you think of Hector's new studio?' asked Mrs Dunbar. 'He's been so busy up in Scotland that he hasn't been able to spend much time here, but he assures me it will become a centre for this new music he's so fond of.'

Molly knew all about Hector Ferguson's ideas for his studio. He had treated her to an account of his plans whilst mixing her a White Lady. He had spoken at some length. The new studio was, in fact, nothing more than an empty room in Soho, with a cloakroom and two box rooms. According to Ferguson, it was ideally placed to lure the hottest jazz musicians from the clubs. They would clamour, he said, to be recorded. They were, apparently, standing in what would be the dynamic heart of jazz.

The odd thing was that she had heard Hector Ferguson on the subject of jazz before and he had overwhelmed her with his enthusiasm. On this occasion, in his new studio with his new recording machine, when he had every reason to be on top of the world, he sounded flat and uninterested. He had said the words, yes, but there was no passion behind them. She shot a glance to where he was standing, back against the wall, smoking a cigarette. He was staring at Major Haldean. He's *nervous*, she thought with sudden insight, looking at the way he pulled on his cigarette. The man's alive with nerves.

With an effort, she dragged her attention back to Mrs Dunbar. What had she been talking about? Oh yes. 'Mr Ferguson's ideas sound very interesting,' she said, adding politely, 'I do

like the decorations.' Mrs Dunbar, she knew, had been the force
behind the Chinese lanterns, roses and wreaths of glossy green
leaves that adorned the newly painted white walls.

'It makes it more of an occasion,' said Mrs Dunbar in a
satisfied way. 'I wanted Hector to hire a couple of waiters,
but he said he didn't want anyone to know about this new
machine until he and your husband were ready to demonstrate
it to the Press. Hector says that the publicity will have to be
handled very carefully, with Mr Carrington being . . .'

Molly felt as if a hand had gripped her heart. She knew
her face betrayed her. She saw Mrs Dunbar's expression change
and heard her voice falter.

Gerry! she thought bleakly. Damn Gerry. Despite everything,
she couldn't get him out of her mind. Life should be good but
not an hour passed that she didn't think of Gerry. And it was
so unfair to Steve. He deserved better. She had tried – really
tried – to forget Gerry, to give the man she was actually married
to the wholehearted attention he deserved. Steve couldn't ever
really appreciate how mixed her feelings were. One feeling she
had isolated was anger, that burning resentment of betrayed
trust. She had *believed* in Gerry. Once before, when he had
been accused of murder – the murder of this woman's husband,
she reminded herself – she had clung passionately to the belief
he was innocent and rejoiced when he was free. Steve had tried
to warn her, but she hadn't wanted to listen. 'I'm sorry,' she
managed to say. 'Please, do carry on.'

'The circumstances are so difficult, aren't they?' said Mrs
Dunbar lamely. 'What does your husband think, my dear?'
she added with an attempt at brightness.

Molly felt as if she'd reached some firm ground in the
shifting sand of her emotions. 'Steve? He hasn't really talked
about it,' she said, looking across the room to where Steve,
his thick fair hair streaked with red light from the Chinese
lanterns, had strolled across to Major Haldean.

Mrs Dunbar glanced about her conspiratorially. 'I was so
grateful to your husband, Mrs Lewis,' she said in hushed tones.
'I know he was instrumental in freeing Hector from that awful
suspicion. I have never felt so desperate in all my life as that
terrible night Hector was arrested. When he was freed, it was
as if I'd come to life again. I can never thank your husband
enough for what he did.' She reached out and held Molly's

arm confidingly. 'I know you have endured a great deal, my dear, but you have a lot to be grateful for.'

And that, presumably, was Mrs Dunbar's tactfully clumsy way of referring to Dad. No one would ever forget what her father had done. How could they, when he had made such a parade of his virtues? She suddenly remembered when she was very small and Dad was very big, a sunlit memory of Dad in the garden. He'd thrown her up in the air with a shout of laughter. Her mother's voice: *Charles, don't drop her!* Molly, helpless with joy, trusted Daddy would catch her and he had. She'd always trusted him until the ghastly truth had poisoned all her memories. That was when the anger had begun. When she had first found out what her father had really been like.

'It'll be much better when Mr Carrington is convicted,' said Mrs Dunbar with brutal sympathy. 'We can forget all about it then.'

Molly suddenly couldn't take any more of Mrs Dunbar. 'Yes, yes, I'm sure we shall,' she lied, backing away. 'Excuse me, I want a word with Steve.'

But Steve, to her dismay, was also talking about Gerry. 'The whole family always had some sort of mental kink, I'm afraid,' he was saying to Major Haldean. 'It's a real pity when you consider how brilliant the Professor was. And Gerry too.'

She saw Major Haldean frown warningly as she approached. Irrationally, she resented the fact that he didn't want to talk about Gerry in front of her. For heaven's sake, what did she want? *I want it all to be different,* a voice deep inside whispered. She was like a child crying for a broken doll, she thought in disgust. She didn't just want the doll to be mended; she wanted it never to have broken at all. She wanted Dad to be good and Gerry to be innocent and it was stupid and she was a gullible fool to have trusted them. Even now, there was a traitorous spark of hope. *Fool!*

'I'm looking forward to seeing this machine put through its paces,' said Major Haldean. He welcomed her into their little group with a smile. 'When Ferguson invited me, I jumped at the chance.'

'Why doesn't he show it to us?' asked Molly fretfully. Once Ferguson had played the wretched machine, they could all go home and she could stop pretending not to mind so very much.

'Let's chivvy him on,' said Steve. He raised his voice and called across the room. 'Ferguson! When are you going to demonstrate our new machine? We're all waiting.'

Ferguson threw his cigarette to the floor and crushed it out with his foot. Molly saw him consciously take a deep breath and straighten himself up. 'I'll do it now,' he said, walking to the table.

The two varnished wooden boxes on the table were approximately eighteen inches high and two feet long, connected to each other by a wire. The front of the second box was faced with fretwork bands covering a thin mesh. Beside them was the Dunbar's gramophone.

Ferguson lifted the needle from the record player and the room fell silent. 'First of all, thank you all for coming,' said Ferguson. 'I hope you all enjoyed the music.'

Beside her, she was suddenly aware that Major Haldean was standing very still. He was concentrating on Ferguson. She clenched her fists involuntarily. The pools of light from the lanterns shadowed his face and coloured his shirt red against his black jacket. Black and red: the colours of a pantomime devil. But he was so *intent*. This wasn't a pantomime . . .

Haldean was on edge about Ferguson and something was badly wrong. He was waiting with so much pent-up stillness she was irresistibly reminded of a hungry cat beside a fishpond. Waiting for the kill.

Ferguson cleared his throat. 'The quality of sound from this gramophone is about as good as can be achieved with any model currently on sale. It simply doesn't measure up to the wireless, does it?'

His carelessness was assumed, she was certain of it.

He patted the larger of the two boxes. 'However, this is the new machine. The second box takes the place of the horn. In my opinion the sound is even better that the wireless. I'll play it and you'll be able to hear for yourselves the radical difference.'

'I hope there *is* a difference after all the trouble you've been to, Hector,' said Mrs Dunbar with a grating laugh. She sounded on edge. She'd sensed that indefinable threat of danger in the atmosphere too. 'It looks very much like an ordinary gramophone to me.'

'Not when you look inside,' said Ferguson. He lifted up the

lid. 'You'll see the difference between this and a gramophone or phonograph. There's no turntable or cylinder but only these two spindles on which the ribbons are placed.' He picked up a small round Bakelite case from the table and drew out a coil of flat wire on to his hand. 'I recorded this earlier,' he said, fixing the case and wire on to the spindles.

Molly suddenly realized just how nervous Ferguson was. His hand, as he reached out to press the button on the machine, trembled. Beside her, Major Haldean drew his breath in.

The sound of a jazz piano, played with considerable flair, filled the room.

Molly felt it was a complete anti-climax. She had expected . . . *What?* Something else. Ferguson was really keyed-up, but all that was actually happening was a group of people listening to a piano. She shook her head in irritation and tried to concentrate on the sound. It really was very life-like.

Even though she wasn't in a receptive mood, Molly could appreciate the clarity of the reproduction. Dad would have loved it, she thought involuntarily and winced. Dad would have loved Gerry's machine. That was a nasty little refinement of irony. There was admiration in the faces round her. She tried very hard to mirror that emotion.

'It's astonishing,' said Jack Haldean with what seemed like genuine admiration. He was a very good actor, thought Molly. His attention was still fixed on Ferguson. 'The piano could be in the same room. What is it? *The Alligator Hop*?'

Ferguson ran his tongue over his dry lips. 'That's right. The original's by King Oliver's Creole Jazz Band. It's one of my favourites. But what do you think of the sound? It's easily as good as the wireless, isn't it?'

'Easily,' said Steve enthusiastically. Molly relaxed, hearing the cheerful lilt in his voice. 'By jingo, it's remarkable. If we can get the price right, we'll make a fortune. Have you thought about potential customers?'

'There's films, of course,' said Ferguson, still with that odd nervousness, 'but I'll leave that side of it to you, Lewis. I want to concentrate on music.' His voice was clipped and Molly could see the muscles in his throat contract as he swallowed. 'It's easy to record and it's easy to play. Not only that, but we can have music at length. We're not limited by the three minutes you get on a record. You could have whole concerts recorded, an entire opera, say, or a symphony, or an entire evening of jazz.' He pushed back a strand of ginger hair and Molly knew he was searching for something to say. 'There could be a very decent profit from the sale of the ribbons.'

'You recorded this earlier, you say?' said Steve admiringly. Ferguson nodded. 'It's very well done. What about speech? Is there any distortion?'

'You can hear for yourself,' said Ferguson. He took another Bakelite case from his pocket and weighed it in his hand. 'I . . . I recorded a poem by Robert Burns to give you an idea of what speech sounds like.' He took out the *Alligator Hop* and fixed the new ribbon into the machine. 'Here goes.'

What followed certainly rhymed, but it wasn't Robert Burns and it wasn't Ferguson speaking. A man's voice filled the room. *'Mary had a little lamb . . .'*

Molly screamed. She couldn't help herself. It was Dad's voice. *Dad's!* For the briefest fraction of a second she thought she had imagined it, but the stunned bewilderment on Steve's face convinced her.

She started towards him, wanting support, and then – it was as if time slowed to a crawl – her shocked disbelief took on the quality of a nightmare. She saw the minute fair hairs on Steve's face stand out as his face reddened and contorted. His teeth showed in a snarl and the dull sheen of his jacket shifted under the light as the muscles on his arms rippled as he sprang forward.

With the movement, time snapped back to its proper speed. Jack Haldean caught him and Steve struck out, desperate to get to the machine. Hector Ferguson caught his flailing arm, reeling back under Steve's furious onslaught. Jack knocked him off balance and forced him down.

All the time, the voice, her father's voice, continued, *'It followed her to school one day, it was against the rules . . .'*

She leapt back as Steve, utterly desperate, fastened his hands round Jack's throat, oblivious to Ferguson's attempts to pull him off. Jack jerked his knee upwards. Steve grunted and slackened his grip. Jack put his fist under Steve's chin and shoved as hard as he could.

Then there were other men in the room. Two policemen and Inspector Rackham. The policemen seized Steve and the

Inspector forced first one of Steve's wrists and then the other
into handcuffs.

With the policemen holding on to his shoulders, Steve stood,
hunched and dangerous, his breath coming in gusts.

'Steve?' she said blankly. '*Steve?*'

'Let's hear the rest of the recording, shall we, Mr Lewis?'
It was Rackham, his voice cool and decisive.

Steve shook himself like a wounded animal about to attack.
'No!' He gathered himself up. 'You can't have that recording.
I've got it. Ferguson sent it to me. I've got it. I destroyed it.'

'And I copied it,' said Gerard Carrington grimly.

And there, standing in the doorway to the storage room,
incredibly, was Gerry. He came forward into the room. At the
sight of him, Steve Lewis crumpled, sinking to his knees.

'You don't understand,' he began. 'It's not what you think.'
His voice sharpened to a shrill whimper. 'I didn't do it! I
didn't!' He reached out and tried to grab the hem of Molly's
dress. She stepped back sharply. She didn't understand what
was happening but for a split second she'd seen another Steve,
a cringing, frightened, frightening Steve. A Steve who wasn't
quite sane. He tried to laugh, tried to look at her with that
special smile of his, and it was a mask. She was scared of
what lay behind the mask.

'Gerry?' she said weakly. 'Gerry?'

He turned to her, apologetic and anxious. 'My God, Molly,
I'm sorry. If there had been any other way, I wouldn't have
agreed to this, but there wasn't.'

She searched his face. His eyes were troubled but totally,
completely sane and full of concern. 'I really am sorry,' he
said. In the silence, Charles Otterbourne's voice continued.
'These are your father's last moments on earth,' said Gerry.
'Haldean told us exactly what it was and where it was.'

'Dad?' said Molly in a whisper. Her voice came out as a
sob as she heard his voice, Dad's voice. 'Listen! That's Dad.
Please, can we listen?'

The recorded voice took on a slightly self-conscious tone.
'*I have chosen Mary had a Little Lamb in conscious
imitation of Thomas Edison's first recorded words. This
remarkable machine is the work of Professor Carrington, who
. . .* The voice stopped and there were the sound of footsteps.
Out of the speaker came the sound of distant birdsong and

the noise of a man breathing. Then came the scraping noise of a chair being pushed back. '*Stephen? I thought you had gone to your uncle's. Stephen?*'

'*I had something else to do.*'

It was Steve Lewis's voice. There was a gasp, then a flat whiz as if a sharp gust of air had been blown through a pipe, followed by a choking, gurgling noise and a thud.

There was a satisfied laugh and Lewis spoke once more. '*Easy.*'

Carrington moved forward, unconsciously shielding Molly from Lewis. 'You murdered Charles Otterbourne and you've done your level best to murder me.'

Molly felt sick. Jack, seeing her eyes blaze in her paper-white face, reached out to her, but she shook him off. Very deliberately she walked to where her husband still knelt on the floor. 'You *laughed!* You killed him and you *laughed!*'

Lewis raised his head and laughed once more. 'So what? You should be grateful. He ruled you, heart and soul. Killing him was the best thing I ever did. I did it for you.'

'No!' Molly started away and buried her head in her hands, stumbling against Gerard Carrington. He put his arm round her shoulders, drawing her to him.

'Hector,' cried Mrs Dunbar in distress. 'Who killed Mr Otterbourne? Who killed Andrew?'

'Him,' said Ferguson succinctly, gesturing to the crouching man. 'Lewis.' Mrs Dunbar gave a little gasp. 'But how?' she wailed. 'I don't understand.'

Jack gestured to Ferguson who switched off the recording. 'He used a silenced gun, Mrs Dunbar, the same gun he used to kill your husband and Hugo Ragnall.'

'There's more on that recording,' said Carrington. 'I know every word of it. It records my father coming into the room and seeing Charles Otterbourne's body. My poor father was beside himself. He took his own life, but you killed him, Steve, as surely as you killed Hugo Ragnall.'

'Wait a moment, Mr Carrington,' Rackham warned. 'Stephen Vincent Lewis, I arrest you for the murder of Charles Otterbourne, of Andrew Dunbar . . .'

Lewis, still restrained by the policemen, got to his feet. 'I know what I've done,' he said wearily. 'What's the point of going through all this rigmarole?' He raised his handcuffed

wrists and then dropped his hands in a gesture of defeat as
Rackham doggedly went through the names and the charge.
'I'm a gambler. I always have been. I know when I've made
my final throw. What do you want me to say? The only one
I cared about was Ragnall.' His mouth trembled. 'We'd been
friends.' He looked at Jack. 'It's your fault. I killed Ragnall
because of you. It's your fault.'

'You did it,' said Jack flatly. 'You had the choice.'

'Choice?' Under Rackham's wary eye Lewis, his face sickly
white, sank into a chair. 'Choice? I'm not to blame. It was
him. Charles bloody Otterbourne.' He looked at Molly huddled
against Carrington. 'It was your fault. I was your husband.
You should have done what I wanted, not him! All you ever
did was dance attendance on your father.'

'You stole the money from the pension fund,' said Jack
levelly.

'You stole it?' whispered Molly.

'Of course I stole it!' said Steve impatiently.

'*You?* Then Dad's not a thief?' Her mouth straightened into
a thin line. The anger, the white-hot anger that had scorched
her ever since that shocking revelation, burned in her chest,
flared and was gone in a flood of relief. Dad *wasn't* a thief.
Gerry *wasn't* guilty. Nothing was broken. Nothing apart from
this white-faced man huddled in a chair. And, oddly enough,
she didn't feel anger but a wave of compassion. Moments
before she'd been scared of what was behind the mask, but
the real tragedy was there was virtually nothing. He'd inflated
himself with deceit, cunning and hatred and now the balloon
was pricked and there was nothing left but this shivering
remnant of a man.

'Steve,' she said softly. 'How could you?'

'I did it for you.'

She shook her head. More deceit. 'No.'

'Yes, I did! Your father prided himself on his business
sense.' Steve laughed harshly. 'I was teaching him a lesson.
If he'd had any idea how to run a business, he'd have been
on to it right away. But no, he was far too high-and-mighty
to bother with such petty details as accounts. I tell you, I
laughed myself sick, knowing how I was getting my own
back. It was the only way I *could* get my own back.'

'What did you do with the money?' asked Rackham.

'Lived, damn it.' A vicious smile curved his mouth. 'Gambled high, and had the pleasures only money can bring.'

'I knew you had other women,' said Carrington. Molly gave a gasp and he held her close.

'So what?' countered Lewis. 'You didn't know, did you Molly? I was good to you. I've always been good to you. Don't forget, I saved the firm. That was my money. I'd won it.'

'Maybe you did,' said Jack. 'But it's money you won gambling with the pension fund. Hugo Ragnall figured out what you were up to.'

'Hugo Ragnall?' Lewis laughed once more. 'Do me a favour. Hugo Ragnall never had a clue. I got him out of a hole and he was grateful to me. That, believe it or not, was sheer kindness. I wanted an ally, someone else who would say, *yes, sir, no sir, three bags full, sir* to that bastard's face and live their own life behind his back. I had it all planned out. That's the only thing that made life bearable, knowing that one of these days I'd see that swine, Otterbourne, pay. As soon as the pension fund business was discovered, it was curtains for him. I knew exactly what I was going to do. I could take the money in complete safety and blame it all on him. It just happened sooner than I thought, that's all. It was clever, you know? I've always been smart. And Molly . . .' His mouth trembled again as he looked at her. 'You should have been happy. I did it for you. I *cared* for you.'

'Don't give us that, Steve,' said Carrington, his arm round Molly. 'The only person you've ever cared about is yourself.'

Lewis's face darkened. 'You bloody foreigner. I cared enough to know what your game was. How dare you look at my wife? *My* wife?'

Rackham dropped a hand on his shoulder. 'Come on, Lewis. It's time we went.'

With Rackham and the two policemen in attendance, Lewis was led out to the waiting police wagon, Jack and Ferguson bringing up the rear. Perhaps it was Lewis's utter acquiescence that made his captors relax their guard for, without any warning, Lewis suddenly kicked out, catching the sergeant in the knee and, wriggling out from their grasping hands, raced into the road.

An oncoming lorry swerved wildly but Lewis was caught, flung into the air like a rag doll, rolled to the other side of the bonnet, and fell into the path of an oncoming car. There was a scream, the shriek of brakes and a horribly drawn out series of thuds as Lewis was dragged along the road. The car swerved wildly, crashed into the lorry, and, amongst the shattered glass and sudden silence, Lewis, one side of his head pulped and unrecognizable, lay still.

SEVENTEEN

Four days after the events in Bridle Lane, Jack had a telephone call from Gerry Carrington. 'It's Molly,' explained Carrington. 'I've told her what I know, but there's plenty I can't explain. Could we come and see you, Haldean?'

'Good idea,' said Jack. 'I'll ask Hector Ferguson too.'

Jack added brandy, lemon juice and a couple of slices of orange to the cocktail shaker and brandished it with a flourish.

'That looks very elaborate,' said Bill Rackham dubiously, handing the drinks to Molly Lewis and Gerard Carrington. 'I think I'll stick to whisky, Jack.'

There were five people in Jack's sitting room on Chandos Row. Jack himself, Bill Rackham, Hector Ferguson and, looking rather tense, Gerard Carrington and Molly Lewis.

Molly took an abstracted sip of her cocktail. 'Thanks. The more I think about what happened, the less I can see how everything fitted together. It's the details I want to know.' She took a deep breath. 'I understand what drove Steve on. He fairly loathed poor Dad. I've come to realize just how much he resented him. Dad controlled everything but Steve wanted to run the firm. I don't know if my father ever promised him anything, but Steve wanted to be in the driving seat. He simply couldn't bear being second in command and he hated the way I worked round Dad's feelings. At the same time, Steve didn't want to leave Stoke Horam. I think he nursed up his grievances. I couldn't understand it at the time, but I think he *enjoyed* hating Dad.' She lit a cigarette and sat without speaking for a few moments. 'It's not really sane, is it?'

'No, it isn't,' agreed Jack quietly.

Her forehead creased in a frown. 'It all seems like a bad dream. I know what happened, but I'm not sure why it happened.'

'Or how you managed to get to the bottom of it all,' put in Gerry Carrington.

'It was a question of fruit,' said Bill.

'Fruit?' asked Hector Ferguson, frowning at the slice of orange in his glass. 'I don't see how fruit comes into it.'

'It was fruit,' said Jack, settling himself into an armchair. 'That, and something my editor said which stuck in my mind. He talked about writing a story around a set of illustrations. The meaning of pictures depended on the words around them and it struck me that was like evidence and interpretation. We'd been shown, in a manner of speaking, a very convincing series of pictures, or evidence, telling us you were guilty, Carrington. But if we changed the words around those pictures, the evidence could be interpreted a different way.'

'And the answer was a lemon?' asked Hector Ferguson.

'Well, it was a raspberry, as a matter of fact,' said Jack, with a laugh. 'I suddenly saw what you might call the big story, the real story, the one thing that lay behind everything else. And the big story is where Hugo Ragnall fitted in.' He glanced across to Carrington. 'Carrington, do you remember when we went to see your Uncle Maurice? We met his housekeeper, Mrs Tierney, as well, didn't we?'

'So we did, poor woman. I was very sorry when I heard what happened to her.'

'So was I. And,' added Jack, gesturing to Rackham, 'so was Bill. It was when we talked about Mrs Tierney that everything clicked into place. We were having breakfast at Stoke Horam, Mrs Lewis, the morning after Carrington had supposedly taken a pot-shot at your husband.'

'Don't,' she said, in embarrassment. 'I know it all worked out for the best, but even now, I feel guilty about it. Steve was in a foul mood, wasn't he?'

'Yes, he was, and for a very good reason. Up till then, he'd more or less arranged everything that had happened, but Carrington had gone beyond his control.'

'He wanted me to come to Stoke Horam, though, didn't he?' asked Carrington. 'I mean, it was Steve who placed that entry in the agony column, wasn't it?'

'Yes, it was. But he wanted you to come to Stoke Horam when he was ready for you. He planned to shoot you, of course, but he didn't want a houseful of witnesses and a garden full of policemen to see him do it.'

'No wonder he was rattled,' said Rackham with a laugh. 'By jingo, at breakfast he was like a bear with a sore head.

The final straw came when he picked up what he thought was marmalade and it turned out to be jam.'

'Jam?' questioned Ferguson.

'Jam with lots of fruit in it,' said Jack. 'Raspberry jam with pips and he was really ratty about it. It was after both of you had left the room, Mrs Lewis, that Mrs Tierney's name cropped up. Mrs Tierney had really liked Steve Lewis. She'd said as much when we met her, didn't she, Carrington? She'd talked about how pleasant and obliging he was and how easy to look after, and, because she was the sort of woman who thought in meals, talked about how much young Mr Lewis had enjoyed his food, particularly a blackberry tart she'd made. Now, we'd just seen Lewis's reaction when he inadvertently put raspberry jam instead of marmalade on his toast. It was more than mere dislike, it was absolute loathing. Fruit with pips in made him ill, he never ate jam, he couldn't stand berries, etcetera, etcetera. He sounded like an entirely different person from the man Mrs Tierney had talked about. And the thought was so compelling it brought me up short. Because if he really was *entirely* different – another person altogether, in fact – then so much could be explained. Why, for instance, were we so sure that Lewis hadn't murdered your stepfather, Ferguson?'

'Because he was at his uncle's that day.'

'Exactly. And Lewis's uncle, Colonel Willoughby, was an unimpeachable witness. But it wasn't Steve who went to Colonel Willoughby's.'

'Hugo Ragnall?' said Carrington softly.

'*Hugo Ragnall?*' repeated Molly in disbelief. 'You mean it was Hugo Ragnall who went to see Colonel Willoughby after he'd been attacked?'

'Exactly,' agreed Jack.

'But he can't have done,' she protested. 'Steve and his Uncle Maurice knew each other. Hugo couldn't simply turn up and say he was Steve. Unless he was in disguise, I suppose,' she added doubtfully. 'But I can't see that working. Even if the Colonel had been too ill to know who had come to see him, Mrs Tierney would realize immediately that Hugo wasn't Steve.'

'Exactly,' agreed Jack. '*She would know.*' He lit a cigarette and blew out a cloud of smoke in triumph. 'You've put your finger on it. *She would know.* And that's when the penny dropped. Because when Colonel Willoughby died and there was every prospect of both you and Lewis attending the funeral, Mrs Tierney would realize that the Mr Lewis at the funeral wasn't the Mr Lewis she'd come to know.' He raised his eyebrows expressively. 'So, I'm afraid, it was curtains for the poor woman. Look,' he added, seeing Molly was still struggling with the idea, 'how did Colonel Willoughby know Steve Lewis was his nephew?'

'He just did,' said Molly, puzzled. 'He'd visited him a few times. When the Colonel came back from India, Steve went to see him.' She coloured slightly. 'I thought it was very good of Steve, as a matter of fact. The Colonel was ill and I thought it was kind of Steve to make the effort to see him.'

Jack shook his head. 'Lewis didn't go and see him. It was always Hugo Ragnall, right from the beginning. Ragnall had good reason to be grateful to your husband, didn't he?'

She nodded. 'Yes. I remember telling you so. A dreadful man came to the house, dunning Hugo for gambling debts. Steve paid him off and covered it up. Dad never got to hear about it.'

Rackham leaned forward to fill his pipe from the tobacco jar. 'Lewis told us himself that he wanted Hugo Ragnall as an ally. When I realized how long Lewis had been planning things, it fairly took my breath away.'

'So Ragnall was in it as well? On the theft of the pension funds, I mean?' asked Carrington.

Jack shook his head. 'No, he wasn't. I think Ragnall was doing Lewis a favour.'

'What on earth sort of reason could Lewis give?' asked Carrington sceptically. 'It's a dickens of a lot to ask someone to pretend to be you.'

'It depends how you ask,' said Jack dryly. 'All Lewis would have to say is that what he really should do was visit his tiresome old uncle, but both he and Ragnall were men of the world and he'd like a few days away with no questions asked, etcetera, etcetera.'

'Yes,' said Carrington thoughtfully. 'Yes, as a matter of fact I can see that being fairly believable.'

'And there we have it,' said Bill. 'Lewis is armed with an alibi, an alibi he'd set up nearly a year in advance. Secure in the knowledge of that alibi, he forged Mr Otterbourne's signature on the cheques and proceeded to rifle the pension funds. When Hugo Ragnall discovered the theft, he talked it over with his friend, Lewis. Ragnall naturally assumed that Mr Otterbourne had taken the money.'

Molly drew her breath in sharply. 'This is the part I find really horrible. I know it's true, because I heard Steve say so.' Her voice broke and Carrington took her hand. 'I really don't think he was sane,' she added after a little while. 'Maybe that's why I've felt so uneasy for the past couple of years. Steve *seemed* so in control, but he'd have odd bursts of really vicious temper. Then he'd get over it and sometimes he could be really good fun. He used to try and jolly me along, you know? He wanted me to be fun too, and I did try, but most of the time I think I was uneasy. That's probably why,' she added thoughtfully, 'I wanted to live at Stoke Horam. It seemed safer, somehow.'

Carrington said nothing but squeezed her hand. She looked at him gratefully, then turned her attention to Jack. 'The day Hugo Ragnall discovered the theft from the funds, he and Steve had a long talk in the garden. Then Hugo vanished for the day and Steve went off to his Uncle Maurice's. At least, that's where I thought he went,' she added. 'I know Dad was cross about it, because you and your father were expected that morning, Gerry.'

'Ragnall went off to Colonel Willoughby's,' said Jack, 'and Lewis put his plan into operation. What he hadn't planned was your arrival, Carrington. On the face of it, it shouldn't have made much difference. Lewis's plan was that Charles Otterbourne should apparently shoot himself. We heard what really happened on the recording. Lewis must have been hiding near the house, with an eye on the study. As soon as your father left the room and Otterbourne was alone, Lewis went into the study and shot him with a silenced gun, leaving another gun of the same type beside the body. Then, back in the safety of the garden, he fired the shot which brought the servants running.'

'And poor old Dad walked back into the room,' said Carrington softly. He put his hand to his mouth. 'My God. D'you know, I was moved by Steve's concern? I knew him, of course, and I respected his war record tremendously, but I'd seen him in some pretty flash company I didn't care for and tended to avoid him. I was so grateful for his support, though, I warmed to him, the devil. But where did Dunbar come into this?' He looked apologetically at Ferguson. 'I thought if anyone was to blame, he was. His attitude was so peculiar.'

'It was peculiar,' said Ferguson. 'It was so odd I made a point of meeting you, Carrington, to see what you thought of it all, and of asking Haldean if he knew the inside story of what happened at Stoke Horam. My stepfather was so unbearably smug, I knew he had to have gained something, but for the life of me, I couldn't see what.'

'What he'd gained, of course,' said Bill, 'was the recording we heard this afternoon.' He indicated Jack with his pipe-stem. 'Once Jack had tumbled to Hugo Ragnall's part in the affair, we put our heads together and worked out exactly where Dunbar fitted into the picture.'

'We were sure Lewis had murdered Otterbourne and why,' said Jack. 'It didn't seem such a leap to assume he'd murdered Dunbar as well. Now why should he do that? On the face of it, Lewis wanted Dunbar alive, so it had to be a secret reason. Blackmail seemed obvious.'

'And,' said Bill, 'as Dunbar's change of mood was apparent about a fortnight after Mr Otterbourne died, it wasn't hard to work out what Dunbar was blackmailing Lewis for.' He looked at Jack with a grin. 'You were jolly pleased with yourself when you worked out that, granted Professor Carrington had been there to demonstrate his new machine, there more or less had to be a recording of Mr Otterbourne's murder, weren't you?'

'It all fitted,' said Jack. 'Dunbar didn't know anything at the time, that was obvious, but Professor Carrington's machine had been boxed up and sent to Falkirk. It must have taken Dunbar about two weeks to play the recording but, when he did, he must have rubbed his hands together and started to collect.' He looked at Ferguson. 'We found the recording in your stepfather's safe-deposit box at the bank, didn't we?'

'We did,' affirmed Ferguson. 'And, although you were fairly confident it'd be there, I was flabbergasted when we found it.'

'I hoped for the best,' said Jack. 'It's the obvious place to keep something small and very valuable. Anyway, Carrington, this is where you come into the picture again. Lewis enjoyed being in command of Otterbourne's. He really did work very hard those first couple of weeks, and then Dunbar decided to spoil the party. Lewis had patience, though. He wanted the recording, but he also wanted your father's machine. He knew it would be a very valuable commodity and was perfectly happy for you to get it to the point where it could be sold. He'd decided to murder Dunbar, of course, but he'd also decided to murder you.'

Molly squeezed Carrington's hand. 'Why?' Her voice faltered. 'I know what Steve said, but it can't have been just jealousy, could it?'

Carrington gave an unhappy wriggle of his shoulders. 'It doesn't seem enough, somehow.'

'It wasn't,' agreed Jack. He looked at Ferguson. 'Your mother is, I think, a kindly soul. With Dunbar dead, there was a good chance she'd have either given or sold the machine back to Carrington, including all the ribbons. If Carrington played the recording, Lewis would be back where he started. But if Carrington died too – well, that's a happy ending. Very happy, in fact, because Lewis can then say that as your cousin and next-of-kin, he was the legal owner of various bits of the machine.'

'He attacked Uncle Maurice the night before Dunbar died, didn't he?' asked Carrington.

'Yes, he did,' said Rackham. 'That puzzled us, you know, because Colonel Willoughby had seen the man who attacked him. He stated it was a stranger. Of course, Lewis *was* a stranger to him. When the telegram arrived from Mrs Tierney to say the Colonel had been attacked, Hugo Ragnall was despatched to play the part of the concerned nephew.'

'And,' continued Jack, 'In the meantime, Lewis had booked into the Marchmont. I'm sure I was right, Bill. I'm sure Lewis was Patrick Mullaney, and he changed his room to be near Dunbar.'

'You're probably right,' said Bill with a grin. 'He certainly had to be somewhere close, so he could watch Carrington leave Dunbar's room. He knew more or less what time you'd be going, Carrington, because Mrs Lewis had arranged to have tea with you. At first, it all went like a dream. The suicide was seen through right away, as Lewis intended. The ironic thing is, that it was the letter he wrote that got you off the hook.'

Ferguson grinned apologetically. 'I added to the fun, didn't I? When I realized I'd walked off with the key, I nearly had a fit. My stepfather was a real swine, you know, and I'd never pretended to have any affection for him. My mother was certain I'd killed him and for a time I felt so guilty, I could almost believe I had. It's ridiculous the tricks your mind can play on you. I was nearly sick with gratitude when Hugo Ragnall turned up with that story of his.'

'But Ragnall *couldn't* have been in the hotel,' said Carrington. 'He was pretending to be Steve at my uncle's, wasn't he?'

'Of course he was,' said Jack. 'Lewis earned Mrs Dunbar's gratitude by finding out the details of exactly what she and Ferguson had done at the hotel, then primed Ragnall with them so he could give a really convincing story to the police. The only place Ragnall slipped up was by allowing too short a time to get up and down the stairs to Dunbar's room. Lewis didn't want you convicted, Ferguson. If you had been, Gerry would have had the machine including, once your mother had looked in your stepfather's safe-deposit box, the damning recording as well. If you were saved because of Ragnall's actions, Mrs Dunbar would be so grateful she'd look very kindly on the idea of a merger once more and, with you cleared, Lewis could try once again to get Carrington convicted.'

'I knew something wasn't right,' said Bill. 'I never dreamed that Ragnall's story was a fairy-tale from beginning to end.'

'But why did Ragnall do it?' demanded Ferguson. 'I can see he didn't mind stepping in for Lewis for a visit to his uncle's, but he must have wondered why Lewis wanted him to put one over the police. That's serious stuff.'

'Because, I imagine, Lewis appealed to his better nature.'

'Did Ragnall have one?' demanded Carrington.

'Oh yes,' said Jack. 'Don't be too hard on him, Carrington. Lewis had convinced him you were guilty. He did a good job of that. He convinced everyone – including Bill and me, I must say – that you had murdered Dunbar in a fit of rage. The more he said in your apparent defence, the guiltier you seemed. I imagine he told Ragnall that he *knew* you were guilty. You were his cousin and he could understand why you'd gone off the deep end, but it was wrong to let another man – Ferguson – suffer for it.'

'I still don't understand Ragnall's part in all this,' said Carrington. 'You said he wasn't as black as I've painted him. All I can say is that on the day we were all supposed to have dinner, the day Ragnall died, I received an appalling letter from him. It was nothing more or less than an attempt at blackmail. I honestly believed Ragnall had been at the hotel on the day Dunbar was killed, and he wanted, so he said, a substantial consideration to make it worth his while not to tell the police what he'd seen. I couldn't understand what he'd possibly seen, but I believed he could tell some very damning lies. He finished by asking me to call at quarter to eight to discuss the matter. I wrote a reply – I can't remember what the hell I wrote because I was blistering – and marched round at the appointed time with the idea of making him eat his ruddy letter and choke on the damn thing.'

'Do you honestly believe Ragnall wrote that letter?' asked Jack.

Carrington's jaw dropped. 'Oh, my God,' he said softly. 'Of course he didn't. It was Steve, wasn't it?'

'Of course it was. Colonel Willoughby had died and Ragnall had outlived his usefulness. What's more, Ragnall knew far more than Steve Lewis was comfortable with him knowing. And, with Ragnall dead, Lewis could make up any old tale about what Ragnall had said about the time you'd left the hotel. He roped me in as a witness. I could testify that you'd come into the flat in a state of absolute fury. Then, minutes later, Ragnall was dead and you, apparently, had shot him. It was much the same trick as he pulled on your father.'

'How exactly was it worked?' asked Ferguson. He looked at Carrington in bewilderment. 'I was there and, even though I know the truth, it was very convincing. We were playing records and chatting in the other room when we heard a shot. How did he pull it off?'

'Some of this is guesswork,' said Jack, 'but I believe it's close enough. Lewis planted two guns in the study. When we heard the shot in the drawing room, Lewis went into the study and ushered you into the hall, Carrington, yes?'

'Yes, he did.'

'And as soon as you were safely in the hall, he shot Ragnall with a silenced gun, put it back in its hiding place, and planted the second gun by the body.'

'But we heard the shot!' said Ferguson in frustration. 'How did he manage that?'

'The shot was on the record,' said Jack. 'The Jack Hylton record that you put on the turntable. There's a nice symmetry about it, isn't there? Lewis was in deep trouble because Mr Otterbourne's murder had been recorded, and he used another recording to land Carrington in it. It didn't matter which record you picked out of the box he gave you, Ferguson, because there was a gunshot on all of them.'

'But he can't have done,' said Ferguson. 'You can't simply record another sound on top of a record.'

'You can if you've got Otterbourne's at your beck and call.' Ferguson still looked puzzled. 'Look,' explained Jack. 'There were six records. He had the master copies at the factory. What I bet he did was play the master into a recording horn and fire off a gun while the record was playing. Then he'd have a new master, complete with gunshot, that he could turn into a lovely new shellac record.'

'Did you find them?'

Jack grinned. 'You can't honestly think he'd go to so much trouble then leave them lying around. He destroyed them, of course. No, he had a set of undoctored records as well, which he was careful to leave in an Otterbourne's box, just like the doctored set. He put the undoctored Jack Hylton record on the turntable, in case we played it. Which, in fact, we did.'

'How on earth did you figure all that out?

'Fingerprints.'

'And it was damn clever of you to think of it, Jack,' said Rackham appreciatively. He turned to Ferguson. 'I couldn't imagine what the devil Haldean was after when he asked me if we had your fingerprints on file at the Yard.'

'*My* fingerprints, Haldean?'

'Don't look so shocked, Ferguson. You'd handled those records. I'd seen you do it and, I must say, for a music lover you're pretty heavy handed. I scooted up to London, went to Lewis's flat, charmed my way in past the workmen who were repairing the ceiling, and there was the box of records. I took it to the Yard and got them to look it over. Your prints weren't on the paper sleeves or the Jack Hylton record and they should have been. That's when I knew we'd been had. However,' he added with a shrug, 'we had a problem.'

'It was lack of evidence,' said Bill. 'I believed you were innocent, Carrington, but if I'd arrested Lewis there and then, we wouldn't have a case. Juries are made up of men and women who read newspapers, and we knew that in the mind of any jury, it would come down to a straight horse-race between you and Lewis as to who was the guilty man. Fingerprints that weren't there seemed such a trifle compared to the evidence Lewis had manufactured against you. Even when Haldean and I played the recording of Mr Otterbourne's murder, it was still very iffy. For one thing, neither I nor the Assistant Commissioner, Sir Douglas Lynton, knew if the recording would be admissible in court. It's a totally new departure and judges can be very cautious about what they'll admit as evidence.'

'And,' added Jack, 'once we had listened to the recording, we realized just how a clever defence counsel could play havoc with it.'

'But Dad's voice was perfectly clear,' said Molly. 'It was obvious what had happened.'

'It was obvious to you, Molly,' said Carrington. 'But you recognized your father's voice immediately. That makes a huge difference. I thought we were really up against it. Haldean and Rackham came to see me the morning after I'd been arrested in the garden at Stoke Horam and told me what they thought was the true state of affairs.' He reached out and took her hand. 'They were certain a recording of your father's death existed and wanted me to go up to Falkirk to finish working on the machine. I agreed, of course.' He looked at Haldean with unspoken gratitude. 'I was knocked sideways when I realized that you and Rackham thought I was innocent. However, once we'd played the recording, we realized we couldn't simply arrest Steve. If he knew – and he'd guess as much – that the recording was going to be played in court, his reaction would be very controlled.'

'We needed to shock him, Mrs Lewis,' said Jack. 'Carrington was unhappy about inviting you to Ferguson's studio, but I thought your presence was vital. You were the only person there who would recognize your father's voice, for a start. If it wasn't for you, Lewis could have pretended it was a recording he'd made for fun. It could easily have been a piece of play-acting and a silenced gun doesn't sound like a shot. As it was, you screamed and Lewis went in a instant from feeling utterly secure – Ferguson had, on our prompting, sent him both the Professor's machine and the damning recording – to being in great danger.' He smiled at Ferguson. 'You were terrific, old man.'

'I only did what you asked,' said Ferguson, rather abashed.

'Don't underestimate yourself. You convinced Lewis that all you were after was the new machine and made him think that, if I was suspicious of anyone, it was you. It was damn good work.' Jack leaned forward and stubbed out his cigarette. 'And, as we know, Lewis confessed, which is what we wanted.'

Molly shuddered. 'It seems cruel, though.'

'We had to find enough evidence to get Carrington off the hook,' said Bill. 'There didn't seem to be any doubt, missing fingerprints or not, that he'd shot Hugo Ragnall.'

'That's something I want to know,' said Jack. 'Why, Carrington, when you walked into the study and found Hugo Ragnall, did you pick up the gun? You must have known it was a frame-up.'

'Of course I did,' said Carrington. 'When I saw Ragnall lying there, I *knew* – really *knew* – that Steve had killed him and I also knew that my prints were on that gun. Steve had a gun collection which he'd insisted on showing me. As soon as I saw Ragnall dead with the gun beside him, I knew why. I was going to fight my way out. I'd had one experience of prison and I didn't want another. If I'd waited to be arrested, I'd have been hanged.' He cocked his head at Bill Rackham. 'I'm right, aren't I?'

'I like to think truth will out,' said Bill awkwardly. 'But it would have been very difficult, that's for sure.'

Carrington leaned forward, his chin resting on his hands. 'You talked about Steve having gone from feeling secure to being threatened. That's exactly how I felt when I saw Hugo Ragnall's body.' He looked at them thoughtfully. 'I fired the gun in the hall so I could escape. I don't know if I intended to hit Steve or not, but I'll tell you this, Haldean. When you stopped me from shooting him in the garden the night I was arrested, I was prepared to kill him.' He smiled wryly. 'You took a pretty big risk, you know, when you got in my way.'

'I thought I was safe enough,' said Jack. 'I trusted you.'

Carrington half-laughed. 'You were right, but I hardly trusted myself by that stage. I'd seen him that afternoon, you know. I got into the house by climbing up to the balcony. I found Molly's room, left a note, then got out and hid in one of the outbuildings. I found a snug little space in the rafters of the laundry. Steve came in and searched the place. He was right beneath me. I came within a whisker of shooting him then, but I couldn't bring myself to do it.'

'That's because you're not a killer,' said Jack. 'I knew that.'

Carrington looked at him. 'Thanks,' he said softly.

'Where did you get to after Ragnall was shot, by the way?' asked Bill. 'We know you went back to your rooms and packed a suitcase, but that's it. We scoured Britain for you. For a complete beginner, you disappeared like an old pro.'

'I holed up in the university,' said Carrington with a grin.

'But we searched there!'

'Yes, but I knew the university routine, remember? It wasn't very difficult to keep out of the way. I knew what was going on because there were newspapers left lying around in the caretaker's room. That's where I saw that entry in the agony column of *The Messenger*. I suspected it was a trap, of course, but I couldn't take any chances, not where Molly was concerned.'

Molly looked at him with shining eyes. 'That was very brave of you. But how did you live, Gerry? What did you eat?'

'I pinched food from the kitchens.'

'Didn't anyone see you?'

'As a matter of fact, they did. One night – it was fairly late and I thought I was safe – I was in the corridor, when the door opened and Dr Austen walked out. I thought I was for it, because there wasn't anywhere to escape to, but he looked at me and said, "Ah, Carrington. I've been reading your notes on waveforms. Very interesting, m'boy. Have you considered the effect of the ratios, rather than merely the numerical differences, on intensities? On the logarithmic scale . . ." And on and on.'

Jack gave a crack of laughter. 'How on earth did you get out of it?'

'I didn't! I had to stand there gravely discussing waveform variations, whilst all the time expecting someone with a better grasp of current affairs to come along. In the end he said, "I really must be going. My wife tells me we have guests for dinner" – it was about ten o'clock by this time – "and she has warned me of a habit of tardiness, which, I fear, is growing upon me. Now what did I have to tell you? I'm sure I've heard something about you recently. What was it? No matter. It will probably occur to me later," and off he went.'

'Would you believe it?' said Bill with a laugh. 'Actually, having met Doctor Austen, yes, I would.'

'That was pretty brave of you, Molly,' said Gerry Carrington later that evening. They were walking down the Strand to Molly's hotel. 'Wanting to know the unvarnished truth, I mean.'

'I knew the truth about Steve anyway,' she said thoughtfully. 'The odd thing was, I wasn't really surprised, you know? Steve could be enormous fun to be with, but it was always a strain. Poor Steve,' she added quietly.

Carrington looked at her sharply. 'Poor Steve?'

'He could have had so much, but he wanted everything. And no one can have everything, can they?'

Carrington sighed. 'There's only one thing he had that I want,' he murmured. Molly looked at him enquiringly, but he shook his head. 'Forget it. It's all too soon.'

Molly didn't say anything for a little while. Then she shook her herself and stuck out her chin. For a moment, she looked exactly like her father. 'Gerry,' she said reflectively. 'Perhaps you could give me some advice. Hector Ferguson's proposed.'

He gazed at her, thunderstruck. '*Hector Ferguson?* Damn me, what the devil does he think he's playing at?'

'I haven't told you what he's proposed,' she said with a laugh. 'He's proposed that the merger between Otterbourne's and Dunbar's should go ahead.'

'Oh.'

'But I told him,' added Molly demurely, 'that I would have to consult my fiancé.'

'But you haven't got—' Gerry Carrington broke off and, swinging round abruptly, caught her arms and held her firmly. 'Molly! Me, you mean? Me? For God's sake, Molly, will you?' He searched her face anxiously then, oblivious of the startled comments from passers-by, gathered her into his arms and kissed her passionately.

She laid her head against his chest. 'Hector Ferguson,' she murmured, 'will be pleased.'